Rebecca Yarros is the No. 1 *Sunday Times*, *New York Times*, *USA Today* and *Wall Street Journal* bestselling author of over fifteen novels including *Fourth Wing* and *Iron Flame*. She loves military heroes and has been blissfully married to hers for over twenty years.

She's the mother of six children and is currently surviving the teenage years with two of her four hockey-playing sons. When she's not writing, you can find her at the hockey rink or sneaking in some guitar time while guzzling coffee. She and her family live in Colorado with their stubborn English bulldogs, two feisty chinchillas and a Maine Coon cat named Artemis, who rules them all.

Having fostered then adopted their youngest daughter, Rebecca is passionate about helping children in the foster system through her nonprofit, One October, which she co-founded with her husband in 2019. To learn more about their mission to better the lives of kids in foster care, visit www.oneoctober.org.

T0349980

Also by Rebecca Yarros

Empyrean
Fourth Wing
Iron Flame

Flight & Glory
Full Measures
Eyes Turned Skyward
Beyond What Is Given
Hallowed Ground
The Reality of Everything

Renegades
Wilder
Nova
Rebel

Legacy
Point of Origin (Novella)
Ignite (Novella)
Reason to Believe

Muses and Melodies

A Little Too Close

EYES
TURNED
SKYWARD

REBECCA

NO.1 *SUNDAY TIMES* BESTSELLING AUTHOR

YARROS

PIATKUS

PIATKUS

First published in the United States in 2014 by Amara,
an imprint of Entangled Publishing, LLC
First published in Great Britain in 2024 by Piatkus

13 5 7 9 10 8 6 4 2

A CIP catalogue record for this book
is available from the British Library.

ISBN: 978-0-349-44255-6

Printed and bound in Great Britain by
Clays Ltd, Elcograf S.p.A.

Papers used by Piatkus are from well-managed forests
and other responsible sources.

Piatkus
An imprint of
Little, Brown Book Group
Carmelite House
50 Victoria Embankment
London EC4Y 0DZ

An Hachette UK Company
www.hachette.co.uk

www.littlebrown.co.uk

To our Little Miss, our maybe Audrey-Grace—
loving you is worth every risk.

Eyes Turned Skyward is a story about finding love and autonomy, but contains some difficult themes and elements that might not be suitable for some readers. These include: Family conflict and estrangement, mentions of family member deaths, military service and deployment, addiction, mentions of suicide, infidelity, hospitalization, surgery, chronic illness, and graphic sex on page. Readers who may be sensitive to these, please take note.

CHAPTER ONE

22. Ditch responsibilities and head to the beach.

*B*reathe and drop the towel. That's what people did at the beach, right? They wore swimsuits and didn't hide behind enormous beach towels. *You can do this.* I could be fierce. I used to be, I just had to remember how.

I sucked the humid Florida air past my lips, tasting salt from the ocean. My heart skipped, and I gripped the towel tighter.

"*She was afraid to come out of the locker. She was afraid that somebody would see,*" Morgan sang next to me, her southern drawl even more pronounced than mine.

"You hush up," I whispered. I was embarrassed enough without her making a scene.

"You promised, Paisley." Morgan tugged at the towel, but I held firm.

I swallowed, trying to keep lunch in my stomach. "I know, and I'll do it. I just need a minute."

Her exaggerated sigh did nothing to calm my nerves. "It's

just a bathing suit."

"It's a bikini, Morgan, which is most definitely *not* just a bathing suit." I dug my toes into the white sand.

"You've got an amazing body. I don't know why this is such a big deal." She adjusted her sunglasses and pulled back her ebony hair, her towel long since replaced by unwavering confidence. I may have agreed to a two-piece, but my boy shorts and a halter-style tankini top covered a heck of a lot more than Morgan's triangle confection. "Look, it's our one day away from everything before classes start. This was your idea."

"Right." Yes, one day of wildness, freedom, where I wasn't just a Donovan. Besides, the beach was the easiest box to check on the bucket list, and I was down to 231 days.

"Paisley, no one cares who you are here or what you're wearing. There are no expectations but your own, just another college girl at the beach. Pretend you're not...you know...you." She waved her hand at me. "Now drop that towel before I pitch a fit."

Pretend. Yeah, I could do that. *Deep breath.* I straightened my posture like Mama was watching and let go of the towel like she wasn't. Now, if only I could have shed my inhibitions with it. Morgan nodded with approval, and we headed toward a group of acquaintances from school.

"Hey, y'all!" Morgan called, laying out our beach towels at the edge of the group. I gave a small smile and wave, then turned down a beer, which Morgan claimed. By the looks of it, they'd all been drinking for a while. I sprawled out on my towel and debated wrapping myself in it. I was never allowed to be this exposed at home. *What would people think?* Mama's voice burrowed through the sunshine.

I ran my finger down the line of my sternum. No, I'd bare this little bit of skin while it was still pretty, before I let the surgeons get their hands on it. And really, it didn't matter what the outside of my body looked like, not when it was failing from the inside.

"You're going to burn that fair skin of yours," Morgan lectured, handing me a bottle of SPF 90. I thought twice, then slipped off my purple watch, stashing it away before slathering the lotion everywhere I could reach. I didn't want it to get all oily.

Oh, now that was a lie. I just didn't want to wear the darn thing.

"You blondes always seem to burn faster." A deep voice spoke from behind me.

I craned my head and lowered my sunglasses. The guy looked like every other college-aged guy I saw, nothing special or descriptive. Maybe being with Will blinded me to other guys, but I certainly didn't get the hormonal rushes Morgan cooed about.

Crud. He was waiting for a response. *Don't embarrass Morgan.* I gave an easy smile. "Sunscreen saves the day."

Sunscreen saves the day? Kill me now.

He gave me the "Wow, you're a total dork" look I knew well but masked it with a smile. "Right. Can I…uh…get your back for you?"

"I'd rather you didn't," I answered, shorter than I meant to.

"Oh, okay?" he said and quickly retreated.

Morgan's sigh reminded me how bad I was at this socializing stuff. "Just because you're pretty much married to Will doesn't mean a guy can't put sunscreen on you."

"Being together for a year isn't married, but I'm not about to let a stranger put his hands on me."

She spread the lotion across my back, careful to cover me completely. "I know, darlin'. How is it being in the same town with him?"

It took me a second to mull that over. "It's nice. I'm still getting used to seeing him more than a couple days every few months."

"Well, y'all rocked that long-distance stuff." She motioned to my Kindle. "Just don't forget about the real world, okay?" She gawked past me to a crowd of guys playing Ultimate Frisbee near the surf. "Like that piece of eye candy!"

I peeked to see what had her drooling like a hound. "You know, there's more to a man than how he looks. You have to know what's—"

Sweet Lord, have *mercy*.

My Kindle hit the sand with my jaw. I'd never seen a man so beautiful, so raw in energy, or so...delicious looking. He stood easily over six feet tall and had no problem leaping for the Frisbee. His blue board shorts hung low on his hips, and his chest was beautifully bare, colored in tattoos that stretched across his abdomen, half his chest, and down one arm. The Florida sun caressed the line of his carved abs, giving him a fine sheen of perspiration that made his skin glow.

His blond hair was cut close, but long enough to wave, and it framed a gorgeous face. Strong nose, angular lines of his cheekbones, a solid chin, and oh...dimples in his cheeks when he grinned. He belonged on a beach. I halfway expected to find a label on him that said "Mr. California." He looked laid-back, even by Florida standards.

My heartbeat sped up, my lips parted, and my hands itched to touch him. Heck, I was shocked my thighs hadn't popped open of their own volition. What color were his eyes? I couldn't tell from this distance, and maybe that saved me from the utter disgrace of admitting that I was attracted to someone other than my boyfriend.

I couldn't remember the last time I'd seen someone and simply...wanted, but I sure did now.

Mr. California's eyes focused on us when Morgan whistled through her fingers.

"Morgan!" I hissed.

"Oh, lighten up, Lee. I whistled; I didn't drop his pants. Not that I'd mind that."

Heat raced through my cheeks, not because her suggestion embarrassed me but because in that second I envisioned myself sliding those board shorts down over his hips and— *No!* What on earth was wrong with me?

Will. Will. Will. I forced his face to my mind, his close-cropped brown hair, his gentle, amber-colored eyes. Yes, Will. Not golden beach god over there.

"You could say hi, Lee," Morgan suggested. "Flirting never hurt anyone."

"No, thank you." First, I wouldn't do that to Will. Second, what would I even say to someone like that? *Hi, I'm Paisley. I'm twenty years old, and my heart is a ticking time bomb. Want to be friends?* I thought not.

"There's Luke! Do you want to hop on the WaveRunners with us?" Morgan asked, waving back at a guy near the water.

"I'd rather not. There's a red flag out." Hence a giant vat of death just hankering to swallow me whole.

"That one's just the warning; the beach isn't closed or anything."

"I'm just not a fan of the water."

"Okay, well, I'm getting your feet in the water sometime today, spoilsport!" She took off with a smile and a wave.

I snuck a glance over at Mr. California, who was surrounded by at least four different bikini-clad girls. It was no surprise; boys like that attracted attention. Heck, I was happy with Will, but Mr. California had *my* attention, too.

I sighed. There would be no reading if staring at him was an option. I traded my Kindle for my hot-pink sarong and stood, wrapping it around my waist.

The pier jutted out over the crystal blue-green water, and I wandered over to it, keeping my eyes fixed in front of me and not on the Frisbee players. That would never be me, running up and down the beach for fun. I couldn't run like that if my life depended on it. Actually, my life depended on me *not* running.

A fresh wave of heat wafted off the wooden boards of the pier before a gust of wind took it away. My sarong billowed out behind me as I explored, entranced by the rhythm of the waves.

When I reached the middle of the deserted pier, I leaned on the railing, my hair whipping me in the face and sticking to my lip balm.

Someone touched my bare shoulder. I turned, pulling my hair off my face. It was one of the guys from Morgan's group. He was massive and scared the daylights out of me when he swayed, obviously drunk, and nearly knocked me over. "You're Lee, right?" he slurred, his eyes vague.

"Yes?"

"Morgan told me to get your feet wet." He bent down and plucked me right off my feet. Ugh. He smelled like a brewery.

My muscles stiffened in protest, and I pushed away from him. "I'd really rather not. I'm fixin' to go read. Could you please put me down?" I tried to be polite, but when he started for the other side of the pier, panic set in.

"She said you'd say anything to get outta going in the water." He laughed, his drawl sounding more sloshed than southern.

"Please, don't!" I cried out, shoving away from him in earnest.

"Oh, come on now, it's just a little water. You can fix your hair once you're out." He leaned his head over the side of the pier, and my eyes popped wide at the twenty-foot drop. "This looks faster than walking over to the beach, doesn't it?"

"No!" I screamed, throwing everything my five-foot-two frame had against his concrete arms. "No! No! No!" I kicked, thrashing in his arms, but there was no give. My heart pounded and my throat closed up.

He laughed, like this was some kind of joke. "Aw, girl, you know you'll love it once we're in! You go first."

He climbed up onto the rail, and I had to say it—keeping

this embarrassing secret was going to get me killed. "Please! I can't swim!"

He wouldn't stop laughing as he swayed unpredictably, leaning over toward the water.

"No, really, I can't!" I stopped fighting and started clinging. He wouldn't drop me over. He wouldn't. Things like this didn't really happen.

His hands gripped my waist and pulled me away from him. "In you go!" It seemed effortless to him, taking away my last vestige of safety, and he tossed me into the air.

Everything stilled. My heart ceased its beat as I was airborne. The fall took forever and was over before I could blink.

I screamed the whole way down.

Cold water engulfed me, and didn't let go. The impact stole the air from my lungs, and I clung to what was left, fighting the instant urge to suck in. I sank, my head far beneath the surface, but I was scared to open my eyes. My feet hit bottom with a soft impact, and I pushed up with every ounce of strength I had, clawing at the water. Momentum brought me to the surface, and as I broke it, I gulped in a breath and screamed for help.

The next wave smothered my cry, hurling me under in a twisted death grip. My body was jerked in the opposite direction of where I wanted to go. Salt water burned my nose. I kicked viciously, reaching for the surface. Where was it? I flipped over again. And again.

No surface. No air. Where was it?

My heart raced in a dangerous beat, too fast. Way too fast. If I wasn't going to drown, I was going to have a heart attack. *But I still have 231 days!*

A wave swept me to the surface, and I flung my head back, desperate for air. I spent a precious second pulling the hair from my mouth to get to the sweet oxygen and took a gasping breath. I couldn't manage a scream before I was swept down again, my mouth full of seawater.

The urge to breathe in overwhelmed every other thought, but I couldn't do it. I swept my hands up, trying to get to air, but the wave wasn't bringing me up this time. No, another one came, knocking me farther down. My chest was going to burst if I didn't let the pressure go. It would be so easy just to let it go. *I'm going to die out here.*

It was supposed to be peaceful, right? Drowning? This wasn't peaceful. This was terrifying, and it *hurt*. I wasn't giving in that easily or drowning because some drunk boy threw me into the ocean. Mama wouldn't survive it. Peyton would have fought…if she'd had that chance.

Her face brought me the fight I needed, those green eyes that mirrored my own. I kicked harder, aiming for the sparkling surface above. *Kick harder, Paisley. Don't give up. Not now.* I heard her voice; lack of oxygen was shutting down my brain. It wouldn't be long before my reflexes took over and I either lost consciousness or sucked in a lungful of the Gulf of Mexico.

Another wave assaulted me, stealing the last bit of oxygen from my lungs. There was nothing…left. Which direction was up? Where…was I? *Don't breathe in…don't…*

I heard my mother's voice, but that was impossible, right? *"Paisley, stop that nonsense. Peyton will always be older. That's never going to change. When you're six, she'll be eight. When you're sixteen, she'll be eighteen. Even when she's eighty-two, she'll be older."*

"No, she won't. She'll be dead."

The wave tossed me into the pier, and I felt the impact on my shoulder before my head struck the wood.

Then I felt nothing.

CHAPTER TWO

*One day I'm not going to fail, and it's going to shock
the hell out of you.*

Holy shit. *Did that guy just throw that pretty little blonde
off the pier?*

I ditched the redhead in my arms and jumped the last two
stairs onto the deck. *Run.* My strides consumed the distance to
the railing where she'd gone over, my arms pumping furiously.
Get there. Faster.

The asshole had thrown her into the water when she'd
begged him not to. What the fuck was he thinking? Goose
bumps erupted over my skin as she screamed, the sound tearing
through me long after the water covered her.

I shoved the juicehead out of my way as he stood there
gawking like he hadn't been the one to drop her twenty feet to
the ocean. The waves weren't fucking around today, obscuring the
normally clear water. I climbed the railing and balanced on the
edge, scanning the water. *Come on, Little Bird, where are you?*

There.

Her blond hair popped above the surface for a priceless second before a wave dragged her under again, but it was long enough for her to cry out.

"Get help!" I shouted at the fumbling idiot, whose slack-jawed expression suggested he might finally understand what he'd done.

Stepping out into nothing, my arms circled to slow my impact. A deep breath, and I cut into the water, submerging with brutal force.

I scanned around me fruitlessly before I had to get to the surface and breathe. One breath later, a wave came in and pushed me toward the beach, away from where I'd seen her. The hell with that. I wasn't leaving without her.

The salt water scraped my eyes as I dove, kicking deeper. *There she is!* Limp, her arms semi-raised, her hair floated in a morbid halo, the blond catching the light from the sun through the water. Fuck. I was not too late. I refused to fail. Not in this.

I swam down to her, looped one arm around her waist, and kicked furiously for the surface, my lungs burning. Give me skates and ice and I'd decimate everyone, but I was mediocre in the water. Mediocrity wasn't something I handled well.

We burst through to the air. I rolled onto my back, pulled her face up onto my chest, and kicked for the shore. A wave washed over us, sending water rushing up my nose, but I brought us back to the surface, keeping my arm like a vise around her. She wasn't breathing, but she wasn't too blue yet.

My legs caught the material of her skirt, and I untied the knot at her waist, letting it wash away. A few dozen sure, solid kicks later, we reached where the waves stopped fighting us and instead pushed us closer to the shore. Just another minute. She could make it another minute.

Stark relief gutted me when my feet touched the sand. I lifted her into my arms, trying to keep her head balanced against my shoulder. *Still not fucking breathing.*

I pushed my way through the resistance of the water. "Dude! Is she okay?" The juicehead asked from shore. He was lucky my hands were busy at the moment.

"Get the fuck out of my way," I seethed, pushing past him. I made it onto the beach and put her down, then checked for breath. None.

Lowering my ear to her chest, I caught her faint heartbeat.

I would have thanked God if I'd believed he existed.

I tilted back her head, and for the first time didn't check out the looks of the woman I was about to put my mouth on. Plugging her nose, I pulled her jaw down, then sealed my mouth over hers, breathing for us both. I counted out the breaths and laid my hand on her chest, checking again for that precious heartbeat.

"Come on, Little Bird."

The seconds slowed to small measures of infinity before she sputtered, water spewing from her mouth. I rolled her to the side as she forced out the rest with coughing heaves, her slight body convulsing.

All of the adrenaline abandoned me, leaving only exhaustion. She hadn't died. She was alive. I hadn't failed. When she finished, I brought her to her back, watching the rise and fall of her chest like it was going to stop any second. I leaned over her as she took a shaky breath.

Damn, her face was as perfect up close as I'd thought. Small, delicate features on top of plump, parted lips. I'd seen her as I ran down the beach, but I figured she'd be a Monet—pretty from afar, but a mess up close—like most of the girls today. I was wrong.

She was beautiful, and not in the fake, made-up way. "Hey, are you okay?" I asked.

"Thank you," she whispered in a sweet southern accent as her eyes opened wide in shock. Words failed me. Green. Holy shit, her eyes were huge and the clearest shade of pale green I'd ever seen, with a ring of forest green on the edges. My heart skipped and then began to pound. I ran my barbell across my teeth, speechless for the first time since...ever and reminded myself that I did not believe in love at first sight, or that insane voice in my head that clearly said, "Mine." Her eyes widened. "Mr. California?"

What? A smile broke out across my face. "Not exactly. I'm from Colorado. Luckily they teach mouth-to-mouth there, too."

She gasped, leaning on her elbows. "Mouth to— I have a boyfriend!"

Indignant. She was offended? "And...he would take objection to me saving your life?"

She blinked several times, her lips parting. *Keep your thoughts off her lips.* "N-n-no. He just wouldn't take kindly to someone else's mouth on mine." Her chest heaved as she sat up, and her eyes glazed.

I yanked the nearest beach towel to us, not caring that it belonged to Masters, wherever the hell he was, and wrapped it around her, then cupped her face with one of my hands, strangely tender. I was *not* a tender kind of guy. Hell, no. I was a no-effort, easy-lay, forget-'em-before-morning guy. "Well, next time I'll make sure to ask him first, okay?"

She nodded, drawing her knees to her chest. "You saved me."

"You were drowning."

A shadow fell on us. The idiot was here. "Hey, man, that was so cool how you—" I turned as I stood, my fist taking my momentum into his jaw. He blinked as he stumbled until his ass hit the sand. "She's fine!" he called over to the small group that had gathered.

"Jerk," she muttered, wincing, and raised a hand to the back of her head.

"Are you okay?"

Her nose scrunched. "I think I hit my head on the pier."

I brushed her hand and hair away to see the swelling goose egg. "You need to get checked out. Let me get you to the doctor, okay?"

She shook her head, her hand hovering above her heart. "No, no doctors."

She muttered something that sounded like, "My parents will kill me." She looked too old to care what her parents thought, but with that sweet-as-honey southern accent, I bet she was raised pretty old-fashioned. The opposite of my fend-for-yourself upbringing.

"Do you want to call your boyfriend?"

She grimaced. "Will wouldn't understand. God, it was silly of me to come here."

"Who are you here with?"

"My friend Morgan, but she's out on the WaveRunner..."

We both scanned the coastline, but I didn't see anyone.

She shrank in on herself, becoming even smaller, if that was possible. She was already fucking tiny, over a head shorter than I was, but rounded in every place I worshipped on a woman. She was...well, damn, she was as perfect in her body as her face.

Her cough dragged my horny mind out of her pants. What the hell was wrong with me? The girl almost drowned five minutes ago. "You need a doctor, just to check you out. I've heard too many stories of people who drown hours later from the fluid in their lungs."

She rested her hand on her chest, her forehead wrinkled like she was thinking, before she nodded. "Okay, I'll get Morgan's keys and find an urgent care."

My mouth dropped. "You're not going to drive yourself. I'll take you..." I wanted to pull some Jedi mind shit to get her to say her name.

"Paisley," she answered. *Jackpot.* "And I don't get in cars with strangers."

I grinned. "I'm Jagger, and since I've had my mouth on yours, I'd hardly call us strangers." A pretty blush crept over her face. She was enchanting. *Enchanting? Just start spouting poetry and shit while you're at it.*

"I guess if you were going to kill me, you would have left me to drown, not pulled me to shore." A devilish gleam sparked in her eyes. "But you did kiss me without consent." Damn. That smile. Killer.

"I promise, Paisley"—I called her by name just so I could feel it curl around my tongue—"if I kiss you, you'll know it." Her smile faltered, and something intangible passed between us. I cleared my throat. "Let's get you to the doctor."

"Okay."

I stood and helped her to her feet. She pulled the towel closer to her. "I need my cover-up."

"I may have cut it loose while I was pulling you ashore."

"Oh. Right." She sighed and led me to her beach spot, then slipped shorts and a T-shirt over those curves. Shame, really. She grabbed her bag. "Ready."

We crossed the sand wordlessly, washed our feet at the little shower sprayer on the octagon deck, and headed to the parking lot.

I unlocked the passenger door of my Defender and held it open. Paisley tossed her bag inside, sank her teeth into her lower lip, and then looked at me. "I can't get in here."

What? "You're going to the damned doctor."

She laughed, and I immediately wanted to hear it again. "No, I mean, I physically can't get up here unless you have a ladder."

"No problem." I put my hands on her waist and lifted her in. *Do not think about sex. Don't do it.*

Too late.

I slammed her door home, climbed into my side, and had my GPS find the nearest urgent care. "Let's go, Lucy."

"You named your car?"

I turned the key, and she purred. "Absolutely. She's the most dependable woman in my life." Lucy had been my mother's last gift to me and the lift kit a to-me-from-me present, my reward for getting the hell away.

Five minutes and a red light later, we were there. She signed in, and I settled into the uncomfortable plastic waiting-room chair. At least I'd remembered to throw a shirt on, but my trunks dripped water down my legs, forming puddles on the linoleum floor as she took the seat next to me.

"Why would your parents kill you?"

"Oh, I'm sure they'd really be okay." She picked at the leather of her purse.

"Let's make a deal. I don't know you, and you don't know me. We've got a few minutes where our lives overlap, so let's agree not to lie to each other. Don't worry about what I think, just tell the truth."

A blush crept up her neck, coloring her skin pink. "They're just a little overprotective. They don't like it when they don't know what I'm up to."

"They don't know you're at the beach?"

She tucked a wet strand of hair behind her ear. It fell beneath her collarbone. "They think I'm unpacking my new townhouse. I have my debit card, so if I pay cash and keep it off my insurance, they won't know I was here. This is what I get for lying, right?" She sighed. "We start classes next week, so it seemed like good timing to get away. No homework yet, and I have the week off of work, and... Oh, I'm rambling." She forced a fake smile and examined her knees.

"I like rambling." Shit. I did when she was the one rambling. "What are you majoring in?"

"You'll laugh." She stole a look sideways at me, and those green eyes chewed me up and spat me out.

"I won't."

"Guess. Go ahead. Guess the most boring major you can think of. Of course, I find it fascinating." She blinked at me all too seriously.

"Underwater toenail painting."

She laughed, and there went that word through my damn head again. *Enchanting.* "No. Try again."

"Antigravitational basket weaving?"

"Oh, you're just about hopeless."

I may be hopeless, but you're smiling. "Tell me."

Her eyes narrowed, like she was judging me, deciding if I was worthy to know her secret. "Okay. Library sciences."

"A librarian." I couldn't stop the images playing in my head: pressing her petite body against the books in the stacks. Shit.

"See, you think it's lame."

"'Lame' is the word furthest from my mind, trust me."

Her smile returned, this time genuine, and I struggled to find anything else to say that wouldn't make me sound like a moron.

She pulled out her phone and sent a text. "Morgan's going to worry when she gets back and can't find me."

"You should call your boyfriend, too. I'm sure he'd want to know what happened." The image of finding her was burned into my brain. Pale, not breathing, lying limp on the bottom of the ocean floor.

"Oh, no. Will wouldn't want to know. He'd be furious."

"Furious that you came to the beach?"

Her fingers flexed across her sternum. "That I came to the beach, that I moved out of my parents' into my own place, that I've had a job now for six months that he doesn't know about... It's going to be an interesting conversation, let's just say that."

"How long have you two been together?" *Why the fuck do you care?*

"Almost a year."

"You in love with him?"

Her head whipped toward mine, her eyes narrowed. "That's none of your business."

Ah, there was some fire beneath that honey exterior. "Well, either you are, but you're a private person, or you aren't, but you don't lie well, and I thought we weren't lying here...so which is it?"

She crossed her arms in front of her chest. I was good at that, finding someone's trigger, setting them off for the hell of it, but that hadn't been my intention here. Fuck.

"I'm sorry. I shouldn't have asked."

Her shoulders relaxed, and her eyes softened. "No, it's just that we were apart for so long while he was at—"

"Paisley?" the nurse called.

"That's me." She raised her hand and stood. "Would you mind waiting here?" she asked, something like fear flickering across her face.

Like I was going to leave her? "Yeah, I'm good. I'll wait for you." I grabbed the magazine next to me and pretended to read as I watched her walk away. I could do that all day.

It took her an hour, but by the time she came out, I'd convinced the checkout lady to tell Paisley it was a free clinic, and I'd handed over my card to cover her. Hell, it wasn't really my money anyway.

"All clear!" she said with a smile, but she looked pale again.

I forced a smile and held open the door, something I always did out of habit, but for Paisley, I *wanted* to.

The Florida humidity closed in as we walked out of the clinic.

"Morgan?" Paisley called out as a girl came running across the parking lot, all legs and cleavage behind a mess of brunette hair, my usual type. *Usual? When did I start thinking usual?*

"Oh my Gawd." She drew out that last word in a deeper accent. "I never thought he would do that!" She threw her arms around Paisley and burst into tears. "I'm so sorry!"

Paisley patted her back but didn't cry. She hadn't shed a tear through any of it. "It's okay, Morgan. I'm okay."

Her friend pulled away and smacked her shoulder. "You have to learn to swim!"

"Okay," Paisley placated her. She turned toward me with a shy smile. "Besides, Mr. California here pulled me out, so some good came of it, right?"

"That's an insult to a Coloradan. You know that, right? And it's Jagger."

Morgan took a long sweep of me with her eyes, something I was pretty used to, but it annoyed me instead of setting off my usual seek-and-fuck response. "Aren't you the hero?" She used a breathy tone of voice I was sure frequently worked like a charm. She swayed over to me, running her fingers up my chest. "Anything I can do to say thank you for saving my best friend?"

Over Morgan's shoulder, Paisley stiffened, and I pulled away. "Yeah, you can thank me by teaching her to swim. It was close." *Too close.*

"Absolutely!" She hugged Paisley again. "Let's get home and unpack?" She skipped across the pavement to a white sedan.

Paisley nodded, then walked to me slowly, her eyes darting across the ground like she couldn't focus or think of what to say. She looked at me when we were a foot or so apart. We stared at each other in charged silence for a moment, and then she flung herself up, jumping slightly.

I caught her tiny frame easily, and she wrapped her arms around my neck, laying her head over my shoulder as her feet dangled. "Thank you for saving me. For seeing me."

I held her tightly, savoring the only time I'd feel this girl against me. She smelled like salt water and Florida sun. "I saw you way before you went into the water, Paisley. I'd say you're welcome, but I'm just thankful I got to you." She loosened her hold, and I let her slip to her feet. Letting go sucked, plain and simple.

She retreated toward the car, keeping her eyes locked on mine. It was everything I could do to let her go, not to demand her phone number, her address, a way to see her again. After all, she'd come to the beach to escape, not to get stalked by me.

She paused with her hand on the door. "I love Will. He's my best friend, a part of my family, and he...he knows what I need. He's good for me." She gave me a smile that about sent me to my knees. "I'm so glad I met you, Jagger."

She opened her door and moved to get in. "Paisley!" I called out, unable to stop myself.

She turned her head with raised eyebrows.

"He's a lucky bastard, and I hope he knows it."

CHAPTER THREE

PAISLEY

8. Keep some semblance of peace in my life.

I parked at my parents' house on Fort Rucker and did a double take. Was that…? Yes, it was. Daddy was going to be frosted when he found out, if he hadn't already seen it. *Maybe I should skip breakfast this morning.*

The fifteen-foot-tall polar bear statue that kept watch across from the museum now stood guard in Daddy's front yard, wrapped in dozens of PT belts. That thing was at least fifteen hundred pounds, and I tipped my hat to whoever had moved it.

At least this wouldn't be boring.

I grabbed my handbag and headed for the house. As flight school class pranks went, this was a pretty good one. This new class had just started, and they were already at it.

Good for them.

I heard Daddy from his office before I even shut the door.

"I don't care what your goddamned schedule says! Get that thing off my lawn! And you'd better handle the responsible party!" His voice echoed through the foyer, but our golden retrievers, Layla and Clapton, didn't move from their prone position, only thumped their tails when they saw me.

"Y'all are some great guard dogs." I bent down to pet them.

"It had better be gone by lunch, Major. Damned polar bear." The phone crashed in its cradle a moment before the French doors opened. "Lee-Lee!" Daddy embraced me lightly. I missed real hugs, the ones so tight I thought my ribs might break. "You ready for breakfast?"

"Famished and wasting away," I joked, patting my belly.

"You girls, all worried about your figures. A man likes curves, my gal." His arm around my shoulders, we crossed through the living room to the kitchen, where my mother finished the gravy.

"Oh, Lee, you're actually here." She smiled. "Could you take the biscuits out?"

"I told you I would be, Mama. We agreed, once a week." I grabbed the nearest pot holder and took the biscuits out of the oven, careful to place them on the silver trivet she'd laid out. "Perfect as always."

"You flatter me. Now, grab a plate, your daddy only has fifteen minutes before they notice he's not an hour early and the world ends."

"Ha." Daddy kissed her on the cheek, his tan T-shirt almost complementary to Mama's blue shirtdress and ARMY WIFE apron. We'd given it to her for Christmas when I was ten, and she still wore it religiously.

"Is Will coming?" Mama asked, setting four places at the table.

"He said he'd be here at seven fifteen." I took glasses down for orange juice.

"Damn, I just might miss him," Daddy muttered.

"Richard! Language!" My mom swatted his backside when she thought I couldn't see. "We are certainly not your soldiers!"

He laughed and winked at her. "Ah, my poor little southern

belles, are my Yankee manners offending you?"

"Lack of manners." She sighed and waved him off with a smile. "Get your plate."

The doorbell set the dogs barking. "Tell that boy he doesn't need to ring the doorbell. He's family," Daddy ordered.

I swung the door open, happy to see Will standing in the entry. He looked good, but I still wasn't used to seeing him in regular uniform. "Good morning, Lee-Lee." He bent and kissed my cheek. "How are you feeling?"

I ignored his question and instead pressed my mouth to his gently. "I missed you yesterday."

He pulled me into a familiar hug. "Sorry, honey, class ran late."

"You wouldn't happen to know about that polar bear in our front yard, would you?"

With a squeeze of my shoulders, he broke our hug and headed in to breakfast. "Yeah, I might need to talk to your dad about that before I go to class."

"Will!" Mom exclaimed as she put the food on the table. "So good to see you."

"You, too, ma'am." He held my chair, and I slid in, sitting between him and Daddy.

"Oh, you know you can call me Mom." She heaped food onto his plate.

My stomach dropped slightly. Was that because he was my boyfriend? Or because he'd been Peyton's best friend?

"Yes, ma'am." Will smiled with that gorgeous sparkle in his amber eyes. Maybe they weren't crystal blue like Jagger's— *Stop!* I nipped that right in the bud. It had been a week and a half since I'd been pulled out of the ocean by Mr. California…Colorado… whatever, but his face wouldn't stop popping into my thoughts or invading the peace of my dreams.

He'd saved my life. It made perfect sense that I thought about him. Right? Just maybe not *this* much. Where was he? Had he headed home to Colorado, like his license plate suggested? Was he in college? Out? What did it feel like to be kissed by a guy with a tongue ring?

"Lee!" Mama snapped.

I found a biscuit crushed in my left hand and heard a beeping sound coming from the kitchen. "Ma'am?"

"Your alarm?" She pointed to the counter where my handbag rested.

I nodded, throwing away my decimated biscuit on the way to the counter. Slipping my cell phone out of the bag, I canceled the reminder. I left the phone in my bag—Mama wouldn't stand for it at the table—and took my seat again.

"Aren't you forgetting something?" She raised an eyebrow.

"I'll take them right after I eat. They make me sick on an empty stomach." I grabbed another biscuit, breaking it in half before placing it on my plate.

"I think you should—"

"Honey, maybe you could just grab them—"

"Magnolia. Will. Give her a break. She'll take them after she eats." Daddy's voice stopped them midcomplaint, and I smiled my thanks at him. He nodded but didn't look happy as he went back to his breakfast.

My mouth watered as I reached for the gravy.

"Oh, Lee, I made you a fruit salad instead." Mama handed the crystal bowl across the table.

I scooped the fruit onto my plate, still eyeing the gravy. "Thank you."

"Have you told Dr. Larondy our decision yet?" she asked, staring at my plate and counting every calorie I wasn't allowed to work off.

I froze midchew, and Will squeezed my knee under the table, sending silent support. I just never knew for whom. Swallowing slowly, I thought through my response.

"I haven't—"

"Lee, you can't put this off." Her voice rose.

"—because I haven't made *my* decision yet."

Well, if that didn't hush her right up. Her fork rattled on the breakfast china. "We decided that the procedure—"

"You decided, Mama," I rebuked, keeping my voice as low and respectful as I could. "I haven't had symptoms since we started the beta-blockers, and while I respect your choice and your wishes—"

"But you don't, not really." *Oh, here we go.* "You couldn't possibly respect us, love us, if you're willing to risk your life like this. Every day you wait is too long. To even think of putting your father and I through this again is just unforgivable, Lee. This is your life we're talking about!"

"Magnolia, enough." Daddy's voice was soft but stern. "We don't have these breakfasts so you can bully her."

I swallowed my response, knowing Mama spoke from grief and fear. Maybe she was right, and I was selfish, wanting to make this decision myself, when it affected so much more than me.

I wasn't just trapped by my condition, the thickening of my heart muscle. HCM might limit me, but the cage I lived in was fortified by my parents' expectations, locked by their grief over Peyton, and gilded by my own need to lessen their pain by whatever degree possible.

The right thing would be to agree with them, accept the half life the internal pacemaker sentenced me to, and make everyone happy. Even Will wanted it, though he said he'd support whatever decision I made.

But the right thing felt unbearably *wrong*. My instincts screamed at me every time I even considered the pacemaker. It wasn't going to save me, and I couldn't explain how I knew, but I did. I was sick of this. Don't run. Don't eat fatty foods. Don't drink. Don't forget your meds. Don't upset your mama, and for God's sake, don't raise your heartbeat. Don't...live, just exist.

The need to flee gripped me, but I stayed put. I had my own place now, with their blessing, and even had one class up at Troy. One helping of guilt for breakfast a week was manageable. I squeezed Will's fingers, and he took the cue.

"The gravy is fantastic this morning, ma'am."

Mama forced a smile and accepted his compliment. I took a couple deep breaths and concentrated on chewing.

"How are classes, my gal?" Daddy asked.

"Good. I love this semester, especially the class at Troy. I think next semester I'll be okay for the rest of the classes I need to take there."

His brow furrowed. "I like it better when you can take the classes here on post."

Activate appeasement mode. "I know, Daddy, but they don't offer all the classes I need down here. It's only a forty-five-minute drive. I don't mind." The commute was a small price to pay to pretend my life was normal once a week. It was a battle I was willing to pick.

"Well, I mind," he muttered, eating his food so fast I'd swear he was being timed.

An uncomfortable silence settled over the table. I couldn't think of a thing to say that wouldn't end badly, so I stayed quiet.

"Will, tell us how your first week went?" Mama asked.

Will slid his hand from my knee like she could see him under the table. "Well, ma'am, it's not West Point, but it's nice to have some freedom." He flashed that grin, the one that had hooked me, and a smile spread across my face as he turned to me. "Plus, the company is much better. It's nice to be close to Lee."

Mama rested her hand on her chest and sighed. "It's lovely to see you two together in person, instead of on the computer. Two peas in a pod."

Will brushed a kiss across my knuckles. "Couldn't agree more."

"Have you given any thought to which aircraft you're going to select?" Daddy asked.

"Yes, sir. I'd like to fly the AH-64."

Daddy's eyes lit up, and he raised his eyebrows. "Ah, the Apache. Good choice. You'll have to rank at the top of the OML after primary to select that."

"Order of Merit list," Will explained as Daddy stood.

"Will's going to have to finish this phase of flight school at the very top of his class if he wants to fly that helicopter, Paisley. There are only a few of those slots per class."

I nudged Will with my elbow like we were back in high school. "I'm not worried."

"How do you like the other lieutenants in your class? Are there many of you?" Daddy carried his plate to the sink.

"Five lieutenants and twenty warrant officers." Color crept up his neck, and he flexed his jaw. "But it should only be four lieutenants."

"What's wrong?" I asked. It took a lot to get under Will's skin.

"Nothing you need to worry about, Lee-Lee." He winked, and I swallowed the urge to tell him again how much I hated when he called me that. Lee-Lee was twelve, gangly, and awkward. I hoped that was no longer the case.

"Okay." I forced out a half smile.

"So about that PT belt–wrapped polar bear?" Daddy asked, zipping his ACU top.

"Yes, sir. I think I need to tell you about that."

He knows who did it? Daddy's hands flexed on the counter. "What do you know, Will?"

"It may have been a class prank gone a little too far." Oh, yes, his cheeks flushed—his tell.

"Your class?" Daddy's voice dropped softly, dangerously. Daddy didn't yell when he was super mad. Oh, no, he didn't need to.

"Yes, sir."

My eyes flickered between Will and Daddy, and my heart picked up a faster beat. "Will, did you put that thing in the front yard?" I couldn't stop the words from tumbling out any more than I could quiet the half of me screaming in hope that he had, that he could break even one rule.

He tore his eyes from my father, meeting mine. "No." He cupped my face with his hands. "I did not do this." He looked to Daddy. "But I know who did."

My stomach turned.

Daddy nodded. "I think we'd best continue this discussion away from the ladies. My office seems more appropriate."

"Yes, sir." Will cleared his plate and took my empty one to the sink. I hurried from the table, standing behind him as he loaded it into the dishwasher.

"You know who did it?"

"Yes."

"And you're going to tell on your classmate?" It hardly seemed like the loyal thing to do.

"A cadet will not lie, cheat, steal, or tolerate those who do." His jaw did the immovable thing that signaled his mind was made up.

"You're not at the academy anymore, Will. Are you sure you want to do this? You're in flight school with these guys for the next couple of years. Aren't you supposed to look out for one another?"

"You think I want guys like this in with me? Being active duty doesn't change that it was wrong. I tried to stop them, but Bateman wouldn't listen. That's a piece of Fort Rucker history that they defaced."

It's a bear.

"No one got hurt, and nothing is damaged. It was a harmless prank. Do you know what Daddy will do? You could get them kicked out over a silly polar bear with a few too many PT belts wrapped around it, not to mention they'll all know you told."

"William?" Daddy called.

Will's spine straightened like Daddy had pulled an invisible string. "I can't expect you to understand, Lee-Lee." He bent down, his lips brushing my cheek. "You'd better get to class. I don't know how long this will take with your dad."

"Remember I have work later. Can I see you tonight?" I needed him to banish the memory of a pair of blue eyes that wouldn't go away. I also needed to resubmit the paperwork to have minor construction work done at the library. Class, work, then Will. Best plan ever.

He grimaced. "I know you told me last week, but I still hate you working. What if it's too much?"

"It's seriously the most heart-happy job I could ask for. Now, tonight?"

"I'll do my best." His grin stole away my annoyance of what he was getting ready to do, and I returned the kiss he gifted me, knowing it wouldn't go any farther with Mama ten feet away. He left me standing in the kitchen.

"That's the kind of man a woman can be proud of, Lee." Mama rinsed her own plate. "You're lucky to have him. Not everyone puts such value on morals."

I received her message—*leave it alone.* "I'm headed to class, Mama. Thank you for breakfast. I'll see you next week?"

Her mouth pursed. "A whole week?"

"We agreed I'd stay here for school and rent that townhouse, but you have to give me a little wiggle room. I'm almost twenty-one." I kept my voice level. Emotions would only earn me a raised eyebrow and a lecture that I wasn't ready to be an adult.

Her gaze flickered to the framed family picture behind me, like it always did when she thought about her. "A week it is."

I hugged her, letting go after one of her signature pats on my back. "I love you, Mama."

Handbag over my arm, I stopped to brush my fingers over

the framed picture in the entryway. Peyton stood in the middle, her pixie face radiant with excitement, dressed identically to Will, on her left, in their gray West Point uniforms, while I hugged her right. Her arms connected us, hopefully approving of what we'd evolved into.

"What would you do, Peyton?" I whispered. "Two hundred twenty days left. What would you have done?"

I missed her so much. A black hole blossomed in my heart, sucking out every breath I'd taken since she'd died, as if I was watching them lay her in the ground. She would've known what to do, but she hadn't needed to make a decision. She'd been free, wild, uninhibited, and paid with her life before she'd even realized there'd been a price. A wretched pang of envy stabbed through me, washed back by the sinking feeling of guilt. She was gone. I was here. I took a couple of deep breaths, pushing the grief where it belonged, in the past.

I almost made it out, but Mama's voice followed me through the front doorway. "Lee! You take your medication right now!"

"Yes, Mama."

CHAPTER FOUR

*You're drowning me, holding me under the rising tide
of your impossible expectations.*

Every curse word I'd ever heard came to mind as the instructors jumped ship. Literally. My heart pounded in my ears, and I had the split-second desire to bail with them. Fuck that. This was my dream, and had been since I'd seen rotors against a blue sky thirteen years ago. I could do this.

Dunker training was a heaping slice of hell.

The pistons released, and the mock helo sank. Water soaked my boots, rushed past my knees, into my lap, and then up my chest. *Wait. Wait. Not yet.*

The pool water hit my collarbone, and I sucked in all the air my lungs could hold. I gripped the seat, my fingers digging in as the water rose over my nose and head. Then they tilted my world on its axis and pitched the aircraft to the right, spinning me upside down. Water forced its way into my nose. This shit sucked.

We stopped moving—it was go time. I fought the panic threatening to force out all my air and concentrated on the harness. My fingers slipped. Double shit. *Calm down.*

A few concentrated movements and the harness came free. I was out of the seat. Hand over hand, I righted myself, made my way to the window, and popped the seal. My lungs screamed, and I released a small amount of air, relieving the pressure. I pulled myself through the window, making sure I cleared the gigantic helmet. I pushed off the outside of the aircraft and kicked my way to the surface, streaming air from my nose.

At least this time it was only my life at stake and not hers.

I burst through the surface of the water, welcoming the rush of oxygen into my deprived lungs. I'd made it.

"Bateman! That was not the proper hand technique!" the instructor yelled.

I swam to the edge of the pool and hoisted myself up, sitting on the edge. "Well, sir," I answered as I unclasped my waterlogged helmet, "since we're sitting here having this conversation, I'm not dead, so I'd have to say the outcome was satisfactory despite me not using your approved hand technique."

I made it out alive, assface. Josh sat farther down the pool ledge, shaking his head at me like we were on the ice and I'd landed in the penalty box again. What? I'd held my fucking temper.

"That kind of attitude can get you killed in a hard-water landing."

My mouth opened, ready to overrun my brain. "Right, and—"

"Jagger Bateman?" a captain called from poolside.

"Sir?"

The steel sheen to his eyes said this was anything but a friendly visit. "Major Davidson would like to see you in his office."

I nodded. "We're done here in thirty."

He shook his head. "Get dried off, you're done. He wants you *now*."

I waited, cover in my lap, outside Major Davidson's office. There was only one reason he'd call for me, a butter-bar lieutenant who'd been in class less than two weeks. He knew. He had to.

The asshole had a long reach. I ran through the possible outcomes in my head. What they'd ask for. What I'd agree to. The inevitable phone call that might keep the shit hole of my family life at bay.

I just wanted to fly. That's it. I couldn't remember wanting anything else. How could I? But one phone call from my father, and it would all end, or even worse—he'd taint it with his help. I'd gotten here on my own merit, lucky enough to do it with my best friend, and I wasn't letting him take this from me.

A cute sergeant gave me the eye as she walked by, but I couldn't muster much interest. One, I knew the fraternization policy and wasn't risking anything for a piece of tail. Two, I'd sworn off women in general. What was the point working my ass off to get here if I let myself get distracted?

Not going to happen. No woman was worth jeopardizing my dream for.

Well, maybe… *Nope, not even that one.*

Green eyes skipped across my memory. Where was she? I should have asked where she went to school. I should have asked her last name. *Yeah, like you're anywhere near good enough for a girl like that.*

I beat my father's voice out of my head. It didn't matter anyway. Paisley was long gone.

"Lieutenant Bateman?"

Here we go. "Major Davidson, sir." I stood, ready to face

my fate.

"In my office, Lieutenant." He turned in to his office, leaving me to follow.

The room was sparse but orderly. He leafed through a file on his desk with one hand and motioned to the seat in front of his desk with the other. I took it. My uniform squeaked against the pleather of the military-issue chair as I shifted my weight.

He took a deep breath, and I held mine. "Anything you'd like to tell me about last night?"

Last night? "Sir?"

"You have one chance to come clean, Bateman. After that you'll be out on your ass. The CG doesn't tolerate liars any more than he does unexpected lawn ornaments."

Wait, this was all about the bear? My breath exhaled in sharp relief. "What exactly would you like to know, sir?"

He leaned back in his chair. "I'd like to know how a fifteen-foot-tall, fifteen-hundred-pound polar bear wound up on the CG's lawn."

"Fifteen hundred pounds? Huh. It didn't really feel that heavy." That thing was a behemoth.

The major's mouth dropped slightly before he caught himself. "So you admit to stealing Sergeant Ted E. Bear?"

Every muscle in my body contracted. *Do not laugh. Don't do it.* "That's really his name?" I kept a straight face. *Booyah.*

His jaw flexed. "That polar bear is part of Fort Rucker tradition, Lieutenant, something you show a fatal lack of respect for."

I kept my mouth shut. Sure, I liked to stir the pot, watch the shit fly. But when it was my career on the line? I knew when to play the good boy.

"Did you vandalize the bear?"

"Technically, he came to no harm. He's standing guard." *With about twenty-three PT belts wrapped around him.*

Major Davidson took a large breath. "Last chance."

Shit. I couldn't lie. There was no one else out there in the hallway; they already knew I'd done it. How? Wait... I was the only one out there. *They don't know about Josh and Grayson.*

"Yes. I relocated Sergeant Ted E. Bear from his post to the CG's lawn." *Boom.* Fell on the grenade. I just hoped it didn't blow my future to pieces.

"How?" The major's eyes were wide—surprised I'd told the truth? Yeah, it was a novel concept to me, too.

"With my truck."

"You expect me to believe that your truck hauled a fifteen-hundred-pound statue three and a half miles?"

"Three."

"I'm sorry?" He leaned forward in his chair.

"It's exactly three miles, not three and a half." They happened to take *forever* when hauling a fucking statue.

"Right. And you did this with your truck?"

"It's a very powerful engine, sir. You'd be amazed what a super winch and a trailer will do."

"Why?" His tone rose in blatant curiosity.

"Never could back down from a dare, sir. Gaping flaw and whatnot."

"A dare? You did this on a *dare*?"

A wry grin escaped. "Looks like it."

"And the PT belts?" He arched a sardonic eyebrow at me.

My thumb grazed the Bateman tag at the back of my cover. "Social commentary on the new uniform policy."

His lips twitched upward, but he stifled it before I could call it a grin. "On a dare. Right. And who helped you?"

There it was. My gaze didn't leave his. My jaw clenched once. Twice. There was no way in hell I was ratting them out. Not going to fucking happen. But I couldn't lie, either. "I didn't need any help."

He laughed. "Son, there's no way you did that alone. Name the others, and there's a slight chance you'll be able to stay in flight school."

And for thirty silver coins... "I alone strapped the bear to the winch. I alone towed that thing exactly three miles."

He smoothed his hands over the papers in my file. "And you alone lifted a fifteen-hundred-pound statue onto the lawn?"

Poker face. "I'm freakishly strong, sir."

"Son, I admire your loyalty to the others, but you need to start naming names, or it's going to get very bad, very quickly."

"Mine is the only name I'll be stating, and I have not spoken a single lie." I didn't. I hooked up the bear. I unhooked the bear. I drove the Defender. The others had nothing to do with those parts. My file slammed shut, smashing my dreams to smithereens.

"You have until end of duty day to change your mind."

Four years of ROTC, a private pilot's license, endless nights studying for the flight aptitude test, and I was about to get kicked out of flight school over a fucking polar bear. Sure, it had been stupid, but seriously. A statue?

The sun beat into my uniform as I sat outside HQ my last five minutes before reporting to Major Davidson. Fuck, I wanted those wings on my chest. I wanted to climb into an aircraft, fly into battle, defend something larger than myself. Now I'd be packing my shit before the weekend.

For the first time in my life, I'd felt like I could do it—break away and make something of myself. As usual, I'd gone and fucked it all up. It was my specialty, after all.

Time was up. I savored the walk to his office, breathing in the scent of possibility for what I feared would be the last time. I knocked on his door.

"Come in."

I hardened my resolve and opened the door. *What the*

hell? The seats in the office were already occupied. *Shit. No.* "Walker? Masters?"

Josh made a face that was half smile, half grimace. "Did you really think we'd let you take the fall for this?"

"No chance. You're not falling on the sword," Masters added. His knuckles were white where he gripped his cover.

"How did you know?"

Major Davidson answered. "Your friends came forward about an hour ago." He turned his back to us and stared out the window. "What am I going to do with you?"

We stayed silent while he deliberated. "You clearly disrespected and vandalized a cherished piece of Fort Rucker tradition, but you showed unwavering loyalty to fellow officers. On the other hand, they came forward of their own volition, showing remarkable integrity. What to do?"

A thousand smart-ass remarks raced through me, but I kept them all to myself. Now was definitely not the time to let my mouth loose.

His head cocked to the side. "You boys have any experience working with your hands?"

"Yes, sir. I grew up building boats," Masters answered.

"Yes, sir," Josh echoed.

"Yes, sir," I added. If you counted the hours I'd put into the Defender, taping my hockey stick, or assembling my dorm room Ikea furniture, then sure, I had experience.

"Perfect. You'll be working off your insult."

CHAPTER FIVE

15. Accomplish something meaningful without Dad's help.

"Have a good day," I whispered to the lady at the counter as I handed her the Wi-Fi password on a scrap of paper.

I grabbed my cell phone from my handbag. Nothing from Will yet. I couldn't wait to see him tonight—another perk of having my own place. I left the phone on the counter and gathered a manageable pile of books. "I'm going to file these away," I said to Alice. She waved me off with a small smile, wrinkling her gently weathered face. She was easily eighty but wouldn't give the library up. It was her home, and I understood completely. It was quiet here. Calm enough that I could think.

"Just got a call—they're sending over a few men to fix up your back room so we can get to that door. They'll be here to check it over and estimate it for us."

My mouth dropped open. "Really? I've been requesting

all summer. Why now?"

"Well, someone up high must have heard you." She patted my hand. "It will be nice to have that storage room put together."

Higher up. Daddy. My stomach sank, but I forced a smile onto my face. "Sure will." I stacked the books and headed for fiction. I'd purposely followed the correct guidelines, completed all the right paperwork, and never mentioned it to him. I didn't want to get this done because he waved his magic wand and made it happen. Even my name tag said Paisley here, just to distance myself a little more from his Lee.

I filed the books, then came out of the stacks, passing the tables where flight school students studied. Fort Rucker, the home of army aviation, was a high-pressure environment. Flyboys who wanted wings had to pass flight school here. That girl in the corner looked particularly stressed out, so I passed her the snack-size Skittles package I'd had in my pocket. "Sugar always helps," I whispered with a wink.

She smiled in gratitude, and I headed back to the desk, taking the small stairs in a couple strides. "Ah, there she is!" Alice's voice was abnormally high-pitched and overly sweet.

Coming around the corner, I smacked right into the reason. Hands steadied me, thank goodness, because once those electric-blue eyes met mine, gravity ceased to exist. "Jagger?" *Oh, no, did that come out breathless?*

His eyes widened before a smile lit up his face. "Paisley?"

I opened and shut my mouth, blinking rapidly as I struggled to find a coherent thought. I must have looked like a fish out of water. My breath hitched, and my lips tingled. I hadn't imagined the effect he'd had on me in Florida; it was real.

This was not good.

"Hey, you know her?" a guy behind him asked.

Jagger's eyes swept over me. "You could say that."

I had to get some distance. The dark jeans and worn Harley-Davidson tee weren't a big enough barrier for me when he stood this close. I moved back, but luckily his hands were still locked on my forearms, keeping me from falling down the steps. "Whoa. I'd rather avoid the doctor this time."

My breath expelled in light laughter. He pivoted away from the staircase, and I retreated. With space between us, I could breathe again.

"You going to introduce us, or just stare at her?" the guy asked again.

"Shut the hell up, Walker." Jagger tore his eyes away from mine. "Paisley, this is Josh Walker."

Josh nodded at me. He was maybe an inch taller, with a gorgeous face and killer smile, but nothing like Jagger's. Then again, I wasn't sure anyone was made like Jagger. *No. No. No. Don't think like that!*

"And that"—Jagger pointed to another guy behind them— "is Grayson Masters." Grayson gave me a miniscule wave with no smile in his gray eyes. He was slightly shorter than Jagger but built like he could charge down a bull, or maybe lift one.

"They're here for your back-door project, dear," Alice whispered loud enough for the entire floor of the library to hear.

Jagger, God bless him, didn't laugh, but a simple glance showed the sparkle in his eyes and a bitten lip. I wanted to bite that lip. *You're so going to hell if you don't knock this off, Paisley Lynn.* "She means clear a path to the back door. Of the library. Right." I hurried past that statement before it could get any more awkward. "The room is a mess." I blinked at him, nothing better to say.

"No problem, we're happy to help," Jagger answered.

"We are?" Grayson asked.

"We are."

"So, you live here?" I spit out, trying to hold on to a

coherent thought.

His smile flipped my stomach. "I do."

I swallowed. "And you work construction?" That would explain the cut muscles.

He hooked his thumbs through his belt loops. "At the moment it seems so, and I couldn't be happier."

I pulled the edges of my black cardigan across my midsection. It was usually cool in the library, despite the sweltering Alabama heat, but I needed more layers than the cashmere to protect me from the energy pouring off him. "Okay." *Okay? Mercy, think of something, anything better to say!*

"Show us the way?"

I forced a smile with closed lips and led the way past the tables of studying students, through the quiet stacks, past the small alcoves and the meeting rooms, to the room with the sign reading AUTHORIZED PERSONNEL ONLY. I pushed the door open and flipped the light switch. The strong smells of dust and paper permeated the air.

"Whoa." Jagger slid in behind me, making room for the other two.

"Exactly." Ceiling-high boxes cluttered the room and left no direct path to the hidden back door. The room was a good size, easily thirty by twenty feet, but we couldn't even see the walls.

"This is not a one-day thing," Josh muttered.

"This isn't a one-week thing," Grayson agreed. "Not with our schedule. We can't even get started for three weeks."

Jagger ran the stud in his tongue along his teeth. That thing was so unbelievably sexy. "What do you need done, Paisley?"

Snap out of it! "What do I *need* done? Or what do I *want* done?"

He leaned against the one cleared section of wall, folding his arms across his chest. One of his tattoos peeked out along his bicep. I had to get out of this room and away from him.

"Both."

Concentrate. I surveyed the absolute chaos. "I need a path cleared to the back door at least. We'd never pass code this way, and I know an inspection is coming. But what I'd want?" I pointed to the walls. "Shelves built and installed there. A workstation there to receive new orders. More shelves built and installed there and there to handle the overflow, and a central space for repair."

Jagger lifted one of the boxes. "Damn, these things are heavy."

"Well, books usually are."

He laughed and set it down. "We'll need to know where all of these things go once the shelves are up."

"I don't mind helping." Control was appealing, but I knew it was going to be a battle with Will.

"Then I guess I'll be seeing you a lot."

A lot. How long could I spend around him without doing something stupid? "Just...make a list of what you need, and I'll see about getting it." I grabbed a legal pad and pen from the long, cluttered table and thrust it toward Josh. "I need to... file some books."

Jagger raised his eyebrows at my hasty retreat. "There's three weeks to get everything together, and then we'll get to work," he promised. "I'll see you soon."

I managed a nod, then fled.

"You didn't lift any of those boxes, did you?" Alice asked, checking out two books.

"No, ma'am. I know better."

"Handsome man, the blond one." She stacked a group of books and slid a sideways look at me. "How do you know him?"

"I've only met him once. I wouldn't say that constitutes knowing him," I answered, taking the stack. "He's just...a guy." *Liar.*

"Well, if I was young enough, I'd say that he's more than enough *guy*."

"I reckon for some lucky girl, he is."

"Well, I'd sure let him leave his boots under my bed."

I was not letting that thought anywhere near my brain. *Too late.* I slipped the books into my arms and headed to file them, trying desperately to ignore the fact that Jagger was actually here. How often had I thought about him since Florida? Not just those eyes, as beautiful as they were, but the way he'd pulled me from the water. He was the only reason I was still alive.

I lost myself in the process of filing books, the quiet monotony. I relished this silence, the way my thoughts could focus or scatter, depending on what I needed. There was no more perfect place in the world for me than the library, surrounded by thousands of stories waiting to be discovered. I filed the last Philippa Gregory and glanced at my watch.

Five until seven. Time to lock up. I walked the floor, clearing the meeting rooms and hidden alcoves so I didn't lock some unknowing patron inside. "All clear," I told Alice as I retrieved my handbag from under the counter. "What about the crew in the back?"

"You just missed them, but I bet if you skip out there, you could still catch him." Her silver eyebrows wiggled.

"No need. I just didn't want to lock them in."

"Mmm-hmm," she replied. "You head out. I'll lock up."

"Sounds good. I'll see you after class tomorrow."

I waved at the door as she cranked the key. I walked under the trees to where my car was parked. Jagger's reverse lights were on across the parking lot as I slid behind the wheel of my car and turned the ignition. It cranked but didn't turn over. *This is not happening.* My car was only two years old; there was no way she wasn't going to start. I tried again with the same result.

No problem. Will wouldn't mind taking a study break to bail me out. I opened my handbag for my cell phone...that wasn't there. *Oh, no.* I'd left it on the desk...in the library... that was locked. Wasn't that craptastic?

The horn blared when I knocked my forehead into it. This was my punishment for looking at someone other than my boyfriend, right? I popped the hood and stepped out of the car. I got it raised and propped and then looked down at the engine, lifting my eyebrows.

"Well, what do you think is wrong?"

I didn't need to look to know that Jagger was standing beside me. "I have no earthly idea."

"Then why are you looking at the engine?"

"Because that's what people do, right? If the car won't start, you pop the hood and take a look."

"But you have no clue what you're looking for."

I tried to unscrunch my facial features. "Well, no."

He laughed. I kept my eyes locked on the hoses in my engine. "Go try to start it."

I slipped between him and the car, successfully avoiding any contact. I left the driver's door open and tried to start it. This time it didn't even turn over.

"Do you have jumper cables?" he asked.

"I don't think so." I'd unloaded everything from the car into my new garage, feeling powerful that I'd even *had* one. I leaned out of the door to see him. He'd turned his Boston Bruins hat backward and was leaned over the engine. "Do you?"

"Ironically, no. I sent them with Ember when she went to Nashville."

Ember? "Oh, well, that leaves me in a pickle."

He lowered the hood and closed it with a *click*. "I'll take you home. Unless there's someone you'd like to call?"

"My phone is in the library." I glanced at my watch.

Twenty minutes until I had to be home for yet another dose of medication. "I don't think Will can get here in time," I muttered.

"I don't think he'll mind if I take you home." He opened my door wider and held out his hand before letting a charming smirk cross his face. "After all, I've had my mouth on yours, right? What harm could a ride be compared to that?"

I tried to fight it, but couldn't stop the slow spread of a smile across my face. I took my handbag with one hand, Jagger's with the other, and let him help me from the car. That small touch was brutal. I hadn't imagined that electric and highly inappropriate spark between us.

He opened the passenger door of the Defender and boosted me into the seat. "Lucy has missed you."

I ran my hand over the dash. "Hi there, Lucy."

"Where to?"

"Oh, I live in Enterprise." It was a tiny town outside the gate, but it was the farthest Mama and Daddy would let me get.

"Me, too. It's close to work." He winked and started the car. Dropkick Murphys blared through his sound system for a few seconds before he could turn the volume down to a non-deafening level. "Sorry." He pulled onto the road, winding us through Fort Rucker's housing.

Memories crashed through me of summer nights, Peyton's laugh, and sneaking out for concerts. "Don't be. I love them."

"Really? They don't seem like your kind of band."

"First, you don't know me well enough to even guess what kind of music I like. Secondly, maybe I have a thing for Matt," I said, naming one of the band members.

"Really?" He swung his gaze in my direction before taking it back to the road.

I laughed. "No, not really. I like them. 'Rose Tattoo' is my favorite."

He shook his head with a smile, and we rode in companionable silence. I gave him directions to my townhouse, and he pulled into the drive. "I live about three blocks from here," he said.

"In the apartments?"

"No, I share a house with Walker and Masters over there." He pointed across the main street. He helped me down, and I didn't shiver at his hands on my waist. Nope, not in the least bit. *Liar.* "So, it's been bugging me for weeks—why can't you swim?"

My cheeks heated, and I dropped my eyes to my pink toenails. "Because it used to scare me, and now...it's too late, really."

"It's never too late to learn how to swim, Paisley." He lifted my chin.

"What? Like I'm going to throw on some arm floaties and head on down to the pool with the neighborhood kids for lessons? Mortifying. I'd rather put out a campfire with my face."

The smile that swept across his face was hotter than the sun-soaked pavement that threatened to burn through my sandals. "No. I'm going to teach you."

"I have a boyfriend," I muttered.

"So you keep saying."

"I'm serious."

"Then it's a good thing sex isn't necessary to swimming." He winked.

"Will wouldn't like it." I clung to whatever reason I could.

"I'm sure Will doesn't want you drowning, either."

"It's not that I don't want to..." Every reason I should was countered with the main reason I shouldn't. But I needed to learn, and he wouldn't make fun of me.

"Look, I know it's odd, and that you don't know me. But I pulled you out of that water. I filled your lungs with my own breath, and if that doesn't make me responsible for you, I'm not sure what does." He curved the brim of his hat. Was it a nervous habit? "I can't stomach the thought of that happening to you again, of me not being there."

"I can only offer you friendship, Jagger." His name tasted as dangerous in my mouth as he looked.

"Good, because that's all I'm asking for, I swear. I'll pick you up at nine tomorrow morning." He drove away before I could change my mind, and I couldn't shake the feeling that I'd started down a slippery slope.

CHAPTER SIX

JAGGER

You saw her drowning. You watched it happen and did nothing about it. Well, except pay for her funeral.

Coffee in hand, I knocked on Paisley's door. I couldn't count how many times I'd picked a girl up at her place, and I'd never been this nervous, friend zone or not.

The door opened, and her roommate smiled at me. "Ah, Mr. California."

"Hey, Morgan."

Her eyes lit up, like always when girls were surprised I remembered their names. Had to love a photographic memory. She stretched her arms above her head, raising her shirt enough for me to see the tanned skin of her stomach. Then she slid her hands down the sides of her waist and smiled. I knew that look in her eyes. It was the same that led to many dropped panties in my general direction. Now usually I'd take that as an invitation and pursue, but she didn't even stir me, even if I hadn't sworn off women.

Fuck. Maybe my dick was broken.

"Morgan! Is that Jagger?" Paisley's voice echoed from behind her.

"It sure is." She moved aside, motioning me in.

I pushed my sunglasses to the top of my head with one hand, holding the cup of coffee from Boldly Going marked "Paisley" in the other. "Hey there!" She walked across the hallway, flustered. "I just need a minute."

The townhouse was immaculate, and bare. I passed the half wall that separated the living room from the entry and glanced around. Everything was beige and white, from the furniture to the carpet. There were no pictures on the walls, no real personal effects besides a few pictures framed on the end tables.

"Morgan, have you seen my—"

"On your dresser," she answered.

"Oh, right!" Paisley bounded from the kitchen toward the stairs, passing me without a glance.

Holy shit. Those legs... Ah, there was the familiar stirring from down below. *Nice to see you, buddy.*

"So, swimming?" Morgan asked, hopping onto the kitchen counter opposite from where I waited.

"Yeah, I want to help her learn."

"Is that *all* you want to help her with?" She batted her eyelashes over her large brown eyes.

"We're just friends, Morgan. I know all about Will."

Her eyebrows shot up. "I'm not sure why I'm surprised, really. Paisley wouldn't carry on behind his back." Her southern accent drew out the words like dripping molasses.

"We're not *carrying on*. I only want to make sure she doesn't drown again."

She cleared her throat as Paisley descended the stairs. "Ready?" The neck strap of her swimsuit peeked out over her tank top, and I had the momentary fantasy of untying it. Right, because I'd gone straight back to ninth grade, hormones and all.

Morgan slid down from the counter, snatching the coffee cup out of my hand and taking a long pull. "Yum. Caramel macchiato is my fave. Thanks!" She smacked a loud kiss on Paisley's cheek and headed up the stairs, pausing to blow me a kiss.

"Hey, that's—" I started, pretty pissed that she was stealing the only nice thing I'd done for someone in...a while.

"I don't drink coffee anyway. Don't worry about it, and I really appreciate the gesture." Paisley half smiled. "I guess I'm ready. And I'm trusting you not to poke fun at me."

"I would never." How easily she said that word. Trust wasn't something I was going to discuss, even in passing. That was something earned.

She pulled her hair into a ponytail. "Just don't take me anywhere I can embarrass myself." She bent over to grab a purple backpack, and I clenched my hands to keep from touching the blond strands that dangled near my fingers.

No distractions. No women. Only friends.

"I have just the place."

"You're certain about this?" Paisley asked from the passenger seat. We hit another bump on the dirt road, and her grip on the oh-shit handle tightened.

"Certain. You want to go somewhere you won't be seen, right?" Ridiculous, but if that's what it took, then...fine.

"Right, but I'm not sure this is a good idea."

I snuck a look at her. Her lips were pursed, and her eyebrows puckered, worry lurking in her eyes. Our bodies jarred as we hit another mud-soaked rut, and I forced my attention to the road. "Don't worry so much."

She laughed, but it was forced. "That's kind of all I do."

My mouth opened, but her phone rang before I could get

a word out. She dug through her purse and caught it before "Shipping Up to Boston" hit the chorus. The girl actually was a Dropkick Murphys fan. Well, shit, if that didn't attract me more.

"Hey, sugar," she answered, sticking my dick in cold water with the reminder that she had a boyfriend. "Yeah, I know."

What kind of guy held Paisley's attention?

The pissed-off tone of his voice came through the phone, but I couldn't make out the words. "I didn't know you were coming over this morning. No, of course you don't need an invite, I just wish I'd...seen you before I left." She giggled, and it damn near killed me. "No, of course not. I know you're upset." There were more words cutting off any attempt she made to get a word in edgewise. "Yes, I know it's on the counter. Will, seriously, don't you think I can keep track of that myself? I don't always need it on. I'll be fine, it's only a swimming lesson."

She told him. Score one point for honesty.

"I understand you're upset, but you need to give me a little wiggle room here." Two more of her deep breaths and we rounded the corner to our destination. "Will. *Will!* Please trust me enough to know what I'm capable of."

Two breaths and the small lake came into view. "I know. I love you, too. I'll call you once I get home." I threw Lucy into park and reached for the door handle as she hung up. "I'm so sorry about that."

I shut my door and made my way around to hers. "You don't need to apologize to me." I helped her down.

"He worries."

"You guys sound like you have great communication." Okay, that was officially the lamest shit I'd ever said, but I envied it.

She propped her sunglasses on top of her head and squinted at me. "We do. We've been friends nearly our whole lives. There's a lot of history there."

Before it could get any heavier or more awkward, I kicked off my flip-flops into the heavy grass. "Are you ready?"

She peeked behind me at the lake. "Wait, you want to swim *here*?"

I shrugged. "One of the guys told me about it. It's secluded, clean, and we have it to ourselves."

She shook her head and waggled her finger at me. "Oh, no, not here. This is not a good idea."

I pulled my shirt over my head and tossed it on the hood of my truck. "This is the idea, Paisley. Get your clothes off and get in the water." Her eyes widened, and I didn't miss the way she raked her eyes down my chest. Was she a tattoo kind of girl? Or was her boyfriend the clean-cut guy she could take home to her mom? "Does the ink bother you?"

She blinked a few times, then jerked her eyes to my face as her cheeks flushed. "No, not at all."

I knew what would come next, the inevitable *what does it all mean* every girl asked. I hadn't told anyone the real translation of the words that stretched across my chest, arm, back, and abs. Those truths were mine and mine alone. "Let's swim."

"No, you don't understand—"

My patience slipped another notch. She was not getting out of this. "If it makes you feel better, I'll get in first, but you'd better be right behind me, or I'm throwing your cute little ass in." I ran at the water, jumping in where it looked deep enough. The cool water slid over my head. I stood, the water coming to my chest. "Get in here."

"No way." She shook her head, her eyes wide with fear. "I've lived here long enough to know you don't swim here. Not with George."

"Who?" I looked left and right. Nothing to be seen but the smooth, barely rippled surface of the water, and the tall reeds that banked it. The mud slid between my toes as I flexed them deeper.

"George. He's—"

"Stop making excuses and get in the water. I can't teach you to swim if you're on land— *What the fuck is that?*" Two rounded eyes appeared thirty feet away, lingering above the surface of the water...coming this way. Fast.

"Get out!" she shrieked.

I didn't need to be told twice. I kicked forward, swimming for the shore as fast as I could, wishing I hadn't come so far out to start with. I made it to the bank and didn't pause in my headlong flight to the car. I scooped up Paisley, tossed her over my shoulder, and barreled for the door.

I swung the door open and shoved her inside. She scrambled over to her seat as I jumped in mine, slamming the door home. "Seriously! What the fuck?"

We both swiveled our heads toward the shore where a very large, very green alligator ambled out of the water and onto the bank. He opened his mouth wide, like he needed to show me those massive freaking teeth, and snapped his jaw shut.

"*That* is George," Paisley said, and she had the audacity to laugh breathlessly. "George is why you don't swim here."

"George."

She reached over the space that separated us, patting my leg like she was soothing a puppy. "It's okay, tough guy, he doesn't eat people."

"He's an alligator!"

She smirked, the corner of her mouth raising just high enough to start my blood flowing to the area of my body I didn't need it to. "American alligators don't eat people. Well, they're a last resort, really."

"You screamed at me to get out!"

"Well, I certainly didn't want you to be his first." Her green eyes sparkled in laughter.

"And to think you trusted me not to poke fun at *you*?" She had the nerve to flat-out laugh, and damn it if it wasn't contagious. My hands flexed on the steering wheel. "You're a handful of trouble, Paisley."

"So I've been told." Her smile killed me.

I threw Lucy into reverse and whipped her around. My shirt went flying off the hood.

"You're going to lose—"

"Let him have it."

"Honey, I'm home," I called out as I dropped my keys and cell phone on the entry table next to Grayson's.

"Fastest swimming lesson ever," he answered, straight-faced, from the kitchen.

"Yeah, well, there was an alligator."

"A what?" He pivoted, almost dropping the marinara-soaked spoon onto the floor.

"Don't ask. Dude, you cook?" I hadn't smelled anything so good since I left— Yeah, not going there.

"Dude," he mocked me, "you don't?" He motioned to the island. "Make yourself useful and start layering lasagna noodles."

"That I can do."

"Good. Maybe I'll make a man out of you yet."

Grayson was hard to get a read on. He'd shown up on the first day of class asking if anyone knew of a cheap place to rent, having spent every last second he could with his family in North Carolina before coming down, so it was take him in or leave him to fend for himself.

I'd taken Josh in as a roommate for the same reason—he put his family first, and I figured that had worked out, so why not take the chance.

I washed my hands and started the base layer, laying the noodles the way Mom had done on the days she'd been well enough to cook. "This all for us?"

"Well, I couldn't get a flight home this weekend." His jaw

flexed. "And I figure we'll be eating like POWs in SERE school next week."

Ah, yes, Survive, Escape, Resist, Evade. Where we'd learn to eat bugs and shit if we crashed our birds. A whole three weeks of mind-blowing fun. "Good idea. Garlic bread?"

He shot me a look that blatantly told me to go to hell. "What do I look like?" He cracked a half smile, which was more than I'd ever gotten out of him, and motioned his head toward the fresh-baked Italian bread on the counter.

The guy didn't miss a beat. "Awesome."

"There's steaks in the fridge for dinner, too."

Holy shit, I lived with Guy Fieri. "Beer?"

He raised an eyebrow at me but didn't bother to answer. Of course there was beer. "There was mail for you." He used his head again to motion to the coffee table, keeping his hands busy with the lasagna.

Once we were finished, I opened the bill and grimaced. At least I knew where she was, even if it cost me a fortune to keep her there. Knowing was precious, because not knowing, worrying about what the fuck she was doing, was agonizing. I'd been there a few too many times.

Yes, five minutes and a large check was more than worth it. I sealed the return envelope and held it to my forehead, the closest I could get without her dragging me down into her private hell. "Anna." I let the ache of missing her in for the smallest second, mourning her loss as if she'd died. But maybe one day... *No.* That thought broke me every time I tried to believe. I closed the door on it with the lid of the mailbox and walked back into the life I'd fought so fucking hard for.

"Can I ask you a personal question?" Grayson asked, sliding the pan into the oven.

"Are you going to anyway?" I threw myself onto the couch, where I intended to stay the rest of the day.

"Yes." He folded his arms in front of his chest.

"Well, then, it doesn't matter what I answer."

"What the hell are you doing with that girl?"

What the hell did he know about Anna? "What do you mean?" I asked carefully.

"Look, I know you and Josh go way back, and he should probably be the one saying this, but he's not here, so I will. She has a boyfriend, Jagger. A boyfriend who is more than capable of teaching her how to swim. What are you getting yourself into with Paisley?"

Paisley. Just hearing her name took over every thought I had. Her smile, her laugh, all made me want everything I had no right to—

"And why didn't you tell her you're in flight school?"

Because then I'll have to tell her when I fuck up and fail out. "Didn't want to."

"Seriously, man. That shit's not cool. And weren't you just going off about how girls during flight school are too much of a distraction?"

I took a deep breath and rubbed the spot between my eyebrows. "You don't think I know that? I'm keeping it as platonic as I fucking can. I know she has a boyfriend, and I'm not chasing her down for sex, so that shouldn't be a problem. I want to make sure she can swim, and then I'll walk away." *Liar.*

"And fix her library."

"That, too." I ripped my hat off and stroked my thumb over the Bruins logo.

His eyes narrowed. "I see the way you look at her, and she doesn't look like the kind of girl who cheats on her boyfriend. She's going to rip you to pieces, and the worst part is she won't have a clue she's done it. Be. Careful." He grabbed his bag and keys. "I'm headed to the gym for a few, so listen for the timer. Burn lunch and I burn you."

I rested my head and stared at the ceiling fan. What the hell *was* I doing with Paisley, and why couldn't I stop? Twice in the last forty-eight hours, and damn if I wasn't addicted to the way she made me feel when I was around her, all hopeful and protective. I needed to find an easy lay and fuck her out of my head.

Something told me that usual tactic wouldn't work this time.

She was already distracting me, making me want things I didn't understand. *I'm trusting you*, she'd said, and the worst part was that I wanted to be worthy of it, perpetual fuckup or not. But she didn't know my history, not from college, not from…before, and that was the only reason she'd put her life in my hands.

Grayson was right. She was going to rip me apart.

And I was going to let her.

CHAPTER SEVEN

31. Put my life in the hands of a total stranger.

My fingers shook as I removed my watch. The pool was silent, as it should be, since it was nine p.m. on a Sunday and long since closed. Major Davidson hadn't batted an eye when I'd asked him for permission to use the facility. He'd even promised not to tell. It helped that he'd finished his assignment as Daddy's aide.

I wrapped the towel around my body and walked out of the locker room to the pool deck. Jagger came out from the opposite side at the same time. How did he *look* like that? He stretched, exposing the mouthwatering lines of his abs. *Friends. Friends. Friends.*

"Ready?"

He flicked his tongue ring across his teeth, the clicking sound reverberating off the walls around me. "Let's go." He backed up, sent me a wicked smile, and then raced toward the pool's edge—despite all the signs that said not to run—and cannonballed perfectly. "Your turn."

I dropped the towel, thankful that I'd chosen my halter-top one-piece, and folded it neatly on the bench. Then I entered in the shallow end, taking even breaths as the water crept up my body. At least it was warm. Kind of.

The water was to my chest by the time I reached Jagger. His smile was reward enough for getting in the pool. "That wasn't so bad, was it?"

No, not if you enjoy things like a thousand spiders crawling all over you, or large vats of water waiting to swallow you whole. "Let's get on with it."

"Why are you so scared of the water?"

"Did your tongue ring hurt?" I shot the question at him like ammunition.

His head cocked to the side, and his eyes narrowed. "Yeah, okay. We can do that. 'Quid pro quo, Clarice.'"

I smiled at his *Silence of the Lambs* reference and relaxed a little. "I can do that. No lies?"

His eyes took on a fierce glint. "I will never lie to you, Paisley. I might not tell you what you want to hear, but I'll never lie. You?"

The question felt meaningful, like one of those moments worth memorizing. "I promise I'll never lie to you, Jagger." I didn't have to tell him everything, just no lies.

"Okay. So, how did you get us in here after closing?"

I couldn't look away from those eyes if I tried. "I asked nicely. I like this game. Tongue ring?"

"The stud? Seventeenth birthday, and it hurt like a bitch, but it was worth it to see the look on my father's face." He grinned and flicked it across his teeth again.

Heaven help me, my entire body clenched, and a stab of pure *want* slammed through me, pulsing low and deep in my belly.

"Fear of the water?"

I swallowed, my mouth suddenly dry despite being surrounded by water. I skimmed my palm along the surface, enjoying the sensation of balancing between two mediums. "I fell into a lake when I was little. It felt like forever until Pey—" I stammered and took a breath. "Peyton saw me and pulled me out, but I never went in again."

His tattoo rippled on his arm as he held out his hand. "Come here." There were letters mixed in with the patterns. C2G? What did that mean?

My heart skipped, and I placed my hand above it out of habit. I took the step that separated us, keeping count of the beats to make sure I stayed on rhythm. *No heart attack tonight.* He gently turned me around. "What are we doing?"

"Floating. Did you really waste your question on that?" He chuckled. "Lie back."

I tensed. "What?"

His breath sent shivers down my neck. "Trust me, Paisley. I won't let anything happen to you. Put your head on my shoulder." He lowered himself shoulder-deep into the water. "Close your eyes and relax."

I inhaled a shaky breath and then gave myself over to trusting him, resting my head on his shoulder.

"Good. Now palms to the sky."

"We're inside."

"Yes, smarty, we are. Palms up."

I stretched my arms out like I'd seen done many times and turned my palms up to the ceiling. I was more aware of his heartbeat than my own, the way his chest rose evenly with every breath. "Feet up."

My eyes flew open. "Can we just do this part for the day?"

He shook his head, his chin rubbing across the top of my hair. "Close your eyes. Ask me another question." His hands drifted along my back until they rested at the center of my waist, supporting what little weight I had in the water.

With his hands on me, it was easier to close my eyes and try to forget I was in a giant tub of death. "Your tattoos. How many?"

He sucked in his breath. "Five individual pieces."

"Do they all mean something? I mean, they're beautiful on you, I'm just wondering if they're art or...something more?" I relaxed, focusing on his hands and keeping my own facing up. It was strangely comfortable to be so intimate with someone I barely knew.

It was stranger feeling as if I already knew him so intimately.

"They all symbolize something to me."

The water swished around my head as he lowered us a little more, but the usual panic didn't set in. "Which one is your favorite?"

"Isn't it my turn?" I heard his smile.

"Sure."

"What's your favorite part of being in a relationship?"

"That's an odd question." I almost jerked, but his hands kept me steady.

"It's mine to ask."

I sighed. "Right. Quid pro quo. Well, I guess I love the ease. I know what his reaction will be to most things, so everything is just...comfortable. Effortless. He knows my worst qualities and doesn't run screaming, and he knows my past because he was there for it." *He knows I could drop dead at any moment.* "What about you?"

He tensed. "I don't know. I've never really had a functional relationship."

"Ever?"

"Ever. I've seen it, though, with my friends." He took a deep breath, raising and lowering my head slightly. "I think I admire the connection between them. They have this...pull, an utter drive to be close to each other, like even a breath separating them is too much."

An ache resonated from my heart that had nothing to do with my condition. "That's what you want."

Four heartbeats passed. "Yes, eventually. I've seen love burn someone to the ground, and I've seen it make sense of the ridiculous. I won't settle for less than that kind of fire."

That was the most irrational thing I'd ever heard, and something in my soul seemed to flicker awake and take notice. "Steady doesn't do it for you? You'd rather chance destruction?"

"If it's between being numb the rest of my life or burning exquisitely for even a moment, I'll take the burn. The best things in life are worth the burn, the risk."

I swallowed the lump in my throat like he hadn't just altered my world. Was I burning? On fire with Will?

"Open your eyes, Paisley."

I did, feeling weightless. "Jagger!"

He laughed, still behind me, my head on his shoulder, but the rest of me was floating. I jerked in fear, sinking immediately. He drew me against him, bringing me vertical before I could go under. I turned around, suddenly all too aware of how personal our conversation had been. How inappropriate when I thought of how Will might feel about it.

I moved out of his arms and pushed through a weak smile. "That was amazing." That need to get away was almost as powerful as the one screaming to get closer. Could he feel this insane tension, or was I losing my mind?

"Yeah, you did great. I think…" He shook his head. "I think we can call that our success for today."

I didn't need to be told twice. I scurried up the ladder and onto the pool deck, wrapping myself in the towel. "So when's our next session, coach?"

He pulled himself up, water slipping down the lines of his muscles. *Breathe.* "I'm working out of town for a few weeks, but I'll call you when I get home?"

Right. I forgot that's why he couldn't start the library project yet. "No problem."

He toweled off his hair and wrapped the cloth around his shoulders like one of those beach models. Mr. California, indeed. "Meet you out front?"

I nodded, retreated to the locker room, and pulled out my cell phone to connect with my real life. The phone rang as I tugged the wet suit down my body with a sucking sound.

"Hey, honey, I'm heading over to your place."

Will's voice soothed the unsettled feeling in my heart. "Sounds great. I'm finishing my lesson and then I'll be home."

"Love you."

I paused, wondering what that really meant for the first time in my life. This was love, right? The steady, easy, solid feeling in my heart? Burning was a ridiculous notion. Who would sign up for that kind of insanity?

I couldn't afford anything like fire anywhere near my heart. "Lee-Lee?"

I cringed at the name. "Love you, too. Be home soon."

I dressed and convinced myself to stop being silly. Love was what my parents had, what gave a foundation to a home. It was sturdy and dependable, not wild or untamed—that was ludicrous. I clicked the lights off and locked the door behind me, pocketing the key.

The sky had gone dark, and the stars dimly winked above me. My hair dripped down my back, and I gave it a squeeze, trying to wring the last of the water out of it.

Jagger leaned against Lucy, and I forced Will foremost in my mind. "Thanks for waiting on me."

That smile nearly sent me to my knees. "Yeah, well, it would be a shame to go to all this work to keep you alive near the water just to have you killed by a roaming alligator."

"He's harmless, you know."

He cocked an eyebrow. "He's a roving menace."

"George only roves his little pond, scaredy-cat." I pressed

my key fob, unlocking my car, and Jagger closed the distance before I could, opening my door. "Thank you, sir." I slid behind the wheel, tossing my bag on the seat next to me.

He leaned in between the frame and the door. "One more question?"

"Yes." I leaned back, all too aware of how close he stood.

"Who is Peyton?" I felt the blood rush from my face. "You had trouble saying that name."

My fingers bit into my steering wheel, my nails impressing the leather. Three heartbeats passed before I dragged my gaze to meet his. *No lies, we promised.* But to tell him? To dig into a wound that barely felt scabbed over?

If there had been annoyance at my refusal, or even acceptance, I could have closed the door, both on him and the answer. But he stood there, looking at me with eyes that saw way too much and not nearly enough, patiently waiting.

"She was my older sister. My *only* sister." The words didn't hurt as they slipped free; instead they seemed to dissolve some weight I'd been carrying.

He gave me a sad smile. "Thank you for telling me. Good night." He shut my door and was at his car before I unrolled the window.

"Jagger?"

He turned, Lucy's door opened. "Yeah?"

We walked a fine line between borderline proper and absolutely not. I stuck my big toe across it, reveling in the honesty he drew out of me. "I'm going to miss you."

He looked at me with a gaze so intense that I forgot to breathe. "Yeah, me, too." He climbed into Lucy and leaned out to grab the door. "You know how that feels, right, missing someone?"

"Sure." I'd missed Will when he'd been at West Point this last year. It was sweet longing to be near him, to talk to him and hear his voice.

"It kind of feels like burning."

CHAPTER EIGHT

JAGGER

There's never been a day where I didn't crave it from you—approval. But now, I could give a flying fuck what you think of me.

"**M**an, how much are you planning on eating?" Josh asked as I shoved another piece of Mellow Mushroom pizza down.

I swallowed. "Shut your face. I'm fucking starving."

He laughed. "I know it was a long three weeks, but you were starving on the last pizza. This is overkill, and we have PT in the morning."

I groaned. I still felt like warmed-over dog shit, but three weeks of SERE training would do that. I lifted my shirt, tensing my abs. "I think I can pass a PT test."

"Put that away, you're turning me on," he joked, sending a text message.

"You get ahold of Ember yet?"

He held his finger up while he downed another bottle of

Gatorade. Dehydrated didn't quite describe us well enough. He wiped his mouth with the back of his hand. "Yeah. I'm headed up this afternoon after formation."

"All weekend with Masters. Maybe we can sit around in silence."

"He's not *that* bad."

"The guy refuses to talk about himself."

Josh cracked a smile. "Well, you like to talk about yourself enough for the both of you." He started toward his room, pulling another bottle out of the fridge on the way. "Hey, did I tell you I found a pickup game?"

"No shit? There's no ice around here." I'd just about cut off a testicle to get in my pads and play. I missed it. The noise of the crowd. The silence in my head. The feel of the blade against the ice. God, the smell in the rink. It was a bitch to go from playing every day in college to nothing.

"Not here, but in Montgomery. Worth the drive to you?"

"Hell, yes."

Josh nodded. "I'll let them know we're interested. I have to pack my clothes."

"What?" I called out. "I figured you spent every weekend naked!"

He flipped me the bird and kept walking. His sex life wasn't ever up for discussion. I respected that, but it didn't mean I couldn't give him shit over it. I tossed the empty pizza box in the recycling pile, grabbed my keys, and headed out. I had two hours before formation; I could make it to the library.

SERE had sucked royally. But the one thing that pulled me through the hours spent in that tiny fucking box? Thinking about those green eyes. I was everything she didn't need: self-destructive, egotistical, and reckless. But damn if she didn't feel like what *I* needed. Even as only friends, I'd take whatever piece of her I could get.

Pumpkins lined the patio of our next-door neighbor's house,

and the little old lady shook her head at me and pointed to the huge USPS box on the patio. They'd delivered the held mail. I picked up the box by the handles and placed it just inside the front door. Well, except the envelope right on top. I folded that one and stuck it in the cargo pocket of my shorts.

I'd deal with that later.

I pulled the door shut, walking the small weed-ridden sidewalk to the driveway. I needed to do something about that with all my spare time. Weeds. Mortgage. Landscaping. Sometimes I wanted to retreat to the apartment I'd shared with Josh the last two years.

I waved politely to our neighbor. "Good afternoon, Mrs. King." She'd made it clear she wasn't happy about having flight school students buy the house next door, like we would immediately haul in a keg and keep it in the backyard. What did we look like? A bunch of immature college kids?

We'd already installed the kegerator in the kitchen.

She pursed her lips under her giant gardening hat. "Those dahlias never looked that sad when the Robertsons owned the house."

I stifled my laugh. "Yes, ma'am. I'll work on that."

"You be sure you do." She grumbled all the way into her house.

Sign up to defend your country? You're an immature kid. But take care of your dahlias? Man, that made you an upstanding citizen. *Reminder—Google dahlias.*

The drive to the library felt longer than it took, even with the stop for another Gatorade, and I nearly fist pumped when I saw her car in the lot. What the hell was wrong with me?

The library door closed softly behind me, and I breathed in the scent of books in the air-conditioning. Even in October it was on. Alabama didn't really have a fall. It was more like, "at least it's not as hot as September."

I hung my sunglasses from the first button on my shirt,

pushed the sleeves up past my elbows, and reminded myself not to run in the library. I rounded the corner—

"May I help you?"

Shit. It was the wenchy one. At least the older lady, Alice, liked me, but this one was impossible. I think her bun was wound entirely too tight. "Is Paisley here?"

She huffed, glancing at the closed bottle of Gatorade in my hand, and pulled an imaginary strand of brunette hair behind her ear. "She's in the back room. You'll have to wait."

I flashed a grin and was rewarded by a miniscule softening of her features. "No problem, ma'am, I can find it."

I didn't wait for her reply, instead headed past the students studying, like I should have been. My palms started sweating... over seeing my friend? What the fuck? I could handle half the sorority girls at school, but this girl had me on my damn knees... in the friend zone. Pathetic as it felt, I was just happy to be on the field.

I slid open the door. A quick scan of the room told me she wasn't in here. "Paisley?" I called out in case.

A pale hand rose from behind a small stack of boxes. "Here."

She sounded like shit. I sidestepped through the maze of boxes. "Hey, I wanted to see if you had that list of supplies to star— *Holy shit!* Paisley?" I dropped to my knees next to where she sat on the floor, her eyes closed, leaning against the stack of boxes while she took quick breaths. I did a quick check. Her forehead was clammy, but she had the energy to swat my hand away.

"Jagger?" Her eyes opened, the green still as brilliant as I remembered. "I'm okay." She gave me a weak smile.

"This does not look okay."

She squeezed my hand, breathing rapidly. "I'm not feeling well. Give me a second to catch my breath. I think it'll just be another minute."

"You think? You're camped out on the floor where no

one could find you if something happened, and you *think*?" I unscrewed the lid on my Gatorade and passed it to her. "Drink. Then we're taking you to a doctor."

She didn't argue and downed almost half of the bottle. "Thank you, but I don't need a doctor. It's over now, and he knows all about it." She closed her eyes and leaned her head back. "I'm really okay."

"Asthma?" I guessed. "I've seen it in a few of my friends, and this is how they all looked after attacks."

"Well, it's…" She sighed and looked at me. "I don't like to talk about it."

So I was right. "It's nothing to be embarrassed of. Can I take you home?" She shouldn't stay after having an attack like that. "Do you need your inhaler?"

She shook her head, rolling it along the box behind her. "I already took my meds. Just…sit with me for a minute while I catch my breath?"

Everything in me clamored to drag her ass to the doctor, but I couldn't exactly force her to go. "Yeah, sure thing." I dropped down next to her so we sat side by side, and the restlessness that had plagued me the last three weeks faded away.

"Questions?" She half smiled over the bottle.

"Already? I've been in the same room with you for less than five minutes, you have me sitting on the floor, you've stolen my drink, and now you want my deepest secrets?"

"Yes." Her eyes threatened to crack me open to the center of my soul.

She didn't make excuses or play coy. It was her most addictive quality, the brutal honesty she leveled on me. "Fine. How long have you been sitting here?" She glanced at her purple watch.

"Twenty-seven minutes. I was actually about to go in search of a drink, so you had pretty perfect timing." She took another long pull of the Gatorade. Lucky fucking bottle. "How long have you been home?"

I glanced down at my Breitling, the one piece of *him* I kept. "Three hours forty-two minutes."

She laughed, the sound stronger, and my smile was an automatic response. "Miss me?"

I shook my head.

She shrugged. "A girl has to try."

"Did you miss *me*?"

Her smile fell, any trace of levity gone from her pink lips. "Yes," she whispered like she was admitting she'd committed a crime.

I rested my forearms on my raised knees, mostly to keep my hands off her. "Yeah. Me, too. It's a little ridiculous, actually." Silence stretched between us, and I fumbled for a question, trying to haul us out of the deep end. "So if you're not a swimmer, why were you at the beach that day?"

"Working on my tan."

"No lies. This is no fun if there's lies."

"It was on the list." She took another drink. Good, her color was returning.

"List?"

She ducked her head, a gorgeous blush lighting her cheeks. "I have a list of things to do before...you know."

My eyebrows drew together. "Before...you graduate college?"

She bit at her lip. "Something like that. So when do we start lessons again?"

"When do you want?" *Now.*

"I have class this afternoon." Her face fell. "Actually I have to leave right around now. Walk me out?"

I stood and then pulled her gently to her feet. She swayed, but her color was returning. "Are you sure you should be going?"

"You have no idea how hard I had to beg to get classes on main campus."

I bent down and grabbed her open purse from the floor. A

panicked look crossed her face, so I handed it over without so much as zipping it shut. Girls were weird about what was in their purses. It's not like I was going to freak at the sight of a tampon. She took it eagerly, slipping it over her shoulder. "You go to Troy?" It was the only local college.

She nodded. "I take one class at main campus and the rest down here. Today is main campus, which is why I'm not skipping it. Not when it's a battle just to get that one."

"Grades?"

She shook her head. "Overbearing parents."

"Ah, right. I remember now. They're not big fans of college?"

"They're not big fans of me being out of their sight. It's a work in progress."

"So why don't you tell them that you're an adult now and live your life?"

She rolled her eyes. "That's not exactly how it works in my family. I respect my parents, and I pick my battles." Her drawl was almost as intoxicating as her smile.

"Would they approve of our swim lessons?"

Her smile quirked up higher on one side, seeming mischievous. "I haven't exactly given them a chance to weigh in."

She seemed steady, but I still walked slowly. I held open the door, and she glided through.

"So you're from here?" I asked.

We crossed the patio to the small path that led to the parking lot. "Yep. Mama was born and raised here. Peyton and I were both born here, too. We moved around a lot growing up, but we always came back to Enterprise. Even when Daddy had to work somewhere else, we came every summer. Mama made sure that we both graduated from high school here, like she did. She said she wouldn't stand for southern girls to graduate in the north. Couldn't have our accents corrupted." She laughed. "I hated it at first, being away from Daddy so often, but I have

Morgan because of it."

"Ah, Morgan. I wondered how she fit into your story."

"She's my best friend. She didn't bat an eye when I had to stay here for college, just gave up going to Alabama so she could be with me. I don't know what I would do without her." She sighed. "So, what's the story with you and the guys you work with?"

"Walker's been my best friend for a couple years now." *My only real friend.* "We've been roommates since we were in college in Colorado. Masters moved in with us right before I met you."

"Ah, and what brought you all the way from Colorado?"

I swallowed. I could admit it to her right here, but what if I didn't make it? What if I fucked this up like I usually did and then had to admit my failure? "A school opportunity we couldn't pass up."

"You're still in school?"

I cocked my head to the side. "I am a student, yes."

"And you moonlight as a handyman." She laughed. "Ah, you're the mayor of Vague-ville. I understand." I loved how her accent made two syllables out of *ville*. It was sexy as hell.

I laughed and held out my hand. "Phone?" She hesitated but handed it over. I was tempted to scan through to find a picture of this boyfriend she held so high. Instead, I opened her contacts and put in my phone number and first name before handing it back. "There. Text me later when you want to schedule another Stop-Paisley-from-Drowning lesson."

She laughed. "Yeah, I'll do that."

My phone rang. I answered it with a swipe. "What's up, Walker?"

"Carter called. Formation got moved up. I grabbed your stuff from home, so get your ass over here." He sounded as annoyed as I felt.

"On my way." I hung up and looked at Paisley. "You sure

you're okay to get to class?"

"Nothing I can't handle. I'll text you?"

"Sounds good."

She drove away, and part of me wished her car was still broken, just so I could get another couple minutes with her. For some reason, I could breathe easier when she was around. Maybe there was something to be said for this friends thing.

I parked Lucy in the closest spot and damn near ran into the building. Josh threw a bag at my chest. "You've got ten minutes."

"Thanks." I threw my uniform on and was almost in the classroom before I realized I'd forgotten my tongue stud. A few twists of my fingers, and I had it out and stored. It was a pain in the ass to keep taking it out, but I wasn't willing to get rid of it permanently.

I took the seat next to Josh, pulled out my green notebook, dropped my pen, then fumbled again trying to get it out from under my chair. "Fuck!"

"What's got your panties in a twist?" He sent me the look, the one he usually shot me to remind me to cool my temper.

"Nothing."

"Oh, and touchy, too? Does it have anything to do with a little blond librarian?" I cut my eyes toward him with my own version of the look. "I saw your car there."

I guess the look wasn't enough.

"Leave it alone."

Josh's eyes narrowed. "You hung up?"

My jaw flexed. "There's nothing to get hung up on. She has a boyfriend."

"He's been friend zoned." Masters slid in behind us, and I crushed the impulse to punch him in the throat. Mostly because he was right.

"I chose the friend zone."

Josh's mouth dropped open.

"What?" I snapped.

He shook his head and pulled his stuff out to take notes. "I've just never seen you hung up on a girl, that's all."

"For fuck's sake. What's it going to take? We're friends!"

He scoffed. "Look, you were there for me, and I'm trying to be there for you. You don't want to admit that there's a problem? Fine."

Well, if that didn't make me feel like shit. Carter walked in, giving me an excuse not to respond to Josh. He was right. I didn't waste time on girls who didn't want me. Hell, I didn't really waste time on girls, and I couldn't remember the last relationship I'd had that didn't end with me handing her clothes and offering to call her a cab.

It came down to that one little word I was incapable of: trust. And, damn, she made me want— *Don't even think it.*

"Glad to see you all survived SERE," Carter said, sitting on the edge of a table at the front of the room. "Well, almost all of you."

Everyone in the class glanced around, looking for who was missing. I counted twenty-four…Rogers. I'd heard him screaming in the box that last night. Guess psych pulled him.

"Bateman, I'm shocked you didn't get the crap beat out of you more often for singing that stupid song over and over."

"Hey, man, the secret of the fox is an ancient mystery." It'd been worth the beating my ribs took to distract Josh. He never did well in confined spaces.

Our classmates laughed, but Carter didn't. Arrogant West Point fuck was never amused. I grinned just to piss him off.

He tapped his ring on the table. "Right. Major Davidson wants accountability before the four-day. Academics start on Tuesday, so please don't slack off this weekend. Also, there's a sign-up sheet here." He lifted a clipboard from the desk. "We've been tasked with the dunk booth for Saturday's Fall Fest, so you each need to pull a time slot."

"Fuck," Josh swore under his breath.

"I'll cover you. You'll be an insufferable asshole if you don't get to see her."

"Thanks, man." He relaxed into his chair.

"No problem."

"Got something you want to share, Bateman?" Carter snapped.

"Nawh, I don't share well. My parents bitched about it constantly," I fired back. Class leader or not, he'd been commissioned one day before me. That didn't make him God.

His jaw flexed. How far could I push before he lost his shit in front of the class? That might be fun to see...

"Don't," Josh whispered, like he could read my mind.

He was right, of course. This wasn't the frat house or the rink. This was my career.

I swallowed the acidic comment on my tongue and instead concentrated on recording the upcoming dates and times Carter was throwing at us. I was getting better at this being-civil shit.

Barely.

CHAPTER NINE

4. Stand up for something you believe in.

"Why, yes, I'd love to be bikini-body ready for Halloween," Morgan drawled, pointing to the publication date. "We need to get this doctor of yours some new reading material."

Laughter shook my shoulders as I swung my feet from the end of the exam table. "Thanks for coming with me."

She reached out from her seat and gave my hand a squeeze. "There's no place else I'd rather be." Her smile was bright, and her eyes the same, but with unshed tears.

"Don't be scared, Morgan. I'm not scared." I wasn't. Resigned, maybe. Sad, even. But knowing I was limited on time made me more driven, more determined to live than anything else. I'd make it through that list.

She wiped away a stray tear and sniffed through her smile. "But you don't have to miss you if something…"

Now it was my turn to squeeze her hand. "One hundred

ninety-two days. Now stop."

She narrowed her eyes. "Why on earth would you think that?"

"Peyton and I were the same weight at birth, had the same hair, an identical smile, and now the same heart. She died 143 days after she turned twenty-one. I know how to do math," I interjected, and pulled the last sticky sensor off my chest from my EKG. I was never going to be the older sister, and it didn't matter if anyone else understood. I did.

"Paisley—"

"My life, my thoughts."

"Well, speaking of your thoughts..." She arched a well-maintained eyebrow. "Just what are you doing with Mr. California?"

"Jagger?" Saying his name elevated my heartbeat.

"Mmm-hmm. Last time I checked you were all but married to Will." She kept going, despite my meanest glare. "Not that I object to Jagger. Gawd, Paisley, you sure can pick 'em. He's utterly delicious."

"We're friends. Just friends!"

"Right, protest much, Lady MacBeth?" She examined her perfect manicure.

"Stop using your major against me, Morgan Elyse Bartley." I sighed, trying to find the words. "He makes me feel...free. That's something I haven't had. He doesn't treat me like I'm about to break."

"That's because he doesn't know you're breakable. I saw that coffee he brought you. You haven't told him about your heart, otherwise he wouldn't be bringing you caffeine."

My cheeks heated, and I started to pick apart the embroidery on the Etsy-made hospital gown Mama bought me. "I don't want him to know."

"And Will?"

My chest tightened unpleasantly. "He knows I'm taking

swim lessons from the guy who saved my life."

"Mmm-hmm. That sure was a long three weeks he was gone for."

"What are you getting at?" I narrowed my eyes.

"When you got to class yesterday, you were all gushy, and you said Will doesn't get home until tonight, so it had to be because Jagger stopped by the library." My mouth snapped shut. "I'm right, aren't I? No judgment, darlin'. As your best friend, I wholeheartedly approve of anyone who brings you to life like that."

"Seriously, he's just a friend."

"And my mama's just a makeup lady." She raised her eyebrow at me, since her mama was the top Mary Kay representative in southeast Alabama. "And what does Will know?"

"He's fine with the lessons. He's actually happy, since he studies so much."

"Right, but does he know that you're falling for Jagger?"

"I love Will! I most certainly am not—" The knocking at the door stopped my tirade before it got off to a proper start. "Come in." I glared at Morgan for good measure.

Dr. Larondy walked in, a nurse wheeling in a laptop cart behind him. "Good mornin', Paisley." He pushed his glasses up his nose.

"Hey, Doc." I put on my best smile.

"No parents today?"

"Nope. They don't even know I'm here."

"You little rebel, you." He couldn't have been older than forty, but the smile made him seem so much younger. "Let's take a peek." He pulled my chart and sighed, which was never a good sign.

"Tell me."

Morgan took my hand.

"Your symptoms are progressing, which, of course, is something we didn't want. Your EKG is showing arrhythmias—

irregular rhythms in your heartbeat. With your hypertrophic cardiomyopathy, the present obstruction, and your family history of sudden cardiac death, well, we need to start a different treatment regimen. How have you been feeling?"

"I tire easily now," I admitted as he scribbled into my chart. "And sometimes it's hard for me to catch my breath, especially when my heart starts to pound, but passing out is new."

"How long were you unconscious?"

"I reckon ten minutes or so?"

"I'd like to start you on some medication to help regulate your heartbeat in addition to what you're already on. We're going to need to schedule a new round of testing and probably a heart MRI so we can get a good look at what's changing and where you sit surgically."

My stomach rolled. "Pacemaker?"

"That's definitely a good option, if that's what you want. It would control your heartbeat, but there's also the internal defibrillator that shocks your heart if it fails."

He went into the details of each, which I already knew, but my mind shut down, choosing instead to concentrate on the bird perched on the windowsill. He could fly away whenever he wanted—why would he stay here? I would fly away. I would soar above everything, choose what I really wanted for my future without thought for my heart's ability to handle it. But that wasn't my life.

I was held prisoner by my own body.

"Paisley?"

"Yes?" I blinked twice.

His lips pursed. "Do you need a minute? I know this is a lot to take in."

"No, I'm here. Sorry."

He nodded. "I know your parents want the pacemaker, but I'm only interested in what you want."

Mama was going to cry. Then she'd scream at me for being

childish, but I knew it was fear getting the best of her. The pacemaker was the more reasonable choice, but I couldn't silence the nagging, unexplainable instinct that it was the *wrong* choice, that it wasn't going to save me.

"Have you given it any more thought since your last appointment?"

"My parents think—"

"I want to know what *you* want. You're almost twenty-one years old, and as much as they'd like to control every aspect of your medical care, they don't. They can't."

I licked my lips, dry from the hospital air, and finally gave voice to what I'd never been able to say aloud. "I don't want to keep coming back. I want this to be over with." Either way.

The bird flew from the windowsill.

"You're going to have to come back. This is something you'll monitor your whole life, Paisley, regardless of the treatment we choose here. Even something as drastic as a transplant would need to be checked on."

You sound like a petulant little baby. "Of course, I'm sorry. I do understand. What gives me the best chance at a normal life?" The life where I could take off my heart monitor, and drink coffee, and run after my kids.

"That would be the surgery we discussed, septal myectomy, where I would remove enough of the thickened area of the heart to eliminate the obstruction. But, given the abnormal rhythms you're experiencing, there's no guarantee you wouldn't develop a branch bundle block or need an implantable cardioverter-defibrillator. There are no certainties here."

I didn't want a bunch of foreign wires in my body, tethering me to a half life. *Oh, Peyton, what would you have chosen?*

"How long do I have to make the choice?"

He set my chart down on the rolling table. "These episodes are only going to increase the worse the obstruction gets, and SCD is a *very real* possibility. We'll try the medication first, but if that fails, we're going to need a decision in the next few months. Six at tops."

One hundred ninety-two days. There were still so many little boxes I had yet to check off the list. I needed every one of those days to live, really live, not just exist. "I need more time."

"And I'm trying to give it to you. Medication first, but the choice is coming at you fast."

"I'll think about it. I understand what you're saying. I know I have to make a choice, and I'm thinking about it, but I'm not ready to decide. Not yet."

"Okay. Well, let's see how the medication goes. Moderate exercise, watch your sodium intake, and be aware of how you're feeling."

"Swimming? I'm taking lessons."

"Perfect. Don't go for laps or anything, keep it—"

"Moderate."

He smiled. "You got it. Okay, I want to see you again in a month." The nurse smiled as she wheeled the cart out of the room, but before he shut the door, he popped his head back in. "The pacemaker isn't the *wrong* decision, Paisley. If that's what you want, we'll do it. It's only the wrong choice if it isn't *yours*."

"Thanks, Doc." Something occurred to me. "Oh, one more thing?" He raised his eyebrows, and I flushed hot, but had to ask. "Um…about…sex?"

He didn't blink, God bless him. "As long as you can climb a flight of stairs and you're not winded—you're good to go."

Morgan walked into the kitchen as I examined the label on my new meds. Less energy, quivering, loss of appetite, nausea, and vomiting. Yay, couldn't wait to see if any of those side effects called my name. First dose was down. I reckoned we'd see soon.

"Choose the darn pacemaker, Paisley."

"No," I replied calmly, taking a sip of the tart orange juice. The more I said it, the easier it became.

"Why not?" She raised her voice. "If it means you live, then why the hell not?"

I took another long drink and gave her my full attention. "I wouldn't expect you to understand."

"Don't you dare condescend me. I've been with you since day one, sat through every late-night internet search, and joined every it's-not-fair cryfest." She folded her arms across her chest, but they didn't cage the tension emanating from her.

"I don't want the wires or the limits, not when there's another option. It just feels *wrong*." I enunciated each word but kept my voice soft. She was about to blow, I saw it coming, but I didn't need to add to it, despite hot, painful anger that coursed through my veins, begging to be let loose on the crap hand I'd been dealt.

"Well, it's a hell of a lot better than cracking open your chest for heart surgery! For the love of God, were you not listening? You could die!" Her voice rose with every word until she was screaming. She slammed her hands down on the counter, shaking the napkin holder.

"Wake up, Morgan, I *am* dying. My heart is going to fail just like hers did!"

"Then suck it up and make the safe choice! None of us want to lose you because you feel like living with a pacemaker isn't good enough for you!"

That stung but still didn't quell the fire raging through me. Mama, Daddy, Will, Morgan... Why couldn't I make them all understand?

"God, I miss being normal! I can't run, or go dancing like a twenty-year-old should, or do a million other things I want to do, have dreamed of doing. I have parents who look at me like I'm going to drop dead on the floor at any minute, which is a distinct possibility, and a boyfriend who barely makes love to me. He won't give me an orgasm because he's terrified, no matter how many times I tell him it's okay! To be honest, I have to beg him to touch me, and *if* he does, which is maybe once a month, his eyes aren't locked on mine, no, they're on this darn watch!" I lifted my wrist. "I've got everyone telling me to get a pacemaker at twenty, to not only accept all of this as my life, but to be *grateful*, because my sister didn't get it. Grateful!"

Her shoulders drooped like the fight fell right out of her, but I couldn't stop the words flying out of my mouth.

"I don't know what I want yet, but I know that there's a fine line between being a respectful daughter and trying to make up for them losing Peyton. Maybe I want to take the chance that I could have a normal life. Maybe it's my chance to follow my instincts when they're screaming that a pacemaker isn't what my body needs. Maybe I deserve to think about every maybe before they slice me open and sentence me to a life I didn't choose because I was too weak and *respectful* to say no. And maybe, just maybe I need you on my side!" My voice broke, like even it couldn't handle the sheer longing within me.

She hugged me tight, her tears soaking into my shirt. "Oh, Paisley."

I took gulping breaths. "Be on my side, because *no one* else is."

CHAPTER TEN

PAISLEY

11. Get inked.

It was now or never.

Will was preoccupied with studying. I couldn't blame him—he wanted to be top of the class, and there was someone giving him a run for his money. He pulled out his flashcard 5&9s to study, and I pulled out my car keys and left him to it.

Jagger would understand, right? He had five of the things. He would help me. Besides, he'd been in and out, prepping the renovation yesterday, and I hadn't managed a single moment alone with him. I missed my friend.

Oh, how you love to validate your reasoning.

Lucy was huge, yellow, and impossible to miss. I parked in front of his mailbox and picked my way across the newly aerated grass. Huh. The flowerbeds were freshly weeded, too.

Nerves tied my stomach into knots. Maybe I should have texted first? But I was here now, so I knocked, and Masters opened the door five heartbeats later. "Is Jagger around?"

"Hey, Paisley. Come on in." Odd how I liked someone I'd never seen smile, but I did.

The door opened directly to the living room, which was immaculately clean for a guys' house. Well, except for the giant bags along the dining room wall. They stood vertically like luggage, but had a weird, trapezoid-like shape to them. Hockey sticks leaned on them, so I figured the rest of that kind of gear had to be lurking in there.

"Paisley?" Jagger's voice triggered butterflies.

"Hockey?" I pointed toward the bags without meeting his eyes. Why had I done this? What was Will going to think when I showed him what I'd done?

"Yeah. Josh and I used to play in college." My eyebrows shot up. "Why so shocked?"

"Hockey just isn't a sport you hear a lot about around here. Were you any good?"

"Yeah. I mean, Josh was better. Is better. But most college guys don't go on to the NHL or anything."

"You still play?"

He moved in front of me, so I had to look up at him or stare at the logo on his shirt. I looked up and immediately regretted it. His eyes drew me in, made me forget things I had no business forgetting. "Pickup in Montgomery when we get the chance. Paisley, you're not here to talk hockey. I'm glad to see you, but what's going on?"

I swallowed. "If I wanted to do something considered a little crazy, would you help me?"

He crossed his arms in front of him, his ink peeking out of his shirtsleeves. "Define crazy."

"I want a tattoo."

His eyes flew wide. "Seriously?"

"I just said it, didn't I?" Okay, so the tremors in my voice gave me away. I wasn't pulling off fearless very well.

"Is this on your list?"

Was he laughing at me? "As a matter of fact, it is, which is really none of your business. My only question is if you want to come with me."

"You need someone to hold your hand." His smirk just about pushed me over the edge. I wanted to trace my tongue along the curve of his lips. Oh, I was going to hell again for thinking about that.

"I want...you," I whispered, the admission slipping free before common sense and decency could stop it. "I mean, I want you there. I figure you have experience and won't be all judgy."

"What does your boyfriend think?"

"He doesn't know." I raised my chin. *Be fierce.*

"And where are you planning on going?"

I shrugged. "I figured I'd go into Dothan and see if I could find a place."

"Jesus Christ, Paisley. You're talking about getting a needle repeatedly jabbed into your skin for some permanent artwork, and you think you'll just find a place? Is that all you think you're worth? Some random shop with their light on? This isn't getting your ears pierced. This is *forever.*"

"It's not like I'm going to pick some cliché rose out of a portfolio. I know what I want, and I'm going, whether or not you come with me." *Please don't make me go alone.*

His jaw flexed, and then he sighed. "I'll take you, just wait." He tapped a few times on his cell phone and set it to his ear. "Hey, Matt. You around? Nawh, man, it's good. I'm loving it. I'm actually bringing someone to see you if you've got an opening. Cool? Yeah. Be there soon." Another tap and the phone was back to his pocket.

"You have a tattoo artist on call?"

He shrugged with a grin. "You don't. Hence why you're here, right?"

• • •

"You ready, Paisley?" Matt asked, sliding into his chair behind where I reclined on my side, my shirt tucked into my bra. I nodded, unable to say much. This was definitely not what I expected. Everything was sparkling clean. It was all so... sanitary.

"Aren't you going to hold my hand?" I looked where Jagger hovered next to me. I felt his gaze on my bare stomach as surely as if his fingers were on my skin.

His grin was contagious. "Do you need a little support?"

I nodded my head, my lower lip caught between my teeth. He took my hand in his and gave it a gentle squeeze. "Ok, I'm ready," I said.

Matt held a mirror to my side so I could see where he'd stenciled my soon-to-be tattoo. "Is this exactly what you want?"

"*Though she be but little, she is fierce.* Yes, that's perfect."

The gun started, and I jumped. "Let's not do that, okay?" he gently said.

I nodded and squeezed Jagger's hand so tight I was pretty sure I'd bust a couple bones. He took it in stride. "Look at me, not at him."

I turned my head away as the gun touched my skin. It wasn't too bad, just an annoying scratch. I could handle this. "Thank you for coming with me."

He brushed a loose strand of hair out of my eyes. "No problem. You a Shakespeare fan?" he asked, motioning to my tattoo with a nod of his head.

My mouth popped open. "You know this is Shakespeare?"

"Jeez, think a little higher of me. I've read *A Midsummer Night's Dream*."

"And you remember this exact line?"

One side of his mouth rose in a smirk, and my belly clenched. Did he have to look like that? "Sure I do. Act three, scene two, Helena talking to Hermia. Would you like the context?"

"Wow."

He laughed, the sound turning my muscles to liquid. "Don't be too impressed. I have a photographic memory."

The needle's itch started to burn. "Aren't you full of surprises?"

His expression fell. "You have no clue."

I tried to concentrate on the blue of his eyes instead of the pain that quickly grew to thought consuming. "So this photographic memory, did it help you in school?"

"My degree is in physics, so it didn't hurt."

"You have a degree in physics and you're remodeling my storage room?" I hoped that didn't sound as condescending out loud as it did in my head. "I mean, not that your work isn't meaningful..."

"I like motion. It's easy to understand, easy to predict once you know the rules." He leaned back, keeping his hand in mine.

I wanted to move away from the persistent burn in my side but knew better. "How much more?"

Jagger took a good look at my tattoo. "About a quarter of the way."

I sucked in my breath. I could do this. It wasn't too bad, but it sure as fire wasn't pleasant.

He smiled softly. "Need a distraction?"

I sank my teeth into my lower lip. "Questions?"

"What do you want to know?"

"You're letting me go first? Really?" Man, that gun was beginning to *hurt*.

"Well, I'm not the one getting tattooed, so I'll have mercy on you." He ran the stud in his tongue along his teeth, and I stared, transfixed. "Paisley?"

"Oh, question. Right. I know you're all anti-relationship right now, but don't you miss having a girlfriend?" *Oh my God!* That was not supposed to come out of my mouth.

He played with the tongue stud again for a moment. I was fast learning that it meant he was thinking. "I've never been a relationship guy. I've learned that the people you let in the closest have the power to hurt you the most, which doesn't really push me toward relationships."

I instantly hated whoever had hurt him. "That's a really cynical way to look at love."

"That's a painful place to get a tattoo. Pretty bold choice for a newbie." He abruptly changed the subject.

I understood loud and clear. "How much more?"

Matt sprayed something cool and soothing onto my skin and wiped it off before he set the gun to my skin again. "No, kids, we're not there yet," he joked.

"You sat through five of these?" I asked Jagger. Pain laced my voice into an almost whine. "I'm such a wimp."

"You're doing fine." I loved the feel of my hand in his. There was no awkward placement of fingers or clammy grip. It felt natural.

"Have mercy on me and let me ask another question?"

Jagger half laughed. "What do you want to know?"

"Tell me about one of your tattoos. Your first?"

Something dark flickered across his face. "How about my last?"

I nodded, willing to take whatever he would give.

He let go of my hand and lifted his shirt, revealing the black scrollwork that cut across his lower abs. My mouth watered at the idea of tracing it with my tongue. *Bad!* I shut that thought down immediately.

"It says, 'I am the master of my fate. I am the captain of my soul.'"

Unable to stop myself, and careful not to move my upper body, I touched the black ink, his skin hot under my fingers. "'Invictus.'"

He sucked in his breath. "It's my turn to be impressed."

"I'm fixing to be a librarian, remember?" I forced my fingers away. "What language is that?"

"Tok Pisin. It's from Papua New Guinea."

"What?" I laughed, despite the pain wracking my ribs.

"Hey, don't move, or you're going to have some very different words over here," Matt threatened.

"Sorry, Matt," I said over my shoulder. "So, is English too trendy for you?" I joked at Jagger.

He looked over my shoulder. "What, Matt, you're not chiming in?"

"Nawh, man. My job is to keep the secrets, not to expose yours."

His eyes flickered to mine. "They're my truths and no one else's. If I want to share them, it's my choice. Well, unless I travel to Papua New Guinea shirtless, I guess."

His wry smile didn't fool me. "How many people know what it means?"

"Just you." He swallowed.

My breath stilled, and it felt like we existed in a time all our own. "Thank you for trusting me."

His face was a kaleidoscope of emotion, changing too quickly to identify. "We're friends."

Before I could respond, Matt sprayed my skin again and wiped it clean. "You're all set, Paisley."

I looked over, scared to see if I'd end up as one of those epic fail posters with the wrong tattoo, but it was perfect. Fierce. "It's exactly what I wanted. Thank you." My voice nearly broke, but Matt took it in stride, cracking a smile.

He slathered on ointment, then bandaged it. A set of directions and a paid bill later, and Jagger and I were on our way back to Enterprise.

I loved my tattoo. I loved every black line, every curve of ink, every feeling that washed over me when I looked at it. I'd never done anything so permanent, or anything that was liable to get my butt whooped. But I wasn't afraid. Peyton wouldn't have been afraid. No, she would have strutted into the house in a sports bra and rolled her eyes when Mama said something.

Maybe I wasn't as fearless as Peyton, but she'd been right. I was fierce in my own right. As if the ink reached deeper than my skin, it seemed to bleed into my soul. I had given up so much in the name of being safe, and not only in regard to my heart. How much was there to give before I wasn't *me* anymore?

"Mission accomplished?"

"Absolutely. Best tattoo guide ever." I gently squeezed his hand, then released it. "Tell me why you have 'Invictus' across your stomach?"

He stared quietly at the road so long that I didn't think he was going to answer, our soundtrack only the chirping of crickets.

"What's with the Shakespeare?"

I smiled. Quid pro quo. He'd never give up something of his own without learning something equally deep. "I read it my sophomore year, and it spoke to me. Peyton was always bigger than life, and growing up with that...well, it makes you feel smaller somehow, and not just in height. She was fearless. The last time we were together, she said, 'I may be wild, Lee, but you're fierce. Your heart is so much stronger than mine.'" I swallowed and closed my eyes for the smallest moment, almost feeling her arms around me that last time.

"Then she slipped this"—I pulled the paper I'd had my tattoo drawn from—"into my back pocket." His eyes darted to mine. "I may be little, but I'm fierce, and I'm going to live every day remembering that. She wouldn't want anything else, and I'm so sick of accepting anything less."

Silence stretched between us while he deliberated. I kept my focus on his profile, letting him know that I expected his trust in return for mine.

"I left my house, my father, as soon as I was legally able to emancipate myself. I abandoned every plan he ever made for me, every expectation that anchored me to his world. I became the captain of my ship."

"The master of your soul," I finished. What could have happened that he would walk away from his family? My parents drove me crazy, but I couldn't imagine not having them.

"Yes. Don't feel sorry for me, Paisley. I can feel pity pouring out of you. I've never once regretted my decision."

I tried to blank my expression. "How old were you?"

"One day over seventeen."

I knew he wasn't ready to tell me why...yet. "Thank you for telling me."

We pulled into the driveway, and Jagger came around to my side, lowering me without brushing the tattoo. My feet hit the ground, and I smiled at him, all too aware of the shiver that raced through me at contact with him.

He cleared his throat. "How did you lose her? Peyton?" I felt the blood in my face race out of it like someone had pulled a drain plug, and he flinched. "I'll understand if you don't want to tell me." His hands lingered at my waist before he drew them back.

I wanted him to know, to put it together as much as I needed him to stay away from my personal nightmare. "She had a heart condition no one knew about. It gave out one morning while she was away at school, and she was gone. Sudden cardiac death. Just like that. No good-bye."

He hooked his thumbs in the pockets of his shorts. "I'm so sorry you lost her."

This was it, my chance to tell him naturally. Right. Now. Chills raced through me, but I opened my mouth anyway. "Jagger, you should know something."

"Yeah?" I saw it then, the flickers of trust in his blue eyes, the slightest opening in the doorway he kept so tightly locked to himself, and I just... I just...

"I really like being your friend."

I chickened out.

CHAPTER ELEVEN

The hardest moment was when I saw you for what you really were...a liar.

My feet swung off the tiny seat my ass perched on. "Come on, little man! You got this!" The kid looked about seven, lifting his leg off the ground as he wound for the pitch. The ball released, sailing through the air, but fell short of the target.

He looked devastated.

"Hey, Dad!" I called out. The guy raised his eyebrows at me, and I tilted my head to the side, motioning to the lever that would dunk me.

He smiled in gratitude and carried the kid up to the red-and-white-spiraled target. "Go ahead, Brody."

The boy's eyes lit up as he looked at me beneath his Iron Man face paint. "You sure?"

"Show me what you got!" I took a deep breath as his little hand flew out, pressing the lever. The seat dropped out from under me, and I plummeted four feet into the tepid tank of water. I surfaced and gave the kid a thumbs-up as I climbed the ladder.

Masters held open the cage door. "Your shift is up."

"Thanks, man." I jumped out of the dunk tank, sluicing the excess water off my hair with the towel he handed me. "I have a couple hours off."

"Why the hell would you sign up for two shifts of this?"

"The kids are cute."

"And that had what to do with Walker skipping out?"

"We got tasked. It's for charity. The guy never gets to see his girl, and I don't mind getting dunked for two hours. He's done far worse for my sake."

Masters nodded. The guy was harder to crack than a nuclear code. "You might want to get your shirt on. The CG is wandering around here somewhere, and you know how he feels about ink." He started to motion to his arm and then his pecs, then gave up and generally gestured to his torso. "You're kind of...colorful."

"What do you think he'd have to say about this?" I flicked my tongue stud across my teeth.

"Jesus, Bateman. It's like you're asking to get kicked out."

He reset the lever and climbed into the tank. Montgomery, a warrant officer from our class, took the money, and the next shift started. Shit, my toes were pruned.

The fair was in full swing behind the CG's house. Guess he didn't mind loaning out his helipad for the day. People wandered the booths, bouncy things had squealing kids, and the smell of fried food made my stomach grumble.

I changed into my cargo shorts in the dressing area and then walked behind the booth where I'd left my shirt and shoes.

"Bateman." *Shit.*

"Major Davidson, sir." He wasn't in uniform, but he stood between me and my shirt, snacking on a bag of peanuts. They were fucking mad about peanuts down here.

"Staying out of trouble?"

"I haven't recently relocated any giant bears, if that's what you mean."

He cracked a smile. "Yeah, that was along the lines of my thinking."

"I was debating one of the stationary helicopters, but you've made me see the error of my ways."

"I somehow doubt that, but I'll take what I can get when it comes to you." He popped another peanut and motioned toward my shirt. "Please."

I walked around him, cursing as water splashed me from Masters getting dunked.

"Well, Bateman, this takes casual to a whole new level."

Fucking Carter. My fist flexed automatically, and I swallowed the need to force his West Point ring down his throat. If he tapped it on his desk one more time... "Just grabbing my shirt, Carter. Nothing to worry about. When are you working?"

He checked his watch. "I'm up after Masters in about an hour. I came by to see how it's going."

I had half a mind to hide his clothes while he was in the tank. Mature? Nawh. Fun? Yup. "Have fun with that." I reached around him and grabbed my shirt.

"Yeah. I'm supposed to be meeting Lee here. You haven't seen her, have you?"

I shook my head, pulling my arms through the shirt. "Never met her, so zero chance of me recognizing her."

"Right."

I put the bottom button through the hole and started on the second.

"We dress for the festivals around here."

General Donovan. *Fuck my life.* "Yes, sir. I was just getting out of the dunk tank."

"General, sir, this is Jagger Bateman. He's another lieutenant in my class." Carter introduced us, looking all chummy with the CG.

The general's eyes looked like they were about to bug out of his head. "Bateman?"

Why is everyone all over my last name today? "Yes, sir."

His jaw flexed, and he folded his arms across his chest. That was not the answer he wanted. "Exactly what are you doing here?"

"Working the dunk tank, sir," I repeated, gesturing behind me like there wasn't a huge fucking dunk tank in eyesight. "Our class was tasked with it."

He looked at Carter. "He's still in your class?"

Carter nodded, and a gleam came across his face. Prick. I had to give it to General Donovan. Other than his arms and that tic in his jaw—there it was again—it was hard to tell he was angry, but I'd grown up with a man skilled at hiding emotion. Yeah, the general was more like livid.

"Major Davidson?"

The major stepped forward. "Yes, General?"

"Can you explain why Bateman is still present on my post? I asked you to handle this."

Well, shit. My stomach dropped fourteen stories and landed in the realm of nausea.

Major Davidson stopped chewing those peanuts. "You told me to handle it, sir. I tasked the lieutenants accordingly. Bateman was willing to take the fall for all three, and the other two came forward of their own volition. I felt obligated to give them another chance."

"I want him gone. Now." He left no room for argument. Carter had the gall to look a little shocked, and then fucking ecstatic. Prick.

"Daddy?" That voice soothed me like nothing else could. Paisley, dressed in the sexiest white sundress I'd ever seen, walked around Carter toward General Donovan. "What's wrong?"

Wait. "Daddy?" My eyes narrowed, and hers widened as she saw me. Her eyes lingered where the skin of my chest was exposed before dragging them to my face.

"Jagger?"

Now Carter and General Donovan stared her down and called her out at the same time.

"How do you know him?"

"You know each other?"

My teeth ground, more pissed at her betrayal by omission than General Donovan threatening to kick me out of flight school. "You're General Donovan's daughter?"

"You're in flight school?" Her mouth hung slack. "Why didn't you tell me?"

"I told you I was in school here. You assumed college. You?"

"You never asked for my family pedigree."

"Lee, how do you know Bateman?" Carter asked his question over again, and this time I put it together. William Carter. Carter was Paisley's Will.

The blood drained from my head, leaving me feeling drunk, and not in a pleasant-buzz kind of way. Oh, no. This was an I've-done-twelve-shots-of-tequila-before-a-game kind of way. I would rather have been cross-checked into the boards with no helmet than hear this.

She gave her forced smile to Carter, the one where she didn't show her teeth. "He's teaching me how to swim."

"He what?" Her dad growled.

"Bateman?" Carter's mouth turned down like he'd tasted something disgusting.

I knew the feeling well.

I buttoned up the rest of my shirt. If I was getting kicked out of flight school, I was at least going to have clothes on. "Hard time believing I can swim, Carter?"

"Wait, you know him, too?" Now it was Paisley's turn to look incredulous.

"He's in my class, Lee! He's Bateman!"

Ah, so he'd been talking about me. Nice to know.

Her gaze snapped toward mine. "You're the one he's competing against?"

"Yes." *And I'll win...if I stay.*

"Get him off my post, Major Davidson. I won't have him here." The general's jaw was set, just like his opinion of me.

"Sir, all due respect, but you told me to deal with him, and I did. He's completed his extra duty and then some. He made a stupid mistake."

"He put that damned polar bear on my lawn!"

I sucked in a breath and closed my eyes before I could see Paisley's reaction. I could handle everyone's disapproval, but not hers. The silence got to be too much for even me, and I manned up and opened my eyes.

Paisley didn't look disgusted. Nope. She had a shit-eating grin on her face. The general may as well have not existed—I couldn't pry my eyes off Paisley's thousand-megawatt smile if he'd told me I was on fire. Then her expression fell, and she glared over at Carter. What the hell was that about?

"Process his paperwork. There's no chance he's staying." General Donovan delivered sentencing and turned on his heel, making it a couple feet before Paisley stopped him.

"Daddy, no! You can't kick him out! He saved my life!"

"Lee-Lee, what on earth are you talking about? Because of the swim lessons?" He shook his head. "I love you, but you don't get a say in these matters."

She glanced at me. "I went to Florida. When I told you I had that appointment with my academic advisor? I really went to Florida with Morgan."

Man, if I thought he'd been pissed before, the shade of mottled red he turned was far worse.

She cleared her throat. "I needed to go. It's hard to explain, but I was thrown into the water. I would have drowned if Jagger hadn't jumped in to save me. He's the only reason I'm still here. He pulled me out of the water, and then he took me to the doctor even after I told him I didn't need it. Thank God he did, because I needed..." She blushed, the color just...enchanting. *Shit, there's that word again.* "I needed to be seen. He saved my life twice in the same day."

She hadn't said a thing. Had she had an asthma attack when they'd taken her to be examined?

The muscle in his jaw flexed once. Twice. "Is this true?" He asked it like a dare.

I wanted to lie, for the sheer satisfaction of letting him believe I was the asshole he thought I was. But I wouldn't make Paisley a liar. "It is, sir. She'd been thrown in by some asshat who didn't know she couldn't swim."

"Language," Carter growled.

I ignored him. "I was just in the right place at the right time, sir. But it's the best thing I've done with my entire life." Her indrawn breath was all I heard.

A splash broke my concentration and jarred General Donovan, too. He looked past me to where I knew Major Davidson was standing. "He stays under one condition."

"Sir?" Major Davidson sounded as confused as I felt.

"You all stick together, Lieutenant? You and your fellow delinquents?"

"Yes, sir." My stomach dropped and my mouth watered, like that second before puking. I really didn't want to see breakfast again.

"How about this—your position on the Order of Merit list for aircraft selection can stick together, too. Wherever you place after the primary phase of flight school is where they do. Fail, and you drag them down with you. Enjoy primary." He walked off, dismissing us all without a word. Major Davidson clapped me on the back and followed.

Enjoy primary. He wasn't kicking me out, but he'd tied Josh and Grayson to my epic-fuckup fate.

"Will Carter, you get your rear in the house. We're fixing to have a few words that shouldn't be spoken in polite company." Paisley shot a glare at Carter and stalked off, leaving him to trail her like a wounded puppy. We really needed to talk, and I moved in her direction until I remembered that Carter was the one with the right to her time. Not me. We were just friends. My shoulders drew up, and my torso tensed with my jaw.

Carter. Will-fucking-Carter. He touched her. Kissed her. Damn it, he knew how she tasted. And he didn't deserve any of it, that ring-tapping asshole.

I spun and slammed my fist into the Plexiglas side of the trailer. My knuckles split open, the blood streaking a garish line across the white material. Pain radiated up my arm, but it never reached my chest, where I desperately needed it to quell the fire like it usually did.

"Bateman, don't do it. That one will sink your career," Masters called from the dunk tank. Paisley Donovan. If my career was the only thing she sank, I'd be a lucky man.

CHAPTER TWELVE

PAISLEY

3. Save someone's life.

"You told on him!" I paid no mind that we stood in Mama's living room and didn't bother to keep my voice down. "You almost ended his career over a statue! Was it worth it to you?"

"It's not just a statue, and it didn't really matter before you knew who it was."

"Oh, now, that's not the truth." My inner five-year-old reared her head. "Jagger is a really good guy, and you could have ruined him. You *would* have ruined him if I hadn't stepped in."

"I did my duty."

"You purposely sold out the members of your class!" It flew out of my mouth too fast to stop.

A stricken look passed over his face. God, why did I say it? Was he right? Was I only upset now because it was Jagger? What did that even mean? "Will, I'm—"

"What he did was wrong, and he doesn't belong here, Peyton!"

I sucked in air reflexively, and it rushed out just as quickly. He'd popped my heart like a balloon, and her name was the dart. "Paisley," I whispered.

"What?" he snapped.

"Paisley. I'm Paisley, not Peyton. I will never be Peyton." Pain walked in and sat on my chest. Heck, it never really left completely. Oh, no, that pain, and the missing her—it hovered right outside the doors to my heart, waiting to crush me with the first memory to surface, even two years later.

"Oh, Christ." He reached for me, but I dodged his hands. "I'm so sorry, Lee. I was thinking about her, how she would have...understood."

I backed away until my shoulder blades touched the fireplace mantel. "Oh, no. You don't get to use Peyton like that. Not ever." His eyes flickered to my left, where her picture sat framed.

"Peyton would have understood this. She would have been right by my side, talking to your father."

An unflattering heat bloomed in my stomach, pushing up my throat, hot and lethal. He was wrong. Peyton's impetuous nature would have kept up with Jagger. *In ways I never can.* "No, Peyton would have been right there with Jagger, figuring out how to get the bear upright on the lawn! She may have been your best friend, but she was my sister. Don't you dare act like you knew her better than I did." I shook my head and threw my hands up. "She wouldn't recognize who you've become. Where's the boy who left for West Point with her? The one with the thick southern accent that *disappeared* while he was in New York? He'd have been out there, too, strapping on the last PT belt. He'd have been friends with Jagger."

His shoulders dropped, and his voice softened. "I may have lost my accent, Lee, but I didn't lose my honor, which Bateman has *none* of."

"His honor had him dive off a pier to save my life, Will. Give the guy a chance. Not everyone goes to West Point." *Or changes like you have.*

"What he did was wrong." His voice was low, hard as concrete.

"The world isn't always as black-and-white as you see it. Jagger pulled a prank. The class prank, if I'm not mistaken, which you are a part of, right? You chose not to participate, which I get, but sinking your classmates?" *Same class.* But if they were in the same class, then why...? Ice ran through my veins.

"Someone has to set the example."

"Jagger was at SERE with you these last three weeks."

His forehead puckered. "Yes?"

"But you...you said you weren't back until yesterday. Jagger came by the library on Thursday."

He paled. "I was...I was home Wednesday night."

I waited for pain to streak though me, but all I felt was annoyance. "I'm sorry?"

"I was home, but I had a ton of work to get done, so I told you Friday so I could get it done and spend all my time with you this weekend. You know how important flight school is to me, Lee."

"So you lied. Honor and all?"

His face crumpled. "God, Lee. I'm so sorry. I didn't think of it like that, I swear. I just didn't want you to come over and see me with my face in a study guide. You deserve 100 percent of my attention, and so I didn't tell you until I could give it to you. I promise that's all it was."

My eyes flicked to his fingers, which always rubbed together when he was lying. They were still. "Well, it hurts. I know we don't have this passionate, insane relationship or anything, but you could have at least wanted to see me." *No burning.*

"I did, I swear. But I didn't want to half-ass my time with you. I won't make the same mistake again."

I locked my right arm to my side, protecting my tender skin as he pulled me into the familiar spot against his chest. With Will, it would always come to this; our friendship meant forgiveness. "Okay. Just remember this moment when you're snapping to judgment on someone else."

"Bateman."

"He saved my life, and he's..." I swallowed. "He's my friend. Can't you please cut him a little slack?"

He cupped my face in his hands and brushed a kiss softly across my lips before shaking his head. "I love you, Lee, but you're too damn trusting. I'll teach you to swim if you want, but please stay away from Bateman. There are two of us in this relationship, not three. This isn't an ultimatum, but I'm asking you not to let him come between us."

I wanted to refuse, to draw my line in the sand just to make me bigger in his eyes, but that wasn't a relationship. He'd asked something I was capable of giving, which meant I needed to be mature enough to give it to him. "I won't swim with him anymore."

"Okay."

I hadn't lied, but I hadn't exactly told the truth, either. I looked at the picture of Peyton's impish grin on the mantel.

"Thank you, Lee."

Lee. I closed my eyes and inhaled the scent of hundreds of summer days, and Will...and home. When I opened my eyes, she was still there, perpetually smiling.

He followed my line of sight. "God, I miss her, too. She really was the best of us."

Usually that declaration made me feel closer to him, acknowledging our shared grief. But today it shriveled a tiny piece of my heart.

Will was wrong. There were already more than two of us in this relationship, and I was the third wheel.

• • •

Boom! One of the players slammed into the glass walls around the ice, and I jumped. Jagger did this for fun? He hadn't responded to my texts, and when I'd gone by the house, Masters told me he was here in Montgomery, playing hockey.

I claimed a seat on the almost empty bleachers and yelped. The bench nearly froze off my girly bits. Maybe a skirt hadn't been the way to go, but I hadn't changed after Sunday services, just jumped into the car. My impetuousness was about to earn me frostbite.

I needed to sort out what had happened yesterday, but I also wanted to see him, which was utterly wrong now that I knew who he was and how much Will despised him. What if he didn't want to see me? What if our friendship, as new as it was, had been squashed by simply knowing how our lives intertwined?

Which one was Jagger, anyway? They looked the same under all that gear.

"I have an extra hoodie, if you'd like it." A girl my age sat down next to me, a black zip-up hoodie in her hand. Her auburn hair was piled in a twist, and the smile she offered reflected in her blue eyes. She was beautiful without being overly made-up, which made me instantly lean toward liking her.

"I usually wouldn't put a stranger out, but I'm freezing," I answered, taking the hoodie. "Thank you so much." I slipped my arms through the sleeves and zipped it up, still trying to figure out which of the giants was Jagger. They all moved so *fast*, like their skates were extensions of their feet.

"No problem. I'm used to the cold." She sipped her Starbucks and turned her attention to the rink. "Who are you here to watch?"

"I'm not sure which one he is," I admitted as a fight broke out. "Oh, sweet mer—" One of the players shoved the other into the wall so hard his skates came out from underneath him and he collapsed, shaking his head. There was something about the way the aggressor tilted his head...

"Bateman! Two minutes for unnecessary roughness!" the ref called out. I couldn't help but smile as Jagger lifted his hands in the air in obvious question of the call.

"I can see his temper has improved," the girl said, her northern accent thick with sarcasm.

"He's something else," I drawled slowly, immediately wondering how she knew Jagger. My eyes locked on his gear-clad frame, noting the *B* on the back of his helmet as he grabbed his water on the way to the penalty box, then ripped off his helmet as he sat down.

"Wait!" the girl exclaimed. "You're here for Jagger?"

As if he'd heard his name spoken, he looked up, his mouth dropping open as his gaze met mine. I smiled through my nervousness and gave him a small wave. "Yes, I suppose I am," I answered without taking my eyes off him. Was he happy to see me? I sure couldn't tell.

"Oh, shit," the girl exclaimed, grabbing my hand. "Blond hair, green eyes, and a sweet little southern accent. You're Paisley."

Okay, *that* got my attention. "How did you—"

Her grin was infectious. "I'm Ember, Josh's girlfriend."

My forehead puckered, trying to remember which one was Josh. "Walker? The one who lives with Jagger?"

"That's him." She pointed out the guy shaking his head at Jagger as he skated past the penalty box. "He's my world." Her eyes swept over me in a kind but obvious appraisal. "You're exactly as Jagger described you."

"He talks about me?" Oh, mercy, I had regressed to high school. "We're just friends," I quickly added, so she didn't get the wrong impression. Not that driving all the way here would give her the right one.

"Right," she answered. "Well, he needs more friends, so I immediately approve."

The timer hit zero, and Jagger flew from the penalty box,

heading straight for the player closest to the goal faster than anything I'd ever seen. He danced around his opponent, stole the puck right from his stick, and charged toward the other goal, speeding around the players coming at him. As if they read each other's minds, he fired the puck to Walker, who easily scored. "Whoa."

"Yeah, it's always like that when they're out there together." Ember smiled and lifted her cup in Walker's direction. "Good job, babe!"

Jagger didn't spare me a glance; he was too focused on the game. By the end of it, he hadn't looked my direction again, and my level of nervousness hit DEFCON three.

"Come on, let's go wait for them," Ember led me to the concession area and stretched. "Good thing I don't have class tomorrow. I actually get to spend some time with Josh."

"You go to Troy, too?"

"I'm at Vanderbilt. Josh and I make the best of what time we get. It's never enough, but we adapt."

"I did that with my boyfriend for a while," I admitted. "He was finishing college the first nine months of our relationship. It's nice to finally be around each other." My voice trailed off. Was it?

"Hard to readjust?" she asked.

I forced a closed-lip smile. "We were never really *together*. I mean, we were friends, but our relationship started long-distance, so we're finding our way around each other now." I stared at the doors that led to the locker room. "Sometimes I think it was easier when we were apart, like the idea of me was easier to love than the actual…" Wait. Was I really saying this to a stranger? "Oh…I am so sorry. I do love him. I don't know why I'd even say that. I must look like a loon." I closed my eyes in utter mortification.

"It makes more sense than you know." She sipped her coffee again, her eyes kind and unjudging. "How did you meet him?"

I liked that she didn't dwell on my outburst. "He was my sister's best friend."

"Was?" She waited a few heartbeats. "You don't have to tell me if you don't want to. I promise I'm not the inquisition or anything."

The first of the players came out of the locker room, but not either of the ones we were looking for. "I have a little bit of baggage."

"Me, too. Dead dad. You?" Her tone was matter-of-fact.

"Dead sister and a broken heart," I answered, just as deadpan.

She nodded her head. I liked that we didn't offer each other condolences, the words we'd probably both heard so much that they didn't even sound like words anymore. I saw Jagger through the glass and stood as he pushed the door open.

My heartbeat sped up, and Ember leaned over to squeeze my hand gently. "He's really good at unpacking, Paisley. You just have to give him a chance."

"It was really nice to meet you, Ember." I squeezed, too, and let go. Three heartbeats later he stood in front of me, his hair still wet from the shower.

"Hey." His voice sent a ripple through me.

"Hey."

"Well, as awkward as this whole situation looks, I think I'd like to get home." Josh tossed Ember over his shoulder. Her squeal of protest and delight echoed off the brick walls. "You good, man?"

Jagger waved him off. "I'll take my time."

Josh smiled. "Appreciate it!"

"Joshua Walker!" Ember's voice faded as they left.

We stood there, staring at each other in a game of nonverbal chicken. His eyes trapped my breath in my chest until I gave in. "I can't do our lessons anymore."

One of his eyebrows rose. "And you drove all the way to

Montgomery to tell me that?"

"You haven't returned a text or a phone call."

He stared at me, peeling back my soul layer by layer until I had to break eye contact. "Are you mad at me?" I asked. He was silent, and it took forever for me to drag my eyes over his chest, fixating on his Led Zeppelin T-shirt and the muscles it clung to.

"Are *you* mad at *me*?" he countered.

"I asked you first." I looked up at him.

"Are we in kindergarten?" His grin broke the tension.

"I didn't lie, I promise. Or at least, I didn't mean to. I just don't like talking about my father."

"I understand." The sudden, solemn set of his mouth said maybe he really did. "I should have told you I'm in flight school."

"Why didn't you tell me? It's not something to be ashamed of."

He looked away. "There are very few things I'm scared of. But the big one? That's failure."

"But you're not failing, are you? Will says you're neck and neck with him for top of the OML. A pain in his rear end, but smart." Actually, Will had a healthy dose of jealousy over Jagger, but it would be the ultimate betrayal to let that secret slip.

He sucked in his breath through his teeth. "I know this sucks, but can we agree not to talk about Will?"

I cringed but understood. We both liked the little bubble we had here. "I think we can do that. But you're not failing."

"Not yet." He nodded toward the door. "I'll walk you out." He rolled his gear behind him and held the door open for me. I tried not to touch him, but he nearly filled the doorway. My skin tingled at every inch we'd made contact.

"What does that mean?" My narrowed gaze locked onto his profile as we walked toward the parking lot. Why was he so hard to get answers out of? "Why do you say that you haven't failed *yet*?"

"I almost got kicked out over that damned bear. Then again when your dad realized I *hadn't* been kicked out. I fuck stuff up, Paisley. I let people down. I walk out. I didn't tell you because then you'd know when I failed. It's what I do."

My hand covered his on my door handle. "You're not going to fail. I don't think you have it in you."

He leaned down to where our noses nearly met. My heart thundered, and my lips parted without thought. "I hate to break this to you, but disappointing people is my specialty."

I didn't back away, or down, like he was daring me to. "You've never disappointed me."

His jaw locked. "Honesty, right? That's our deal?"

I nodded, despite my hesitation. "Honesty."

"My disappointing you is inevitable. It's only a matter of how far I fall down the fuckup trail, and whether or not you give me another chance. Look at where we are. You can't even swim with me because your boyfriend hates me, and that's just the beginning. I fuck things up."

My thumb stroked over his hand absently, like it wasn't my decision. I chose my words carefully. "I preemptively forgive you for whatever it is you think you'll fail me at. That's what friends do, Jagger. They forgive each other when they make mistakes." The intense heat in his eyes stilled the breath in my chest, and in that moment every future I could imagine seemed open, possible, even though I knew better. "In fact, I brought you something."

I opened the door and pulled the small box from the driver's door, handing it to him. His brow puckered, and mercy, it was cute, boyish. "Your first flight is this week, right?"

"Yeah, our first flight with our instructor pilots." He opened it and took out the shiny nickel I'd placed in there last night. "Paisley—"

"They call that your nickel flight," I explained, cutting off anything he was going to say, mostly because I wasn't sure how to handle it—how to handle him. "You're supposed to give your IP a nickel for your first ride, and it's extra luck if it's your birth year."

He examined it closely, his eyes lighting up when he saw that I'd correctly guessed his birth year. "How did you know?"

"I didn't, just a guess. I have two other nickels in the car in case I was wrong."

He wrapped his arms around me, our bodies flush, and kissed the top of my forehead slowly. Chills morphed into flames as they raced down my spine, and I sinfully imagined what those lips might feel like on mine. "Thank you," he whispered against my skin. My arms wound around his back, and I ignored the dips and curves of his muscles as best I could. Which was not at all; they consumed every thought. I let myself sink into the feel of him for a moment.

This attraction to Jagger, the longing, the craving to be near him, it was wrong, and Will deserved better. "I...I have to go." I scrambled back.

"Paisley, don't."

I fumbled with my door handle. "Why do we always have these conversations outside my car?" I muttered. "I have to go, Jagger."

"We always have these conversations outside your car because you're always trying to leave. You could try finishing a conversation, you know."

An unladylike snort escaped me. "That's not the least bit true. These...talks happen because I've already stayed too long. I'm sorry about the swim lessons."

"He..." Jagger took a deep breath. "Carter can't be that big of a dick. He's a pompous asshat, but he doesn't want you to drown."

"Will is going to teach me himself. He's not what you think he is. He's a good man, a good friend."

"Friend? Is that seriously how you think of him?"

"He is my friend!" I shouted, and then gasped, my eyes darting around the empty parking lot to make sure I hadn't caused a scene. "That's the base of any real relationship, what makes it the strongest, so don't mock it. And he's not up for discussion, remember? Wasn't that your request?"

The muscle in his jaw twitched, but he withdrew slowly, his hands reaching for the sky before they clasped the back of his head. "Well, I'm your friend, too. And a friend says something when the other's dating a douche bag."

I didn't try to stop him from walking away. Mostly because I couldn't give him a good enough reason to stay.

CHAPTER THIRTEEN

JAGGER

*Maybe one day you'll be proud that I took a chance—
hung everything out there on the line. But you'll
probably only be more pissed that it wasn't your
damned line.*

Three fucking weeks, and I'd only seen the top of Paisley's head at the library. Whenever I was working there, she avoided me like the plague. The only way I'd known she'd even seen the back room were the organized supplies on the new shelves.

We were a day or two from finishing, and then I'd have no excuse to see her anymore.

"Hey, where are you? Because it's sure not here," Josh asked.

I blinked twice and woke the fuck up. "I'm here." I tapped my pen on the desk, stretching my legs out in front of me, wondering how much of the lecture I'd missed.

Our instructor, Mr. Givens, looked at the clock, and I

followed suit. Mondays always seemed the longest, but today was dragging ass.

"Who do you think it will be?" Josh asked in a whisper.

Carter turned from his seat ahead of us and shot Josh a glare, like he was the noise police. I shot it back, and it turned icy on his part. What the fuck did he have to be so angry about? He got to keep Paisley, while I lost my friend. I swiveled my finger in a circle, and he took the hint and turned around, but not before he shook his head. He disapproved of my choice of finger, apparently.

"It's close," Masters said.

"My money's on Jagger."

That earned Josh a snort from Carter. He tapped his ring on the desk for good measure, like he needed to remind us that he'd graduated West Point.

"Good bet," Masters replied.

I ignored them both and concentrated on the PowerPoint ahead of us. Not that I didn't already know this shit. It had been committed to memory since I picked up a book on the principles of flight when I was thirteen. Regardless, I made sure to take a look at each slide as he presented them.

"I'm sure you're all wondering what's going to happen this afternoon for the flight schedule," Mr. Givens segued. My grip tightened on my pen so hard I was surprised it didn't break. First solo flight went to the highest on the OML, which was a pretty closely guarded secret. Not that we didn't all try to keep tabs on test scores to figure it out ourselves, but this would be the only real way to measure before the official list was posted at selection. "You solo flight when you're ready, not because it's your turn." He pinned the schedule to the board. "Those of you who are ready are listed on today's schedule, along with who your stick buddy will be for the remainder of primary." He smiled like he hadn't altered our entire lives, announcing that we'd also be assigned our pilot partners. "Enjoy your lunch. Meet here at thirteen hundred."

He walked out, and chairs screeched as the class rushed the board. I hung toward the back, flipping Paisley's nickel over in my fingers. I knew all about the nickel flight tradition and had given my IP a different one. The shiny coin in my hand was the first gift I'd been given in six years; I wasn't letting anyone have it.

Josh came over grinning, clapping Masters on the shoulder.

"Well, did you make the varsity football team?" I asked.

"Hell, yes, and I scored Grayson as my stick buddy. But you—"

"Are you fucking kidding me?" Carter's exclamation cut Josh off.

"What's wrong, West Point? Didn't make the cut?" I called out. Josh elbowed me in the ribs, but that didn't stop the smirk of satisfaction crossing my face as Carter glared at me.

"Fuck you, Bateman. Looks like we'll be seeing enough of each other as it is. I'm going to grab lunch with Lee."

Hearing her name out of his mouth squeezed my chest like a vise. My fist clenched, and I couldn't manage to draw a full breath until he was out of my sight. "He's an asshole."

Josh raised his eyebrows at me. "Good news or bad?"

"Both," I answered.

"Looks like you solo first."

My head snapped toward his, looking for any indication that he was messing with me. "Are you serious?"

"As a heart attack." He smiled, mock-punching my shoulder. "Good job, man."

First. I was going to solo first. Top of the Order of Merit list. I had a shot at an Apache, and not fucking my friends over. "That's..." I couldn't find the words. "Where's the bad in that?"

Josh laughed. "I'll meet you at the car."

Nearly everyone left, either ecstatic about soloing in the

afternoon or utterly dejected. I didn't have a problem getting to the schedule or finding my name in the first slot. Hell, yes. This was everything I'd been— *What the fuck?*

"This should be interesting," Grayson said, standing next to me.

I'd gotten Will Carter as my damn stick buddy. Fuck my life.

I juggled our drinks—two beers and a sweet tea—like a professional frat boy and headed to our table. Masters accepted his tea with a nod, because speaking more than the required amount of words might kill the guy, and Josh gave me a half smile. "Thanks, man."

We all relaxed and drank as our classmates ambled in, grabbing drinks at the bar and dragging chairs over to join us. Once over a dozen of us were there, some with girlfriends or the occasional wife, we had to combine tables. The bar filled quickly for a Friday night, with both flight school students and local girls. A couple of them were eye-fucking me from their bar stools.

"What's with you?" Josh asked. "I get to be pissy. It's been two weeks since I've seen my girlfriend, but what's your excuse?"

I shook my head and wiped the condensation off my glass. *Beverages, people...everything sweats down here.* "Nothing, man." I spun the nickel on the table.

"Bullshit." He scoffed.

"Let it go."

"I've known you for three damn years, Jagger. All you ever talk about is hockey and helicopters, so you're going to have to explain why you're not jumping through your ass in joy right now. You soloed first, man, *first*! I get the little chastity vow you've self-imposed, but you've got two hot girls over there dying to make your lap their seat, and you look like your dog just died."

"I don't have a dog." I couldn't explain what I didn't understand myself.

"You know what I mean. I know it blows that you've got Carter as your stick buddy, but at least you guys will push each other."

Push each other right off a damn cliff.

He leaned forward and dropped his voice, "You know you can talk to me."

"He said to let it go," Masters answered quietly. "Sometimes voicing something gives it power over you. He's got to acknowledge his own shit storm before he lets someone else witness it."

I raised my beer in salute and drained half the glass.

"Dude, you speak?" one of our classmates asked Masters, looking dumbstruck.

Masters glared in response.

"Masters no speak. Only grunt," replied Montgomery. The street-to-seat nineteen-year-old kid had the nerve to make monkey motions at Masters. Why the hell did they let babies into flight school?

"How was that solo-cycle ride, Montgomery?" I countered.

"Fuck you, Bateman." The kid turned bright red. He'd ranked last on the OML, soloed last, therefore had to pedal the infamous solo cycle down the airfield.

Persley cleared his throat. "Right. Anyway"—he raised his voice and his glass—"here's to us, for all completing solo flights without burning one in!"

A cheer resounded, drowning out the music. "And here's to Bateman for soloing first!" Josh slapped my back and lifted his glass to another cheer.

"To Bateman." Carter's mocking voice grated as he took

the empty seat directly across from me. I spun the nickel and kept my eyes focused on it.

"Congratulations, Jagger."

I stopped the nickel midspin, seeing Paisley standing behind him. She'd come. She never came to these things. She wore a fitted top the same green as her eyes, and it might not have shown off that amazing rack she had, but it was sexier than anything the spandex sisters at the bar were wearing. She smiled, and my fucking heart stopped beating momentarily, then hammered.

Get a grip.

I clenched the nickel in my fist and answered her smile with my own. "Thanks, Paisley. Want me to grab you a chair?" I threw out the olive branch.

"She doesn't need a chair." Carter wrapped his arm around her waist and pulled her into his lap. "Do you, Lee-Lee?"

I arched an eyebrow at the nickname. It sounded ridiculous, like a five-year-old child instead of the beautiful woman in front of me.

"I'm fine," she said softly, as if she was answering my thoughts and not his question. She blushed and tucked that soft blond hair behind her ears, then wound her arm around his shoulders like she was happy to be there. *Of course she's happy to be there. He's her damn boyfriend.*

Dropkick Murphys came on the jukebox. Paisley smiled as "Rose Tattoo," her favorite song, started to play. She arched an eyebrow at me, and I gave her a small nod. *Yes, it's for you.*

Carter locked eyes with me, turned her head, and kissed her, never wavering in his gaze. "Yep, she seems pretty fine to me."

"Well, I'm glad one of us is," I responded without thinking. Shit. My mouth was going to get me into trouble. That familiar pressure rose in my chest, and I knew this was not going to end well. Too bad I didn't give a shit enough to stop it from happening.

"What does that mean?" Paisley shot at me, her eyes narrowing.

I gave her my best mocking smile. "Well, Carter has a pretty girl in his lap. I'm feeling like I might need the same kind of treatment." I winked at the prettier of the girls at the bar, the one with her tits hanging out, and she giggled. That was more like it. I turned to Paisley. "That a problem for you?"

Her jaw flexed twice. "Nope. Why would it be?"

"Oh, this is priceless," Masters muttered under his breath and finished his drink. "Another?"

"That'd be great."

He stood as the busty little brunette swayed over to us, her hips arriving before the rest of her. "Hi there," she said with a breathless southern accent and a slow, sultry smile.

"Hi there yourself," I answered with the grin I knew could drop her panties before we hit the parking lot.

"Mind if I take a seat? I was gettin' all sorts of lonely over there." She batted her eyelashes, and Paisley made a sound that was half snort, half growl.

"Not at all. I'm Jagger, and you're...?"

She smiled, her makeup cracking at the corners of her mouth. "I'm Marjorie." She moved to take Masters's seat.

"I'm sorry, Marje, but that's Masters's seat. Seems to be a full house tonight." Paisley's sweet drawl had a distinct, intriguing bite. How far could I push her before she reacted?

"Oh, Paisley Donovan. I didn't barely see you there all snuggled up on...Will Carter, is that you?" Marjorie's smile didn't reach her eyes, which matched Paisley's.

Carter lifted his beer in greeting. "Marje."

I scooted my chair back as Masters handed me a fresh beer. "Small towns are fascinating."

Marje took the opening and sat in my lap, her skirt riding over her thighs to where my jeans were the only barrier between us. "You don't mind, do you? Those chairs are a little cold." She threw puppy-dog eyes at me.

"I wouldn't get too comfortable. Jagger's sworn off women," Paisley drawled.

Marjorie sent me a sly smile. "Jagger doesn't seem to mind me. Do you, darlin'?"

"Not in the least." Not if it forced Paisley into some sort of dialogue. Anything was better than radio silence.

"Maybe he's just sworn off the pale, boring ones. How is life in that little...library of yours, anyway?"

Paisley's smile could have sweetened Grayson's tea. "Still full of books. We've got some you might like, pictures and all."

Josh whistled, and I took a deep drink of my beer, my eyes boring into Paisley. "I think that's southern for 'the claws just came out,'" Josh whispered.

I turned my cap backward. "I'd have to agree."

Carter leaned away from Paisley. "Play nice, Lee."

Fucking Carter.

"So you're a flyboy?" Marjorie asked, turning to look at me.

"I'm in flight school," I answered, tipping my glass toward Carter. "I'm actually Carter's stick buddy."

Carter blanched, and Paisley whipped her head, whispering something I couldn't make out. From the look on Carter's face, it wasn't pleasant. "I was going to tell you," he answered.

"Will Carter, a pilot! All those times we snuck out to... watch those helicopters take off at night, and now you're flying one. Imagine that!" Marjorie's voice dripped sugar. "And of course you're first in your class, right?" She turned to me. "He always was."

I leaned my head to the side and arched my eyebrow at Carter, whose glare could have sunk the *Titanic*. "There's one prick in my way," he answered, and then grunted in pain. Paisley's elbow reappeared on the table.

Marjorie giggled, a high-pitched sound that more

resembled a helium-sucking donkey. "Where on earth did you lose your accent to, Will Carter?"

Paisley bit back a smile, catching her lower lip in her teeth. Damn, I wanted to suck it free. My hand clenched, catching Marje's thigh in the process. "Oh, you can do that again." Marjorie smiled over her shoulder and rotated her hips across my groin. Paisley's smile vanished.

"I spent a few years in New York. I think I left the accent there," Will answered.

"Maybe you should fetch it," Paisley muttered.

Marjorie picked up my beer and drank the last quarter of it. I was too busy watching the changes on Paisley's face to give a shit. "Imagine. You two together!" She sighed. "Isn't that just perfect? Who would have ever thought?" Paisley's eyes narrowed. "I mean, sure, we all knew Will would end up with a Donovan girl, all right..." Paisley sucked in her breath. "Just had him pegged for the pretty one. Shame about your sister, God rest her soul."

Paisley motioned to stand, but Carter locked his arm around her waist, keeping her firmly in his lap. "Relax, Lee-Lee."

"Well, I'm empty," I said, standing quickly. Marjorie slid off my lap, barely catching herself on the edge of the table. "Paisley, can I get you a drink?"

"She doesn't drink," Will answered.

"But she does talk," I snapped.

Paisley swallowed, her eyes still zeroed on Marjorie. "I'd love a lemon water, Jagger. Thank you."

"Of course, Lee-Lee Donovan can't be caught drinking," Marjorie teased. "Whatever would her daddy say? Now her mama—"

"Marjorie Jenkins!" Morgan's singsong voice was more than welcome in my ear as she came around the table, putting her purse in front of Paisley. "My goodness. Did you forget the other half of that skirt at home? I mean, I know Auburn invited you not to return, but that's no reason to think fall didn't actually come. That skirt looks a smidge cold for November, and a smidge trashy with that freshman twenty. Not that we don't completely support your stress eating, bless your little heart."

Marjorie huffed. "Morgan, fancy seeing you here, tagging after Lee and Will. Guess nothing changes there."

"Morgan—" Carter failed to keep the peace. Personally, I was ready to find the popcorn until I saw Paisley's face. She had her swimming face on, the one that said she'd rather be doing anything else, but she'd tough it out.

Morgan's smile was bright…and frightening. "And imagine finding you in Oscar's, trying to pick up flyboys to haul your ass out of Enterprise. Guess we're both creatures of habit."

"This shit is better than *Jerry Springer*," Josh muttered, joining me at the bar.

I ordered our drinks and leaned against the counter. "She's upsetting Paisley."

"I thought that was your goal."

"Pissing her off and hurting her are two different things." And Carter wasn't doing a damn thing to stop it.

"You are walking a fine line, Jagger." Josh thanked the bartender for his beer and took a drink.

"It's what I do best."

Morgan must have finished off Marjorie, because she huffed and swayed her hips in my direction.

"I think I'm going to head home." She batted her eyes at me and trailed her fingers down my chest. Nothing stirred below. "Maybe you'd carry me?"

"Carry?" Josh about spit out his beer.

"Southern for 'take,'" I explained, and held up my beer. "Sorry, Marjorie, but I've had a few too many of these to get behind the wheel. I can call you a cab, though."

She pouted. "Well, if I can't convince you tonight..." She reached behind me and pulled my cell phone out of my pocket. A few clicks and her number was stored. "Give me a call sometime. I'm a lot more fun than any of the girls"—she threw a pointed glance back at our table—"you'll find round these parts."

On her tiptoes, she brushed her lips across my cheek. It was almost worth it to see Paisley turn a mottled shade of red. God, she was cute when she was pissed. "Good night, Jagger."

"Night, Marjorie."

She swayed out of the bar, and I carried our drinks to the table, sliding Paisley's water toward her. "Lemon water, as ordered."

"Maybe you should keep it," she drawled. "Seems you could use a cooldown. Or were you planning on using that number she gave you?"

"Lee," Will snapped.

At least she paid attention. "I'm not the one perched in my boyfriend's lap," I countered. "So, if I want to call a lovely young southern lady, I think that's my prerogative, right?"

"Damn straight!" Montgomery answered, reminding us that we weren't as alone at the table as we felt.

"Poking the bear, Jagger," Grayson said under his breath.

"'Lady' is the last term I'd ever use in conjunction with Marjorie Jenkins," Paisley said, "and that's being kind."

"Lee, bad-mouthing people doesn't suit you," Carter added.

"Don't defend that piece of trash just because you belonged to the Marjorie-got-me-off club in high school, Will," Morgan interjected, pulling a chair over to sit next to Paisley. "It wasn't very selective."

"Really, Morgan?" Carter flushed.

Morgan raised her eyebrows. "Don't act all surprised. I don't mind calling out truths, and I'm happy to ruffle your feathers."

Carter fidgeted. Holy shit. She did ruffle him. Not in the pissed-off sense I usually saw, but in a more unsettled kind of way.

"Can we please stop discussing Marjorie Jenkins?" Paisley asked.

"Sure, as soon as you tell me why you had to drag her through the dirt," Carter answered. "You're better than that, Lee."

My breath hissed out through my teeth.

"You know what?" She turned in his lap. "If you'll kindly excuse me, I need some air." She stood, taking her purse from the table.

"Lee—" Carter stood.

"Don't you dare, William Carter." She pointed her finger at him and marched out of the bar, the picture of gorgeous indignation.

"You dated her sister first?" Josh asked, his eyebrows arched.

Carter shook his head, and Morgan answered for him. "They never dated, but they were best friends. He and Lee got together last year after Peyton died."

Her sister's best friend. Pieces started clicking together in my head, and it wasn't a pretty picture.

"Could you maybe not give out details on my relationship?" Carter barked.

"Could you maybe not treat her like she's five? By grace, twenty minutes with you and I need a drink." Morgan's chair squeaked as she pushed away from the table and headed to the bar.

I took another sip of my beer for fortitude and looked at Carter as I stood. "You're an idiot."

His glare went arctic. "Go ahead, chase after her. It won't end well. She needs space because she doesn't like confrontation. How do I know? Because, unlike you, I've been in her life more than five damn minutes."

"You really think it took me five minutes to understand Paisley? It took me less time to save her life. I knew what kind of woman she was the moment her eyes opened. She's a fighter." I leaned over the table toward him. "And funny, that first breath she released? It was mine." I didn't waste another second, just weeded my way through the crowd until I got outside.

Finally, Alabama had reached a moderate temperature. I pushed up the rolled sleeves of my blue button-down. It didn't take long to find her, leaning on Will's truck, only one empty space away from where I'd left Lucy. Her hair hung in soft waves past her shoulders, the gold catching the light from the street lamp. Leave it to Paisley to make a parking lot off Rucker Boulevard beautiful.

"Don't ask me if I'm okay."

I leaned against the cool metal frame next to her, tucking my hands in my pockets, mostly to keep them from touching her. "Okay."

Her head swiveled my direction. It didn't matter how many times I'd looked into her eyes; I was lost, spun out of control. "You're really not going to ask?"

I pressed my lips together to keep from smiling. "You're kind of fun when you're pissy."

"I am most certainly not…that."

"You can say it, you know."

She crossed her arms in front of her. "I'm more than aware of what I can do. It's not about the ability."

"What's it about?"

"Restraint, and knowing when to use it."

"Restraint has never been my strong suit." My gaze flickered to her lips, pale but shiny from her gloss. *Stop. Friends, only friends.* Shit, I even sounded weak in my head.

"Yeah, I could tell that with Marjorie perched on your lap

like a baby bird waiting to be fed." Her chin came up, and damn if that wasn't sexy.

"You're my only Little Bird," I promised her.

"Why do you call me that?" she bit out through clenched teeth.

"Well, you did kind of fly at our first encounter. Why don't you tell him that you hate when he calls you Lee?"

She squeezed her eyes shut and rubbed her temples. "I don't hate it."

"Yes, you do. I just can't figure out why you don't tell him. He's an ass if he hasn't figured it out by now. Hell, he's an ass, period." *Shit.* I hadn't meant to blurt it out.

"You don't know the first thing about him." She pushed off the car, and I quickly took hold of her wrist.

"Don't go." Shit, was that desperation leaking into my voice? "I've missed you."

She shook me off. "I can't be here with you. I can't do this." She gestured between us, like there was an invisible string tying us together. "Whatever *this* is."

"You can't have a friendship outside your relationship? It's that weak? Worth turning away a friend? You act like I don't know him, but I'm with him every day! He's completely wrong for you."

Because *I* was right for her. I wanted her—wanted to be with her. Admitting that was as thrilling as it was terrifying, and I had no idea what to do with it. But I sure as hell wasn't going to let her think Carter was her only option.

She took another step back. "Will knows me in ways you don't—you *can't*. He knows every scary, damaged part of me, and he still loves me. That's the kind of man he is."

"Damn it, Paisley, listen to yourself. You act like you're some charity case! You think I can't handle those pieces of you?" I moved forward to close the distance between us, and her eyes widened, like she'd felt the shift in our relationship that I had. "I know you from your soul to your skin. Just being friends with you..." I flicked the stud in my tongue across my teeth, trying to find the right words. "I've never been more intimate with a woman, and that includes every girl I've ever had sex with."

She retreated until she bumped into Lucy. "This conversation is over."

I didn't stop until my toes met hers, my chest nearly brushing the rise of her breasts. "Why, because it suddenly doesn't fit in your neat and tidy friendship box?"

"We are *friends*, and you don't get to make judgments on my relationship." Her head bumped the glass of the window as she craned her neck to look at me.

I braced, then tested my theory. "He treats you like a little sister."

"You hush." She squeezed her eyes shut. Damn. I'd been right.

I lifted her chin, but she still wouldn't open her eyes. "He sure as hell didn't stand up for you against Marjorie."

She swallowed but didn't speak.

The need to reach her clawed through me, to make her see what I did—that she was worth so much more than anything Carter or even I could offer her. I dragged my eyes away from the delicate arch of her lips. Rather than backing off, I caged her in, leaning my forearms on the glass on either side of her perfect face.

"Tell me, when he touches you, kisses you, does your skin sing for him?" I could barely choke the words out. Just thinking about Carter holding her, touching her, made my stomach churn. "Does your blood rush, your lips part just thinking about his kiss? Does your body vibrate when he's close, remembering every orgasm he can wring from you?" I crossed the friendship line, sliding my fingers along her collarbone to rest inside her shirt, above her galloping heart.

Her eyes flew open, and her lips parted. I wasn't near her breasts, but I was still too close. "Your heart doesn't pound like this for him, does it?"

"That...that is none of your business." We were so close her breath hit my lips in little bursts.

"Does he treat you like a little sister in bed, too? Is that really what you want? A platonic sex life with a guy who uses you as a replacement for your older sister?"

She sucked in her breath and jerked away from me, escaping my arms. Her eyes narrowed. "Go to hell, Jagger." She walked off, leaving the parking lot silent but for the cars going by.

I hit my head lightly into Lucy's window. "I'm already there, Paisley."

CHAPTER FOURTEEN

PAISLEY

7. Go completely off course.

I slipped the Steinbeck novel into place and made sure the row was even. We were just shy of—wait, I checked my watch. No, time to close up now. I'd avoided Jagger this whole week, and their project was finished, our storage room a model of organization and access. Dang, I hadn't even seen him leave. Now if I could decide if I was pleased with that decision or not. I ran my fingers along the spines as I turned the corner of the bookshelves.

"Does he treat you like a little sister in bed, too? Is that really what you want? A platonic sex life with a guy who uses you as a replacement for your older sister?"

Jagger's words ripped through me again, shredding the pretty paper my relationship with Will had been wrapped in and revealing the banged-up truth beneath it.

Ugh, I hated him for seeing our weakness by watching us for twenty minutes.

I shooed out a couple of guys studying near the doors. "I'm so sorry, gentlemen, but we're closing up for the evening." I gave them a friendly smile and walked them to the doors after they gathered their things.

I hadn't finished Alice's routine, but I wasn't a fan of leaving the doors open past closing, so I turned the key and locked myself inside. *Beep, beep, beep.* The alarm sounded on my cell phone as I slipped off my ballet flats. Once I choked my meds down, I locked the front door, too. *One more to go.*

I turned the doorknob to the storage room and opened the door. "*Dang!* Jagger, you scared the living daylights out of me!" My hand clutched at my chest in reflex.

He slung his black messenger bag across his body and gave me an icy smile. "Sorry. I was just packing up." His jeans hung low on his hips, and when he hooked his thumbs in his pockets and stretched his shoulders, his worn concert tee rose above the waistband, giving me a peek of what had been burned in my memory since Florida.

"We're closed." One day I would not say the most ludicrous things around this man. Today was apparently not that day.

"Well, I'm glad you didn't lock me in. That probably would have screwed my weekend."

"Big plans?" *Please say no.*

"Yeah, I thought I'd have a party or two. There's this really cute brunette two houses down, and Josh and Masters are both gone for the weekend. Nothing like having the house to myself." Anger washed off him in waves, and it was all directed at me.

Well, I could sure as sin give as good as I got. He wasn't the only angry one here.

"Then I guess it's too bad you're not done working here."

"What the hell are you talking about?" He looked around, trying to find the flaw that wasn't there. "We finished. We did everything your daddy told us to, and now we get to go back to our real lives." Fire flickered in his blue eyes, and my breath caught. He looked primal, raw, and I wasn't sure I was capable of handling him.

"Those shelves are a disaster." I laid my palms on the huge wooden worktable in the center. "Nothing is organized, and I'm pretty sure that table over there"—I pointed to the corner—"is fixing to fall apart at any second." I looked over my shoulder. "Is this really the best you can do?"

His eyes narrowed dangerously as he crossed the three steps that separated us. I counted them with my heartbeats. "First, you're the one that did the organization, and second, this room is perfect. We're done. Josh, Grayson. Me and you. All done."

Ouch. "How do you expect to become a pilot with this lack of attention to detail?" I needed to draw his blood. "You really can't see that?"

"Yeah? Well, at least I can see what's right fucking in front of me." He spun me around, and as I gasped, his lips landed on mine.

He took the opening, sliding into my mouth as his hands did the same with my hair. He held me to him, stroking the roof of my mouth, pulling away just to dive back in.

My shock lasted a heartbeat. Maybe two. Then I rubbed my tongue against his and pressed closer. His groan vibrated through his chest, and I was swept up in everything…Jagger.

He pressed me into the table, bringing our bodies flush. He was massive, surrounding me as he drove me breathless with soft lips and hard kisses that tasted like peppermint. Need ripped through me like a shock wave, and I heard a moan. Oh, God. It was me. Yes, those were my hands at his back, fisted in his T-shirt, pulling him closer. That was my body arched into his, and the friction felt so *good*. He consumed me, owned me, and I loved it because in that second, I owned him, too.

I took his hair in my hands as his fingers drifted to my waist. On tiptoe, I tried to get a better angle, to feel more of him. Kissing Jagger was as necessary as breathing. He lifted me by my rear, setting me on the table. Yes. That's exactly what I craved—a better angle. I drew his lower lip into my mouth and sucked on it, then ran my hands down his chest and under his shirt to finally caress the lines of muscles there. Perfect. Every line of him was carved, tight, and trembled under my touch. He growled, pushing me down onto the table as he slid over me, dragging his chest across my breasts.

More. I locked one of my ankles behind his thighs as he settled over me, pressing his hips into mine. He was hard against me, and I rocked into him, aching.

His kisses drugged me, taking my mouth again and again, and I lost myself in every touch, every sensation as my heart beat as wildly as I felt. He kept his hands on my face, bracing his weight on his elbows, his mouth never leaving mine, and his tongue ring didn't disappoint. Hunger rushed through my veins, all stemming from the magic he worked with his kiss. My whimpers mixed with a moan or two from him.

"Paisley," he whispered against my lips. "You're so damn sweet."

His words sent heat rushing through me, pooling low in my core, desire inflaming every nerve ending in my body. I arched into him, kissing him with the same urgency that was unraveling me.

BEEP. BEEP. BEEP.

Stupid watch! I took my hands off his back long enough to press the silent button, unclasp it, and toss it to the side. It skidded along the table before falling to the floor. Who the hell cared about my heart rate when Jagger was kissing me? The world could burn down before I formed a logical thought. There was only Jagger on top of me, surrounding me, anchoring me.

My heart raced, pounding in delight, and I reveled in the utter abandon of kissing him. Will would never let me take off my watch, or kiss me like this. He was too focused on my heartbeat.

Will.

Oh. *Hell.*

I ripped my mouth away from the heaven of Jagger's. "Stop!" I gasped.

He jerked his head away, his eyes flaring wide. "Paisley?"

"Jagger, we can't."

He pushed up, caging me in his arms. "Why the hell not?"

"Oh my God." I covered my face with my hands. "What have I done?" I sat up slowly, tucking my hair behind my ears with shaky hands. In less than five minutes, I'd become something I loathed, abhorred.

I'd become a cheater.

He stood at the edge of the table, a breath away, and pulled me gently, bringing me to the edge of the table. "Don't do it. Don't you dare say his name. Not now when I can still taste you." His voice was sharp, but there was something underneath it I couldn't bear to hear—hurt.

My fingers lingered on my lips swollen from his kisses.

Will. Will, whom I loved. Will, who didn't deserve what I had just done with Jagger.

I cried out, unable to hold in the pain of my own betrayal. Tears pricked my eyes, welling and falling in quick succession.

Jagger wiped away the tears with this thumbs. "God, Little Bird. Don't cry. Please, don't cry."

I didn't even deserve Jagger's hands on me.

I pushed, and he retreated enough for me to slide out. As soon as my feet hit the floor, I ran for the first time in two years. If it caused my heart to stop, then it was only what I deserved.

I slid my key into my front door, on autopilot, and turned the handle. It was still locked. I turned it again, and it opened. Ah, it had been unlocked. Will was here.

Oh, God. Oh, God. *Oh, God.*

I dropped my keys into my handbag, where they chimed against the unused set from the library. Ugh. Alice left me in charge for one night, and I couldn't even get the library locked up right. No, I'd just left…him…standing there. I leaned against the wall, the back of my head hitting it with a *thump*, and closed my eyes, trying to blink away the tears.

"Lee-Lee?" Will called.

I drew in a stuttered breath. "Hey, I'm here." I pulled myself together the best I could, slipped off my shoes, and walked down the short hallway. A quick turn to the living room, and I was in front of judge, jury, and executioner.

He sat on the couch, manuals spread out all around him. I took a moment and memorized him, the soft fall of his brown hair, the way he chewed on the end of his pen cap as he looked over his 5&9s for the training helicopter. He was such a *good* guy. He deserved so much better than me. So much better than someone who couldn't contain her lust for someone else—no, someone who didn't lust for anyone else. I had failed him on so many levels.

He didn't look up, just flipped the page, completely lost in his studies. "Hey, Lee-Lee. How was your day? I ordered from Mellow Mushroom, so it should be here in about twenty minutes. I wasn't sure if you felt like cooking."

How normal it all seemed. How easy it would be to simply let it stay that way, to hide what I'd done. "I kissed Jagger."

That certainly got his attention. His head snapped up, and the pen dropped from his mouth. "Excuse me?"

"I kissed Jagger." I enunciated every word, letting them rip me open so I could feel the measure of pain I'd caused us all.

He shook his head, like he could shake my words from his ears. "You kissed Jagger. Bateman. Jagger Bateman. My asshole stick buddy? That Jagger Bateman?"

"Yes." I rubbed the skin of my wrist where my watch usually

resided. Apparently I'd left that behind with my morals.

"Wait. He kissed you? Or you kissed him?"

"Does it matter?" My drawl was more pronounced as I drew out the words.

"Yes." His voice wasn't hard. Oh, no, it was soft. Quiet.

"He kissed me—"

"That son of a bitch!" He jumped to his feet, heading for the door.

"—but I kissed him back. I am just as much to blame."

Will looked from me to the wall, his expression slack, his mouth hanging slightly agape. "You kissed him back?"

My nails bit into the skin of my wrist. "Yes."

"You liked it."

My cheeks heated. "Yes." I'd loved every second.

"What the hell am I supposed to do with this? What does this mean?"

"I don't know, but I had to tell you."

He fastened his hands behind his neck. "Do you feel better now that you have it off your chest?"

Shame burned, coming up my throat like acid. "Mercy. No, Will. This isn't something I planned."

"Well, what *is* it, Lee-Lee?"

"He... I...it's complicated."

He dropped his hands and backed away until he reached the end of the couch. "You can't be seriously considering starting something with him."

Protectiveness swept through me and took over my mouth. "And what if I am?"

"You're kidding!"

"I'm not," I said softly. "It's not in my nature to go around kissing people who mean nothing to me, Will. You should know that."

"Are you trying to break up with me?" He crossed his arms in front of him.

Was I? "I...I don't know. I haven't thought that far. It just happened." Could I stay with Will? Was it even a possibility now that I knew what blatant desire felt like?

"No. We're not breaking up, Lee. I'm not losing you over a one-time lapse in judgment. Not when we've come this far and been through so much together. What do you think Pey—"

"Oh, no, Will!" I shouted, anger coursing through me instantly. "Don't you dare bring her into this. She's in every part of my life. I carry her in my heart every day, and you don't get to use her in this. Peyton would tell me to be happy and push me to take a chance. And you know what? She'd want you to be happy, too."

"I am happy!"

"Sure seems it."

"You're not happy?" His eyes flickered between mine, like he was searching for something.

"I love you, Will. But you and I both know there's something missing here. You treat me like I'm made out of glass. Even making love is a constant worry for you! Tell me the last time you've let yourself enjoy sex, because it wasn't with me. Not with the constant checks to my heart monitor and holding yourself back."

"So this is *my* fault? You kissed someone else because I'm not good enough in bed for you? My stick buddy? I fly with him every day, Lee-Lee!"

"Stop calling me that!" I closed my eyes and concentrated on calming my racing heart. All of this because of one kiss. One kiss brought my world tumbling down around me. One kiss transformed me into something I hated and broke the man I loved into pieces. One kiss that I could still taste and couldn't bring myself to regret. Oh, I was surely headed to hell in a hand basket over the likes of Jagger Bateman. "I love you, Will. I have always loved you. You've been the one I could depend on. I never meant for this to happen."

"I want to know exactly what happened."

Images skyrocketed through my brain. Jagger on top of me, his eyes devouring me, the feel of his mouth caressing mine, the way he shot lust through me as though he'd injected a needle. "No, you don't."

"You let him touch you!" His anguish ripped me apart. "You kissed him!"

"Yes." I deserved this. I deserved whatever he wanted to throw at me as long as he didn't bring up Peyton again.

"Do you regret it?"

"Will..." Lying was something I couldn't—wouldn't—do.

"Do. You. Regret. It?" His voice shook me to the core.

I bit my lower lip, still tender from Jagger's kiss, and shamefully, I wanted more. "No," I whispered.

A cry ripped from his throat. "I love you! I'm careful with you! I know how to take care of you! Why, Lee? Why?"

Because there's something in me that can't stay away from him, that's drawn to him like a bleepin' magnet. "I don't know. But if I loved you the way you deserve to be loved, there's no way I would have kissed him back." I walked toward him. "I don't deserve your forgiveness or your understanding. What I did was appalling, and I don't expect you to understand or absolve me."

He stroked my cheek. "And if I want to? If I want to say, 'I forgive you,' and we go back to life as usual?"

I pulled away. "We just...can't. It shouldn't have happened, but I can't go back." *Not now that I know what a kiss is supposed to feel like.*

"I'm not letting you go this easily. People make mistakes."

Ding! Ding!

"Pizza's here," I whispered. Such a normal activity happening during the second-biggest upheaval in my life.

"I got it." Will slid past me, taking out his wallet, and opened the door. "How much do I owe— What the *fuck* do you think you're doing here?"

"She told you." *Jagger!* I raced down the hall, but Will's frame blocked the door. Jagger stood a good four inches taller, and saw me easily over Will's head. "Your watch. I know you like to wear it." He held it up.

Will snatched it out of Jagger's hand and narrowed his eyes at me. "You took your watch off? What the hell were you thinking?"

My chin rose. "That maybe I wanted to experience something without it telling me I shouldn't."

He grabbed my wrist and fastened the watch with quick, rough hands. "Reckless." He turned to Jagger and shoved him with both hands. "You make her reckless! You have no thought for what she needs, you selfish bastard!" He followed Jagger out on to the porch.

"Will!" I scurried to get out from behind him. "Don't!"

Too late. Jagger locked eyes with mine as Will swung, his fist connecting with Jagger's face in a sickening thud that sounded nothing like movie effects. Jagger's head snapped, and he seemed to blink it off. He thumbed away the drop of blood from his lip and rotated his jaw. "I deserved that for kissing her when she belonged to you, but you won't get another one in."

Will cradled his hand. "I'm going to end you."

"Will, please…"

"You're seriously defending him?" Will shot at me over his shoulder.

Jagger looked at me once, then locked his jaw and shook his head at Will. "She's blameless, Carter. It was all me."

"That's certainly not what she says."

Jagger's eyes flew wide as they met mine. His shoulders tensed, his arms hanging loose with fists clenched. He broke my stare. "I take all her responsibility."

"Ha! If you only knew what responsibility for her even means! You're the most selfish, arrogant asshole I've ever met!"

"Yes. But that doesn't mean I'm not capable of being with someone—" He looked at me. "Being with you, Paisley."

My heart flipped, did somersaults, and landed in my stomach. He wanted more from me than just that kiss.

Will swung again, but Jagger sidestepped as Will tumbled past him. "I'm not going to hurt you, Carter, but you're not hitting me again."

"*Argh!*" Will cried out, rushing Jagger, who took the impact of Will's shoulder to his stomach as the two came barreling into the house, taking out the entry hall table. It skidded down the hallway in pieces as Jagger flipped his weight and anchored Will to the wall.

"Fucking stop!" Jagger yelled. My heart raced, and I fanned my hand over my chest, wishing there was something I could do to make them stop before someone got hurt.

"Will you two knock it off?" My head swam, and I suddenly couldn't catch my breath.

"No!" Will shouted. "You don't get to win this one. You don't get her, too!" He swung again, and Jagger simply moved, prepared. Will's fist put a hole in my drywall. "Damn it!" He pulled his hand from the wall, turned, and charged again.

Beep. Beep. Beep.

Will skidded to a stop a few feet from Jagger, his eyes finding mine in panic. "Deep breaths, Lee."

I silenced the alarm, closed my eyes, and slowed my breathing, taking deep pulls of oxygen that calmed my heart rate. "I'm…fine." Three more breaths, and the pounding eased, and the dizziness faded. "Really, I'm fine."

"'Fine' is the last word I would use to describe any of this. You're not fine, I'm not fine, and he"—he pointed his finger toward Jagger, who had moved to stand by me—"is the most fucked-up person you could ever choose to be around." He walked into the living room, gathering his things by the sound of it.

I couldn't chance looking at Jagger. I didn't want to see those eyes or even contemplate everything that had happened. I wanted to live in denial, ignore that I'd ripped the gravity out of my world. I wasn't even in free fall. Oh, no, I floated in a place where physics didn't apply. I was lost.

Jagger reached over and squeezed my hand, centering me.

Will passed us without a second look, his backpack across his shoulder. "I'm not giving in this easily, Lee. I'll be around when he fucks up and leaves you broken."

He walked out without shutting the door, taking the last year of my life with him.

"Paisley?" Jagger questioned softly, but I refused to look into his eyes. "I meant it. Forget everything I said about distractions. I want to be with you."

"I just need you to go, Jagger. Please?" I drew in on myself and dropped his hand.

"I don't want to leave you alone."

I stared at the shattered remains of my entry table. "I need you to give me some time."

I looked into the mirror and saw his reflection. We locked eyes, and electricity passed between us like it always did, some unspoken connection that had just cost me what I'd thought was my future. "You get a day. That's all I can survive. I'll be here in twenty-four hours."

He walked out.

CHAPTER FIFTEEN

JAGGER

*Sometimes there are things bigger, greater than
yourself, and I'm sorry that you haven't found that yet.
But I have.*

Three minutes until exactly twenty-four hours had passed.
Thank God it was Saturday, and I didn't have to deal with
Carter.

That was going to be an epic treat on Monday when we flew
together.

Two hours of sleep was all I'd managed. Every time I'd
closed my eyes, I'd seen her under me, arching toward my
mouth. I'd felt her hands in my hair, tasted her on my lips.

One fucking kiss, and I was addicted.

I'd also been a royal asshole and wrecked her yearlong
relationship. He was wrong for her anyway, but I hadn't exactly
made it a smooth exit for her. *What if she didn't exit?*

I stopped that thought before it could consume any more
of my head. She couldn't go back to him, not after the way

she'd reacted to me—us. *What if you're the only one who felt it?*

"Shut the hell up," I muttered to myself. Great, now I was losing it.

The number on the dashboard clock changed, and I headed for the front door, a single peony in hand. My stomach turned over, and my palms dampened as I rang the doorbell.

"Hold on a second!" Morgan's voice was muffled through the door.

Don't puke. It took forever for her to get to the door. Her brown hair was in a messy knot at the top of her head, and her eyes were rimmed red.

"You look like hell." The words were out of my mouth before I thought. Shit. "I'm sorry. I mean, you look like you need a good night's rest?"

"Well, aren't you just the example of chivalry," she drawled with arched eyebrows. "Lee isn't here."

I checked again to make sure I wasn't hallucinating. "Isn't that her car in the driveway?"

Morgan looked past me. "Yes, but she's in Birmingham for the weekend."

"What is she doing in Birmingham?"

"Treating a broken heart."

My stomach clenched. "Is she alone?"

Morgan shook her head, and a part of my soul threatened to shrivel up. "No, but she's not with Will, either. Her mama is up there with her."

"Oh, thank God. Are you trying to kill me?"

She ripped the sunglasses off, and her eyes narrowed. "Kill you? Kill *you*? You might be the biggest bastard to walk the planet at the moment. I get it, you're hot, and she was hooked from the minute you walked down that beach. And sure, you've got that whole savior thing going for you, but you ripped her whole world apart in ways you know nothing about.

So yeah, maybe I feel, as her best friend, I get to give you shit."

Damn. She didn't pull punches. "I didn't plan it. I mean, yeah, I've thought about it pretty much since I pulled her out of the water, but I respected that she was in a relationship. But then I found out it was Carter, and I couldn't *not* fight for her. Not when every fucking cell in my body screams out that she belongs with me."

"Just..." She sighed. "Ugh. Jagger, give me that. I'll deliver it." She took the flower and then hauled her bag out of the doorway. She locked the door and then turned to me. "Look, we both know they were horribly wrong together, but that doesn't mean that *they* knew it. Yesterday morning, she would have married him if he'd asked, and you eviscerated that whole future."

"By kissing her."

"By existing. Lee isn't typical—"

"You don't have to tell me that. She's extraordinary."

"Shut up and listen." She jabbed her finger at me. "She doesn't let people in easily, and until now, she hasn't had to. She's had me, who's known her basically all her life, and Will, who watched her grow up. Will, who may treat her like a child, but he's a great guy and he's sure as hell there to pick her up when she needs it. You took that from her."

As if I didn't feel like shit already. Well, the part of me that wasn't ready to hurl from the excitement of just having a chance with her. But yeah, the other part of me? Shitty.

"So you'd better be ready to step up, because she doesn't need some little flyboy. She needs a man strong enough to handle his own shit and carry her."

What was I missing here? It was something she wasn't going to tell me—I'd have to hear it from Paisley. At that moment, resolve unfurled within me, stretching from my chest through my appendages, until it reached my fingers and toes. I felt... strong, capable, and determined.

"Let me worry about Paisley. I can handle more than you can imagine."

She pushed past me, headed to her car. "That's the easy answer, Jagger. Think about it, and if you're not ready to stand up, don't show up. She'd be better off without you."

She didn't bother to say good-bye, just threw the bag into her trunk and took off.

A thread of hope wove itself around me. If there was one thing I hated, it was being underestimated. I could do this. I could be with Paisley, tackle anything for her. Flight school was tough, but my grades kept me neck and neck for top of the OML. She wasn't going to be a distraction; if anything, she was my incentive to prove myself.

Dropkick Murphys sounded, and I pulled out my phone, holding my breath. The Seattle number sucked away any hope that it was Paisley.

"This is Jagger."

"Mr. Bateman?" The female on the other end had that tone, the one that preannounced bad news.

"That's me."

"I'm calling about Anna—"

"Yes?" My stomach dropped, and I braced my hand on the side of the Defender.

"I'm so sorry, sir, but I need to tell you she walked out this morning. She's gone."

Not. Again.

"It's been two weeks, what do you mean you can't find her?" My cell phone took the brunt of my anger. A couple heads on the library walkway turned in my direction, and I lowered my voice. "This is what I pay you for."

"She really doesn't seem to want to be found this time."

"I don't give a damn what Anna wants. Check her credit cards, her bank account, and call every ex she has." The thought of her staying with any of those disgusting assholes turned my stomach. Why didn't she call me? She always called me.

"I already have," Paul snapped. "This is my sixth year of doing this, Jag. Cut your shit and trust me. Unless you'd rather hire another PI."

"You know you're the only person I trust. Just fucking find her." I stabbed the end button and ignored the gawking reflections of the guys behind me as I swung open the door. I took my cover off and locked my anger in a box like it belonged to someone else, because it did. "Hey, Alice."

The aging librarian smiled. "Hi there, Lieutenant Bateman. We sure have been missing you round here."

"I have actually missed being here. I went to put some furniture together this week and realized I'd left my tool bag here." *The night I kissed Paisley.*

"Well, you just hop on back there and grab it."

"Thank you, Alice." I took the steps two at a time and walked to the storage room. The study alcoves were nearly empty, and the door to the storage room was propped open. My bag still sat on the worktable. I picked it up and took a look around the room with a healthy dose of pride. We'd done this, taken a huge mess and transformed it into something useful, needed. The excess books were organized neatly, no doubt Paisley's work.

"Don't you, forget about me," she sang, dancing into the storage room, and every muscle in my body froze. Her arms full of books, she kicked the door closed and kept singing. She had earbuds in and scooted past, her back to me. She tried to be careful, but the books tumbled out of her hands onto the center table. She swung her hips along to the music. Her jeans highlighted every curve, hugging her ass like a wet dream, and her fitted sweater was a shade darker than her eyes.

Finally. After two weeks, I felt like I could breathe. The rush of sweet oxygen filled me, and I watched her for a few seconds more, pretending she wanted me there...pretending she wanted me at all.

Her silence since the kiss spoke volumes.

"Will you— Oh my gosh!" she shrieked as she caught me watching her. One tug of the cord, and the earbuds fell out. "Jagger! How long have you been there?"

I grinned, so damn happy to be near her. "Long enough to guess that you've been watching *The Breakfast Club*."

Her cheeks turned pink. "I may have had a John Hughes marathon this last week."

"It shows."

She tucked her hair behind her ears, and my hands itched to run the strands through my fingers. "So..." she mumbled, leaning against the table.

The table I'd kissed her on. "So..." I tried to think of anything but the sound of her whimpers when I stroked the roof of her mouth with my tongue. Well, shit, now that was all I could think about.

"Thank you for the flowers," she said quietly.

I ran my tongue across my teeth, but my stud was out, since I was in uniform, and it didn't have the same calming effect. "You mean the ones I've left on your doorstep every day?"

She held my stare. "Yes, those. They're beautiful."

"So are you."

"Jagger—"

"Just don't, Paisley. I got the message loud and clear. I really don't think I can handle any more rejection. Not being there the day after? Yeah, I can understand that, but fuck, I've managed to have civil conversation with Carter, but you won't see me?" Not that it had been pleasant, but we'd come to a decent agreement to leave the personal shit outside the aircraft. Neither of us could afford for our scores to drop because we couldn't manage to be professional.

"I was gone most of it."

"In Birmingham?" Her eyebrows shot up. "Yeah, Morgan told me."

"She did?" She rubbed her fingers across the center of her chest—her nervous tell.

"Yeah, said you and your mom were off mending your broken heart or something." I twisted my cover in my hand. "I didn't mean to wreck your relationship, or you. It just... happened. I swear it wasn't premeditated. Not that I hadn't thought about it, because kissing you seems to be all I think about when I get around you, but that night..."

"Don't," she begged, her eyes shutting tight. "That night... I've never felt..." Her shoulders slumped. "What I did, kissing you, that was wrong."

Fuck. Twist the knife a little more.

"Not because I didn't want it. I think we both know there's something here. But I've never betrayed someone. I hate what I did to Will, when he's done nothing but try to take care of me."

"I understand." I set the tool bag on the table.

"But you can't. Not really. Maybe one day you'll understand what he's done for me." She covered her face with her hands.

I gently pulled them away. "Don't blame yourself for this. I'm the one who kissed you."

Our eyes locked, and there it was again, that electric current that shot from my heart, through my dick, until it anchored in my very soul. "I wanted you to. I knew the entire time we were friends that it was dangerous, that I was attracted to you."

My stomach jumped. "Was?"

"Don't be stupid, Jagger. Of course I'm still attracted to you. You look like"—she scanned her eyes over my body—"that. Every woman with a pulse is going to be attracted to you."

A corner of my mouth quirked up. "There's only one pulse I'm concerned with, and she doesn't seem to want me."

We stood in a stalemate for more breaths than I could count, gauging each other's reactions, both uncertain of what to say next.

"I can't be with you."

Fuck, that hurt. It would have doubled me over if I hadn't been holding her hands. I stroked my thumbs over her soft skin. "You're going to have to give me a reason."

She pulled her hands away, like she'd just now noticed that I held them. "You have no idea what you're getting into with me. I'm not..." She played with her watch, sliding it along her wrist. "Jagger, I'm not a good idea for you."

"I'm not really a walk in the park, either." I forced a smile. "Underneath this handsome yet mysteriously inked exterior is someone who doesn't trust anyone or anything. You don't know everything about me, either. I'd say you and I are pretty well matched."

"As friends."

"That's all you want." *Tell me I'm wrong. Please.*

She gripped the edge of the counter. "That's all I can give you."

Fuck. I locked my jaw and nodded once, not because I was okay with it, but because it was the only motion I was capable of making. There was nothing I could say that wouldn't come out like begging, and I refused to beg a woman whose mind was already made up. I'd learned that lesson a long time ago.

I took my tool bag and got out of there as quickly as possible, ignoring when she called my name in a soft, morose sigh.

What the hell. I'd stood up to my father, carved a life for myself, and yet I was literally running away from a pint-sized blonde who didn't have a mean bone in her body.

I threw the tool bag unceremoniously into the truck and

speed-dialed Josh.

"What's up?" he asked.

"Gym."

The other side was quiet for a couple breaths. "I'll grab Masters and meet you there."

"Okay."

"Jagger, don't hit anything until I get there."

"Yeah." I hung up, carefully placing my cell phone in the cup holder so I didn't hurl it through the window.

The drive was short, and the hard rock blasting through my speakers did nothing to quell the absolute rage boiling within me. I threw Lucy into park, grabbed my just-in-case gym bag, and headed inside.

Josh entered the locker room, Masters on his heels, as I was lacing my shoes, ready to go. They were both already dressed for the workout.

"Ready?" Josh asked.

I didn't have to say anything. We walked toward the punching bag, and Masters took off to the weights. The guy was massive for a reason.

Josh held the bag, and after my hands were wrapped, I slammed my fists into it. Hit by hit, the vibrations sang up my arms, releasing the anger, the hurt, the frustration. After a few minutes, my heart pounded, the tightness in my chest eased, and my punches slowed.

"This have anything to do with the peonies in your car?"

I hit the bag again. "She wants to be friends. Just friends." I punched between each word. "Friends don't kiss like that."

"Ouch." He waited a couple more hits. "What are you going to do about it?"

I stopped, my chest heaving. "What the hell can I do about it? Beg?"

"Yes."

I scoffed at him. "Right. So I can humiliate myself while

she rejects me again. No fucking way."

"Then you don't deserve her."

I stepped into the punch, throwing my full weight behind it. The momentum took Josh over, slamming him into the mat. Shit. Before I could apologize, he stood and took hold of the bag, ignoring that I'd just knocked him on his ass.

"You'd beg? Seriously rip yourself open and beg?"

"Did you not see the shit I crawled through for Ember?" He looked at me like I was an idiot.

He had a point.

"Jag, the good ones are worth begging, pleading, and basically mutilating your heart over."

My laugh bordered on self-deprecating. "I don't know why the hell I'm so pissed. Honestly, it's for the best. This is what I wanted, right? I have jack and shit to offer her." I wiped the sweat off my forehead. "I don't have anything left of a heart to mutilate."

"Bullshit. That hurt you're feeling? That fear that she meant it, that you can't talk her out of it? That's what you need to hold on to. The anger is going to get you nowhere." He grinned. "Besides, I remember someone buying me a pair of knee pads and telling me to suck it up and take as much as Ember could dish out for however long she needed to get her shit together."

I hit the bag again, focusing on technique and not blind anger. "Yeah, well, everyone but you saw the way she looked at you, the way you two basically orbited around each other. But not everyone is you and Ember."

Josh pulled the bag out of my reach, effectively stopping my punches, and waited for me to look at him. "Don't be fucking stupid. It took me all of half a second to pick up on the vibe you two put out at the library. Let alone the ice rink, the bar, you name it. So take your own medicine. Suck it up and swallow as much as Paisley can dish out for however long she needs to get her shit together. Don't beg her, convince her. She's not Anna, Jag. She's not going to walk out on you."

He might as well have punched me. I blinked. I hadn't thought to compare the two women, but with the shit going on with Anna...yeah, it bled all over Paisley.

"You two girls done already?" Grayson asked, walking over. "I need a spot."

"You go ahead. I need to find some knee pads." I walked off the mat feeling like I'd dropped fifty pounds on it.

Now I only needed to convince Morgan to help me.

CHAPTER SIXTEEN

PAISLEY

9. Celebrate my twenty-first birthday.

This week's breakfast had been exchanged for a Saturday night dinner, since Daddy had been TDY in Washington most of the week. The bad thing about dinner? There was no specific end time. Breakfast was simple, a little *hey, I have to get to class*, and I could escape. Dinner? Not so much.

I rinsed the last plate and slid it into the dishwasher. "That should do it for the dishes."

"Swore he'd be home by six, today of all days," Mama mumbled to herself.

"Oh, it's no big deal. We both know he'd be here if he could. I'm really not mad." It wasn't the first birthday he'd missed, and it wouldn't be the last. Luckily I was old enough to understand that the good of the many outweighed the need of a few.

"Well, can I take you to a movie or something?"

I stifled a smile. There was nothing Mama hated more than going to a movie theater. She ran for hills the first time her shoes came in contact with a spilled soda. "No, ma'am. This was just perfect."

She gave me a soft smile. "It's so nice to have you close."

My cell phone alerted me with a text, and I dried my hands on the hanging towel. A quick swipe of my finger, and Jagger's name appeared on my screen.

Jagger: *A little mouse might have said that it's your birthday.*

I bit into my lower lip to keep from letting out a squeal of delight. Friends. We were friends again. That was the deal I'd offered, and I guess he was taking it. It didn't matter that I wanted more. I would only hurt him—distract him—and I could never let that happen.

Me: *It sure is.*

Jagger: *Want to go have a real 21st birthday?*

Me: *What makes you think I'm not already having a huge, mind-blowing party?*

Jagger: *Because you didn't invite me, so it couldn't possibly be a good party.*

"Who's making you smile like that?" Mama hung up her apron and turned her inquisitor eyes on me.

Dang it. "A friend, Mama."

"Mmm-hmm."

I ignored the tone of her voice. She knew something was wrong between Will and me, but I hadn't told her we'd broken up. Since we'd spent over a week in Birmingham between scheduled and rescheduled tests, she'd let me off the hook. Well, at least until the results were in. Until then I had 143 days—and I was going to use every one of them.

Luckily, I'd Skyped into class, or my GPA would probably be circling the drain.

Me: *Maybe I'm in the middle of a raging rave right now.*

Jagger: *Yeah, I heard your mom really knows how to throw down.*

Me: *How would you know?*

The dogs barked a heartbeat before the doorbell sounded. "You have to be kidding me."

Mama raised her eyebrows at me as she headed for the door. "Are you expecting company? It's about time Will came around."

"No, Mama—"

I made it to the entry hall when she opened the door. "Oh. Morgan. It's lovely to see you."

Wait. What? "Morgan?" Hopefully my voice didn't sound as disappointed as I felt.

"There you are! Let's go, birthday girl!" She tugged me out the door. I barely managed to grab my handbag off the entry hall table. "Nice to see you, Mrs. Donovan!"

"You too, dear. Lee…"

"Yes, I'll take my meds!" I answered, laughing while I tried not to trip over my own feet as Morgan tugged me down the stairs. "Morgan, what on earth are we doing?" We skidded around the front porch, and I gasped as the driveway came into view. Lucy. Jagger.

He leaned against the yellow paint job, his baseball hat on backward, wearing jeans I wanted to peel off and a fitted Dropkick Murphys shirt. *Just friends.* No, I could not spontaneously lick his abs to see if he really tasted as good as he looked.

Then he smiled, and I remembered the urgent press of his lips with mine, the way he whispered my name. I swallowed and played my friends-only mantra through my head. "Jagger?"

"Get in, Little birthday Bird."

Morgan skipped ahead of me and opened the back door, since I saw that Masters already occupied the passenger side. "Where are we going?"

"Does your list say anything about unexpected journeys?"

"I'm not a hobbit."

He pushed off Lucy and walked toward me. A breath of space separated his hand from my cheek before he thought better of it and put it down. "Well, how about I promise that you can check a box off your list if you get in the car? If what I've got planned isn't on it, then you pick something, and we'll check it off."

"Friends?" I needed that line clearly delineated.

"Fucking knee pads," he muttered, closing his eyes briefly.

"What?"

"Yes, I even brought Masters and Morgan as chaperones."

"I'm not really dressed for anything..." I looked down at my simple, fitted V-neck tee, infinity scarf, and ballet flats.

"You look incredible. Now get in the car."

I went.

Nearly two hours later, the bouncer smiled at me and said, "Happy birthday," as he tagged my wrist with a green band.

I grinned and showed off my prize to Morgan, who rolled her eyes. "Don't go getting any ideas, Paisley Lynn."

"I still can't believe you got us tickets." The opening band was on stage as Jagger wound us through the small arena in Panama City. Dropkick Murphys. Incredible.

"When I saw they were coming, I couldn't pass it up." We grabbed drinks at the concession stand, then made our way down the steps of the arena. "You sure just water?"

"Yeah, just water." Alcohol was a giant no-no, which just about frosted my cookies tonight. What was the use of turning twenty-one if I couldn't have a single drink on my birthday?

"Sober on your twenty-first. It's a crime."

"I like to break stereotypes," I answered as we came closer to the stage. "Where are our seats? Did we pass them?" He led me forward until the front row was all that was left. "No way. No way!" I jumped a little and threw my arms around his neck. "Thank you!"

His arms wound around my back. "Only the best for the birthday girl." His lips grazed my ear before I withdrew.

We found our seats as the band took the stage, but I was out of it the minute they started to play. I lost myself with nothing between me and the music, and Jagger next to me. I sang along with every song until my voice was hoarse, the energy in each verse winding me higher and higher until I felt invincible.

It was perfect, and then it was over.

Jagger took my hand and led me through the crowd on the way out. Once we cleared the bottleneck at the doorway, he dropped my hand, and I frowned at my own disappointment.

"Well?" He held Lucy's door open for me.

"That was amazing!" My face hurt from smiling so much. "The perfect birthday, thank you!"

"Ready to head home?"

Energy hummed through me. "Is there anywhere we could go down here to dance?"

"Lee?" Morgan questioned. "Dance? Really?"

"Club La Vela is here," Jagger offered. "It's pretty legendary."

"Like the-biggest-club-in-the-nation legendary," Masters commented.

"It's my birthday," I all but begged Morgan. "Have you ever heard me want to go out?"

She shook her head and pulled me aside. "No, but do you think it's the best idea?"

"Yes."

Morgan sighed. "Just keep it within reason."

"Oh, come on. This is *me* we're talking about."

CHAPTER SEVENTEEN

You've always seen my loss of control, my recklessness as my biggest weakness. Maybe, just maybe, it's my greatest asset.

The Thanksgiving-weekend crowd packed the club, and the music was loud, pumping through me in rhythm with my heartbeat. Paisley leaned across the bar, her ass in the air, and I glared one of the eager assholes away. Her perfect lips closed around the straw of her third drink, and that wink she just gave me said she was definitely feeling it.

Morgan slid behind her, having been dancing the whole time. "Enough!" she yelled, trying to be heard above the thumping bass.

"I'm twenty-one, Morgan. Give me a night!" She threw her arm over Morgan's shoulder and hopped off the bar stool, wavering a second before she steadied.

She glared at the empty glasses in front of her. "Three? You know better!"

"Morgan, give her a break. Most twenty-one-year-olds are blasted and puking by now. We're lucky she's still conscious." Masters rolled his eyes over his sweet tea.

"Well, she didn't tell you that drinking interferes with her medication, did she?" Morgan asked.

"Her asthma meds? I had no clue." *Shit.* I was the one who'd offered her the first drink.

"Asthma? *Oof!*" Morgan picked up her left foot, rubbing the insole.

"You okay?" Paisley asked.

She grimaced through a smile. "Yeah, just...stubbed my toe. Damn peep-toes." She glared at Paisley.

"I think I'll be okay for one night, Morgan. Checking off boxes and all." They had some kind of silent girl exchange where they spoke through hand gestures and eyebrows. I needed an interpreter or another beer.

"I want to dance!" Paisley declared, wiggling her ass. She'd ditched the long-sleeved tee in the car, opting for the low-cut tank top I'd bought her at the concert, and now I wished she'd kept the other one on. The curves of her breasts were too visible, too close, and way too much. "Jagger?" She turned those green eyes on me and didn't look away while she pulled her hair into some kind of knot on her head. Sexy little tendrils escaped, framing her face.

"Dance?" I croaked.

That grin just about destroyed me. "Friends dance."

She slid past me, catching my hand and pulling me onto the already crowded floor, and I followed after her. I kept a respectable distance, which in a club this packed meant about an inch or two. The couples around us writhed to the music, more than a few in various stages of base running.

She raised her arms above her head and closed her eyes in abandon, her body moving with the beat of the music. She was exquisite and erotic in the same breath, and I was hypnotized.

Her eyes opened at the same moment she brought her arms down and put her hands on my chest. Her eyes lifted in open challenge, which I blatantly ignored until she grasped both my hands and put them on her hips.

Okay. I could do this. I fought the impulse to grasp her curves and pull her to me, and I succeeded...until she brought her body against me.

"Fuck," I hissed as she slipped one of her legs between mine, straddling my thigh.

"That's better," she purred.

I gave in and moved with her, careful not to let my hands slip to that delectable curve of her ass that I'd been drooling over all night. Like she'd read my mind and decided to test my resolve, she turned abruptly, giving me her back, and pushed into me. Her hands roved up and down my thighs, then reached behind her to stroke the sides of my abs. *Did she just—* Yep. She lifted my shirt and ran her hands over my bare skin.

Her touch burned me, the heat spearing through my body and concentrating in the one area I couldn't exactly hide while she was grinding against me. Damn it, in less time than it took the song to change, I was hard as the poles holding up the bar.

Paisley finally figured it out, gasping and stilling her movements. My fingers flexed on her hips, waiting for her to react. One breath. Two. She turned her head toward me and met my eyes. Her pupils were blown, covering most of the green in her eyes. I knew it was the alcohol, but she was blurring my judgment, especially when her lips parted and she dipped a few inches and then rose, rubbing against my dick.

I groaned, and she picked up the beat. Sweat broke out on both of us as the song changed. The tiny drops along her skin reflected the colors from the lights.

She brought her arms up, bending at the elbows to stroke the slick skin on the back of my neck and raising her breasts. I looked away, knowing there was a line, and she may have been dancing right across it, but I couldn't. Not while she was drunk.

Her watch beeped, close to my ear. She didn't seem to hear it, so I brought her wrist in front of her face, rubbing my thumb into her palm. She stilled long enough to turn off the beeping and then turned in my arms and pressed against me.

"You're killing me, Paisley," I growled into her ear.

She giggled, dragging me farther over the edge. "Tell me something. Do friends kiss?" Then she took my earlobe in her mouth and set her teeth lightly to the skin.

Holy. Shit. "Depends on the kind of kiss." I tried to keep my brains in my head and not my pants.

She pulled back a couple inches and her gaze dropped to my lips, her tongue slipping out to wet her own. "What about this?" She balanced on her toes and kissed me. The pressure of her lips was sweet against mine, despite the groping going on around us. She dragged my lower lip in a soft bite as she withdrew slowly.

"Don't I get a birthday kiss?" she slurred.

Her half-lidded eyes locked with mine, and yeah, the alarm blared in my head that she was acting on alcohol, but I was intoxicated simply by her. I met her halfway, gripping her hip in one hand and cupping her face in the other. My mouth slanted over hers, and she opened for me as my tongue slipped beyond the barrier of her teeth to caress hers.

She tasted like pineapple from her drinks, and I couldn't help but kiss her deeper, longer. She pushed against me, and I barely suppressed a groan. I hadn't imagined it in the library; kissing Paisley was better than sex with any other girl I'd ever been with. Her grip tightened on my neck, and my hand shifted to her ass—to support her, I justified. She went all soft and pliant, ready for whatever I wanted. That moment of her absolute surrender—the moment I'd usually declare victory and head to the car to get laid—it jarred me more than any slap could have.

This was Paisley, the same girl I'd pulled from the water. The same girl I knew didn't give kisses lightly, let alone initiate them on a very public dance floor. This was the alcohol acting, and while I could pull the douche move and argue that I'd been drinking, too, it just wasn't good enough for me, and was far less than what she deserved.

There weren't enough curse words for how hard it was, but I managed to break away. "That is most definitely not a friend kiss."

"But it's fun." Her smile slipped past tipsy and into the realm of drunk.

I kissed her forehead, lingering in the scent of her hair and tinge of salt in her skin. "Let's get you home, Little Bird."

Someone behind me pulled Paisley's arm from around my neck, and I nearly punched them before I realized it was Morgan. She flashed Paisley's watch in her face. "Twice, Lee. I know it's your birthday, but let's not overdo it."

My forehead puckered as Paisley glared at her best friend. "Are you my mother?"

Morgan sighed. "You're so fun when you're drunk."

Paisley giggled. "I am not"—she snorted—"drunk."

"She's a lightweight." I laughed.

"Other than the beer Will fed her the summer we were fifteen, this is the first time she's had alcohol." She fought it, but a smile grew from a quirked lip to a full-blown grin. "Ah, my Lee." She cupped her face. "It's not often that I'm the responsible one, but you're drunker than Cooter Brown."

"What?"

Paisley threw her arms around me again, laughing. "That's southern for 'take the girl home.'"

"Gladly." I looped my arm around her waist and walked out, collecting Masters in our wake. He unlocked the doors, and I boosted Paisley up.

"Sit with me?" she asked, and because I was stupid, or

masochistic, whatever, I agreed. Truthfully, I was starved for her, and would take just about anything I could get. I buckled her in as Morgan and Masters took the front seats.

The lights along the highway illuminated her face as we left Panama City Beach. Leaving her lap belt on, she leaned over, put her head in my lap, and looked up at me. The music from the front seat made us feel isolated.

"Why do you want to fly so badly?"

Of all the questions she could have asked, at least this one I knew the answer to. "My father took me to an air show when I was ten, and there was an Apache there. The pilot put me in the cockpit and it just felt like...home. Like that was where I was meant to be. I remember looking up through the glass and seeing the rotors against the blue sky and thinking that was how I wanted to spend my life. Then the next year, on my birthday, my mom had a private ride set up for me. Not in an Apache, of course, but from that moment, that was all I ever wanted to do—fly."

"'For once you have tasted flight, you will forever walk the earth with your eyes turned skyward, for there you have been and there you will long to return.'" She smiled softly. "Da Vinci."

My thumbs slipped across her cheeks. "Yes, exactly like that."

"Your mom, is she proud?"

My smile faltered. "Quid pro quo."

"Of course."

"Why are you so hell-bent on friends only? Is it because of Will?" If she was going for my deepest secrets, I was going for hers.

She let loose a huge sigh. "Ah, Will. It's not so much about him. I mean, in a way. It would call my morals into question if I jumped from him to you, right? But more than that, I don't want to distract you...or hurt you. Not knowing how badly you want to fly. It's not that I don't want you, Jagger. I'm just scared

I'd destroy you." She nuzzled the side of her face into my hand while I tried to recover. "Your mom?"

Of course. My instinct was to deflect, to kiss her into forgetting she'd asked, or to deny outright. But I wanted her. Every part of her. Which meant I was going to have to show her every part of me, even the ugly sides, and just pray she didn't run. "She died when I was sixteen. Fell off her bedroom balcony and broke her neck on impact. It was the stupidest way for a woman like her to die. She was beautiful, and smart, and so...alive, always seeking out the next thrill, never content with, well, contentment. Oh, and she made the best brownies." I left out the part where her white nightgown had been soaked in her blood when I looked over the banister.

"Oh my God, Jagger. I'm so sorry."

I forged ahead, not letting the emotion in, but I wanted— needed her to know. "My father...he wasn't around much, even when I was little. He showed up when he needed us, and left us to our own devices a lot of the time. Nothing changed after she died."

"Is that why you left?"

My jaw flexed, and I ignored that one. We weren't going near that...near Anna. "For my sixteenth birthday, my mom got me flying lessons. I took my final check ride the day I turned seventeen and legally became a commercial pilot."

"You left the next day."

"That's why this is easy for me now. It's never been just about flying, and always about Apaches." I pressed my lips together to keep from telling her anything else.

"Thank you for tonight, for telling me."

I stroked my fingers down her cheek, and let my thumb brush across her lips. "Happy birthday, Paisley."

"One more question?"

"You're killing me." Damn those eyes and her ability to draw shit out of me.

"I know, but if you had your choice, with me...what would you choose?"

The alcohol made her bold.

"What do you mean?" I dodged.

"Friends? A relationship? A steamy fling? What?"

I swallowed, wishing she was sober for this kind of conversation. "You said just friends, and I'm trying to respect that. I know you just got out of a relationship."

"What do *you* want?" she asked again, a little plea in her tone.

I stared down at her and saw the two possibilities clearly. I could leave my defenses intact, play the friends card and continue on. Or I could take a chance at being wrecked, burning myself to the ground. Who the hell was I kidding? I was already on fire for her. My heart had screamed out *mine* the moment I carried her from the water, and hadn't quit since.

"Jagger?" her voice was softer.

Fuck it.

"I want everything, Paisley. I want your smiles, your laughs, your kisses. Yes, I want to be your friend, and more. I want to feel your arms around me at night, taste your kiss for breakfast, and I want to hear my name on your lips when I make you come apart. I want to study on the couch while you do your homework. I want to fight with you and make up with you. I want to shoulder the burdens you're carrying, even the ones you still won't tell me about, and I want...I want everything."

She stared at me, tiny breaths exhaling from her parted lips. "And if I can't give you that? If the most I can be is friends?"

I bent down, the angle awkward, and kissed her, only tracing the seam of her lips with my tongue lightly before raising my head. "That's the thing. I'll settle for any part you want to give me. That's how badly I want every part of you."

"I don't want to be broken," she muttered, her eyes finally losing the battle and fluttering shut.

"You're not," I reassured her, stroking her hair from her face, knowing she'd passed out.

It wasn't clear, but I heard her mumble, "One hundred forty-three days, Jagger...one hundred forty-three days."

CHAPTER EIGHTEEN

PAISLEY

26. Take a road trip.

Christmas Eve—118 days. I finished the bow on Daddy's present just after lunch and carried the package over to the tree. I stood and admired the tree, watching the way the lights caught in the colorful ornaments.

I loved Christmas, and this year everything about the season seemed to slip by between studying, finals, and spending time with Jagger. Not that we'd crossed over that friends line again. Oh, no.

He'd appeared the morning after my birthday with a giant bottle of water and Tylenol. Then he sat through all the *Twilight* movies while he studied next to me, only looking up to make sarcastic comments about sparkly beta males.

We'd spent our time studying next to each other, talking, swimming, and spending every available moment together up to a good-night. The last month had been the best and most aggravating of my life. The best, because he was near me at every available opportunity. The most aggravating because the more I wanted him, the more I knew I shouldn't.

My cell phone buzzed in my back pocket. I thumbed open the screen and smiled.

Jagger: *Merry Xmas Eve. Looks like snow here 2night. Jealous?*

Me: *Insanely. Having fun in Nashville?*

Jagger: *Kind of. I miss my friend.*

Me: *Miss you, too. Tell Ember I said hi.*

Jagger: *Will do, Little Bird.*

Me: *What are you hoping to get for Christmas?*

Jagger: *U in a big red bow.*

Me: *You're incorrigible.*

Jagger: *I prefer tenacious, driven, determined.*

Me: *LOL. Go celebrate.*

I sighed, the sound horribly melodramatic, and wondered for the millionth time if I was an idiot for not being with him. My cell phone sounded again, this time with the alarm for my meds, and as I popped those three pills, I was more resolute in my decision.

I had 118 days, and losing a friend? That was recoverable. But losing someone you loved? That would destroy Jagger. My test results had been in for over two weeks. The obstruction was getting worse, but the medications were slowing my heartbeat, keeping me relatively symptom-free. Maybe that was a curse, to feel blissfully unaware as my body fell apart while I was still in it. If I was dying, shouldn't I feel it?

The dogs barked as the front door opened. "Ah, Will!" Mama announced. *What in the world?* "I'm so glad you're here. Lee!" she called out as I rounded the corner into the entry hall. "Look who's here to see you."

She whispered in my ear as she passed, "You fix this, Lee. It's just not right. He's family."

I grimaced but didn't answer her. "Hi there."

He smiled, but it was reserved. He waited until Mama left and then motioned to the staircase. We both took a seat. "Your mom told me I needed to come over and talk to you."

"Of course she did. Never could stop meddling."

"Everything okay?" he asked. "Finals go all right?"

"Yeah, nothing much has changed. Still carrying a four-point-oh. You?"

"I'm good. I think I've edged out Bateman on the OML, so I've got that going for me."

I ignored his jab. "You've got more than that going for you."

He squeezed my hand. "Man, do I miss you. Being apart for a month has been awful, but really good for me, too. It gave me time to think."

"I've missed you, too," I responded honestly.

He cleared his throat. "Okay, so this is awkward as hell, but why aren't you dating him?"

"Is that really your business?"

He laughed. "Girlfriend or not, you've always been my business, Lee. Besides, Peyton made me promise to look after you, and I always will."

My gaze jerked to his. "What?"

He squeezed my hand. "You were right, as much as I didn't want to admit it. I love you, but it isn't the kind of love that either of us need, or deserve."

"I'll never be Peyton."

His amber eyes sparked with a flash of pain. "You're not Peyton. You're unique. You. Being with you…I thought I could hold onto her, onto everything we had growing up."

"You loved her?" I asked, finally needing to know.

He swallowed. "Yeah, I did. But it was never reciprocated. We never dated, or so much as kissed. When she asked me to watch after you, loving you just came naturally. I'll always love you, Lee. You were just so much faster to realize we weren't right."

I leaned my head on his familiar shoulder. "I'm so sorry about how it happened."

"Me, too, but if it hadn't happened like that, we'd still be together, and that's not what's best for either of us." His arm came around me. "Now stop avoiding the question. How do you feel about Bateman?"

That was the million-dollar question lately. "I'm...he's... ugh."

"That clear about it, huh?"

"I want him more than anything, but he can't love me."

"You're easy to love. As much as I can't stand that cocky fucker, he's got it bad for you. I know all about the flowers, and the lunch meetings, and the fact that he pretty much devotes every waking minute to you." I sent him a questioning look, and he grinned. "Stick buddies, remember? So what's the big deal? I thought that's what every girl wanted."

"And if he falls in love with me? One hundred eighteen days, Will. What kind of heartless monster would I be if I took his love to be happy and then left him like that?"

"Don't you keep saying that. You're not Peyton. You're not on her time line."

"You don't know that." I did. I felt it in my bones, the same way I knew a pacemaker wasn't going to save me. I was never going to be older than my sister.

"Neither do you. Does he know yet?"

"No."

He sighed. "You need to tell him. Don't throw away a chance at being happy, really happy, just because you're scared. Trust me, you'll regret it more than anything else." He kissed my forehead. "You deserve better than him, Lee, but don't let me deter you. We all deserve to make our own decisions, our own mistakes."

"You think he's a mistake?"

"What I think doesn't matter anymore. I meant what I said.

I'll be around when he fucks up. I'll pick you up and dust you off. But when that happens, the question is, will you feel foolish that you let it happen?"

Jagger's voice echoed in my ears. "No. I'll be thankful I took the chance and burned."

Will's smile was sad as he stood. "Then that's your answer, Lee. Merry Christmas."

"Merry Christmas, Will."

We locked eyes as he opened the door. "She...Peyton would tell you to go for it. She'd say something absolutely horrendous about how good-looking he is and tell you to jump it."

I laughed. "She sure would."

He nodded at me once, then shut the door behind him.

His footsteps hadn't even faded from the door before Mama was in the entry hall. "Well, are you two made up? Is he coming for dinner tonight?"

I stood. "No, Mama. We're over."

"What? How is that even possible? This is Will we're talking about!" She put her hands on her hips, and I settled in for a nice long lecture.

"Then you date him," I said as Daddy walked out of his office.

"Well, I never! Will Carter is the best thing for you, Lee! He's already a member of this family."

The guilt didn't work this time, because Will had already cut the tethers. I was free. "You cannot hold onto Peyton by keeping me with Will. He's not going to bring her back."

Her head jerked like I'd struck her. "That's not at all the case, young lady."

"Isn't it?" I asked softly.

"Lee," Daddy warned.

"Mama, there's someone else, someone I want more than breathing. Someone who makes me feel alive, who might not know every detail about me, but who knows who I really am and doesn't wish I was Peyton. Please, just let me be happy."

She shook her head. "Will was the only person we trust with your health."

"You need to trust *me*."

"Well, given the absolutely ridiculous decisions you're making regarding your condition, it looks like that won't be happening. You're going to have to move to New York with us."

"Magnolia!" Daddy growled. "Have you lost your mind?"

"New York?" I asked, my gaze darting between the two of them.

Daddy put his arm around me. "I've been here for over two years, Lee. I'm being transferred to West Point in the summer."

"We had considered letting you stay here, but without Will watching over you, you're just going to have to come with us."

I sputtered. Another PCS. Another move. "My life is here. I'm in college, and I have a house, friends. I don't need to go with you."

"That's your choice," Daddy agreed with a squeeze.

"No, it's not!" Mama shouted. "If you're hell-bent on staying here, we'll cut you off. No help for tuition, or rent, or books, or life. Your insurance will expire, and you'll be on your own."

My mouth dropped open. "You're that desperate to keep me on a leash?"

"You need one! It's been another month, and you haven't given Dr. Larondy the okay to do the pacemaker. You're being childish, so we'll treat you like a child. Life is too short to jeopardize it!"

"It's *my* heart, Mama! Mine! My life, my decision!" Life was too short to straddle the fence, and her comments pushed me in the opposite direction of what she'd been hoping.

"Then make the right one!" she screamed, her voice harsh and breaking. "Call me evil, but I just don't care what you want. Not when you're being ludicrous. I have already lost Peyton!" Her breaths came in heaves, shaking her shoulders.

One of the dogs whined, breaking the silence. Daddy shook his head at Mama.

"Well, you just lost me, too," I said over the lump in my throat. I hugged Daddy. "Merry Christmas, Daddy."

"She doesn't mean it, Paisley. She's just scared. We would never do that to you," he whispered. "Merry Christmas."

I gave him a squeeze and walked out the door. It took me an hour to pack, where I ignored every text and the six phone calls Mama placed to my cell phone.

Instead I placed my own, and hoped she'd have room for one more for Christmas.

I left Morgan a note, since she was with her parents, and got on the highway, but not before I stopped at the store for the last thing I needed.

The drive was long and quiet. I didn't listen to music, just let my thoughts sort themselves out. Pacemaker, surgery, death—these were terms being thrown around like I needed to choose between strawberry and vanilla ice cream. But everyone who declared it an easy decision wasn't the one who had to make it. Dr. Larondy had said I had some time before I had to choose, and I was going to use every second of it.

I just wanted to live, and not the half existence full of limits and doctor visits, but truly live, like those boxes on the list demanded. If I could live these next 118 days and finish the list, then I'd consider one of their solutions, but I wasn't going to feel unfinished when they cut me open and tried to fix me.

I took each turn the GPS said to until, five and a half hours later, I parked across from a really nice condo complex. I zipped my coat as the first snowflakes fell and grabbed my bag from the trunk.

Wildest thing you've ever done. Loony tunes, and I couldn't be happier about it.

My heart felt fine climbing the stairs, but my belly was in knots as I opened the door to the hallway. I compared the number with the address in the text message, swallowed, and knocked.

"What, did you forget your key?" he said through the door, and my breath caught.

"Good thing they knocked," a female voice said. "I mean, imagine if we'd been busy!" She laughed, and my stomach lurched. Who was that? What if he'd gotten tired of being only friends? What if I'd made him wait too long, and he was no longer interested? The locks slid open, and then so did the door.

The young woman who answered was beautiful in a way I never would be. Her golden brown skin was flawless and contrasted with her light green eyes. "Can I help you?" she asked with a genuine smile.

"I...I was just looking for someone," I stammered, afraid that the chance I'd taken was about to be on the stupider side of the things I'd done.

"Paisley?" His incredulous voice came from behind the girl.

I forced a trembling smile as Jagger gently moved the girl out of his way. "Hey."

His mouth hung open for a second, and I drank him in greedily. He'd been gone for four days, and given the daily contact we usually had, it felt like a lifetime. His long-sleeved shirt molded to his muscles, and his jeans followed suit. "I just...I wanted..." I shook my head and forced out a smile. "I didn't know you'd be...you know"—I gestured to where the girl stared at us in confusion—"busy."

"With Sam?" His eyebrows puckered and then arched. "Oh, Paisley, no. Sam is Ember's best friend. We used to live next door to each other in Colorado. Just a friend. Come in."

I shook my head, unsure for the first time since I'd stopped at that store in Daleville. "Friends like we are?"

Jagger came into the hallway, shutting the door behind him. His gaze raked down my body, hot as ever, and I cursed the parts of me that jumped to life. Especially if he'd been having friendly relations with that beautiful girl. "God, I've missed you."

"Friends like we are?" I repeated, needing to know. Standing across from him, knowing what I wanted now, was the sweetest torture.

"No one is friends like we are." He folded his arms over his chest. "I'm thrilled to see you, but why aren't you with your family?"

I dove headfirst. "I wanted to be with you."

His breath hitched, and his eyes narrowed slightly in confusion. I needed to make myself clear. "I want to be with you, Jagger." I enunciated each word slowly, and then unbuttoned my belted black trench coat, revealing that on top of my white blouse and jeans, I'd tied my chest with a giant red ribbon. "Merry Christmas."

A heartbeat passed, then two, three, and four, before a smile slowly spread across his face. He was incredible, both inside and out, and maybe mine. "But I need to tell you something first."

"Later." He reached out like lightning, cupping my neck and pulling me to him, crushing his mouth over mine. I leaned into his kiss, looping my arms around his neck, and kissed him like I'd fantasized about for the last month. I sucked his tongue into my mouth and was rewarded by a groan.

He spun and pressed me against the door. I hitched one of my legs around his hips, and he ran his hand down the back of my thigh, lifting me so I was at face level.

"Tell me you mean it," he growled into my neck, alternating licks and nibbles that had me arching to give him better access.

"I mean it," I gasped. This was the best road trip ever, and I hadn't made it past the front door yet. My hands threaded in his hair.

"You're mine?"

I would have laughed if he hadn't looked so apprehensive. "Yes."

"Say it."

A shot of pure lust fired through me at the demand in his eyes. "I'm yours, Jagger."

"Thank God," he whispered against my lips before sinking into me. He tasted like warm peppermint from the mints I now knew he was addicted to, and his tongue sent delicious shivers down my spine to pool deep in my belly. He angled my head, kissing me deeper, and I whimpered, desperate to get closer to him.

He was everywhere, overwhelming every sense, inside my mouth, holding me up by my rear and yet still cradling my head like I was something precious. I rocked my hips into him, and he sucked his breath in through clenched teeth. He gave one slow thrust against me, rubbing my inseam along my pelvic bone, and I just about yelped. If he could cause that kind of reaction with our clothes on, what would it be like once they weren't? Wait. Was I even ready for that? I'd only ever slept with Will.

He pulled away, stroked his thumb over my cheekbone, and smiled. Charged seconds passed while we stared at each other, grinning like fools.

"You say it," I ordered, needing a bigger declaration than his tongue in my mouth.

"I've been yours from the second your eyes opened on the beach."

My gaze dropped to his lips. I wanted his mouth back, so I took it. He quickly sank into me, his tongue stroking the sensitive place right behind my teeth, and I fell into his rhythm. I gathered the fabric of his shirt in my hands and pulled it upward, needing the heat of his bare skin caressing mine. It caught between us, but came free to his chest with a few motions. *Yes.*

"Whoa. I guess they aren't interested in Chinese?" A male voice broke through the haze.

"I'd say not. But how do we get past them into the house?" a female answered. Josh and Ember.

Jagger walked backward, his biceps flexing as he easily carried my weight, until he was across the hallway, my knees pressing into the neighbor's wall. Then he kissed me again, uncaring that we'd just been caught like a pair of hormonal high school students. I heard the faint sound of the door opening and closing.

"Jagger—" I muttered into his mouth, but he all but ignored me until I pushed his chest.

"What?" he asked, kissing down my neck to that magic spot that was pretty much a button to pop open my thighs. Wait, they were already open. Even better.

"We're in the hallway."

"So?"

I lifted my head and arched an eyebrow. "The hallway, Jagger."

He rested his forehead against mine. "I wait forever to kiss you, and now you dictate where I can do it?"

He lowered me until both my feet hit the ground. I'd never been more aware of our height difference. "How about anywhere but the hallway?"

He grinned, catching the tip of his tongue between his teeth, and lord help me, it was sexy. Sinfully so. "Deal." He kissed me once more, softly. "That doesn't count."

I tried to compose myself, but I was flushed, my hair mussed, and now I had to face the people who'd caught us making out.

"You're the most beautiful woman I've ever seen," he muttered into my neck, brushing my hair aside as we stood before Ember's door. He ran his tongue along my skin, and chills erupted on my arms.

"Hallway, Jagger."

He laughed. "Yeah, yeah."

We walked into the condo to the applause of Sam, Ember, and Josh. "I'd give that a nine-point-two. I have to deduct points for clothing still being on," Josh called out.

My cheeks heated to the point I thought flames might erupt at any second. Jagger took my hand, kissed my knuckles, and bowed.

He winked at me as he came to full height, and I melted. He was incredibly sexy, magnetic, reckless, a touch devious, and a whole lot mine.

Merry Christmas to me.

CHAPTER NINETEEN

She had her days, you know? Where everything was great. Fine. I wanted to spend eternity in those days. But then she would spiral and take the rest of us down with her.

Dinner long since done, we all lounged in the living room, haphazardly fitting onto Ember's sectional. I had Paisley curled around me, her head tucked into my chest. I pressed a kiss to her hair simply because I could. She was mine. She'd driven from Fort Rucker and tied a damned red bow around herself. Best. Christmas. Ever.

"You hear from your mom, Sam?" Ember asked.

She nodded, mouth full of popcorn.

"How much longer?" I asked.

"Six months. Honestly, I should have stayed behind in Colorado. But she wasn't paying for it, so it was come with her to Campbell or fend for myself."

Paisley's eyes darted over, but she didn't say anything. Her manners would never let her pry. But Sam saw, and she gave her a half smile. "I failed out of school, so my mom pulled all of her financial support unless I came with her. She deployed, and now I'm stuck here."

"Let me know if there's anything I can do for you," Paisley offered, and the crazy thing was I knew she meant it.

Deployed. That word meant something different with Paisley in my arms. I still had roughly eighteen months in flight school, but it would inevitably come, and I'd leave...and pray I'd come home to her. *Don't think about that.*

"Sam, you're always welcome in Alabama. I have an extra room and all, just say the word," I offered.

She raised her beer in salute and a nod of thanks.

Paisley cracked a yawn that triggered my own. "You ready for bed?" I asked.

She nodded.

"Good, me, too." I grinned down at her. She smiled, but there was something off about it. "You okay?"

"Perfect!" Her voice wavered.

"You guys take the guest room. There's a queen bed in there," Sam offered. Paisley tensed and gave me the public, closed-lip smile. "I'll camp out on the couch."

"I wouldn't want you to do that. We can find a hotel," I protested. Paisley was going to snap in half if she went any more rigid.

"It's Christmas," Ember argued. "Take the freaking guest room."

"What, you're not going to offer to go all girls one room, boys another?" I joked with Josh.

He shook his head, rubbing circles on Ember's back. "You're hot and all, Jag. But I think I'll stick with Ember. She's softer."

She smacked him with a pillow. "Last door on the right, Paisley. If you need anything, just ask."

"Thank you so much for having me," she said, manners in effect.

I grabbed my bag from the corner and threw hers over my shoulder, walking to the guest room as she followed. She entered the room and stared at the bed, crossing her arms in front of herself and holding her elbows.

Ah. Gotcha. I shut the door, set both bags down near the dresser, and tugged my shirt over my head. Her breath hitched, but the lust-filled haze that usually came over her eyes wasn't there. Oh, no, that usual appreciation had been replaced by apprehension.

"Aren't you going to get undressed?" How far would I have to push?

"Wh-what?" she stammered.

"Well, you aren't going to sleep in your clothes, are you?" I unbuckled my belt, and her eyes grew impossibly wide, like a deer caught in the headlights. Teasing her was too damn fun.

"Clothes?"

I went for the kill and dropped my jeans, kicking them off so I stood in only my boxer briefs. "Well, sex is kind of impossible in your clothes."

She took three quick, gasping breaths. "Oh, I...maybe... Um..."

She turned to the door, ready to bolt, and I made it to her just in time to keep it closed, pressing my arm to hers but nothing more. "Relax, Little Bird, and tell me what's on your mind."

She turned in my arms, still in full runaway mode. "Jagger, I love being with you, but I don't think I'm ready to...be with you, if you follow."

I feigned a look of shock. "You mean you didn't just drive to Nashville for me to strip you down and worship your body until we were both limp from orgasms?"

A spark lit in her eyes, and she raked her gaze down my

abs before retreating, only to be blocked by the door. "Well, I mean…"

"Don't people have sex the first day they decide to be in a relationship?" I tried, but couldn't hold out, and laughed. "Paisley, come on."

She turned as red as the bow she'd been wearing, which was now tucked away safely in my bag. "You're joking." She took a deep breath. "Sweet heavens, you're teasing me!"

I wrapped my arms around her. "It took you long enough to realize it."

"I feel like an idiot."

Barefoot, she didn't reach my collarbone, but I could smell her apple shampoo from here. "I just wanted to see when you'd push back."

She narrowed her eyes. "You were testing me."

"Yep." I moved my hand to her face, brushing over her smattering of freckles before running my thumb along her porcelain cheekbone. "No matter what, we don't lie, right? That's always been our deal."

She covered my hand with hers, leaning into it. "Right. No lies."

"I'll never push you into anything you don't want, especially not sex. But you have to be open with me, or this is going to be impossible."

She smirked. "Jagger, I would like to not have sex with you tonight."

"Well, there went my evening plans. Guess I'd better go watch some TV."

"Ha. Ha. You're funny!" She pulled out her pajamas, and then we took turns in the bathroom, readying for bed.

I'd never been in such a domestic scene with a girl. She even borrowed my toothpaste.

Lights out, we climbed into bed, and I pulled her into my arms. She was so tiny, yet fit beside me perfectly.

"You know I've slept with Will—"

"Yes," I bit out, refusing to think about Carter's hands on her skin, his body over hers. Nope, that would earn him a busted face when we got back to class, which wasn't exactly fair.

"He's it, Jagger, and it wasn't exactly...thrilling."

Not thrilling. Hell, yes. I was good at two things: fucking and flying. I'd wipe away the memory of that asshat one orgasm at a time, or two. Sex was easy. I'd been doing it since I was fifteen. But with Paisley? That was in a different realm, a different dimension. Shit, I was going to give myself performance anxiety, just thinking about it.

"So, I'm a lot less...experienced than you are. It's not something I treat lightly. I know you think of it a little differently, and I don't want to disappoint you."

Her admission sliced away my bravado, and for the first time, I wished I hadn't slept with so many girls, that I'd come to her a little less experienced. A lot less experienced.

"I've never been in a real relationship." My hand spanned across the curve of her waist, reassuring myself that I was in one now. "Sex, sure, but I don't know what it's like to really trust a woman, or to make love to one. There are some things you are way more experienced at."

"We'll figure it out." She brought my hand to her lips for a kiss.

"Just clue me into what you're thinking, Paisley. I promise I won't let you down."

She tensed under my hand. "There are things about me that you don't know."

"There are tons of things about me that you don't know," I countered. "Are you ready to tell me yours?" I wanted to tell her as much as I wanted her a million miles away from it.

"Not yet, and I know that's not fair."

"Then don't. Let's do things backward, start with"—I

swallowed—"trust. No miscommunications, just trust, and then we'll fill in the blanks as we're both ready." *Holy shit, I said it.*

She relaxed, her body forming to mine. "Jagger?"

"Mmm-hmm?" I'd never spent this much time in bed with a woman with her clothes on, let alone one who wanted to talk, but I'd listen to Paisley read a phone book if she wanted.

"Does no sex mean no kissing?"

I didn't need to be asked twice and slid her under me. I lingered above her for a few breaths, drinking in how exquisite she was. Her hair spread all over her pillow, and her lips were full, parted. The straps of her tank top caressed her collarbone, and the skin of her chest was flawless, rising with each breath she took. I refused to look lower, where her breasts rested. There was zero chance I was fucking this up the first night I had her.

"Want to know the biggest reason I'm okay waiting to make love to you?"

"Yes," she whispered.

"Anticipation is the best part. Wondering where every kiss will lead."

She tangled her legs with mine. "Oh, yeah?"

"Definitely." I stole a glance at the clock—12:04 a.m. Slowly, I lowered my lips to hers, brushing across them lightly. "Merry Christmas, Paisley."

She smiled against my lips. "Merry Christmas, Jagger."

She kissed me then, the softest, warmest caress I'd ever had. I wrapped her in my arms and stayed awake longer than she did, my mind racing.

I'd never felt anything as right as having her in my arms, her lips moving with mine. It was a sense of home that I hadn't felt since...well, too long.

I drifted, jerking awake only to reassure myself I hadn't been dreaming and Paisley was really here. I caressed the line of her hip, my hand sliding easily over her satin pajama pants, and finally gave in, breathing in the scent of apples.

The cell phone jolted me awake, and I rolled to the side, momentarily confused as to where my left arm was. Ah, under Paisley's head. I blinked into consciousness, reaching for the phone. Unknown on caller ID. I swiped the phone on, gently disengaging my arm.

"Hello?"

"Jag?"

Holy shit. I sat at the edge of the bed, instantly aware. I leaned over, resting my elbows on my bare knees, trying to decide if I was about to cry with relief or puke up dinner. "Anna?" The whisper was all I could manage.

"Oh, Jag." She sniffled. Was she drunk? High?

My stomach clenched. "Anna, where are you? Tell me. I can be there in twelve hours." I reached for my pants, pulling them on in one smooth motion.

"I'm okay. You don't have to worry about me." The noise of a party infiltrated the background.

"Don't have to worry? Anna, I worry about you every fucking day." I kept my voice low so I wouldn't wake Paisley, and tugged my shirt over my head. "Please, tell me where you are."

"I miss you. I miss seeing you smile. Are you happy?" Her words started to slur.

"Anna, I won't ever be happy unless I know where you are, that you're safe."

"Would you come see me if I told you? Would you stay with me?"

My eyes closed of their own volition. "Of course I would come. I'll get on the first plane." But I wouldn't stay. I knew

I'd get dragged down before I could pull her out. I forgot all sense of time and priorities when I was with her. "Just tell me where you are."

I opened my bag and dug around for socks, calculating my distance to the airport.

"Oh, Jag. I love you, but I'm no good for you." Her speech grew heavy.

"Anna, you're as much a part of me as my own skin. There's no good, no bad, just us. Please, for the love of God, tell me where you are. I'm so damned worried." She had to tell me. I couldn't not know if she was hurt, or broke. "At least let me send you money."

"You're better off without me."

"No. I'm never better off. I need you. I will always need you! Tell me where to come, and I'll be there." That sense of foreboding crept along my skin. This was going to end like usual.

"Do you still love me?"

I paused, looking over to where Paisley slept, the first real chance at happiness I'd had. But she was safe. Anna wasn't, and this wasn't a choice between them. "I will always love you, no matter where you are or what you do. Can you understand that? You're never too far gone."

"You can't save me."

"I can if you'll let me." Her heavy breaths were nearly drowned out by the thumping bass in the background.

"Merry Christmas, Jag. I love you so fucking much." Her voice broke on a sob, and the distinct beep told me the call had been ended.

"Merry Christmas," I whispered to her, even though she couldn't hear me.

I lifted my phone, needing to throw it, to destroy something, anything, but if she called again, I'd need it. Who the fuck was I kidding? She wasn't going to call. I slid down the wall and collapsed, my head on my knees.

I sat there for another forty-two minutes, watching each tick by the light of my cell phone, praying it would ring again, that she'd call from an unblocked number, and I could track her down.

One call and I was in a dive, the only question being what kind of rock bottom I'd hit. I was supposed to protect her, to keep her safe. I'd promised her. I'd failed, ever the quintessential fuckup.

The sheets rustled. "Jagger?" Paisley sat and turned her head until she saw me. "Everything okay?" Her hair was wild, falling around her and catching the small rays from the streetlight like a halo. She hadn't even been mine twelve hours, and I'd nearly left her to chase a ghost.

I shook my head.

Her feet made no noise as she came to me. "Do you want to talk about it?"

I shook my head again.

Her lips parted, and her eyes practically dripped sympathy as she held out her hand. "Then come to bed."

I took it, then stripped to my boxer briefs before climbing in next to her. She burrowed into me and lifted my hand to her waist, like she'd known touching her would bring relief. It did. She wound her fingers through mine and wiggled across the scant inch that separated us, pressing her body against me shoulder to toe.

Her breaths evened out into sleep, and I ran my fingers over her bare shoulder, savoring the soft skin. I fucked up almost everything in my life, but not her. I couldn't let any of my shit storm touch her, mar her in any way.

Anna was the cycle I couldn't manage to break—wouldn't break. But what if it cost me Paisley? What if she didn't understand?

I swallowed the fear, refusing to let it steal tonight, the

heaven of holding her, when I'd been waiting so long. It crept in anyway, causing me to clutch her just a little tighter. I should have been ecstatic watching her sleep in my arms, but I could only focus on one fact.

Now I had something to lose.

CHAPTER TWENTY

13. Drive recklessly.

"Ah, you came prepared!" Ember sat next to me at the rink.

"I'll get the hang of this." I zipped my jacket.

She offered me a steaming cup from Starbucks. "I don't drink coffee, but thank you kindly for the thought."

"Jagger told me while you were up at Christmas. It's hot apple cider."

I took it from her gratefully. "I think I love you."

"Now that," Sam said, stealing the third cup from the carrying tray, "is my latte. I'm not sure I've missed these chilly Josh-watching dates, Ember." She slid past me in stylish skinny jeans and boots, taking the other seat next to me.

"You like it and you know it," Ember jibed.

"Well, now that drooling over Jagger is off the table..."

My gaze snapped to hers, one eyebrow raised. She got the point, and started laughing. "Oh, sweet little Paisley. I'm so glad you have some spunk under there!" She touched my arm in all seriousness. "I'm not interested in Jagger, I promise. I just wanted to make sure you really were."

"Because driving to Nashville was just a little jaunt and all," I said sweetly. "Christmas just seemed like the right time to alienate my parents for a little hay roll."

She sputtered out her coffee. "Good God, you southern girls can say 'go to hell' with a smile on your face, huh?"

"Don't worry, you're not being insulted until someone blesses your heart or calls you sweet."

She rested her feet on the chair in front of her. "Well, now that's cleared up."

"Are your parents talking to you yet?" Ember asked, eyes glued to Josh as he skated toward the goal. It was their third game this week, and their last for a while, since leave was over soon.

"Barely. It's actually kind of nice." I sipped the cider, relishing the warmth. "They're throwing their annual party tomorrow night, so we'll see how they take the Jagger news."

"They don't know you're dating Jagger?" Ember asked, her eyes darting to mine.

"I figure tomorrow night is the best time to tell them. Too many witnesses for Mama to go postal, or Daddy to toss him off post."

"They're not Jagger fans?" Sam asked. "I mean, that tongue piercing of his and those tats...I guess he's not really the guy you take home to Mom."

Again, I couldn't help but wonder what the history between them was, and she saw it on my face.

"Next-door neighbors, remember? Plus, girls on campus talked. Josh may have been a little man-whorish in his day, but Jagger...I've never seen him with the same girl twice."

Ember cleared her throat. "Sam *meant* to say that we've never seen him in a committed relationship, and it's so nice to see him maturing. Don't let her scare you." She reached around me and tugged on Sam's hair. "Don't be a wretch, Samantha."

"But I'm good at it."

I laughed. "You remind me of Morgan, my best friend. Y'all would definitely get along."

"Did she get kicked out of school, too?"

I shook my head. "No, but she's a kindred spirit. Come down to Alabama, and I'll introduce you."

"You want me that close to Jagger?" She waggled her eyebrows at me.

I took a long pull of my cider. "Don't push your luck. But Josh and Jagger have made friends, you know…"

"Oh, hell, no. I'm staying away from anything in a uniform."

Jagger stole the puck and flew down the ice. He nailed his shot, scoring. I jumped out of my seat, squealing like a crazy woman.

He fist-bumped Josh and waved at me before another play.

I was the only one on my feet, and my cheeks heated, despite the freezing temps. I smoothed my coat and sat, keeping my gaze on the ice.

Both Sam and Ember broke out in laughter. "Oh, you've got it bad," Sam said between gulps of air.

I let loose a smile but didn't argue. They were right.

Jagger came through the doors of the rink, and I didn't hesitate, just skipped over to him and jumped. He caught me easily. I didn't even reprimand him for manhandling my rear in public— my mouth was too busy kissing him.

"So, you guys coming home or planning on sleeping here at the rink?" Josh joked.

I broke away. "Want to go do something with me?" I asked Jagger.

"Whatever you want."

"That's a dangerous offer, Jagger Bateman. I might want to paint your toenails pink." I loved being held eye level with him, so close I could lose myself in those electric blues.

"Then I would probably have to keep my socks on at all times."

"Hey, Jagger, I think you've got your damn hands full with that one." Ember laughed, looping her arm around Josh's waist.

"Yeah, yeah." He waved her off, and they headed out the door with Sam.

"What did you have in mind?" Jagger walked us toward the door, despite my dangling feet.

"Oh, just checking off some boxes."

"One day I need to see this infamous list. I'm beginning to think you just add things as you want to do them."

"Wait until you see number fourteen." I smiled, then slid down his body and headed to the car. Something told me he wouldn't have a problem producing a mind-blowing orgasm.

"Seriously?" he asked, his knees nearly pressed to his chest in the tiny go-kart. "This is on your list?"

I buckled my belt and winked at him. "It's a suitable environment for driving recklessly."

"I'm never going to get used to you, am I?"

"I hope not." I lowered my sunglasses as the light turned green. Flooring it, I zoomed out ahead of the other racers, who were all at least ten years younger. Jagger caught me easily at the first turn, accelerating through it where I braked.

That was the way he did everything, speeding ahead when common sense said to slow down. One of the kids rubbed my left side, and I hit the gas, the force sliding me back in my seat. I kept the pedal to the floor, eased up before the curves, and accelerated out of them, darn near keeping pace with Jagger.

The speed whipped the loose tendrils of my hair, and the wind stole the moisture from my lips. I edged out the kid next to me, moving to the center of the track so he couldn't get beside me again. We took the overpass at full throttle, and I crept up on Jagger, nearly on his bumper.

I registered the steepness of the last curve and took my foot off the gas. Jagger maintained his speed, kept control when the car skidded to the side, and accelerated out of the turn. Even with the brake off, I felt the force pull me to the left, and a trace of fear touched me. I wasn't wearing a helmet. I checked my watch, and my heart rate was still in good parameters. Funny, I had a ticking time bomb in my chest, but I was worried about a helmet on a go-kart track.

Jagger came in first, pulling in between the concrete barriers that marked the starting lanes. I parked behind him, unclicked my seat belt, and stood.

He helped me out, and I caught the dismayed looks of some of the kids he'd just smoked. Apparently he did, too.

"Sorry, guys," he apologized, turning his baseball hat to the front again. The white of the cap contrasted to his tan skin and made his eyes seem even brighter blue. "What?" He caught me staring.

"Mr. California," I mumbled with a smile.

He kissed my cheek as we walked off the track and past the attendant. He stopped and passed a fifty-dollar bill to the guy. "Hey, man, let the kids go again. It wasn't exactly a fair matchup."

Well, if that didn't just melt me.

The attendant nodded, one earbud still in, and stopped the kids as they followed us out. I looped my arm around Jagger's waist as the kids yelled out their thanks.

"You kept up," he said with a smile.

"You should see me on an ATV. I more than keep up." *At*

least I used to.

"I'll keep that in mind. Skee ball?" he asked, taking me into the arcade portion of the park.

"Oh, I'd hate to wound your ego," I said with mock sorrow.

"My ego has pretty good defenses." He flicked his tongue stud across his front teeth and smiled. He had to stop doing that before I jumped on him...again.

He was careful to respect the boundaries I'd vaguely outlined a week ago in Nashville, but with every kiss, I wondered what it would be like with him. Sure, I liked sex, but I hadn't lied. I'd never seen the big deal, or the reasons people had affairs and were ruled by this lust nonsense. I'd never had trouble keeping my head in bed, but Jagger made me lose all sense of reason with a simple kiss. My only thoughts were always *more* or *closer*.

Like right now.

"—can take it. Paisley?" He jarred me from my growing obsession with his mouth.

Oops. "Hmm?" I asked, like he hadn't just caught me openly ogling him.

His thumb grazed my lower lip. My tongue swept across the tip without thought, catching a hint of salt. His eyes darkened as his gaze followed.

He took my hand and led me through the nearly deserted arcade, popping quarters into the enclosed racing game. His hand swept aside the curtain and tugged me into the darkened space after him. Instead of taking his side of the bench, he sat directly in the center. One hand on my lower back, he guided me, and I was all too happy to put one knee on either side of him.

I fit my hips to his and kissed him, unable to keep my hands to myself another minute. His hat fell to the bench as my hands tangled in his hair. How did this keep getting better? I couldn't get enough of the press of his lips, the stroke of his tongue, the way he made the world around us disappear.

My breasts tingled where they pressed his chest, and I shamelessly adjusted my position to get as much full-body contact as possible. My heart kept pace with my breathing, both seeming to stop and start around each kiss.

His hands flexed at my waist and ran the length from my ribs to my hips. I arched, leaning my head back, and he took the opening, caressing my neck with his mouth. A jolt of pleasure jumped down my body, and I *wanted* him. Wanted like I'd never thought I was capable of. I rolled my hips into his and was rewarded with a rumble of a moan against my throat.

My fingers slipped down his neck to dig into the tense muscles of his shoulders. One of his hands threaded through my hair, while the other one slipped beneath the back of my shirt, caressing bare skin.

His fingers lingered on the hollow of my spine, lightly tracing patterns. Every nerve ending on my body sizzled to life. I couldn't still my hips over his, and the kisses grew longer, more intense. We were a mess of hands, teeth, and tongues.

The game behind us reached its limit, alerting us that it wanted more quarters even though the virtual cars hadn't left the starting line. I giggled into our kiss, thinking we sure had.

He shook his head at me, the grin bringing out his dimples. I bet those got him out of more than his fair share of trouble, and probably got him into more than his share of girls. The smile faded from my face. My thoughts ran amok and refused to listen to reason. Even worse, my mouth opened.

"How many girls have you slept with?" I cursed my tongue.

His face transformed into an impenetrable mask. "Why?"

"I think it's a reasonable question, especially if we're going to be in a relationship." I moved my thumbs in circles along his biceps, trying to take the sting out of my unplanned assault on his past.

His jaw ticked. "We *are* in a relationship, Paisley." His eyes slid shut, and he sighed like he'd been defeated, his head falling to the fiberglass shell of the game.

"Then don't I have the right to know?" I had to know. Sweet lord, I didn't want to know.

"What will the answer give you?" His eyes stayed shut.

My heart pounded at an acceptable rate, but I couldn't tell if it was from our impromptu make-out session or anticipating Jagger's answer. "Knowledge."

"Is the answer going to change how you feel about me?" His eyes opened underneath a puckered brow. I smoothed my fingers along the lines in his forehead.

"No," I whispered. "It doesn't have to be now, if you're not ready." That seemed to be our mantra when it came to our pasts. "But I need to know eventually." A corner of my mouth tilted up. "I can give you my whole list right now, if it would make you feel better. I've kissed five boys my whole life, and slept with one."

"Only five guys have kissed you?"

"My first one went to Billy Gerrison during a scandalous game of spin the bottle when I was fourteen. Will scared off most of the guys in high school on account of being Peyton's best friend, and then there were a couple guys my senior year. Then..."

"Carter."

"And there's the whole sordid history of Paisley Donovan," I joked. "See, it's not that hard." His reluctance was enough to make me want to breathe into a paper bag. How many could there possibly be? He was twenty-three. A dozen? My God, two dozen?

"This is that important to you?" He had on his serious face.

"I need to know."

"And if I told you that I don't know? That I never marked my bedpost?" He held my hips like he was scared I would run away.

I leaned away from him a little. "You can't even guess?" Oh, that came out harsher than I intended.

"I could try." He looked past my head and darted his eyes left and right like he was calling up memories. "There was high school," he muttered. "And then college...I just didn't keep track. It wasn't about numbers, it was just a physical gratification kind of thing, no emotion involved. I don't do attachments."

"*Didn't,*" I corrected.

"What?"

"I hope you're kind of attached to me, otherwise I'm not sure what we're doing here." I tried to keep my voice level. "I don't care about what you did or who you were, Jagger, as long as that's not who you are now. I'm not judging you. I just want to know how many memories I'm competing with, being compared to. If you were...safe?"

His eyes cut right through me to the heart of every insecurity. "I'm very attached to you, Paisley. I haven't felt so connected to another human being since..." His eyes unfocused, seemingly hazed for a moment before he snapped back. "Since I left my family." He cupped my cheek. "I don't know how many there were. A lot, and I wish I had the same numbers you do, but I don't. I wish I'd always interpreted sex as you do, but I haven't. I can tell you that I was safe every time. I've never had sex without a condom."

I let out the breath I hadn't realized that I'd been holding. "Okay—"

"I'm not finished," he interrupted, both of his hands now holding my face. "As for your last concern, who you're competing with? Paisley, there's no competition, no ghosts lurking in the corners of my heart, no standard I could hold you to, because you blow every single memory out of the water like it never existed. Kissing other girls was just a step in a very well-rehearsed little dance. Kissing you fucking consumes me. There's no room for anyone else."

"When was the last time?" My stomach clenched, and my heart thudded in my throat.

"None since Florida."

I arched my eyebrow at him, wordlessly asking.

He shook his head with a wry grin. "It wasn't meeting you, though I know that would be the awesome line you'd want to hear." He tucked a strand of my hair behind my ear. "It was saving you. Seeing how quickly life could just be...over. I've wanted nothing more in my life than to fly Apaches, and there I was at the beach, scoring another girl in a bikini. My priorities were wrong. Then you were thrown in, and when I saw you, my first thought was that I was too late. You were already gone, this vivacious girl who'd been reading just a few minutes before..."

"You noticed," I murmured.

"Want to know the color of your bathing suit that day? Because I can tell you that, too."

"You have a photographic memory, you cheat."

A grin flickered across his face. "I'd made it into flight school, but I was wasting my time, my energy on girls who meant nothing. So I stopped. No women. No distractions. I decided to concentrate on what really mattered."

"And me?"

"You matter."

"I'm a distraction."

His gaze dropped to my lips. "Only the best kind. And I like to think of you as more of a reason to succeed."

I kissed the furrows on his forehead. "Thank you, for telling me about the others."

"Has it changed anything?" His eyes were wary.

"No, I promise. Do I approve? Of course not. Does it scare me a little? Absolutely." He turned away, and I gently brought his face to mine. "I'm not going to hold your past against you, as long as you don't hold mine against me."

"Deal." He pressed his lips to mine. "I don't know how to do this, how to be in a relationship. I don't know if I'm calling you too much, or too little. I don't know if I'm supposed to feel this way, all borderline obsessed, or if I'm a total nut job. I think most guys figure this out in junior high." He rested his forehead on mine, and I tried to match his slower breaths.

He looked at me, unguarded, and a sweet pressure settled in my chest that I was too scared to name. Not this soon. I was over my head and yet never more comfortable in my skin, my thoughts. "You have been perfect. Don't think about what you should be doing. I want *you*, not some fake version of what you think I want."

"And my track record for fucking things up?" He smirked, but his eyes didn't hold a trace of the humor his mouth did.

"You have never let me down, Jagger."

"Maybe...maybe you could be my exception." His voice was low, laced with faint hope.

With the rules I'd broken, the feelings I had in that very moment, I felt like...me, and not just the watered-down version I'd become since diagnosis. Jagger made me want things I'd long since given up on for my future. There was no alarm on my wrist, no one telling me exactly what I had to be doing for my own good. He was living, breathing freedom. "Maybe you're mine, too."

CHAPTER TWENTY-ONE

JAGGER

I know what you're thinking. Eventually I'll screw it up.
I always do.

"You don't have to do this." Paisley squeezed my hand. "If you're uncomfortable…"

"I'll be fine." Now that was funny. Uncomfortable at a formal party? If she only knew. But she didn't, because I hadn't worked up the balls to tell her yet. I adjusted the knot on my tie, wishing it was just a little looser, or better yet… off. We stood outside her parents' house, watching as couples parked their cars and moved toward the front door.

Paisley wore a simple black dress, a strapless number that ended just above her knee. Her hair was swept up in some style that showed off her neck and made it way too accessible. Luckily I wasn't amateur enough to leave hickeys, because the soft skin at the base of her neck was easily becoming my favorite place to worship.

"Are you sure this is the best way for them to find out about us?" I asked.

She scrunched her nose, which was impossibly cute. "Well, no. But at least in public you're not going to get shot or anything."

"I've seen your dad pissed. Are the guns locked up?"

She laughed. "Want me to go in first and make sure?"

I ran my thumb over her knuckles and led her toward the lion's den. "Nope. We do this together."

"Do you want to wait for Josh and Ember?"

Every officer had been invited, and I'd basically blackmailed Josh into coming. "They're running a little late due to the shower running out of hot water. It was something about getting stranded with soap in their hair."

She raised her eyebrows. "They were both in the shower?"

A wicked grin erupted on my face. "Yes."

"That doesn't seem...practical."

I locked eyes with her, letting all my carefully banked desire for her pour out in a glance as I drew us into the shadows, out of sight. "Practical? Since when does sex have to be practical? Just think, Paisley. Your wet, naked body pressed between me and the tile, which you like, because it's cold and your body is on fire. Me taking your weight in my arms so I can fit you to just the right angle where I can lick the water off your—"

She covered my mouth with her hand. "I understand." Her cheeks flamed, and her eyes darkened as she moved her fingers away from my lips. "You make waiting really hard, Jagger."

"If you think that's hard..."

"Seriously!" she squeaked.

"Well, it's my job." I smiled, trying to calm my body from the very vivid fantasy I'd just painted. "You're supposed to play the genteel southern lady and ward off my advances."

She stretched on her tiptoes and put her lips to my neck, just above my collar. "I think I like your job better." I groaned, and she giggled. "Let's get inside."

We mixed in with the crowd and crossed the threshold. Major Davidson greeted us in the entry hall. "Bateman?" His eyes darted to Paisley and widened when he noticed our joined hands. "Paisley? Well, this is going to be an interesting evening." He laughed. "You two kids enjoy yourselves."

That did not make me feel better.

"Lee! You made it!" A woman with pale blond hair, about Paisley's size, tugged her hand, pulling her to the side of the room. One look at her heart-shaped face and I knew she was Paisley's mom.

"Yes, Mama. I promised I would."

"Well, after that stunt you pulled at Christmas, I wasn't sure we could depend on you." The woman's eyes had switched from kind-mother vibe to sharp in two seconds.

"I went to where I was wanted," Paisley answered, her voice still demure. She moved closer to me, and it didn't escape Mrs. Donovan's notice.

Her narrowed eyes took in every detail of my attire, and I sent a quick prayer of thanks to my mother, who'd taught me the difference between a three- and four-button blazer. There wasn't a single stitch out of place that she could pick on. Finally she met my eyes with an icy glare. "And you would be?"

"Mrs. Donovan?" a uniformed major called from her side. General's aide, if I had to guess.

Her face transformed instantly, the lines softening into a smile. "Major Beard, is he ready for us?"

The way she shifted so quickly between her private face and public one sent chills down my spine. Paisley's smile was close-lipped, and her eyes darted to mine, silently asking for understanding.

What wasn't to understand? I'd grown up just like this. Only in a bigger house with bigger sharks.

I smiled. "Don't worry."

"Yes, ma'am, he's ready for you," Major Beard replied. "If you'll come with me?" He gestured with his hand toward the spiral staircase.

"Lee-Lee, you look beautiful this evening." Carter's voice shredded my already frayed nerves. He leaned forward, brushing his lips across her cheek, and my fist clenched. *Calm the fuck down*, I warned my inner Hulk. I didn't need to explode into a giant rage monster at the moment.

"Thanks, Will. It's good to see you," she answered, still holding my hand.

"Lee," Mrs. Donovan ordered, her sweet voice at odds with the look she cast our way. "I'm sorry, but this is family only," she said to me.

"No, ma'am, I understand." I brought Paisley's knuckles to my lips and brushed a soft kiss across them. "I'll be right here."

"Will?" Mrs. Donovan motioned him toward the stairs.

Well, if that didn't take tonight from awkward to flat-out hostile.

"Mama—" Paisley warned.

Carter shook his head. "Not this year, ma'am."

Mrs. Donovan smiled genuinely at Carter and said, "Well, next year," with a pointed look in my direction. *Nice.*

Paisley rose and brushed a kiss across my lips. It wasn't passionate, or even sexy, but the symbolic claim that she meant it to be. It struck home, if the melodramatic sigh from her mother was any indication. I stroked my thumb across her cheekbone. "Go."

She took a deep breath and then followed where her mother led, her heels giving her a couple inches over her.

"Didn't think I'd see you here." Carter stood next to me. "This isn't exactly your scene."

I bit back the assholish retort that immediately came to mind. "Paisley asked." I walked the very thin line we'd drawn with each other.

General Donovan waited at the top of the stairs as the ladies walked up. The entry hall was now overcrowded—those who couldn't fit watched from the living room. Mrs. Donovan wound her arm around her husband, and he held out his other for Paisley, lightly kissing her forehead. She hugged him, a look of relief on her face.

Huh. I'd thought he was a raging asshole, but it looked like he was the one Paisley gravitated toward.

"She might want you, but I still think you're nowhere good enough for her," Carter said.

"That makes two of us."

"Welcome!" General Donovan silenced the crowd. "I'm old army, raised by a father who was even older army. On New Year's Day, tradition stated that every officer called upon the general's house to bid him happy New Year. All day that damned doorbell would ring, and being the oldest son, well, I had to answer it every time." The crowd murmured a laugh. "We've lost a lot of traditions as our army has modernized, if you will, but accepting callers on New Year's Day has always been one tradition that my wife and I like to keep alive. Instead of asking you all to ring our doorbell all day long tomorrow, we figured we'd just get it out of the way by hosting you tonight.

"We're honored you're bringing in this new year with us at our home. Tonight we say good-bye to the old and welcome in the possibilities of the new."

I looked at Paisley, and my heart jumped. She was already smiling at me.

She was so poised, but her smile was genuine, unlike her mother's, and that smile was all mine. She had faith in me. She wanted me, and not just for a piece of my body, or the money the girls in high school had known about. She knew who I was in my soul and didn't try to fix my flaws or glaze over them. She simply understood, forgave, and moved forward.

I needed her. At some point in the last few weeks, she'd

become like gravity, anchoring me. I found her nickel in my pocket and rubbed my thumb across the shiny metal. She hadn't just given me a gift, she *was* my gift, for as long as I could keep her. And I *would* keep her. I'd be worthy of her, not because she asked me to—she'd never ask me to change—but because she deserved the best man to hold her, understand her, love her.

I stopped breathing, my chest on fire, burning, wanting to catch this one moment and hold it, just in case I fucked this all up. I needed to remember this exact second with clarity for the next fifty years of my life—the moment I looked at the girl who was literally way above me and saw the rest of my life. The moment I realized I had fallen in love with Paisley Donovan.

The audience started clapping, and General Donovan kissed Paisley's cheek before turning to his wife. Apparently I'd missed the rest of his speech. My chest hurt, reminding me that I needed to breathe. I didn't just suck air into my lungs, but purpose, silently vowing that I would do anything it took to stand here, to be in her world.

Her father's eyes scanned the crowd, smiling, especially at Will. His expression clouded for a moment when he saw me, and he whispered in Paisley's ear. Her eyes locked onto mine, and her smile faded as she nodded.

"Holy shit, do I wish I could witness what's about to happen." Carter laughed. "Good luck. Hopefully I see you on the flight line. If not, it's been an experience flying with you." He slapped my shoulder and disappeared into the crowd as the Donovans descended. I'd been raised around much more powerful people, so the sweat clamming up my hands was completely unjustified, right?

They beelined for me, not stopping to shake hands or mingle. My brain started a countdown, like one of those apocalyptic movies where the nuclear weapon has some bored, feminine voice counting down destruction. Ten. Nine. Eight.

"Now, Lee," was all I heard as General Donovan walked right past me, opening the French doors to what looked like an office. Seven.

"Deep breath," Paisley said, clasping my hand and leading me in. Six.

"We're not to be disturbed," General Donovan ordered Major Beard as he and his wife took a position near his desk. Five.

"Yes, sir." He closed the doors behind us with an ominous click. Four.

The wall on one side was lined with bookcases, all filed alphabetically. The guy had a serious stick up his ass when it came to organization. Awards and guidons hung on the other surfaces, reminding me that I was most definitely out of my league. He was a two-star general, and I was a butter-bar lieutenant.

Three. Two. One. "Lee, why don't you introduce us to your new friend." Mrs. Donovan crossed her arms in front of her cocktail dress.

Paisley stepped in front of me, like her tiny frame could protect me. I reached around her waist and pulled her to my side. There was zero chance I was hiding behind her like we'd done something wrong.

"She doesn't need to. I already know who he is, and this isn't the first time he's been to our house, just the first time he's been inside." *Boom.* Detonation.

"Mama, Daddy, this is Jagger Bateman." Her voice was sweet and clear, totally at odds with the slight tremors that shook her hands.

Mrs. Donovan ignored the introduction. "What do you mean, he's been here before?"

"Jagger's the young man who saved my life in Florida."

"He's the one who decided our front lawn needed a visit

from the polar bear." General Donovan kept his tone level.

"What?" her mother yelled.

Paisley just kept on rolling. "He's also here for flight school—"

"Lee! You know we have rules about dating students!" her mother snapped, her cheeks turning as red as her dress.

"You didn't mind when it was Will," she answered.

For a few seconds, we all stared at one another, the only sound coming from the party just outside the doors.

"I'm sorry we had to meet like this," I said, taking advantage of the only quiet minute I might get. "But yes, I'm Jagger. I met Paisley in Florida, a little unconventionally. I had no idea who she was." I looked down into her eyes and sighed. "Honestly, I don't think knowing would have stopped me."

"This is ridiculous!" her mother seethed.

"We met again at the library and became friends," Paisley explained, her eyes still locked onto mine. "Then, more."

"Lieutenant Bateman," General Donovan growled.

I fully faced them. "Sir, I'm sorry to upset you, but I'm not sorry about Paisley. I'm crazy about her."

She sucked in her breath, and I wondered if I'd ever said that to her, or just thought it in my head. I looked down at her. "I am, you know."

Her eyes sheened. "I am, too."

"Oh, stop acting like a pair of besotted fools." Looked like I wasn't winning her mother over any time soon. "This is completely unacceptable, Lee."

"What is?" she asked. "Me being happy? Moving on from Will?"

"Will Carter is perfect for you," her father argued. "We completely respect your decision to take a break from that relationship. But this boy?" He pinched the bridge of his nose, and I saw the ring. "Will is a fantastic young man that you've known for years. He's strong, reliable, and a trusted part of this family."

Fucking great. I was compared to Carter all day long on the flight line and now with Paisley's parents. I couldn't get away from the ring knocker. "Let's not forget a West Point graduate," I added, and then damn near bit my tongue off.

General Donovan tried to cut me down with a look. I didn't shrink, hell, no. I straightened my shoulders.

"And where did you go to school, Lieutenant?"

"University of Colorado," I answered with no shame. I'd gotten into that school on my own with a GED and a damn good essay. After all, I'd walked out on my entire past, so it wasn't going to tag along anywhere.

He quirked one eyebrow. "Well, not every man can get into West Point."

"Sir, not every man who gets in *chooses* to go." His eyes narrowed. Fuck. Six years, and I'd never made a slip like that. "Theoretically speaking." *Right. Good cover. Not.*

He kept his eyes trained on me like he was picturing a little red laser dot on my forehead. "I don't approve of this."

Paisley's chin lifted. "I'm not asking you to."

"You would do this without our approval?" Her mother didn't try to hide her shock. "I didn't raise you to be so disrespectful, young lady."

Paisley swallowed. In Florida, she'd been more concerned with their disapproval than her own health. I gave her waist a squeeze, trying to convey everything I couldn't say aloud. *I support you, no matter what. If this is too much for you, tell me.*

She covered my hand with hers. "You don't seem to approve of much in my life right now, Mama. I love you, but I'm going to have to respectfully ask you to accept my choice."

"You're making absolutely asinine decisions! If your sister only knew what you were doing. You're supposed to be more rational than this. You're supposed to make the choices that are good for you, and not just the ones that might feel good that very second. Stop being such a child, Lee."

I took a deep breath. *Down, Hulk, down.* "Please don't talk to her like that."

"Paisley," she said softly.

"I'm sorry?" her mother shot at both of us.

"Say it. Paisley." Suddenly, this fight wasn't about me anymore. Paisley had opened the barn door on something I knew nothing about.

"Lee, what on earth are you talking about?"

"This is not the time, Paisley," her dad said. His eyes cut to his wife, and his mouth flattened. The concern etched on his features made him seem more like a worried dad and less like the commanding general.

"I need her to say it, Daddy. Even if it's just this once." Her mom's mouth opened and shut a few times, and Paisley's shoulders dropped. "You can't do it, can you? That's why Will calls me Lee, too."

"Pa—" Her mom choked back something that sounded like a sob, and her dad put his arm around her.

"You don't say it, because you're afraid you'll say Peyton's name instead, and you'll be reminded that she's gone and you're stuck with me. I'm the one who didn't play sports, didn't excel at anything but reading. I'm the one who didn't shine, didn't bring you recognition, didn't make you proud. If I didn't love her so much, I'd hate her for what she's done to me."

"Lee—" Her mom shook her head. "This is not the time. For heaven's sake, girl, we have guests."

"You lost your daughter, and I'm so sorry, Mama. But I lost my sister, my best friend, my absolute idol. Then I lost my name." She stared somewhere on the floor. "Then I lost me."

"Paisley, stop," her father pleaded. I couldn't look away from her, from the sad strength I knew came from a place of such grief that you had no choice but to rebuild using the very ashes you'd been burned into. I wanted to stop the flow of pain coming from her mouth, but I'd never been prouder of her for setting it free.

"You need to calm down, Lee. This isn't good for you," her mother snapped.

"Oh, please, Mama. Like I'm going to drop dead of a heart attack for being *honest*. I've stood in her place. I've been with the man who loved *her*. I have come to every family breakfast, worked on base, and only taken classes on main campus once a week, just to keep you content. I ignore everything I want, because it's what you need. But please, Mama." Her voice broke, but she stood straighter than ever. "Please understand. Jagger is the only person in my life who knows me as just Paisley, and not Lee. I choose him. I choose him over living in Peyton's shadow. I choose him over Will because I finally understand what it is to want someone so badly that you're willing to risk what we're going through this very minute. I choose him because he makes me feel alive, and amazing, and *me*. He makes me remember who I am. And I choose him over you because he can say my name without making me remember that you'd rather I'd died instead of Peyton."

She choked out the last word through tears, pushing me away from her and bolting from the room like it was on fire.

Holy shit. Her words hung in the air like floating land mines, daring the first person to cross the field. In one breath she'd breathed life into my heart and destroyed her parents'.

"She's..." Her mother swallowed, her public face on. "She's prone to melodrama."

"Unbelievable." It was the only word I could spit out before I chased after her, weaving through the crowd in the entry. The music was loud enough to assure we hadn't been overheard.

Paisley raced up the stairs. I'd crossed the foyer and hit the first step before his hand caught my elbow. "What the hell did you do?" Carter fired at me.

"Me? This isn't about me. It's more about you, and using her for a stand-in for her sister for the last year. Fuck, Carter. She's amazing, and you couldn't look past her dead sister long enough to love her for who she is." I pried his fingers off my arm with deliberate motions, careful not to snap on him in a house full of officers. Bar brawls were one thing. Destroying another lieutenant in the home of the commanding general was a career ender.

He paled. "You don't know *anything* about it, Bateman. Nothing. Don't act like dating her for a week gives you half of the shit you need to know."

"I know she deserves better than she's gotten!" I yelled over my shoulder as I took the stairs two at a time. Her skirt disappeared into the second room on the left, but she closed the door before I could get to her. "Paisley?" I tried the door handle, but it was locked. "Let me in."

"I just need a minute."

A minute. I could give her that. She'd just unloaded two years' worth of anger in one conversation. I could give her a minute.

"Lee, you open this door *now*," her mother shouted, appearing next to me. "Don't you run off from me like this conversation is finished!"

I took another deep breath, hoping to flush the anger, to find my happy place before I did some verbal damage to her mother. Paisley was my future, which meant I couldn't burn the bridge in front of me, even if it was currently covered in freaking locusts.

"No," Paisley replied.

"Stop acting like a petulant toddler and open this door!" Her voice escalated, and I looked over the railing to see if she'd been heard. I didn't care, but Paisley would. Will stood at the bottom of the stairs, glaring at me.

"This is all your fault," Mrs. Donovan yelled at me.

"I love how everyone assumes this is about me. Look at how you're treating her." I kept my voice soft.

She shook her head and narrowed her eyes at me. "I knew the first time I heard your name out of Will's mouth that I wanted you gone, away from our family."

"Will?" I laughed, envisioning Carter whining to her mother that I'd made a move on Paisley. Hell, yes, I'd made a move. "Carter may be a god in your eyes, but he didn't love her like she needs."

"Will Carter is a man of honor who had the guts to come forward when you put that monstrosity of a bear on my front lawn!"

Everything in me went still. Deadly. Every ounce of anger I'd felt today on Paisley's behalf, at her father for immediately hating me, her mother for treating her like shit, focused into one thought. "He told."

"I've never been more proud of him." Her chin rose.

I was moving before another rational thought entered my brain. "Jagger! Don't!" Paisley's voice registered like an echo under the water. Everything in my brain fogged except the one person at the end of the stairs. Will-fucking-Carter.

I launched at him from a few steps up, pulling some aerial WWE shit. We landed in the entry hall, people scattering as we slid across the tile floor. My fist slammed into his face, and his head bounced off the floor. I stood slowly as he wiped the blood off his lip. "You think I want a traitorous asswipe like you as my stick buddy?"

"Traitorous?" he asked, gaining his feet. "You stole my girlfriend!"

"You turned us in for the class prank. The class you *lead*! Who the hell wants a leader they can't trust? Sure as hell not me!"

"Stop!" Paisley shouted, coming down the stairs, her

mother hot on her heels. "Jagger, don't hurt him!"

I grinned like a homicidal maniac. "See, even she knows I'll kick your ass."

Carter yelled and rushed me. I let him, wanting to have another excuse to fucking demolish him. We took out the catering table in the middle of the foyer. The trays scattered to the floor, the noise nothing compared to the roaring in my head. He got in one punch to my cheek, but I swung hard with my right, catching him in the temple so hard he fell off me.

"No!" Paisley screamed, but I was too far gone for it to register. I didn't wait for him to react, delivering another hit to the other side of his face. Symmetry was a beautiful thing.

Carter grabbed a tray, moving so quickly I didn't recognize it until the pain wailed through the side of my head.

I got in two more punches, blood dripping from my face onto his.

"Enough!" Arms pulled me up and locked my own behind me. I struggled against them, ready to finish what he'd fucking started. "Calm down. You're about to kiss your helicopter and your girl good-bye, Jag." Josh's voice came through the haze, quiet enough that only I heard him.

Carter yelled out a war cry and charged, throwing his shoulder into my stomach. Josh and I both skidded to our asses, landing beside the front door, my arms wedged behind my back. Carter swung once, twice, and pain erupted through my face.

"Jesus Christ!" I heard Major Davidson before I saw him pull Carter off. "That's quite enough!" He hauled Carter across the foyer, then unceremoniously shoved him into a chair.

Josh and I managed to stand, my arms still held captive. He knew me too well.

My chest heaved. Slowly the haze cleared, and I surveyed the damage. Carter held his head, but glared at me like he was ready to go another round.

Food was scattered everywhere, the trays lying haphazardly along a line of dress shoes. I closed my eyes for a moment, taking in enough oxygen to power my brain and not my fists. "You okay?" Josh asked quietly.

I nodded, and he released my arms.

Then I turned to look at Paisley. Her mouth hung agape, her eyes huge, frightened. Then she slowly closed her mouth, the line tense, shook her head, and walked right past me to Will. *Guess the guy who starts the fight doesn't get the girl.* I might have kicked his ass, but he'd won this round.

CHAPTER TWENTY-TWO

Oh, forget it. Not everything has a flippin' box.

Will was a mess, his face already swelling and blood trickling from one nasty cut above his eye. Jagger had beaten the crap out of him.

"He's right, you know," Will whispered brokenly, so only I could hear him. "I shouldn't have told. I should have been there, too."

"I know," I whispered, my hand going to my head, which felt like it wasn't attached to my body. Nausea hit me hard. I shouldn't have taken those meds on an empty stomach. Rookie mistake.

"Lieutenants!" Daddy yelled in *that* voice, the one that commanded attention over parade fields. The one he'd never used in this house. "Office. Now!"

The room cleared. Will stood slowly, and I couldn't bring myself to look at Jagger as he walked by. *Who is he? Do I even really know?* I'd never seen someone with that much rage in his body. He'd hurt someone I cared about, not that Will hadn't deserved it. But did anyone, really?

My heart pounded, the beat forceful, and my stomach turned.

"You okay?" Ember whispered.

I sat on the stairs rather ungracefully, but happy I hadn't collapsed to the floor. I laid my head on my knees. "I'm all right." Crud. I even sounded breathless.

"You don't look it," Ember said.

I glanced up as the staff came into the foyer, cleaning up the mess that covered the floor. Mom glared at me, but with everything that had transpired tonight, she knew better than to start again. We'd both firmly dug our trenches, as she confirmed by shaking her head at me like she couldn't believe I'd let this happen in her house.

My mouth filled with saliva. *Oh, no.* I barely made it to the powder room in time. Thank God there hadn't been a line. I heaved what was left of my lunch into the toilet. When my stomach was empty, I dry heaved until sweat broke out on my forehead.

"Paisley?" Ember called through the door.

"Just a minute," I replied, as chipper as possible when kneeling on a bathroom floor. I stood slowly, my knees wavering, and cleaned up quickly.

"Sit down," she ordered, taking my elbow as I walked into the entry.

"I'm just really tired." I felt sluggish, like my heart wasn't even going to try to keep up with me. *The new meds.* I was getting hit with the side effects.

"Can we take you home?" Josh asked, sitting on the other side of me.

"She is home...kind of," Ember answered. "Do you want me to get your mom?"

"Oh, she's the last thing I need. Yes, please, take me home.

I'm incredibly tired."

The glass doors to Daddy's office swung open. Will and Jagger stumbled out, both holding ice packs to various parts of their bodies. I didn't want to see either of them.

"Lee," Will started, his tone that apologetic one he used right before he started an it's-for-your-own-good speech.

"No. I don't want to hear it." I looked up, focused on Jagger. His face looked like a Picasso painting, swollen in places it shouldn't be and turning colors. They both did. "Not from either of you."

Jagger's head snapped like I'd slapped him. "Just go home," I told him. "I can't even begin to think of what to say to you after that."

He walked over slowly and took my hand, turning it palm up. He placed something cool and circular in the palm, then closed my fingers over it and walked away. The door clicked shut.

I opened my hand to look, but I already knew he'd given me back the nickel, and I knew what he was asking.

He needed me to stand by my word not to abandon him like everyone else he'd walked away from. I clenched the nickel in my hand as the countdown was called out from the living room. Ten. Nine. Eight.

I stood, wobbly but capable. Kind of.

Seven. My feet felt impossibly heavy, but I ran to the door and swung it open. "Jagger!" I called out, unable to run any farther. Six. Five. Four.

He turned and ran toward me. Three. Two. He caught me in his arms as the voices finished the countdown inside.

One. "Happy New Year," I whispered and kissed him.

He lifted me easily, holding me close with one hand under my hips and the other tight across my back. "Happy New Year," he replied, and kissed the breath out of me.

Thank God he held me tight.

Because I didn't have the strength to stand on my own.

...

Something warm pressed against me and wrapped around my stomach. My heart beat normally, and I sent up a little prayer of thanks. It took a couple tries, but I lifted the steel curtains of my eyelids only to be met by more darkness. A clock on the unfamiliar bedside table read 3:43 a.m., and the wall I faced was bare but for the window. It was covered by thick drapes that opened only wide enough to let in a small stream of light. I had no idea where I was, but the scent that enveloped me was familiar.

"Jagger?"

He rolled to hover just above me. "You fell asleep on the way home, so I brought you here. Paisley, I'm sorry about tonight. I was so angry, and when your mom told me Carter was the one who ratted us out, I just lost it. It was inexcusable. I apologized to your father as soon as we got into his office. I won't ever let you down like that again," he promised. "What I did to Carter…"

"You destroyed his face," I accused softly. "Not that you look much better." I skimmed my fingers over the dark splotch of color on his cheek, and he flinched.

"I've always…had a temper, but I've never attacked anyone like that, I swear. It was the first time, and the last." He looked into my eyes like they were the measure of truth.

I didn't know how to respond to that. He'd been wild, and physical violence wasn't anything I handled well. "It's not okay, and I can't pretend that it is. You…you can't ever do anything like that again."

"I won't. I promise. Did it cost me you?" The light was dim in the room, but enough shone through to make out the fear shooting through his wide eyes.

A dozen heartbeats passed before I could answer him. If

anything, tonight showed me how little time I had left to make my choice. But what time I had? I was going to give it to him. "No. I'm not going to walk away from you over this. Not when I promised you forgiveness." The nickel. He'd actually kept it.

He sighed, his whole body sagging along my side. "You won't be sorry. I swear, you won't regret this. Any part of it."

My eyelids felt ridiculously heavy. "I could never regret you." I rested my hands over his heartbeat. His forehead dropped to touch mine, his breath sweet in my face like he hadn't even been asleep. It felt so good to be in his bed, in his arms, safe and cherished, not stifled.

"I'll fix it with your parents. I know they're important to you, but I might need your help. Family isn't something I know a lot about since mine is pretty nonexistent." He kissed my cheek softly, pulling me into his side and draping his arm across my hip. "Sleep, Little Bird. I've got you."

I threaded my fingers between his, leaving my hand on top as my eyes closed. "I've got you, too, and I'll be your family."

For the next 110 days.

Bacon. The smell woke me. I stretched, my hand smoothing over Jagger's empty pillow, and opened my eyes.

I sent a quick text to Morgan, climbed out of bed, used Jagger's bathroom, and checked my face. No makeup, but the bags weren't as bad today. Lying in bed all yesterday, wrapped in Jagger's arms for a movie marathon, had definitely done me some good. Now, if they hadn't all been the Army of Darkness movies, it might have been just perfect.

It would have been exquisite if he'd not kept himself under complete control and only given me soft, quick kisses.

I put a bra on under my tank top. There was no way the girls were getting free range at breakfast. Voices carried from the kitchen, and I came around the corner from the hallway to see Grayson at the stove, turning bacon while Jagger beat eggs. Ember sat on Josh's lap, sipping coffee.

"Morning," I said, coming behind Jagger and slipping my hands around his waist. He tensed, and my fingers felt every ridge of his rock-hard abs as I hugged myself to him. A low pang of desire hummed through me, not entirely unwelcome.

He leaned into me and hummed a moan as I pulled him tighter. "Morning, Little Bird."

I pressed a soft kiss to his back and then left him to the eggs, stealing the seat across from Josh and Ember. "You headed back today?"

A small, sad smile flashed across her face. "Yeah, a little later. I don't have class until the day after tomorrow, so I'll stay here as long as I can."

Josh flexed his arms around her, putting his nose to her neck like he needed to remember how she smelled.

"I would, too," I agreed quietly, sneaking a look at Jagger as he joked with Grayson.

The doorbell rang, and Jagger made it there before me, opening it for Morgan. "Good morning, folks!" She handed Jagger a basket full of bagels.

"Um. You shouldn't have?"

"Darling, I'm southern. We don't come over empty-handed." She flashed him a smile and squeezed my hand, leading me down the hallway. "Here." She handed me three bottles. "I didn't want to keep coming over randomly, so I brought them all."

I hugged her. "Thank you."

"He still thinks it's asthma?" She raised her eyebrows and cocked her head to the side, letting me know what she thought about that.

"I'll tell him," I promised.

"When?"

"Soon." I led her to the bedroom, took my meds, and stashed the bottles in the duffel bag full of my clothes that she'd brought me yesterday.

"My goodness. So Mr. California sleeps in a king-size bed, does he?" She ran her hand along the comforter.

My cheeks heated. "Yes."

"And is he?" She looked at me under her lashes.

"Is he what?" I asked.

"King-size?" She held her hands out an absurd distance from each other.

I smacked her shoulder with the back of my hand. "Morgan!"

"Well, inquiring minds want to know." She wiggled her eyebrows.

"I can't tell what I don't know." She beat me to the door, laying her body across the doorknob like a sacrifice.

"Lee. For the love of all that is right and holy, please tell me you're not holding out the goods." She clasped my hands. "You need to have sweaty, hot sex with that man so I can live vicariously, because my *gawd*!"

"I'll be sure to tell him that you vote yes." I stifled the smile as best I could, but it snuck out.

"And you vote no?" Her mouth dropped. "Because he can leave his boots under my bed any time."

I laughed. "Not that it's any of your business, but I'm considering."

"And what happened to your live-every-day blah, blah, blah?" she mocked me.

"It's kind of battling my don't-sleep-around inner angel right now."

"Well, tell that prudish wench to shut the hell up. You surely deserve a piece of that. Especially since the doc cleared it."

"Did you girls want breakfast? Or is there a pillow fight going on that I don't know about?" Jagger's voice came through the door. "I mean, I'm cool with that, but an invite would be nice."

Morgan sidestepped, and I opened the door to lift an eyebrow at him. Then those dimples made an appearance, and I just shook my head with a sigh. "Feed me?"

"Absolutely."

I introduced Morgan to Ember, and we all crowded the little table, devouring breakfast. I ate quickly, making sure I didn't get nauseous from taking my meds on an empty stomach.

"So, Masters, how was your trip home?" Jagger asked between mouthfuls.

"It was home," he responded, not looking up.

"No, no, way too many details, man." Jagger waved his hand at him. "Anything more and we might actually get to know a little about you."

Grayson grunted and polished off his orange juice.

"Did you make the reservations?" Josh asked.

"I did. We have three quads at noon," Jagger answered, and then cringed, peeking at me through one almost-shut eye. "Sorry, Paisley. You were asleep, and Josh asked if we wanted to go four-wheeling, so I answered for us."

My mind skipped over the list. Number twenty-nine: get back to nature. "Actually, that sounds perfect." Morgan raised an eyebrow at me. "It's not physically taxing," I mumbled at her.

"Mmm-hmm. Just be careful."

"Morgan, would you like to join us? I'm sure you could ride with Grayson," Jagger offered.

Grayson looked impassively at Morgan. I hadn't seen him look at a girl with anything but dispassion since I'd met him. Morgan wasn't an exception. "I'd be happy to take you." Even I could hear the manners talking.

"Oh, no, thank you. I'm more of an indoor girl." She checked her phone and squeaked. "Ooh! Speaking of which, it's pedicure time. Lee, you sure you would rather drive around in the woods than get pampered?"

Hmm. Hang out getting my feet painted, or press my body

against Jagger? "Yeah, I think I'll stick with Jagger."

"Your loss." She tossed me a wink. "Thank you for breakfast, boys," she called out, taking her leave.

"You ready for a ride?" Jagger asked.

Oh, was I.

"You know how to drive one of these?" Josh asked me as we sat parked on the outskirts of the jump park, waiting for Jagger and Ember to return from the restroom. We'd been riding a couple of hours already, and the feeling was finally returning to my rear.

"I spent every summer of my life in southern Alabama," I answered.

"So that's a yes?" He looked over at the jumps.

"Well, I certainly don't own my own riding gear and helmet just because I look cute in pink," I answered with a smile.

"Ouch." He slapped his hand over his heart. "You know, that southern accent of yours can be very deceiving. Your words might sound all cute, but they sure have a bite."

"Oh, just spend an afternoon with my mother."

He shook his head. "Not volunteering for that."

I laughed. "Me, either."

"Grayson?" he asked.

"Go ahead, I'll wait here," he answered, crossing his arms over his massive frame.

Josh motioned with his head toward the all-dirt track that filled the football field–size area in front of us, and I nodded, clicking my visor down.

We took off, tearing around the track. Josh was the faster one, but I kept up without being reckless. Controlling the quad gave me a heady sense of power. I might have been physically weak, but this machine was not. It could run where I couldn't, so

I let it.

I opened up the throttle, keeping pace with Josh, squeezing the seat with my thighs to make sure I stayed on when I took a turn a little fast. I didn't have as much weight to anchor me.

The wind whipped past me, an obscure noise outside my helmet. The hum of the motor and my breath pulsing within my helmet were all I registered. Josh pointed toward the jumps, and a slice of apprehension cut through me, prickling my skin. I'd never jumped before. This was a stupid idea, even for the sake of number thirty—take a leap of faith. Definitely on the doc's no-no list, but I felt great, and didn't I know my own body best?

Ignoring the sinking pit in my stomach, I gave him a thumbs-up anyway. Josh took the first jump, a small one, only a heartbeat or two in the air. I swallowed that lump in my throat and followed him, clenching my knees around the quad. I hit the jump, launching into the air, and concentrated on keeping my rear on the seat.

A heartbeat later, my body jarred, returning to earth. *I did it!* "Eeeee!" Josh gave me a thumbs-up and looked for another jump. We took that one, too, and the lump in my throat dissipated, leaving only the pride that I'd done it all by myself.

If there had been a country to rule, a kingdom to conquer nearby, I was pretty sure I could have done it. I felt utterly invincible. I glanced at my watch; my heart rate was within guidelines.

Josh aimed for the biggest jump there, a mammoth thing that I had no business attempting. But I was invincible, right? Living for just this moment. So why not?

He gassed it, taking the jump at dizzying speed. I followed so quickly behind him that I didn't bother to count his landing. I was already airborne. My heart hammered dangerously in my chest, my only companion in the absolute silence. Josh landed, nearly losing his grip on the quad. *Oh, no.*

My wheels struck the ground mercilessly. I hung on at impact, but physics kicked in. The quad bounced, recoiling, and my body with it, pulling with a force I couldn't combat. That heartbeat lasted an eternity. My fingers lost their grip on the handles when the rest of my body had already given up the fight.

This was going to hurt.

CHAPTER TWENTY-THREE

PAISLEY

14. Yes, please.

I watched the quad fly ahead of me with an odd curiosity, physics propelling it forward. The ground rushed up, and I remembered the basic rule of falling off—roll.

I didn't fight my momentum as my body crashed to earth, instead I worked with it, landing on the diagonal and rolling limply, trying not to tense.

The impact crushed my theory of invincibility. Pain erupted in every cell of my body. The world turned end over end, a bizarre kaleidoscope of red Alabama clay and blue sky. I closed my eyes and surrendered, simply waiting for it to be over. Too many flips later, I stopped.

Rocks dug into my back, and I couldn't breathe. No attempt to pull the air into my lungs helped. My chest heaved, desperate for oxygen.

"Paisley!" Jagger's hoarse cry cut through my panic.

He leaned over me and flicked open my visor. He looked

as crazed as I felt, his eyes wild. My mouth opened and closed, my lungs still screaming, and my heart anything but amused, slowing down dramatically.

"Damn it!" he yelled, unfastening my helmet. "Does your neck hurt? Your head?" he asked quickly.

I shook my head. If it hurt, I couldn't feel it. I just wanted to breathe. He nodded, locked the muscles in his jaw, and took my helmet off, keeping my body as in alignment as possible.

The cool air hit my face, but still nothing. His hands were steady as he ripped the zipper open on my jacket. His hands ran over my rib cage, feeling for anything out of place with gentle hands. "I think…" He looked into my eyes, cupping my cheek. "I think you just had the wind knocked out of you. Try to relax."

Relax? I forced myself to fall into the soft tone of his voice. First a small stream of air made its way into my lungs, then larger and larger breaths, until my ribs expanded to full capacity.

He dropped his forehead to mine and deflated next to me.

I took in breath after breath, smiling at the sky, and then I started laughing. Not just little giggles, either—oh, no, big, heaping laughs. Jagger pulled back, his mouth agape. Then I snorted and laughed harder for snorting.

"What the hell is so funny?"

I moved each of my legs and then my arms. "I'm fine," I said in between outbursts. "I just sailed off the quad, but I'm fit as a fiddle!" I couldn't help that I found the irony hilarious. I could survive an ATV accident without a scratch, but my heart would eventually fail.

God had a sense of humor.

"Oh my God, Paisley, are you okay?" Josh asked, leaning over.

I nodded, but couldn't stop my hysterical giggling.

"What the fuck were you thinking?" Jagger shouted at his friend, coming to his feet. "You want to pull insane stunts like that, you do it with your girlfriend, and sure as hell not mine!"

My laughter died.

"Man, I'm…" Josh looked down at me, the lines of his face tight and his eyebrows close together as he took in a shaky breath. "I'm so very sorry."

"What has gotten into you?" Ember shouted.

Josh closed his eyes and took a deep breath before turning to his girlfriend. "It looked like fun, and we'd already taken the other jumps."

I gripped Jagger's forearm for support when the blood rushed from my head from standing too quickly. "I followed him, it's not his fault." My heart pounded, enjoying the return of oxygen, but there was no breathlessness. I wasn't even tired today. "I'm okay. All ten fingers and toes accounted for."

"Well, I'm not!" Jagger yelled at me.

My gaze snapped to his, my mouth dropping open. "Jagger…"

"I don't want to hear it." He pointed to where my quad had landed, miraculously still on its wheels. "I'm taking you home. *Now.*"

I thought twice about growling at him, but sighed instead and headed for the quad. It wasn't his bossiness that made me, but the fear in his eyes when he'd peeled off my helmet.

We were on the trail before I could say good-bye to anyone. He hugged the curves but kept our speed moderate, safe. His muscles were tense under my hands, and his head would shake from side to side every minute or so, like he was arguing with himself.

He made an abrupt turn to the right, taking a lesser-worn trail to where it looked like a dead end. Then he pushed farther into the woods, stopping only when there wasn't a sound besides us. We sat there in silence for a moment, his chest heaving beneath my hands.

I unbuckled my helmet and placed it on the rack behind me as I slid off the seat. The fallen leaves beneath my feet didn't crunch. Southern humidity didn't really allow anything to crunch, but at least it would have been some kind of noise. "Go ahead."

He unsnapped his helmet and pulled it off violently. "Why?"

"Because you're fixing to blow up anyway." I crossed my arms over my chest.

His gaze remained unfixed ahead of him, his hands pushing in on the sides of his helmet like he could burst it in his lap. "That. Was. Stupid." He ground out each word like it had been torn from his throat.

"I know." I settled in for the lecture.

He swiveled his head, finally looking at me. "Do you?" he asked in a whisper. "Do you know how easily you could have been…" He blanched. "God, Paisley!"

My feet moved before I could stop myself, and I reached for him, cupping his face with my hands. "I'm okay," I whispered. "I'm fit as a fiddle." My smile was forced but there.

"Fucking luck, that's all that was." He shook his head. "You don't get it. That moment I saw you fall, when you hit the ground? Everything in me just stopped, like my heart couldn't beat if yours didn't."

I sucked in a breath, tears stinging my eyes. "Don't say that."

"I've been on my own for six years, Paisley. I've walked away from everyone I've ever cared about, basically killed off my own heart, and still none of that prepared me for the instant I thought I lost you. Nothing in my life prepared me for how much I would love you."

The words hung between us, sweetening the taste of the air on my tongue, calming the beat of my heart, and igniting a deeper fire than I ever thought possible. "You love me?"

"You can't do something like that again—"

"You love me." A myriad of emotions crashed through me with the subtlety of a tornado. Elation. Fear. Hope. Devastation. Everything I wanted and everything I was terrified to lose sat in front of me.

"—because I can't take it, and if that makes me a—"

I stopped his words with my mouth, kissing every feeling into him that I couldn't say. His lips were warm, soft, and open. I took advantage, running my tongue along his teeth, darting in to slide along the stud in his tongue.

His shock became a groan. His hands went to my bottom, easily lifting me so that I straddled his lap, facing him on the quad. I arched into him, my breasts pressing against his chest, and my fingers threaded through his hair.

He tilted my head to the side and took control, devouring me one kiss, one nibble at a time, driving me slowly crazy. He gave just enough to keep a steady hum of energy coursing through me, the tingles in my lips turning to a steady pulse between my thighs. I'd push for more, and he'd pull away, maddening me. Finally, he drew my lower lip out with a soft bite. A noise escaped me that sounded suspiciously like a whimper.

His eyes darkened, and all playfulness evaporated as he took my mouth again, this time holding nothing back. His lips slanted over mine, kissing me deep, thrusting his tongue in a hypnotizing rhythm, and I lost myself in the sensations I only felt with him. His hands moved up my sides, pausing questioningly over my breasts. I pushed them into his waiting hands, and we both moaned.

"Skin. I need you to touch me," I murmured against his lips.

His mouth never left mine as the zipper slid down, revealing my fitted V-neck underneath. The first press of his hands wasn't enough for either of us. The cool air hit my stomach as he lifted my shirt over my breasts, leaving my jacket on for the chill. Thank heavens for front-clasp bras—one snap and he was finally holding bare skin. Between the temperature and his hands, my nipples hardened. His fingers ghosted across them, inflaming the little nerve endings, and I gasped.

"Perfect." He rolled my nipples between his thumb and forefinger.

"Jagger," I shamelessly begged.

"What do you want?"

The hunger I saw in his eyes sent a delicious shiver down my skin. I'd awoken something in him I hadn't seen yet, and I wanted it.

"Paisley, what do you want?" His gaze dropped to my breasts in his hands, and I didn't miss his indrawn breath, or his erection growing where my thighs rested just over his.

"Your mouth," I answered, refusing to be embarrassed. The heat that stung my cheeks told me I might have not been successful.

He groaned, like my words had stroked him. A second later, he cupped my butt, lifting me for access. At the first touch of his lips to my skin, I trembled. He dusted kisses at the tops of my breasts, the sides, and underneath, leaving no inch of skin untouched. I slipped my hands under his jacket, indulging in the play of his muscles under his shirt as I braced myself on his shoulders. "Jagger." His name was a whispered plea.

Finally, he sucked one of my nipples into his mouth, his moan sending vibrations through me like lightning. He alternated deep pulls and gentle laves of his tongue, savoring one breast, then the other. I cried out when he gently used his teeth, and his grip tightened, holding me up when my arms buckled from the unexpected pleasure.

He lowered me slowly, my extra-sensitive skin dragging along his shirt, and kissed me until I was seated again. I couldn't still the movement of my hips against him, desperate for the friction between my thighs. "We should head back," he whispered, his tone weak.

"We should stay a little longer," I suggested, my fingers dipping under his shirt to explore the lines of abs I'd been drooling over since that first day. Did he have *any* fat on him? Warm, velvet skin draped over cords of muscle, giving me a new understanding of "washboard." His eyes closed when I traced the little lines, lifting his shirt the same way he did mine. My mouth went dry, and my tongue ached to taste every inch, follow every tattoo. "I'm never going to get over seeing you like this, getting to actually touch you," I whispered more to myself than him.

He pressed one of my hands over his heartbeat. "Anything I am is yours. Please, touch, because there's no way I'm keeping my hands off you."

I kissed him, trapping our hands between us. My hips rolled, grinding over his, and he hissed. His arm banded around my back, pulling me flush against him. Skin on skin set a fire running through my veins, burning a path through me that led directly to my core. The further I slipped into the haze of desire, the less inhibited I became. I pushed him onto his elbows, but he didn't complain as I climbed over him, tasted the skin of his chest and flicked my tongue across his nipples. His moan reverberated through his chest and sent the headiest wave of power through me.

His fingers deftly undid the braids in my hair and then tangled in it, clenching as I traced the tattoo that ran across his lower stomach, just above the tantalizing line of his jeans. "Paisley." His voice was hoarse. How far could I push him until he snapped? Did I want to find out? *Yes.*

I ran my fingers along his waistband, the black of his boxers peeking just above. My breath hitched, but it was excitement, not apprehension, that had me biting my lower lip. I flicked the button of his jeans open and pulled the zipper down. He jerked, but I didn't look up. He was hard, hot, and straining to escape his boxer briefs. My belly clenched, wanting nothing more than to have him inside me, so deep that I branded him. Mine.

My hand squeezed him gently through the material, and I was rewarded with a very guttural "Fuck," drawn out the length of his breath. "Maybe now isn't—"

I squeezed again, running my thumb along his shaft until

the head of his erection slipped free of his boxers. My fingers swirled around his tip once, twice, and then I replaced them with my tongue. "Holy shit!" His grip tightened in my hair, and I met his shocked, incredibly turned-on stare as I sucked just the head into my mouth, tasting a hint of salt as I explored the ridge with my tongue and lips.

With a growl, he lifted me off him and sat up in one smooth motion. His eyes were wild now with barely controlled lust—the same that had ahold of me.

"No?" I asked with a coy shake of my head.

"No," he barked. His eyes closed. "I mean, yes, *God, yes*, but not this time." My disappointment was short-lived as his fingers gripped a hip and the base of my neck, and he pulled me in for a scorching kiss. "I can't wait to try everything with you," he whispered in my ear. He licked and sucked his way along my neck. "But right now I want to kiss your skin, memorize the way you smell, the way you feel under my hands." *Yes, please.* He popped the top button free on my jeans. My eyes flew open, meeting his. He moved his hand slowly, watching me for the first sign of resistance, the first hint of "no."

I didn't even think it.

Thank goodness I'd worn a respectable pair of black lace panties, because his hand was in them. My thoughts ceased when his middle finger stroked down across my clit. I called out his name, and my hips bucked in response. He slipped lower, to where I opened for him and let loose a ragged sigh.

"Fuck, you're wet."

I whimpered and rocked toward him, hoping he'd continue. I'd never felt this urgency before, this burning need.

"Have you touched yourself before, Paisley?"

I waited a few seconds and nodded, my cheek scraping the stubble on his jaw. We'd agreed, no lies. That didn't mean I wanted to talk about it, though. As if in reward, his fingers stroked me, putting firm pressure on that sweet little bundle of nerves, and I cried out, the sound carrying through the woods.

"Is that the only way you've ever gotten off?"

I hesitated, and then nodded.

"What I want," he whispered against my lips, "is to feel you come around my fingers. I want to know how tight you are when you get there, so I can fantasize about how you'll feel when I finally get to be inside you."

His words were the dirtiest thing I'd ever heard, and *mercy*, I liked it. "Please," I whispered.

He took control of my mouth as he stroked through my folds, keeping a rhythm in both that had me keening. I thrust my hips against his hand, shamelessly seeking more contact. One of his hands lifted me under my butt, pulling my thighs on top of his. Then he delved deeper, the angle allowing him to insert a finger inside me.

I gasped, and he swallowed the sound. He dragged that finger along my inner walls, listening for my reaction, waiting for it to hitch. When it did, he withdrew it, only to thrust two inside. "Jagger!"

He took each of my cries and then pressed the heel of his hand against my clit while he worked me with his fingers, curling them to hit a spot that had me moaning with each thrust, unable to keep quiet.

Every sensation in my body concentrated where his fingers were, locking my muscles, building and intensifying until I wanted to scream from the sweet tension. His tongue, his lips, his fingers...so many sensations rolled into one general feeling of sheer bliss.

"Let me feel you come, Paisley," he begged, and I was powerless against him. He thrust his fingers inside me once more, meeting me as I rocked my hips into him, and when he rubbed the heel of his hand against me with the perfect pressure and whispered, "I love you," I shattered, clenching around his fingers.

I screamed his name, my hips shamelessly bucking as my world narrowed to Jagger. He kissed my breath from me, like he could inhale my orgasm, and stroked the aftershocks from my body with deft, skilled fingers. I tightened around him when another wave hit, and he groaned.

"Amazing," he said, his eyes raking over me. He withdrew his fingers and snapped my jeans, trembling slightly. "You're so beautiful."

I flushed at his praise and rolled my thumb over his exposed erection. He groaned and took hold of my wrist, pulling me away. "You sure?" I asked him. "I don't want to leave you hurting."

His grin was enough to make me think about unbuttoning my jeans. "God, Paisley. You can't…I'm not going to be able to control myself. I'll be buried deep inside you faster than you can blink, and I know you're not ready for that. Plus, selfishly, I'd like to not be on an ATV our first time."

I nearly shook from his words, for the first time thinking to check my heart monitor. My pulse was elevated, just outside desired parameters, but I felt great. What would sex with Jagger do to it? Already I'd felt more in these few moments than I ever had before.

We righted our clothes, and he kissed me like a starving man just before I put my helmet on. "Let's go home," I said, smiling at him.

"Yeah, let's," he agreed.

I climbed behind him, trying not to jump when the vibrations from the four-wheeler rubbed my overly sensitized flesh. Jagger turned us around, and we headed toward the path.

I knew I was only supposed to check each block off the list once, but mercy, number fourteen deserved further exploration.

CHAPTER TWENTY-FOUR

*Even now, I bet you're trying to think of a way to
punish me, but the truth is, I've lived in hell for so long
that there's nothing worse you could do.*

The seconds ticking by on the wall clock were the only
sound in Major Davidson's office the next day as Carter
and I both stood at attention, facing his empty desk. Block
leave was over; it was time for the hammer to drop.

"Bateman," Carter started, his tone remorseful.

"Don't," I snapped.

The door opened, and Major Davidson walked in, setting
his coffee down. "Lieutenants."

"Sir," we responded in time.

I stared at the plaque just above his head until he said, "At
ease." We both visibly relaxed. "Well, gentlemen, I don't think
we really need to rehash the events from New Year's Eve, since
I saw the whole thing."

Here comes the axe.

"What do you have to say for yourself, Bateman?"

"No excuse, sir."

Carter's head snapped in my direction, but I still ignored him. I'd take what was coming. I deserved it.

"Carter?" Davidson asked, his tone tight.

"No excuse, sir."

Davidson pinched the bridge of his nose and mumbled something that sounded like, "It's too early for this shit." He took a deep breath, his gaze flickering between us. "Well, what the hell were you thinking?" We glanced at each other, then back to Davidson. "Somebody answer."

"So, we *are* going to rehash New Year's Eve?" I asked, clarifying.

"For the love of God, just explain why it is you two idiots decided that beating the crap out of each other during a formal gathering at General Donovan's house would be acceptable?"

"He started it," Cater grumbled.

Are you fucking serious? "I did." They both looked at me like I'd lost my mind. "Well, I did. I'm not the one who got in the last sucker punch, but I initiated it."

Carter looked at the floor momentarily before lifting his head. "Is this about the polar bear, or Miss Donovan?"

"Both," we answered simultaneously.

"The only reason your asses aren't out on your...asses is because General Donovan feels some sort of responsibility, seeing as it's his daughter."

A swift sense of relief swept over me. I wasn't getting kicked out. Then again, neither was Carter.

"In light of what's happened, I think we need to reassign you as stick buddies." He started flipping through a file on his desk.

"Sir?" Carter spoke up, no doubt thrilled. Major Davison raised his eyebrows at him, and Carter rushed ahead. "I'd like to keep Bateman. He's the second best in the class and pushes me, sir."

"Second best, my ass," I snapped without thinking.

"You two are going to give me ulcers," Davidson mumbled.

I couldn't deny Carter's logic. Flying with him drove me to fly perfectly and answer every question right, because if I got it wrong, I knew he'd be on my heels with the correct one, ready to show me up at the earliest opportunity. "He's right," I spoke slowly.

Davidson's eyes narrowed. "You're not getting a second chance at this. If you can't make this work, I'm done with both of you. Are you sure?"

"I'm sure," I answered.

"Definitely, sir," Carter chimed in.

He shook his head, mumbled something about us being more difficult than toddlers, and excused us. We both put on our covers as we walked out onto the flight line, the Alabama sun warding off the January chill.

"What happened?" Josh asked, jogging over with Grayson.

"We're still in," Carter answered.

"I didn't ask you," Josh snapped.

Carter scoffed. "Jesus. What the hell is it with you guys? I'm still your class leader, one of the only other lieutenants in our class, and you still can't—"

"Can't what?" Josh interrupted. "Respect someone who has zero sense of loyalty? You wouldn't last a day in a real platoon."

"And what the hell would you know about it?" Carter shot back. "I've spent the last four years of my life dedicating myself to the military."

Josh shook his head. "Un-fucking-believable." He flipped Carter off and headed to his assigned helicopter.

"What?" Carter asked.

"He's already got a tour in Afghanistan and a Purple Heart, you dipshit," Grayson answered. I wasn't sure what caught me more off guard, Carter having no clue about Josh, or Grayson swearing.

Carter tensed. "Watch your language." Apparently for

Carter, it was the swearing.

"Or what?" he added, his massive arms folded across his chest. Grayson wasn't someone I'd ever want to tangle with, not just because of his size—the guy was impossible to get a read on. "You'll knock your pretty little ring on the table and act like that entitles you to lead us?"

"It does!"

Grayson laughed, sending my holy-shit meter off the charts. "Get over yourself, Carter. You have a West Point education—good for you. But our date of rank is exactly the same, and just because my ring is from the Citadel doesn't make you any more fucking special."

Carter's jaw dropped, and I found mine in the same state. "Man, you went to the Citadel?" I asked. Holy shit, I really knew next to nothing about him.

Grayson shrugged his shoulders at me with a definite hint of humor in his eyes, then turned to follow Josh. "Want to know what's going to kill you now, Carter?"

"You're probably going to tell me," Carter spat back.

"Wondering which one of us they really asked to be class leader first," he called over his shoulder.

Carter deflated like Grayson had stuck a pin in him, and I whistled low. "Damn."

"Get to the aircraft, Bateman. Let's get this run-up started," Carter said.

I removed the engine cover and shook my head at the REMOVE BEFORE FLIGHT flags that marked it. *Duh*. Carter was quiet as we checked off procedures and volunteered to let me fly first—something he never did.

As I took off from the airfield, Carter in the backseat, our instructor fired out an easy 5&9 question on fuel limitations. "Carter?" he prompted when he didn't offer a response.

For the first time since I'd met him, Carter got the answer wrong.

...

Shit. I was going to be late for dinner with Paisley. I pulled into my drive, hitting my brakes so hard that my bag slid off the passenger seat and hit the floorboards. I killed the ignition, grabbed the bag, and made it through the front door in record time, even managing to toss Mrs. King a wave as she made an offhanded comment on the landscaping. Again.

Lady, it's February. Hit me up in April, for crying out loud.

"What's on fire?" Grayson asked from the kitchen as I kicked the door shut.

"I'm wicked late," I yelled on the way to my room. I dropped my helmet bag by my dresser and stripped out of my uniform before throwing open my closet doors. I grabbed the first collared shirt I saw but paused when I saw Paisley's sweatshirt hanging next to it.

A wide smile spread across my face, and I stroked my fingers down the sleeve. I liked seeing her stuff there next to mine. The girl was perpetually cold, and it seemed easiest for her to keep a few things here. Like a few sets of clothing, a toothbrush, a hairbrush...that kind of thing. Josh had recommended giving her a drawer or something, but that seemed official, and a little over a month into a relationship wasn't exactly "official" territory. Then again, what the hell did I know? I'd never been in a relationship before, but I liked it.

This was the happiest I ever remembered being. I was staying in flight school, still in the race for top of the OML, and I was so in love with Paisley that my heart threatened to jump ship when I thought about her.

Life was pretty damn perfect.

I dressed quickly and shoved my wallet into my pocket as I headed down the hallway.

"You out?" Grayson asked from the dining room, his books

covering the table.

"Yeah. You doing okay?"

He nodded. "Exams are killing me, but I'll push through."

"Thank God." I leaned on the table and saw his notes. He gave me a what-the-hell look, and I laughed. "Man, I've seen you fly. If you had my photographic memory, you'd be kicking my ass."

He grunted. "Yeah, well, I don't, so I get to study." He dismissed me, delving into the books.

"Is your family coming next Monday for Family Day?"

He didn't look up. "Just to watch me fly the training helicopter? No. They can't afford to make the trip twice. They'll come down when I graduate. Yours?"

"Fuck no," I replied instantly.

He raised his eyebrows at me, looking up. "Do you...want to talk about it?" he asked slowly.

I laughed. He looked like he was in physical pain. "No, and the answer will always be no, I promise."

"Right on." He dropped his focus to his work. "Have a good time with Paisley. You lucked out there."

I caught the longing that snuck into his tone. "Is there someone at home for you?" I asked. "You go home every chance you get, but you don't really say anything."

His jaw flexed, and the grip on his pen tightened. "Want to talk about your family?"

"No," I repeated. He looked up, silent, and I got the message. His love life was like pretty much everything else for this guy—a no-fly zone.

"Good talk." I waved, shaking my head as my cell phone rang. Paisley. I smiled as I answered. "Hey, Little Bird, I'm on my way to you."

"Hi. I'm sorry to call you so late, but I'm actually not there."

"Are you okay?" Panic squeezed my heart. "Are you having an attack?"

"I'm in Birmingham, but I'm okay. Some routine tests ran late, and the doc wants to run some overnight."

"I'm coming," I answered, headed for my room.

"Don't you dare! It's three hours away, and you have class tomorrow."

I pulled down my duffel bag and started throwing enough clothes in it for a couple days, tossing her sweatshirt in for good measure. She'd want it if she had to be stuck there. "I'm coming, Paisley."

"Seriously, Jagger. You wouldn't get here until nine thirty, and that's not counting traffic. They're releasing me in the morning."

"You don't want me there?" Holy shit. I was going to be sick.

"Of course I do." Her voice was soft. "I just don't want you driving this late when you won't be able to see me anyway. Visiting hours are over at ten, and Morgan is already pushing it." *She had Morgan take her, not me.*

"I don't like you being in the hospital and not getting to see you." I swallowed; the idea tasted like sand in my mouth.

"Me, either, I promise. Tell you what. If they keep me another day, will you come?" she asked.

I sighed, squeezing my eyes shut. "Of course. I'll leave as soon as you tell me I can."

"Thank you," she whispered. "I'm so sorry about dinner. I should have called you earlier. I just didn't realize how late it'd gotten."

"Little Bird, a date is the least of my worries. Are you really feeling okay?"

"Yeah. I actually feel great, which I think is why he likes to poke at me. Now you'd better study."

"I don't need to study." I laughed.

"Go read your books, Jagger. I'm not going to be the reason you don't get an Apache."

"Ooh, you're sexy when you're all stern." And sexy when she

laughed, and read a book, and even fucking slept.

"Don't you start." A new set of voices came in through the background. "Jagger, the nurse is here. I have to call you back."

"Okay. I love you. Let me know what you need." I paused, leaving that door open, again.

"I will. Thank you, honey." She hung up without walking through it. Again.

It had been a month since I told her I was in love with her, and she hadn't said it back. I tried not to let it bother me, but there was this little nagging voice in my head that beat the shit out of my self-confidence every time she left my declaration hanging there solo.

It also kept me from sleeping with her. She'd been putting out signals that she was more than ready, but apparently I was the romantic one in this relationship. I wanted the words before the deed. Probably because I'd never had them.

My phone rang again, and I smiled, answering without looking. "Hey," I answered. "Change your mind?"

"Jagger?"

I checked the caller ID. It was Paul. "Hey, man, what's going on?"

"I've found her."

Anna.

My perfect life had morphed into fucked up in ten minutes.

CHAPTER TWENTY-FIVE

JAGGER

*God, she was worth it the whole time, and she's worth
it now. Let me make myself clear: I choose her over
you, and I always will.*

The sky over Chicago was black as the literal midnight it was.
I skipped baggage claim and instead found Paul standing
near the exit. Easily a head taller than everyone around him
and built like a linebacker, he was easy to spot. He shook my
hand and gave me a North Face coat, tags attached. This wasn't
our first go-round.

"You ready?" he asked, taking my duffel bag and lifting it
over one of his massive shoulders. Paul was only ten years older
than I was, and I'd known him just as long.

"As ready as I ever am." He led the way out to his Range
Rover, and I climbed into the passenger seat, putting my
backpack at my feet.

He threw my duffel bag in the back and took the driver's
side, pulling out of the airport as I buckled my seat belt. "Did

you bring it?"

I patted the bag between my feet. "Five grand junkie-finder fee, in cash."

He whistled. "Is it traceable?"

"Nope. I earned it all."

"Good. Buying the house was risky." He cut his eyes sideways at me.

"I'm not going to spend my life scared," I fired back.

He cracked a smile. "Good."

I rubbed my hands over my face, trying to wake up. He handed me a Red Bull from his cooler compartment, and I accepted gratefully.

"So you AWOL or something?"

I shook my head, swallowing the energy drink. "Emergency leave." Major Davidson had been anything but happy when I'd called him on a Thursday night, but he'd met with me. One look at my face and he'd signed the leave form. I had a week. Just enough time to get her taken care of.

Just enough time to royally fuck myself in class. I'd take a hit on every assignment, pretty much knocking myself out of first place.

I pushed flight school out of my head. It was thousands of miles and a world—a life—away. That wasn't even who I was right now. No, right now I was nothing outside of Anna. *Please let this be her.* We pulled into a neighborhood I only wanted to see from the air. "Damn," I muttered, taking in the broken streetlights and rusted-out cars with busted windows.

"Oh, yeah. It's a gem," Paul answered. "Sometimes working for you makes me wish I'd just stayed your bodyguard. At least we didn't end up in places like this."

"Now if we could only keep her out of them."

"That's my prayer," he answered.

I gritted my teeth against my usual answer, that in order for a prayer to work, someone had to be listening.

He parked the SUV outside a dilapidated house that definitely wasn't setting the high end of market value around here. "Ready?"

Paul took the small leather pouch from me, slipping it inside his jacket as I zipped mine up. The Chicago air froze the snot in my nose as we walked to the front door. I hated this part, and it didn't disappoint. My stomach clenched as Paul knocked on the torn screen door.

The wooden door swung open. "Can I help you?" a voice slurred from inside.

I sidestepped him to get a look, and cringed. The guy was rail thin and pale, wearing dirty jeans and a ragged henley, but it was his face that jarred me. His cheekbones protruded, and there were open sores along his cracked lips and up one side of his face. "Are you Steve?" I asked.

"You the guy looking for Anna?" He blinked his droopy eye slowly.

"Yes." My pulse pounded.

"You got the money?"

I nodded, but Paul answered. "You get it when we get her."

He rocked on his heels a couple of times, his eyes darting between us. "Swear you aren't cops?"

"We're not fucking cops!" I snapped. Each second stripped a little more of my civility away, but spooking this guy was detrimental to the goal. "We brought you a nice little present for finding Anna, that's all."

He looked between us again and then opened the screen door, backing away as we walked inside. The living room was empty except for a threadbare couch, the three people passed out on it, and a coffee table cluttered with contents I didn't want to examine too closely.

Paul took up position behind me as I followed Steve through a small hallway to a bedroom. He opened the door and flicked the light switch on and off a few times before muttering,

"Damn light." Instead he pulled the string inside the open closet, lighting the room enough to see the huddled mass in the corner, the whiskey-colored hair I knew so well.

"Anna."

The carpet felt spongy beneath my feet as I stumbled toward the mattress and fell to my knees next to her. Her hair was a stringy, limp mass as I brushed it from her face. It had been a year since we'd done this last, and though it showed, she was still Anna. Her Van Morrison–worthy brown eyes were open, unfocused, but her breathing was steady. "I'm here, Anna, I'm here."

"Do I get the money?" Steve asked, bobbing unsteadily in my peripheral vision.

I nodded, keeping my eyes locked onto Anna. A roach scurried out from the coarse blanket she was under, and I choked back vomit. "Shit!" I ripped the blanket from her and flung it across the room. Her emaciated frame was covered in a barely there pink tank top and a pair of black sweat pants, and her arm—fuck, her arm had a tourniquet banded just above her elbow. I snapped it apart and skimmed my thumb over the track marks that marred her arm. How the hell did she have any usable veins left? "Get my bag," I ordered Paul—how easily my voice reverted to that tone.

"You gonna take her?" Steve asked, fingering through the money in the package.

"Yes." I couldn't keep my hands off her face, stroking her hair, feeling the steady thrum of her pulse beneath my fingers.

"Bag," Paul said, putting my duffel next to me on the floor. I took out a pair of my socks and put them on her bare feet, cursing that I hadn't thought to bring her anything. I should be better at this by now.

I rummaged through the bag for a shirt and grabbed a fist full of maroon—Paisley's zip-up hoodie. I lifted it to my nose, closed my eyes, and breathed her scent in, clinging to the knowledge that I had someone, something that hadn't been tainted by this. *Paisley.* How would someone as good, as sweet as she was, come close to understanding this?

I put Anna's arms through the sleeves like a child and zipped it up, covering her. Next, I put my own jacket on her, and then lifted her into my arms. She was sickeningly light. "Let's get you out of here."

"Jag?" she murmured, her glazed eyes focusing on mine for just that second.

Every muscle in my face tensed to keep the tears at bay. I was not going to break down, not when there was something to be done. "I'm here. I told you I would come."

A smile ghosted her lips. "How do you just get prettier? That isn't fair."

I pressed my lips to her forehead.

"My Jagger." Her head rolled onto my shoulder, and her eyes closed.

I tightened my hold on her and walked out of the decrepit house.

"Just you and me. Promise?" Her voice drifted off.

"Always, Anna. You and me." I secured her in the backseat of the Range Rover. At least no one had stripped it while we were inside.

I closed Anna's door and leaned on the frame of the car, the chill of the metal biting through my shirt faster than the frigid air. I welcomed it, the slight bite that grounded me in this moment, reminding me that I was really here. I'd found her.

This time.

A primal sound ripped from my throat and my fists shook, aching to destroy something. I shoved my hands into my jeans pockets to keep them contained, and my fingers skimmed across Paisley's nickel. I'd promised her I'd control my temper, and I owed it to her. My head slammed against the car, and I stayed there a minute or two, trying to process it. My success at finding Anna. My failure for letting her fall as far as she had. The relief. The resignation that this was never going to end until she chose it for herself.

The engine roared to life, jarring me from my pity party. I sucked in a glacial breath and let it numb me from the inside out. Then I got in the car, ready to take the other half of my soul to rehab. Again.

"You look like shit," Paul said, handing me a cup of coffee. It was the only drug allowed in this place.

"Thanks." I rubbed my free hand across my face and took a drink, welcoming the caffeine, and dropped the 5&9s into my bag. Study time over.

"Anything yet?" He looked at Anna asleep in the hospital bed. The bed was the only hint that this room wasn't in an immaculately decorated house.

"Not since the worst of the withdrawals passed."

"Worse than last time?" He stretched out in the armchair parallel to mine and kicked his feet up on the coffee table.

"Five days." I kept my voice flat, but Paul knew. He'd been with me since this started, since before, really. He'd watched her slow decent into hell just like I had, both of us powerless to keep her from poisoning herself.

"Favorite line?" he asked, trying to bring our usual, morbid levity into the situation.

"This time, hmm…" I thought hard. "Definitely the *I hate you*s, but those are nothing new. But her telling the nurse she was going to use the stethoscope to slingshot her ass back to the hippie commune she apparently was born in was nice."

"Ah, she's not digging the holistic approach?"

"That's a negative. Then again, I'm not sure I'm down with the lack of…everything, either. I've been cut off from civilization for the last six days." They confiscated every cell phone at the entrance, and there were no landlines in the building except the ones for emergencies. No internet, no TV, no game systems. But there was a shit ton of yoga, if that was your thing.

"Why don't you go out past the property line and make a call?"

I shook my head, concentrating on the rise and fall of Anna's chest. "I promised her I wouldn't leave. If I'm not here when she wakes up, we've got no chance of keeping her here. As it is, I have one more day before I have to get home to Rucker." Home to Paisley.

She was going to kill me, and I deserved it. I hadn't spoken to her since Friday night, and that had been a hurried message on her voice mail that I had an emergency out of town and I'd call her when I could. Talking to her was more crucial than air, but at this point I'd screwed up so royally that I had to do it in person. I'd been consumed with one thought—*get to Anna*—and everything else had faded until I had her here, admitted.

Anna was my Achilles' heel, and I was going to have to beg Paisley to understand once I could explain it to her. *Now just figure out how the hell to do that.* I'd run through just about every scenario possible, every way to tell her, to crack the window into my past and help her absorb that sometimes it bled, hemorrhaged, really, into my present.

"Just call. It will only take a few minutes, and I can stay with her." He saw me hesitate. "Jagger, that's your real life in Alabama. This isn't you anymore, and I couldn't be prouder of what you've done in every aspect of your life. Now get to a damn phone and call your girl."

The need to hear Paisley's voice was a physical ache that affected every limb, every finger, even my tongue. I flicked the stud over my teeth and rethought my whole "in person" position. Maybe I just needed to talk to her, to remember my other life, and she was waiting for me. Fuck it. I wanted my cell phone, a quiet room, and a sweet little southern accent in my ear. I stood and made it to the door handle before Anna stirred.

"Jag?"

I deflated like a popped balloon and plastered a smile on my face before I turned around. "Hey."

Paul excused himself as Anna sat up, blinking the sleep out of her eyes. She was still gaunt, even worse after going through withdrawals, but she was clean. Her hair was pulled into a messy knot at the top of her head, and her T-shirt hung too large on her frame, making her seem younger than she was. "Are you leaving?" The panic that radiated from her eyes stopped me dead in my tracks.

"No," I answered, sitting next to her on the bed. I cupped her cheek in my hand, running my thumb along her pocked skin. It didn't matter what she'd done to herself; she was permanently sixteen to me, more vibrant than any girl or woman I knew or had known since. I chose to believe she was there, under the sagging skin and open sores, still my Anna, just a little worn at the edges. "I do have to go home tomorrow," I said softly.

"I'm your home," she protested in a soft whine. "You always say I'm your home."

"I know, and you are. But I'm in flight school. If I stay any longer, they'll set me back a class, or worse, I'll fail out." I picked up her hand and gently squeezed her bony fingers. "I don't have a choice."

Her mouth pursed. "You always have a choice. You could stay. We could get an apartment. I know I could stay clean if you would just stay with me." Her eyes turned to liquid pools, a trick she'd learned early on got to me.

I closed my eyes and took a steadying breath. "We've tried that, Anna. I just end up down the rabbit hole with you, and I'm done. You need to get clean here. There's no time limit, you're paid for as long as you need to stay, but we can't keep doing this."

"Is it because of her?" she asked softly.

My stomach clenched. "Her?"

"The girl with the sweatshirt. The one you put me in? It's a girl's hoodie, and it smells sweet. Have you…found someone?"

Our eyes locked, and I couldn't lie. "Yes, but she's not why I can't stay. I'm in flight school. You know how much that means to me, what I've given up to do this."

"You've never chosen another girl over me." Her voice dropped to a whisper, her eyes losing their focus.

I lifted her chin. "I'm still not. This isn't a competition, Anna."

"Does she know about me?"

I shook my head. "Not yet."

She let out a pitiful laugh. "I wouldn't want to tell her, either. I'm a drug addict, right? A high-school-dropout embarrassment that you waste your time and love on and who just won't go away."

"That's not true. I love you, Anna. Nothing is ever going to change that."

"But she is!" she shouted, drawing her knees to her chest. "You said you'd never love another girl, that I was the other half of your soul. You promised!" Her hands ripped into her hair, and I drew them away gently.

"In all fairness, I think we were nine when I promised that."

She pouted, the look the closest to my Anna as I'd gotten in almost seven years. "It still holds."

A smile spread across my face. "You look like such an imp when you do that. Stop being a pain in the ass. I love you. I will always love you. There is no force on earth, no other woman in the universe who will replace you. Ever. But I can't stay here with you. I'm not what you need right now."

"I hate you," she whispered.

It stung but didn't cripple, not like it usually did. "Yeah, well, I hate me, too. I'm so sorry. I'm sorry I didn't see what you were doing until you were so far gone. I'm sorry about the late-night parties, and the girls, and making you feel like you didn't have any other recourse." My throat threatened to close, but I pushed through, needing to say it. "I'm sorry you felt abandoned, but I can promise that you never were, and you never will be. If I could go back..."

She narrowed her eyes. "You'd what? Stop me before it started? Get me through rehab successfully that first time? Or maybe just before I whored myself out when I ran out of money?"

Nausea struck hard, nearly doubling me over. I blocked out the images she put in my head, so I could breathe. "I would have stopped it all, been whatever you needed. I'm sorry I was young, and stupid, and didn't realize until it was too late. And as for money, you know I'll give you whatever you need. Please—" My voice broke. "Anna, don't do that. You're worth so much more than that, and it's dangerous. Let me take care of you."

"Not with *his* money. I'd rather take my clothes off than take his money." Her eyes sparked with life, and though I wanted to soothe her, I was just as happy to see her passionate about something, even if it was hatred.

There was a knock at the door. "Come in," I said as the heavyset nurse entered.

"Anna Bateman?" she asked. Anna's eyes widened before she nodded. The nurse verified the name on her bracelet with the chart and then switched her IV bag. "I'll be around to check your vitals in a little bit."

"Thank you," I said, since Anna's manners wouldn't.

The nurse nodded and slipped out.

"You told them my last name was Bateman?" She smiled.

"Yeah, it was less risky than telling them your real one."

"I like being a Bateman. I'll have to think about that. Tell you what. I'll keep it if you agree to stay."

"I can't stay! I have a life in Alabama, and you need to get clean and stay there for once."

"Maybe I don't want to! Did it ever occur to you that I'm fine? That I'm happy the way I am without you trying to fix me?" Tears welled in her eyes and ran down her cheeks. I closed my eyes against the assault. Nothing had ever affected me like her tears did. "I'm never going to be okay. I'm a lost cause, so I don't understand why you just won't lose me, too!"

I stood, concentrating on keeping my knees steady. "You are not lost! I will always search for you. I will always pull you back. I will always find you!" My skin felt tight, dry as I rubbed my face in my hands. "Fuck, Anna! You have to help. You have to take one damned step on your own, because I can't keep walking for us both. I can't keep you clean. You have to do that yourself—want that for yourself."

"Stay. Please?" she begged. "Don't leave me."

For a second, we were sixteen again, wrapped around each other, clinging to the only sure thing we'd always had while our world was shredded in front of us. That sixteen-year-old boy should have stayed, should have been what she needed. But he hadn't, and the twenty-three-year-old man who stood in his place couldn't. Not when I knew that staying with her would mean forsaking everything I'd worked for—my independence, my career, my general sanity. "I can't." My hand rested on the doorknob. "I have a training bubble after selection next month." *If they don't kick me out for failing after missing six fucking days.* "I'll come then, I promise, but I can't stay. Not now."

"I can't do this without you," she whispered.

I rested my forehead on the door frame and held off the guilt that lured me to stay here. Then I pictured Paisley. Her smile, her kiss, the way she surrounded me with acceptance and inflamed every one of my senses while soothing me at the same time. "You can't do this with me, Anna. I can't be your crutch, not anymore. I've gotten you here. I've given you every tool you need, but we've been doing this dance for seven years, and it's time for you to stand."

"You're leaving me...for her. C to G, Jagger! You swore!"

I lifted the short sleeve of my T-shirt to expose the tattoo on my right arm and pointed to the lettering in the center. "C to G. I'm here! I mean it. But I can't do this for you. You have to do it yourself. I can't get clean for you."

"You're choosing her over me!" she cried out.

I opened the door to the hallway and didn't turn back around. "No, I chose you when I came instead of staying where she might have needed me." A mistake I'd never make again. "I've taken care of you, Anna, like I swore I would. But now I need you to choose you, too. I can't stick around and watch you kill yourself like this anymore."

The door closed behind me, putting enough space between Anna and me to breathe.

CHAPTER TWENTY-SIX

PAISLEY

1. Fall into desperate, soul-consuming love.

The smell of popcorn filled the townhouse, and I dug out a package of M&M's from the hidden stash of candy I kept behind the flour. After all, I'd read somewhere that mass amounts of chocolate gave your brain the same chemicals as an orgasm. I'd probably need to eat the whole darn factory to get even half of what Jagger did to me. I climbed off the shelves in the pantry, pulling my flannel drawstring pants back up to my waist and adjusting the straps of my tank top.

"Ooh, is it movie night?" Morgan asked, skipping into the kitchen, dressed in form-flattering jeans and a low-cut top.

The clock said eight fifteen, and I rolled my eyes at her. "Not for you, it's not. Go on, get out, Morgan."

She leaned over the kitchen island. "I'd rather stay here and keep you company."

"No. You're not going to miss out on anything on my account."

She arched an eyebrow at me. "Are you going to call your boyfriend? Or are you still avoiding him?"

The problem with avoiding telling Jagger about the tests was that it meant I hadn't seen him, or touched him, or kissed him. I was close to a high-school prank hang-up call. The microwave dinged, and I removed the bag, careful to only hold onto the edges. Once the bowl in front of me was full, I popped a few tablespoons of butter in the microwave to melt. I mean, if my heart was going to give out anyway, I might as well.

"Paisley. You have to tell him."

I nodded, dumping the bag of M&M's on top of the hot popcorn. Another ding, and the butter was ready for drizzling.

"Paisley!" Morgan slammed her hands down on the counter in front of me.

My head snapped up. "I know! It's just…" My eyes darted from the calendar marked with the next appointment. "He doesn't treat me like I'm broken."

"You're not broken."

"Oh, please. Everyone else sees me as a cracked little vase. They just keep handing me back and forth, careful not to press on the weak spots, keeping me high on the shelf where I can't *breathe*. Jagger…he's like a shot of pure oxygen. I don't want to lose that."

"You're not going to stop loving him just because you tell him. He's not going to walk away, not with the way he looks at you. That boy is head over heels, and he deserves to know."

"I never said I was in love with him." I focused on the popcorn bowl, methodically tossing it to distribute the chocolate and butter.

"Oh, darlin', you didn't have to." Morgan grabbed my hand. "You wear your heart in those pretty green eyes of yours. You can't fool me."

Tears pricked at my eyes. "But I don't want to love him! That's silly, isn't it? That I'm ridiculously happy, but won't admit it?"

"Yep, stupid, especially for someone who counts down her days like some morbid Advent calendar." She grabbed a handful of popcorn. "When did you realize it?"

When did I realize it? I thought and simply...knew. "When he told me that he'd rather burn for just a moment, to really experience love than live a lifetime safe without it." I sighed. "It was like...he was meant for me, you know? Because that moment might be all I have to give him."

"It doesn't have to be like that."

"He shouldn't love me. He needs someone who can jump out of planes with him and hike mountains in Nepal. He doesn't need to be saddled with some sickly girl who can't do anything but focus on her heartbeat." I ripped off my watch and slammed it into the counter. "He shouldn't be with me."

"Nepal? Love isn't exactly rational, and neither are you at this moment." She picked up the watch and checked that I hadn't broken it. "He won't leave you, Paisley. If that's what's really scaring you, don't let it. Jagger is a fighter, and he'll stand by you."

I swallowed, imagining the pacemaker surgeries, or the small electrical shocks he could get if I chose the internal defibrillator. He'd live in waiting rooms and doctors' offices. He'd look at me like a heart condition and not...me. I swallowed, damning the situation I'd gotten us both into. "Morgan, I'm not scared he won't stand by me. I'm terrified he *will*."

"Stop—"

But I couldn't stem the word vomit. "Especially now. I feel fine on these new meds, like I could conquer the world, and yet I'm like the one in one-freaking-billion whose enlarging heart doesn't stop growing when the rest of me does. He doesn't deserve this!"

She tilted her head and raised her eyebrow. "He deserves to be happy, the same as you, and he deserves to know the truth.

Now, quit your damn whining before the violins start playing sad songs in our kitchen."

"Ugh. I made such a mess."

She smiled like a Cheshire cat. "But what a fine mess to be in. Jagger Bateman is in love with you. And you're in love with him. Do you know how rare that is? That the person you love feels it, too? Trust me, it doesn't happen as often as you think."

We were so close to perfect, and one heartbeat away from tragedy. Sixty-six days. How was I going to spend them? "I love him so freaking much."

Morgan jumped like we were fourteen again. "*Eek!* Now jump that!"

My cheeks heated, and my pulse leaped, either from embarrassment or thinking of getting my hands on Jagger. Probably both. "You really think that's the best idea?"

"What did Dr. Larondy say?"

"That as long as I could walk up a flight of stairs without getting winded, I'm okay for sex."

"And did you not walk up our stairs to get changed just a few minutes ago?"

I narrowed my eyes at her. "Morgan, go find someone and walk up your own stairs."

She giggled, swatted my backside, and grabbed her handbag from the counter. "Don't wait up, dear!" The door opened, and I reached for the popcorn. "Ooh, imagine that!"

"What?" I answered, popping four salty, buttery, warm M&M's in my mouth. I closed my eyes and moaned as the shells cracked and the melty chocolate escaped. So good.

"Holy shit, that's hot. Would you like me to leave you and your popcorn alone?"

My eyes snapped open at Jagger's voice, and I swallowed, then ran my tongue across my teeth to make sure I wasn't about to talk with a chocolate-coated smile. "Hey," I said softly, not sure what else to say, since my breath left me at the sight of him.

He was dressed in full uniform, his boots heavy as he walked across the tile floor toward me with a vase full of pink peonies. "Happy Valentine's Day? I didn't even realize what day it was until I was in the middle of that makeup test." He put the vase and his cover on the counter, then ran his hands across the top of his hair. It was long, almost too long, and I loved it. He left a foot or so between us, a spark flickering in his eyes that made me feel like we stood at the edge of something big, and I wasn't sure I wanted to know what it was. "I'm so sorry I left like that, that I didn't call." His voice was low, regretful, and sincere.

"There were no phones in Chicago?"

A smile tugged at the corners of his beautiful mouth. "Actually, there were not. I kind of had it confiscated and didn't get it back until late last night. By then I just wanted to see you and explain in person, but I had class all day, and a test to make up."

I took a deep breath. "I think we both have things we need to explain." I moved toward him until our toes brushed and I had to crane my neck up to see him. With my bare feet and his combat boots, our height difference was even more exaggerated.

He swallowed and nodded. "There's a lot you don't know about me. Things I haven't told anyone, things I don't have control over. And I want to tell you, but..." He flicked his tongue across his teeth, his absolute tell. Too bad that tongue stud wasn't in.

"But you're not ready for me to know?" I understood all too well.

"I don't want you to look at me differently and suddenly see someone else...someone you couldn't ever want." *I could say the same exact thing.* "There are ugly parts of me, Paisley. Sins I'm still paying for."

"Is that where you were this week? Paying for those sins?"

Two heartbeats passed while his jaw ticked. "Yes, in a way."

"Did you cheat on me?" I asked softly, using intonation to

make sure he knew I didn't think it was possible. "Did you sleep with someone else? Touch someone else?"

"Fuck, no. How could you even..." He shook his head. "That's not a possibility. You're the only woman I want." My smile must have tipped him off, because he rolled his eyes. "You're killing me, Paisley."

"We agreed to default to trust, so that's what I'm doing."

"You have every right to know what's going on—"

"Let's not talk about it tonight," I offered.

His forehead puckered. "Don't girls always want to talk?"

I shook my head, my hair tickling my bare skin. "I missed you something fierce, Jagger. I just want to be where you are tonight. We can sort out everything else later." *I don't want to tell you my secret, either.* No, I wanted tonight, and I was going to take it.

His eyes softened, relief evident as I stayed my own execution. I rose on my tiptoes and cupped his face in my hands, running my thumbs across the sharp stubble that had grown since his morning shave. "You don't have to worry. Whatever it is, it's not going to stop me from wanting you...from loving you."

His lips parted, and his eyes turned hungry. "Say it again."

"You don't have to worry." I smiled.

"Not that part." I glimpsed the vulnerability he hid so well. He was so adamant against attaching to anyone, to any kind of relationship, so he didn't love anyone, but it also kept anyone from loving him.

He was starved for it.

Guilt slammed into me. I'd known I loved him for months and couldn't say it, even when he did. Couldn't make that promise that I'd be here for him to love. I'd accidentally withheld the one thing he needed desperately.

"Paisley?"

I grazed my thumbs across his lips and searched his eyes. "I love you, Jagger Bateman." My lips met his in the softest kiss we'd ever shared. We clung there for a moment, and I reveled in the love unfurling through my chest, radiating through me.

He slowly brought his hands to my waist but didn't deepen the kiss. "Say it again," he begged.

"I love you," I whispered and kissed him again. "I love you." I brought my lips to his cheeks, his chin, the skin of his throat, punctuating each kiss with an "I love you" until his hands tightened on me, his grip turning possessive.

He brought his mouth down to mine, this time stroking his tongue inside with a tenderness he'd never shown before, drawing a moan from my throat. "I need you." His voice snapped any tether in my mind.

"Yes," I answered as hunger awoke in my belly. Three words, and I was ready to strip in my kitchen.

His hands skimmed down my back to my rear, and he lifted me easily. I wrapped my legs around his waist, my arms around his neck, and kissed him with every ounce of love I could pour into him. He walked us up the stairs, pausing just outside my bedroom to lean me against the wall. He didn't pounce like I'd come to expect; instead, he ran his fingers down my cheek, looked into my eyes like he was making love to my soul, and I liquefied. "I love you, Paisley. I love you so much that I don't understand how I could have taken a single breath before I found you. I came to life when you did on that beach. I don't want to live another day that I can't tell you that."

I arched up, bringing my mouth to his. "You can tell me that for as long as I live," I promised him, then threaded my hands into his hair and kissed him like this would be the only chance I had. The wall was great leverage as I rocked into him, getting as close as I could, but it wasn't enough. I needed his skin. My fingers made short work of unzipping his uniform top, pulling it from between our bodies. He balanced me against the wall to free his arms from the top. My fingernails grazed his skin as I lifted his tan undershirt, revealing the lines of corded muscle and deliciously inked skin I was dying to taste. My mouth opened on its own accord and fastened to the skin above his heart, sucking a small bruise into the surface, like I needed my own mark to compete with the other swirls of ink.

He hissed and leaned into me, forcing my head up, and tugged his shirt over his head. *Oh. My. God.* His dog tags rested against his skin, bare from neck to waist. A uniform had never turned me on, but half a uniform on Jagger? I was going to spontaneously combust. I tested the resistance of his chain and reeled him in for another kiss, savoring the way his grip tightened on my hips. "Bed," I whispered as I pulled away.

He groaned and fumbled with my door handle for a second before he got it open. He flipped on the light, then carried me to bed. He lowered me until I rested on the soft white comforter in the center of the four-poster bed. The white canopy draped across the top contrasted with Jagger's tan skin as I looked up at him, trying to swallow my heart, which had jumped into my throat. "You're beautiful."

His smile echoed mine, bringing out his dimple. "You're biased."

My hands dipped along the planes and angles of his back, memorizing every line. He sat on the bed next to me and made quick work of removing his boots, then slid his weight onto me and set his lips to my neck. My body came to life, arching toward him as I moaned. "I like this spot," he whispered, and proceeded to lick and suck every inch of my neck. A wave of heat ran through me, leaving goose bumps in its wake.

My hips rolled into his, and he kissed me slowly, winding his fingers through my hair and holding me to him like I was something precious. Then he kissed a path down to my chest, grazing his teeth lightly over my breasts. The hard points of my nipples stood out through my tank top, and he kissed each in turn. "Skin," I begged.

His hands followed the lines of my body until he reached

my waist. He looked into my eyes and waited for me to nod, and then lifted fabric over my head when I raised my arms eagerly. His dog tags tickled the hollow of my throat as he lowered himself over me, finally skin to skin. Fire licked at me where we were connected, only to rage even hotter when he raised himself and took off his necklace.

"My turn," I said, and pushed him to his back.

He grasped my hips as I covered him, and he kissed me so thoroughly that my body hummed. It didn't matter if I was over or under him, he could still control every shiver of my skin. I traced a path down his neck with my fingers, hovering over the tattooed flames that licked from his back over his shoulder and transformed into words. "This one?" I needed another piece of him.

"'What matters most is how well you walk through the fire.'" He paused for the barest of moments. "I got it when I felt... settled, like I'd made it through leaving..."

I didn't push. Instead I outlined the words with my tongue. "Bukowski?" I asked against his skin.

He sucked in when I kissed the sensitive spot where his collarbone met his neck. "It's so sexy when you talk librarian to me."

I giggled, but all thoughts of laughter fled as I stroked my hands down his torso, savoring each carved line of his stomach. I held his gaze and lowered my head, kissing the delectable path that led into his pants. I relished every indrawn breath, the tensing of the muscles beneath my tongue. "Paisley." My name sounded so good when he said it like that. I flicked open the buttons on his pants, and he growled, flipping me to my back. "You're killing me."

"That's the idea." I lifted my chest so that my breasts rubbed against his skin, and he consumed my mouth until I couldn't think, only feel the slide of his tongue, the sweet pressure of his thigh between mine.

"I'm trying to go slow. Cooperate." He turned his attention to my breasts, using his tongue and lips until I gasped his name. Each pull sent shots of lava through my veins, pulsing and gathering between my thighs, and all I wanted was to ease the ache. His hands glided down my sides until his thumbs hooked into my pajama pants. He kissed my stomach, ran his tongue over my belly button, and then kissed his way to my waistband.

I lifted my head to see why he paused, to see the question in his eyes. "Yes," I whispered. My elbows supported my weight, and I lifted my hips, allowing him to slide my pants the rest of the way off. He didn't look away from me but held my eyes as he dragged my panties down my thighs. There was nothing but love, almost reverence in his eyes. I lifted my legs out one at a time, placing them on either side of him.

His gaze raked over me, turning from sweet to hungry. "Fucking perfect, every inch of you." His praise warmed me to the tips of my toes.

I drew my feet up along his pants and pushed them down. "Off."

"Bossy." He smiled and stripped them off, leaving his boxer briefs all that separated us. Then he slid between my open thighs and stroked the bare skin of my torso with his. I groaned at the contact and looped my ankle over his hip as he kissed me, a new urgency fueling the speed and pressure. He was losing some of that control, but I wanted him to lose it all. He'd been soft and slow since the ATV, and I wanted *that* Jagger again.

I skimmed my nails over his skin until I gripped his butt through his briefs. "Paisley," he whispered, and I arched, rubbing his erection against me. It relieved some of the ache, only to leave me throbbing when he pulled away. His self-restraint was incredible, but I was done with it. As he sat on his knees, I followed him, kissing the taut skin of his stomach. "I'm trying to go slow, and you're making that impossible."

"Good," I mumbled into the waistband of his boxer briefs.

His breathing sped up as my hands moved to his thighs and gripped the bands of muscle there. "You feel incredible." His fingers tangled in my hair and gripped when I grazed my thumb over the outline of his erection.

He pushed me onto the bed, thrusting against me in one long, delicious slide. "Stop that, or I'm going to snap, Little Bird."

I reached between us and squeezed his length. "Snap already, because I'm on fire for you."

He growled into my neck, and his kisses changed from languorous to abandoned. Yes. This was what I wanted. I needed him reckless, wild, uninhibited with me. No more caution or restraint. He reared back on his hands and looked at me with raw need. I whimpered and lifted my hips, the ache between my thighs becoming unbearable.

"I tried to go slow, to do this right," he warned. Then he attacked, sliding his fingers into my folds and holding me open as his tongue licked over my clit.

A cry ripped free from my throat as he stroked over me again, flicking and caressing, then sucking at me. Oh, God. I was going to die from the havoc that tongue was wreaking. This was...was...there were no words. Desperate for contact, I wound one hand through his hair and the other tangled in the sheet above my head, like it could hold me to the earth while he spiraled me out of control. He blew on me, and my hips bucked. "Jagger!"

"What?" He dragged his tongue over me slowly. "More?"

"Yes!"

"You taste amazing," he said against my clit, and the vibrations sent another surge of pleasure through me. My hips rode his mouth as he caressed me, unable to control my own movements. My breaths came in gasps. "What do you want?"

"More," I whimpered.

"How?" He reared up over me and turned my face to his,

looking in my eyes. I had the feeling he was always going to challenge me here, and I was more than ready for it.

"I want your hands on me."

He slipped a finger inside me and stroked. "Like that?"

"Yes. More!" He looked almost feral as he slid down my body, locking my eyes as he slipped in another finger and thrust. I cried out and then went speechless when he kept time with his tongue against those nerves. Pressure built low within me, so tight I was afraid I'd break apart.

I called his name over and over, unable to think of any other word. Then he pressed up with his fingers, sucked my clit into his mouth at the same time, and I exploded around him. Lights flashed behind my eyes as I clenched around him again and again, until I fell limp.

He kissed my throat and then my lips, every muscle locked and rigid. "Watching you do that is the sexiest thing I've ever seen. You're extraordinary, Paisley." His breathing was ragged, his hands firm, but I felt a slight tremor race through him as he stroked my curves, kick-starting another fire in me.

I looked into his eyes so there could be no misunderstanding. "I want you, now."

"You're sure?" Sweat beaded on his forehead, and his breath hit my lips in pants.

"Now."

He handed me a condom, and I rolled it over him, squeezing as he hissed in pleasure. He took both of my hands in his and raised them above my head as he slid his erection between my sensitive folds. "You're so damn wet." He groaned.

I brought my knees up to cradle his body and waited for him to press inside. Instead, he kissed me, rubbing his tongue with mine in the same rhythm he slid against me below. I groaned into his mouth and rocked back into him. "That feels amazing," I told him as he did it again. "But you—"

"Trust, Paisley, remember?" He stroked his hands down

my arms until he palmed my breasts, then tweaked my nipples, rolling them expertly as I moaned. The ache between my thighs began to pulse again, then throb as he skimmed his fingers over me. He found a rhythm against my clit, stroking, rubbing, and pressing, until I was coiled tighter than a spring.

"Jagger!" I cried out, losing every semblance of control.

"Paisley." His voice shook.

"Please," I begged.

He kept as close to me as possible, resting his forehead on mine and swallowing my gasp as he finally nudged the head of his erection inside me. "I love you," he whispered.

"I love you," I promised. He slipped another inch inside me, and I clenched down on him, burning slightly where he already stretched me.

With a strangled groan, he snapped, sliding into me to the hilt. I gasped at the exquisite pressure of having him inside me, filling every part of me and pushing for more. "God! You're so tight. You fit like you were made for me," he said against my mouth, his breathing erratic as he gave me a much-needed minute to adjust.

"I was." My lips trembled under his, needing the pressure to ease. I rolled my hips and moaned at the friction.

"Don't. Just let me hold this…" His eyes were squeezed tight, fighting to stay still, determined to go slowly with me.

I kissed him, sliding my tongue into his open mouth and stroking the roof of his mouth at the same time I thrust my hips. "Jagger," I pleaded, my nails sinking into his skin.

He pulled out, almost to the tip, and then slammed home. Pleasure ripped through me, so sweet I tasted it. "Like that?"

"Yes!"

He did it again, and again, setting a hard, deep rhythm that drove me higher and higher in the spiral. I couldn't remain passive, and dug my heels into the bed, arching into him, meeting him thrust for thrust. He didn't increase the pace, even when I begged him to, just pushed harder, deeper. Our breathing matched the intense pace, and we gave up trying to kiss, simply tasting the passion that lingered between our open mouths.

He never once looked away, the blue of his eyes darker as he stripped my soul clean with every thrust, every gasp and moan. My cries became desperate, and he finally sped up, his hips pistoning into mine with perfect pressure. "I... I..." I tried to speak but couldn't form a thought. Other than "yes," and "more," which I cried out frequently.

He rubbed his thumb over my clit as he thrust into me. The rhythm was punishing as he drove us toward completion, sweat dripping off us both. I couldn't fathom that I could do it twice, but as he rubbed again with a hard thrust, I came apart in his arms, crying out into his mouth. He swallowed the sound with a devastating kiss, and thrust faster, finally uncontrolled. Another deep push, and he shook, calling out my name as he came.

Then he collapsed over me and rolled us to the side so he wouldn't crush me. "That was..." He struggled to catch his breath. "That was amazing."

"More than amazing." I smiled, realizing I'd just had two orgasms and my heart was fine. Pounding, but fine. "Astonishing and perfect."

"Just like you." He kissed the tip of my nose.

Exhaustion swept over me as he climbed out of bed to clean up. My body started to shut down, demanding rest, and gave in fully when he pulled me against him, resting his arm over my waist and tucking my head beneath his chin.

"You're stuck with me now, Paisley Donovan. I'm never letting you go," he whispered into my hair.

My eyes popped open, because I knew that he might not get a choice.

CHAPTER TWENTY-SEVEN

JAGGER

One day I'm going to be happy, and it will have nothing to do with you.

"Are you sure about this?" I asked her as they harnessed us together, over a hundred feet above the ocean. Was this crane stable? It didn't feel stable. Hadn't I just done this a few months ago? Why did it feel so different now?

"Well, it's a little late to back out now," she giggled into my chest.

"Yeah, I wanted to back out a week ago when you suggested this. But you ambushed me in a sex coma, where I'm defenseless. You didn't lie about your weight, right? I know girls do that, which is just fucking ridiculous, but you have to be honest here. Were you honest?" I tipped her face up to mine to see her laughing. "This is not funny."

"This is very funny," she answered, reaching up to brush a kiss across my lips. "Yes, I was honest."

"And your asthma?" I whispered into her ear.

"I was just at the doctor. Asthma doesn't remotely play into this, I promise."

My jaw clenched. "This is an absurd list, Paisley. What on earth ever made you want to bungee jump?"

She arched an eyebrow at me. "Didn't you say you were just here in August? And in Colorado? How many times have you jumped?"

She had me there. "Six times, but that's me. You've never struck me as the kind of woman who likes to throw herself off giant towers and then snap back with a rubber band."

"Well, it's actually not something I ever really *wanted* to do, but kind of something that seemed..." Her eyes widened, like she finally understood that we were standing on the edge of a very dangerous little box to check on her list. Her throat worked as she swallowed. "It's a bad idea, isn't it? This is such a bad idea."

Her breathing picked up, and I kissed her softly. "Yes, it's a bad idea. An utterly, horrendously bad idea."

"But fun?" A spark of excitement passed through those green eyes, and I couldn't help but grin.

"Yes. It's exhilarating. But if you want to change your mind, I'm all for it," I promised her, running my hands along her spine.

"Yeah, lady, because in about two minutes it's too late." The guide secured the carabiners to our harnesses.

She took a couple rapid breaths, looked up at the sky and then to the edge of the bridge, but not down. Then her eyes locked onto mine, radiating panic. "No, I want to do this."

"You sure as hell don't look like it." I turned to tell the guide to unhook us, that there was no way I was throwing the love of my life off a bridge, but she brushed my cheek with her fingers.

"No. I might not want to do this, but I have to. I need to. For me." She bit her lower lip, her eyes set with that determination I utterly adored. "Besides, you'll keep me safe."

I wrapped my arms around her, pulling her into my chest

and kissing the top of her head. "I won't let anything happen to you," I promised, but my stomach clenched. Doing wild shit for the rush had always been fun, but involving Paisley, risking her, wasn't something that sat well with me. Especially not when she looked like she wanted to be anywhere but there. Why the hell had she make a list of crap she didn't actually *want* to do?

The guide gave us the last rundown, explaining what was about to happen. With every sentence, Paisley squeezed me tighter, until I was held in a five-foot-two little vise. "This isn't safe if you have epilepsy, heart disease, or if you're pregnant." The guide raised his eyebrows at us.

Paisley pregnant? We'd been safe these last two weeks, and there was no chance, but the thought didn't make me want to vomit. No, that news would just give me an excuse to get a ring on her finger. *Holy shit, that escalated quickly.*

"No, I'm not pregnant." I felt her jaw tense against my chest.

"Then by all means, step to the side and have a good time. Remember to keep your hands and feet inside the ride at all times, and don't forget the tabs on the rebound unless you like hanging upside down."

We moved to the edge. She looked up at me, forced out a shaky smile, then laid her head over my heart. "I love you," she whispered.

"Well, good. I don't bungee jump for just anyone," I answered with a kiss on her hair. I tightened my grip on her as the guide counted down. Then we jumped—and let gravity take over. The wind rushed past us as we plummeted toward the ocean below, the only sound Paisley's high-pitched scream. Adrenaline rushed through me, firing every nerve, every sense: the smell of the ocean rising to meet us, air rushing past our bodies, and the feel of the woman in my arms.

We hit the end of the rope and recoiled like a rubber band, but my stomach stayed in free fall. Paisley screamed again, but her tone changed until she was laughing. It was the most beautiful sound I'd ever heard. Well, next to her screaming out my name when she came. I think that was always going to take the top spot. I held her tighter, bracing her head as we fell toward the water, remembering how much the secondary snap had hurt my neck the first time I did this.

"This is amazing!" she yelled as we bounced again.

My heart thundered in my ears, and a laugh unlocked the tension in my muscles. She let go of me, her arms stretching wide above her head in abandonment as she yelled out in joy, release, exhilaration. "I am invincible!"

Invincible and infectious. I let myself enjoy the rush tearing through me. It was only amplified by the perfection of her. I loved her, and not just in a girlfriend way. Hell, not even in a wife way. No. I loved her like the tide loved the moon, vital to sustain the life within. I slammed my eyes closed, both reveling in the feeling and terrified because I couldn't imagine ever going back to the way it was before. Somewhere along the way, she'd become my gravity, holding me to the earth by her sheer existence.

Loving Paisley had the same effect on me as my first helicopter ride—I simply knew where I was supposed to be, whom I was supposed to become, and I was meant to be hers.

She ran her fingers along the sleeves of my shirt as we slowed to a vertical stop. I wound my fingers through hers and dipped my head, kissing her as we hung suspended. She met my tongue with her own, tasting like the strawberries she'd been eating as we arrived for the jump. Was I ever going to get tired of this?

She gasped into my mouth, then rubbed her hands over her eyes. "Jagger...my head."

I pulled the tab we'd been told about, and the ropes shifted, bringing us upright as the winch cranked us back up to the deck. "It's the blood pressure," I murmured against her hair. "Better now?" She nodded and rested her head on my chest. "How do you feel?"

"Amazing!" Her grin triggered my own.

They reeled us up, and we sat back, enjoying the aqua water of the Emerald Coast of Florida. "Hey, look." I pointed down the shoreline where a small line jutted into the water. "That's where we met."

She kissed my neck. "That's where you saved me."

"You're almost ready to head back there and swim. Maybe a few more times in the pool and I bet you could handle the ocean."

"You just want to get me wet and naked."

"Who said naked?" My grip tightened on her as they cranked us the final few feet to the deck.

"I did." She turned her face up to mine and kissed me until I forgot there were two men waiting to unhook us. Luckily, they cleared their throats, or we might have hung there for a while.

I let her sleep as long as I could, wrapping myself around her because I still couldn't believe she was mine. Maybe one day I'd get used to saying that, knowing that she loved me. Until then, I'd just hold her while she napped. Once my phone hit four thirty, I pulled myself away from her, closing my bedroom door behind me.

"How is she feeling? She seemed tired," Grayson said, looking up from his study seat at the dining room table. Our final check rides were this week, and I hadn't cracked a 5&9. After my week in Chicago, Carter was edging me out, but I'd take him down.

"Yeah, she's wiped out. We're supposed to meet her parents in two hours, so I can give her another half hour or so." I pulled a bottle of water out of the fridge and drained it.

"Ah, General Donovan. You know how to pick your women, man."

I cringed. "Not women. Just woman. She's the only one I've ever picked, and she's worth it. You know, as long as I can survive our first family dinner."

"I'll keep you in my prayers. Do they know about her bungee expedition today?"

I shook my head. "I've never been that scared."

"Because it's a stupid thing to do? Tie yourself to a rubber band and bounce?"

"Yeah, well, I almost didn't let her. I'm telling you, I'm turning paranoid."

His pencil clicked against the table as he put it down. "Worse than when you saved her from drowning?"

"I didn't love her then."

He nodded. "Yeah. That love stuff heightens everything else, too. It's like an amp."

I threw the empty bottle into the trash and didn't ask why he knew about it. "I can't help but feel like there's something she's not telling me. Which is fair. We both have things we don't like to talk about, you know? She doesn't know all of my shit, I can hardly expect to know hers."

"But you want to."

"She won't let me in. She changes the subject when we open the door to any of it."

His gray eyes studied me with a perception I couldn't escape. "Then you make her listen to yours. You're both too concentrated on staying flawless for the other, not giving anyone a reason to run away because everything is shiny and perfect. Nothing stays shiny and perfect for long when it's used. Unless you want this relationship of yours in a pretty glass case, you have to show her your cracks, your flaws. Show her that no matter what hers are, you'll stay. Show her there's nothing to be scared of, and she'll let you in."

"Jesus, did you major in psych?" I asked, grabbing another bottle of water.

He shook his head. "Marine engineering."

"And that taught you about women?"

"Nope. Four sisters took care of that."

"What?" I started laughing. "You're like this giant red puzzle, so there's no way to know where the pieces go."

"I'm not much of a people person."

"Oh, you think?" My eyes glanced to the clock. "I have to wake her so she can get ready." I started to walk down the hallway.

"Jagger?"

I turned around, my eyes slightly widened. He'd never called me by my first name. "Yeah?"

"That fear you felt? Don't lose it. It will remind you what she means to you, because the second you become complacent..." He looked away and took a deep breath. "Life is short, man. That's all."

"Someone fucked you up." Another puzzle piece fell into place.

He picked up the pencil and lowered his head to study. "No. I did that all myself."

I knew he'd closed the subject. Hell, I was impressed I'd gotten that much out of him.

Paisley gave me a sleepy kiss as she woke, smiling at me. "Time already?" She stretched to reveal a tantalizing strip of smooth skin at her stomach. I bent down, swiping my tongue across her belly button. "None of that," she murmured, her fingers threading through my hair. "I won't leave this bed."

"Sounds like a plan to me." My hands skimmed underneath her shirt to her ribs.

"Sure, until my father comes looking for us."

Well, there went that erection. "Yeah, up you go."

She laughed and swung her feet over the side. Her fingers braced her temple.

"You okay?" I tipped her face up and handed her the bottle

of water I'd brought her.

"Yeah, just sat up too fast. You sure you don't mind if I use your shower?" Her open mouth on the rim of the bottle had my full attention.

I groaned at the thought of her naked in my shower. "Oh, no, feel free. I'll just stay out here and think about licking water off your skin."

Her lips parted. "That sounds pretty perfect." She stood, so close to me that her breasts rubbed against my chest. "Maybe you want to join me?"

Fuck, yes. "Only if you want to cancel our reservations." *Please cancel.*

She sighed and slid past me. "I wish! Part of being a Donovan—we don't cancel family dinners. Give me a few minutes, and I'll be ready."

I went to find something—anything—to do so I'd keep my hands off her body. I'd never slept with the same girl twice, and never really wanted to, but Paisley was turning into something I could never get enough of. Monogamy was strangely awesome. I'd already learned what turned her on, where her boundaries were, which ones I could push, and which ones of mine I let her push. I felt like I'd traded a ton of traveling carnivals to live at Disney World. It was definitely the happiest place on earth.

I killed time quizzing Grayson for our check ride. He got most of the answers right, but lifted an eyebrow at me when I missed one he got purposely wrong. Fine, I was distracted.

Once it was time, I dressed up—gray slacks, a light blue shirt, and my burnt-orange Hermès tie, just for fun. I ran my fingers over my hair and did a quick survey, making sure there was nothing out of place. This was my chance to make it up to Paisley's parents, to show them I was capable of not acting like a Neanderthal. I thought about taking my tongue stud out, but didn't. After all, it was nothing compared to seeing me take down their favored son in the entry hall.

The bathroom door opened, and I caught sight of Paisley in the mirror. *Fuck me.* My mouth went dry. She wore a red dress that wrapped across her breasts, leaving the neckline low enough for me to start drooling. It fitted to her waist with a belt and flared out at her hips, ending at her knees. It was far from the most revealing dress I'd ever seen on a woman, but it was certainly the sexiest. Her hair curled softly down her back, and I wanted nothing more than to wrap my hands in it.

"We're never going to get there on time." I let my hunger for her show in my eyes. She skirted around me, giggling as I stalked her back into the bathroom, but I caught her from behind, wrapping my arms around her and kissing her neck. "And you smell amazing, too."

She leaned her head away, giving me a better angle on her neck, and I took full advantage, running my lips in a line down to her collarbone. "As much as I would like to continue this, we're going to have to get there." If her nails hadn't bit into my forearm, I would have thought she was unaffected. Her breathing hitched as I sucked lightly on the hollow of her neck. "Jagger..."

She turned in my arms and kissed me, pressing her body to the full length of mine. Her tongue stroked across my lips, and I sucked it inside, groaning at the taste of her, the feel of her under my hands. I backed her against the wall next to the towel bar. Then I took her face in my hands and kissed her, using every ounce of skill I had to make her forget her own name.

In the process, I forgot mine. She arched into me, her fingers tangling in my hair, pulling me closer in a grip that bordered on painful, and I loved it. My hands skimmed the dress to her neckline, slipping inside her bra at the same time to gently palm her breast. This wasn't enough. I wanted my mouth on her, my fingers inside her, pumping her to an orgasm. Why wasn't one touch ever enough? She moaned, leaning into me. I gently pinched her nipple, and she gasped into my mouth.

"We're going to be late if you keep making sounds like that," I promised, caressing her with my thumb.

She looked at me, her eyes half open and hazed by desire. "How fast can you be?"

I quirked up the corner of my mouth. "I think that might be the first time a woman has ever asked me to be quick."

She leaned into my hand. "Yes or no? Because I'm on fire."

"Fire?" I rolled my hips against her and sucked in my breath at the pressure she rolled back.

She tugged my lower lip with her teeth, then licked her tongue across it. "Burning, Jagger. Help a girl out? You told me you preferred the burn, right?"

My mind slipped back to that night when I'd wanted her so badly and she'd belonged to someone else. Not anymore. She was mine. I growled, lifted her by her ass, and slammed the door shut with my foot as I put her on the vanity. The kiss was open, carnal, full of lips, teeth, and tongue, and I was immediately as hard as the granite her ass was perched on. Not that I hadn't been semihard since she got in the shower. It was kind of a permanent condition when she was in the same room.

Never breaking our kiss, I sent my hands skimming up her thighs. God bless the South, she was wearing a fucking garter belt. I fingered the lacy tops of her thigh-highs and had to count back from ten to control myself. She'd reduced me to fifteen again without even trying.

"Fast?" I asked as my fingers inched toward her center.

"And hard." She slid toward me, bringing my hand to her panties. She whimpered as I ran my thumb just along the edge. "Jagger?"

"Hmm?" I mumbled, my mouth full of the soft skin on her shoulder.

"Don't wrinkle the dress, okay? We don't have time to go home to get another."

The absolute turn-on of taking her out in a dress that I'd

personally wrinkled warred with my need to not piss off her dad. The latter won. Kind of. I flipped her in my arms, lifting her dress to lie flush against her back. Then I shuddered, leaning her over the vanity at just the perfect angle. She had on a pair of red lace boy-cut panties with the words "remove before flight" across her delectable ass. They were instantly my favorite pair. "Fuck, Paisley. I thought you southern belles wore good-girl underwear." The perfect globes pushed back at me, and I couldn't help but stroke my palms over them.

"I went shopping, and those are the good-girl ones." She smiled, then leaned back and kissed me hard. "Now, Jagger."

I kept one arm banded around her waist and lifted her against me. Then I slipped a bunched-up towel in front of her hips so I didn't bruise her on the granite. "Well, I have to make sure you're ready for me," I teased, running my hand up the back of her thigh and absorbing her shiver.

She wiggled, moving my hand to the small scrap of lace covering her. Very wet lace. "Fuck," I whispered, my teeth grazing her neck.

I slipped my fingers underneath and stroked her, lightly rubbing her clit until she bucked in my hands. She was slippery and swollen, and I was the luckiest bastard on the planet. I made quick work of my belt and unbuckled my pants, pulling myself free of my boxer briefs. "Shit, condom," I mumbled, reaching around Paisley to the drawer. I tore the package open with my teeth and covered my erection, my hand nearly shaking.

"Please?" She moaned, leaning her head on my shoulder, trusting me to keep her upright. I pushed her panties to the side and slipped one, then two fingers inside her. She spasmed around my fingers, making these little sounds from the back of her throat that pushed me closer to the edge.

"Look at me," I demanded. Her attention turned to the mirror, watching our reflection. Her cheeks were flushed, her green eyes bright, and her mouth swollen from my kisses. That mouth made the sexiest "oh" as I positioned at her entrance and then pushed inside slowly.

Her breath came in tiny gasps, her eyes sliding shut as I crept into her inch by inch. I gritted my teeth, trying to think of anything besides how perfectly tight she was. "Open those gorgeous eyes, Paisley. I want you to watch me fucking you."

Her eyes flew open, and I slammed the rest of the way home with a groan. "Yes!" she cried out, the sound reverberating off the tiles. I flicked the fan switch on to help muffle her cries, knowing she'd be mortified if she realized Grayson could hear how vocal she was. Her cries were my favorite thing about making love to her. She lost every inhibition.

I pulled out again slowly, watching the different expressions cross her face, then brought myself in again just as unhurriedly, savoring every nuance of her response. She wiggled her hips, and I grinned at the desperation in her eyes. God, I could do this slowly all day if it made her look like that. I might die, but I'd do it.

"Jagger!" she snapped at me, her eyes spitting fire.

"Say it." I ran my tongue along her neck. "Say what you want." I locked my jaw, holding onto my control by willpower alone.

Her breasts heaved against the neckline of her dress, and I almost came just watching her, fully clothed, rocking onto me. She locked eyes with me in the mirror, panting through her red lips. "Please."

"Please what?"

She pushed back, and I retreated, stealing her leverage. "Ugh," she whined. "You're going to make me say it."

"Yes." She had to say it soon, or I was going to break, especially if she didn't stop wiggling.

"Why?"

"Because I've never heard you say it." *Come on, Little Bird, say it. Take me. That's all I need to hear.*

She went absolutely still and locked eyes with me in the mirror. Then she dragged her tongue across her lips and raised an eyebrow. "Just once," she drawled. Who was really in control here? "Fuck me. Now."

She was.

Holy. Fucking. Hot. My control snapped, and I thrust into her, then pulled out in a driving rhythm. Our eyes never lost contact as I slammed into her, each thrust better, deeper than the last. This was my heaven. Her breaths turned choppy, her keening cries short and high as she arched. "More!"

I ran my hand between her hips and the counter, pulling her even harder against me, then stroked across her clit, alternating rubbing with little flicks. Her legs started to shake, and I pressed down with two fingers. She flew apart in my hands, screaming my name and triggering my orgasm as she clenched down around me. My knees nearly gave out, but I kept us upright, breathing harshly against the skin of her neck. I found her mouth and kissed her gently. "I love you," I told her as I slid out and lowered her feet to the ground. That was the biggest difference. No matter if it was soft, slow, hard, fast, or even a little dirty, I was still making love to her. I left a piece of my soul with her every single time.

She turned in my arms and returned the kiss. "I love you more."

I stood there, grinning like a doofus as I cleaned up and tucked everything back in where it was supposed to be. She ran a brush over her hair and made sure her dress didn't advertise what we'd just been doing. I didn't need the dress to tell me. It was in the flush in her cheeks, the sparkle in her eyes, her swollen lips.

We were twenty minutes late when we pulled into the country club parking lot. I tossed the keys to the valet and lifted her down from Lucy.

"Can you tell?" she whispered as we walked quickly through

the marble foyer toward the dining hall.

She wavered, and I pulled her close, whispering in her ear. "Tell what? That I just bent you over my bathroom counter and fucked you senseless?"

She blushed and playfully smacked my chest with the back of her hand. "Jagger Bateman, you watch that mouth of yours. We're in public."

I grinned, considering what she'd just said to me in private. "You like that mouth of mine. On you. Even in public." She wavered again, and I gripped her waist tighter. "Are you sure you're okay?"

She nodded, but her breath was shallow. "I'm really okay, I promise. I just need to sit."

"Tell me if you want to get home and rest, okay?" She nodded, and I straightened to a respectful distance as we entered the dining room, keeping her hand tucked in mine. She spotted her parents and waved. The table was set for six. Three of them were already there. Of course he was here. "Hey, y'all," she greeted them. "Sorry we're late."

I pulled her chair out for her, and then shook her dad's hand. "General Donovan." I smiled at her mom. "Mrs. Donovan." And nodded to Carter. "Carter."

I did my best to ignore the subtle dig, especially since I'd been inside Paisley twenty-two minutes ago. *I win.* I even sat next to him.

"Will, it's nice to see you," Paisley said with a tight smile.

"We have an important guest coming that I wanted to introduce you both to," her dad answered. "Ah, there he is!"

Her dad left the table to greet the guest, who'd entered behind me, but I was too focused on Carter's dropped jaw to turn and look. "See a ghost, Carter?" I joked.

"Holy shit, that's Senator Mansfield," he said, like he was in the presence of God.

"Ah, so good to see you, Donovan!" The voice ripped

through every defense I'd built in seven years. It was impossible. Not here. Not with Paisley. Not when she didn't know.

"Jagger, are you okay?" she whispered.

I looked at her and brushed my lips against hers one last time as Jagger Bateman. "Paisley, I'm so sorry."

"What? Why?" she asked softly, brushing her hand along my jaw. I leaned into her touch for a moment and then leaned back, scrambling to put up the walls that might save me.

He stood across from me, the look in his eyes familiar and calculated as he assessed me. His suit was impeccable as always, his blond hair flecked with enough silver to give him a carefully cultivated mix of youth and experience.

"I'd like to introduce you both to Senator Johnathon Mansfield, the ranking member of the Senate Armed Services Committee," General Donovan introduced him.

"Ranking for now." He laughed. "Remember, it's an election year, and who knows, I might be out of a job come November."

That's why he was here—locating the weakest spot in his armor. Me.

"I've seen the polls. There's nothing to worry about there, Senator. Let me introduce you to two promising young men." He gestured toward Carter first.

Carter stood and shook his hand like he was meeting a celebrity. "I'm Lieutenant Carter, sir. I saw you speak at the academy. It's a pleasure to meet you."

Paisley's eyes flickered to me, undoubtedly wondering why I hadn't stood up, or so much as acknowledged him.

General Donovan cleared his throat, raising his eyebrows at me. When I didn't move, he spoke, "Senator, this is another new lieutenant, my daughter's boyfriend—"

"We don't need an introduction, General. Do we, Prescott?" The name sliced me to the quick, peeling away the last seven years like they'd never existed and leaving my nerves gaping and raw. "It's good to see you."

"Jagger?" Paisley asked softly, her hand coming to my knee in question and support. I sucked a breath in and came to life at her touch. "Who's Prescott?"

"I am, or I was." I swallowed and turned my attention, looking him straight in the eye like I wouldn't have dared seven years ago. "Paisley, meet my father."

CHAPTER TWENTY-EIGHT

PAISLEY

35. Find out what I'm really made of.

The table fell silent, eyes darting from the senator to Jagger. The resemblance was striking. Jagger's thigh was tense under my hand. This was the man he'd emancipated himself from? The one who'd left him to fend for himself after his mother's death? Pieces snapped together in my head, aligning themselves like well-stacked books. His father had worked away from them. He'd visited when it suited or when he needed them to "show their faces." Jagger's need to prove himself, to achieve his goals without his dad's help—it all made perfect sense.

I only knew two things about the man in front of me—that he'd gone to extraordinary lengths to ambush Jagger, and that he'd done something to make the man I loved hide himself.

Every muscle in Jagger's body locked except for his jaw, which ticked with his accelerated breathing. I needed to get him out of here. "I'm not feeling well, Jagger. Would you mind taking me home?"

His gaze snapped from his father's to mine, wild but concerned. "Paisley?"

"Ah, that's right. You go by Jagger now," his father said as if he'd forgotten.

"Take me home," I said softly. My heartbeat quickened, my light-headedness returning with such force that I wasn't lying. I didn't feel well. I'd stupidly done too much today.

He nodded once and stood, helping me with my chair. "General and Mrs. Donovan, Carter." He turned to his father. "Senator. I'm afraid you'll have to excuse us."

"Well, that's a pity, since I came all this way to surprise you." His smile didn't fool me.

Jagger's hand tightened on mine, but I forced a smile at his father. "I'm terribly sorry, Senator, but something at the table just hasn't agreed with me, and Jagger is the kind of gentleman who takes care of me when I'm not feeling well. His mama sure raised him right."

We left the senator with his mouth agape and walked from the dining room, those at the table speechless behind us. "I know you have questions," Jagger said quietly. "Just let me explain."

I stopped him in the empty foyer, just under the chandelier. "Default trust, remember? You had your reasons for not telling me."

He rested his forehead on mine, his shoulders sagging. "I don't deserve you," he whispered, the words coming out strangled.

I squeezed his hands in mine. "It doesn't matter to me how you grew up. I love *you*, Jagger Bateman."

"There's more that you don't know."

I glanced behind him to make sure we were alone. "Would you rather do this in the car?"

"Now. I'm not putting this off anymore. He's only here because there's an election soon, and I'm his biggest liability.

I...I blackmailed him for my freedom. The only reason he didn't fight the emancipation was because I signed an agreement that I'd never go public with what really happened." He paused for three heartbeats. "My mom didn't just fall off her balcony. She jumped."

I gasped. "Oh, Jagger—"

He shook his head but didn't pause. "It was accidental, that wasn't a lie, but she went over that railing by choice." He looked toward the chandelier and took a deep breath. "I can't believe I'm about to tell you this in a country club with both of our parents in the next room."

"We're good at awkward timing." I took his face between my hands, bringing his eyes to mine. "I'm here. No matter what." My heart wouldn't calm, and I struggled to keep my breathing steady and my voice even.

"She was high, but there wasn't an autopsy done. Mom was into just about anything she could get her hands on. My father couldn't have that getting out, so he took care of it like he did everything else, and we buried the truth with her body. His greatest liability became his springboard, and he rode the grief boost all the way through the next election."

"Was there a witness?"

"Yes." I waited. "Me. I was there. I couldn't reach her in time."

"Jagger." I whispered his name as a tear slipped down my face for what he'd been through. What I was going to put him through. "I need to tell you—"

"Let me just get this out, and then I'm all ears, Little Bird. I didn't leave him over Mom or his abandonment. Hell, I'd been taking care of things for years while Mom spiraled. I left him because of what he did to Anna."

"You can't seriously walk away from me," his dad called, striding into the foyer.

Jagger's head snapped up and out of my hands. "I can, and

I will." He turned to face him. "Did you miss that memo when I left? You're not welcome in my life."

"Jagger, let's go," I whispered. Who was Anna? What did she mean to him? My head spun so fast that I felt dizzy.

The senator smiled like Jagger had said he'd love to join him for dinner. "Why on earth are you still going by Jagger? I thought that phase would wear out. I never should have given in to her on that, but she was determined for your middle name, and I loved her."

Jagger tensed. "You loved her money. I won't buy your front-page bullshit."

"I loved your mother, but she had an addiction. That wasn't her fault."

"Yeah, and who gave her the first hit? That's on you."

All trace of amusement fell from the senator's face. "Six years, and this is what you want to bring up?"

"Seven next month, and I don't want to bring up anything. I want you to leave me alone."

"Stop acting like a child."

Jagger laughed, the sound empty. "Like I was *ever* a child."

The muscle in the senator's jaw ticked, just like Jagger's. They looked so alike—the same blond hair, glowing skin, strong jawlines. Except the senator's eyes were brown.

"What the hell do you want from me?" Jagger asked.

"Do I need a reason to see you? At least appreciate the lengths I went to for this to happen. Not that you were that hard to track down."

"I've been careful."

His dad laughed. "Son, you changed your last name to your mother's maiden name and didn't bother with your Social Security number. How careful could you really be? You graduated in May, took a pit stop in Florida, and reported to Fort Rucker after buying a house in Enterprise. Did I miss anything?"

"Why are you here?" he asked again.

"Come on, Prescott. You can't be that surprised. I raised you smarter than that. How could you possibly think I wouldn't keep track of you? I knew when you got into CU, when you applied for flight school..." He grinned, and my stomach turned over, nausea flooding my mouth with saliva.

"You had nothing to do with that!" Jagger shouted. "I got here on my own."

"Are you so sure about that? What are the odds of two lieutenants getting chosen for aviation from the same ROTC class and going to flight school at the exact same time? I'll tell you what they are—about as common as a senator placing a phone call."

"No," Jagger said, his certainty slipping. My heart hammered in my ears, but I ignored it, tightening my grip on his hand.

"This is where you say, 'thank you, Dad.'" The senator adjusted his pocket square.

"Get the fuck out of my life," Jagger growled.

His father tsked. "In public? Prescott, we raised you better than that."

"*You* didn't raise me. Mom did, or tried to when she wasn't wasted or zoned out on her medication."

His father's eyes hardened. "Looks like you're doing well enough, though. Latching on to a general's daughter was a good move for your career, but gutsy to split your focus while you're in flight school, don't you think?"

I sucked in my breath, and Jagger stepped to the right, blocking me. "We're done here."

My head started buzzing like I'd had too much to drink, and my watch blinked. I turned off the alarm and leaned into Jagger, trying to calm my heart. I needed to lie down.

"We are *not* done!" his father hissed. "I left you alone for nearly seven years after you dropped that ridiculous letter on me about how wretched I was. I gave you time to get over your tantrum, to be out of the public eye. I let you use your ridiculous new name."

"Let?" Jagger's voice rose, and my eyes flickered to the doors, wondering how much longer we could make it without causing a scene. "You don't *let* me do anything. I control my name, my trust fund, and my future. Remember? You are nothing to me but a biological contribution."

I concentrated on my breaths, trying to slow them down, but the buzzing only got worse.

"Of course I remember. I signed the damn papers, didn't I? I let you leave your preparatory school, turn down your appointment to West Point, and attend some middle-of-nowhere third-tier school all in the name of tracking her down. Was it worth it?"

Her? I looked at Jagger, who was quickly blurring in my vision. *Anna.*

"Yes," he seethed. "She has always been worth it, you bastard. She is beautiful and smart, and deserves far more than the shit you threw at her!"

I wavered on my feet and grabbed ahold of the large table we stood next to for balance. A feeling of unease settled into my heart. He'd told me he'd never been in a functional relationship before. Was Anna the dysfunctional?

"She's a washed-up drug addict who did nothing but pull you under, drowning you. I did what I had to in order to save you."

"Save me?" Jagger shouted, his voice booming across the foyer. "Losing her destroyed me! First Mom died, and then you ran Anna off. She was all that was holding me together!"

"She was ripping you apart! She still is!" His father took a deep breath and smoothed the lines of his lapel. "I thought I could trust you to make better decisions, Prescott, but when I learned that you raced off to be with her last month…"

I tensed. He'd been with her last month? My hand slipped from his, and I turned toward the table, using both hands to hold my weight. It was getting more and more difficult to stand, my head clouding. He spent that week with another girl, and it *hurt* my heart physically.

"Is that why you're really here? Because Anna wouldn't sign your nondisclosure? Do you want to know where I found her? On a dirty mattress in a roach-infested house where she'd prostituted herself to get by. Is that what you wanted for her? Were your expectations of me really worth what you did to her?"

I'd gotten to the point where I couldn't look at the two of them arguing, and the flowers on the table had gone out of focus, multiplying in my vision. My breaths came in tiny gasps.

"I did nothing to her! She is exactly what she chose to be, and I'll be damned if she drags you under with her again. I don't care that you still love her!"

Love her? I leaned heavily on my arms and looked at Jagger's back. The pain was crushing my chest.

"Still love her? Fuck you, Dad. I never stopped. I'm not like you. Anna is the other half of me, and if you couldn't love her for who she was, then you should have loved her because I did, I do! Mom loved her, too."

"Well, there's a judge of character for you," he quipped.

The other half of me. No. No. No. He loved someone else. He'd lied. He'd told me I was the first girl he'd loved. God, how many other girls had he said that to? Was that how he got me? Another notch on his bedpost? Another conquest? I wasn't anything to him, not when the other half of him was another girl. He loved her like I loved him. Everything spun in my vision, and my arms ached from holding my weight. I slipped, knocking the vase of flowers to the ground. The sound of shattering glass halted their fight.

"Paisley?" Jagger asked, turning around.

I stumbled away drunkenly, my feet somehow finding their way to the door. I pushed open the bar and fell into the evening air. I tripped on the cobblestones but caught myself on one of the pillars. He loved someone else.

My Jagger, but her Prescott.

"Paisley!" he shouted, running to me.

"No!" I screamed, throwing my arm out in front of me to keep him away. "Get away!" I pulled the arm back to clutch my chest. Why was the physical pain from a broken heart so bad?

"Stop and let me explain!" He blurred in my vision, but I thought he looked stricken, scared. Pain radiated from my chest, through my shoulders, and into my arms. I couldn't breathe, couldn't think, let alone focus on his face.

"We're not going to do this, remember? No misunderstandings!" He reached for me, and I fell into him, not for want but weakness.

"You love someone else. That's not a misunderstanding," I whispered. I couldn't catch a breath. Why was it so hard?

"Yes, Little Bird, but I love you more. Stop crying, please, and listen." He wiped away tears I hadn't realized had fallen. "Anna is my sister. My twin sister. But she's an addict like my mom, and I didn't want to expose you to that. I didn't want you to see that I'd done almost every drug she had, just never gotten addicted. I was lucky, and she wasn't."

"Your sister?" I whispered, my knees giving out.

He held me up, cradling me gently. "Yes. You're the only woman I love, Paisley, I swear it. You're my fucking everything."

Relief, sweet and pure, sang through me, but the pain was still there, crushing my ribs, moving into my jaw. Shouldn't it feel better? Shouldn't—

Oh, God. Not now. I'm supposed to have fifty more days! "Jagger, I have to tell you," I whispered, my weight completely collapsing against him.

"Paisley?" He wavered out of my vision. "What's wrong?"

"My heart. I should. Have told. You." I forced out every word, but then pain wracked me again, and I wasn't sure I was going to survive it.

"What? Paisley...no, what do I do?" His words came through jumbled, and I wanted to concentrate on him, but I couldn't think of anything but the pressure pulverizing my chest.

"My heart," I managed to whisper, fading. This was it. I had been right—I was never going to be older than Peyton.

"What?" He looked all around and started screaming in a voice I barely recognized. "Someone call 911! Help us!" His hand left my face, fumbling for something. "I need help! We're at the Enterprise country club, and I think my girlfriend is having a heart attack."

"I love. You. Jagger. More than I ever—"

Another surge of pain pressed through my chest, crushing me like a vise. There was no air, no beat, no thought but pain.

Then I felt nothing.

CHAPTER TWENTY-NINE

JAGGER

*Some things are worth holding onto, Dad, fighting
for. I'm just sorry you never found it. That's your loss.
Never mine.*

One. Two. Three. Four. I counted compressions in my head, remembering to lace my fingers as I worked over Paisley. I thought of nothing but pushing her chest down rhythmically.

"Can you tell me her status?" The voice came from my phone, where it had crashed to the pavement on the other side of Paisley. I made it to thirty, then tilted her head to open her airway, breathing for her. I didn't have time for the dispatcher.

My father grabbed the phone. "He's doing CPR. The girl looks to be in her early twenties."

I continued compressions, placing my hands above the mark I'd already rubbed into her skin. It was the same shade as her dress.

Fingers brushed across Paisley's jugular, accompanied by a sharp intake of breath. I caught the gleam of a West Point ring on his hand just before he took the phone from my father. "She's in full cardiac arrest. She has HCM, but until now has shown minimal symptoms. There is a family history of SCD. Her records are filed electronically. Paisley Lynn Donovan."

"Twenty-eight, twenty-nine," I counted out loud. Her dad took over breathing so I didn't have to stop compressions.

"Come on, Paisley. Don't you dare do this," Carter begged in a strangled voice I barely recognized. "You're the fierce one, remember? Fight."

I concentrated on each thrust of my hand, catching the small sucking sounds she made as air dragged into her lungs when I pushed just right.

Her chest cracked beneath my hands, a sickening *pop* sound. "Shit!" My hands flew off her. "I broke something!"

"Probably a rib. Keep going!" General Donovan ordered.

Bile rose in my throat, but I kept it down and returned to compressions, trying to ignore that I'd just broken Paisley's tiny body. "Let's go, Little Bird. We know how to do this, right? CPR is nothing new to us. We're old pros." *Don't puncture her lung. Don't puncture her lung.*

Wails came from behind us. Her mother? I didn't check, just kept pushing down on her chest, forcing blood to circulate through her body. Where the fuck were they? How long could it possibly take to get an ambulance here?

"Two minutes," General Donovan answered, my phone up to his ear. I must have spoken out loud.

We went through another few sets of breathing before we heard the sirens. "They're here!" her mother cried.

The ambulance stopped, the paramedics rushing us. Her dad filled them in while they took vitals, but I didn't stop compressions. I couldn't. They slid a board underneath her. "Sir," said one of the paramedics, braced on one knee next to me. "Sir, we've got it from here."

He covered my hands with his own, and mine fell away.

They lifted her into the ambulance, the paramedic continuing compressions. "We're coming with her," General Donovan announced, helping his wife into the rear of the ambulance while he took the front seat. "Bateman, we're headed to South East."

I nodded, because speaking wasn't going to happen. I didn't even have the strength to get off my knees. What the hell just happened? She had been okay, right? We'd just been bungee jumping today. We'd had mind-blowing sex an hour ago, and now she was strapped to a gurney?

Fuck. Did I cause this?

My heart jumped as the doors to the ambulance slammed home. I couldn't keep up with them, but I could get to the hospital soon after. I palmed my cell phone and gripped Paisley's abandoned purse when a shadow fell over me.

"Prescott?" My father hovered, blocking out the last of the sunset.

I stood, fishing my keys from my pocket. "Go away."

"I came here for you, son. Given what's just happened, I think you could probably use me around right now."

His eyes softened, but I was too schooled in his bullshit to give in. "In the scheme of what's just happened, you are absolutely nothing to me. Anna and I aren't going public, and it's not because you don't deserve to lose but because you're not worth the effort or the press in our lives. Go back to Washington and forget I exist, or that Anna does. You're really good at that. I have to get to the hospital." I turned and headed for the truck. He followed me.

Carter honked his horn next to where Lucy was parked and stuck his head out the window. "Let's go!"

"I'm not leaving until we talk, Prescott."

Damn, he was actually following me. I slipped my key into the door and turned. "Maybe Prescott would have bowed down to you, given you anything for five fucking minutes of your time, but that's not who I am anymore. I changed more than just my name, Dad. Now get the hell out of my way before I run you over."

"Sign this, and I'm gone."

"What?" I threw open Lucy's door.

"Your nondisclosure. Sign it in your new name, and I'll leave. But be warned, I'm not coming back. If you want to see me, you'll be the one making an effort. I don't beg, Prescott. I'm the last of your family."

"Paisley and Anna are my family." I ripped the paper from his hand, took a pen from my glove compartment, and signed my name. "Get the hell out of my life." I shoved the paper at his chest.

He stepped to the side, and I pulled out, speeding before I left the parking lot.

"Here." General Donovan held out a cup of coffee, and I took it but didn't drink. Three hours and fifty-one—no, fifty-two minutes had gone by in this waiting room with no word since they'd taken her. I'd worn a path from one end of the room to the other, and gone through every possible scenario—none of them pleasant—in my head before he settled into the seat next to me for the first time. "You didn't know."

I shook my head, tapping my feet in a rhythm only my racing pulse understood. Yeah, I needed caffeine like a fucking hole in my head.

"You really should drink that," he suggested and took his own advice.

The thought of swallowing anything made me want to hurl, but the smell masked the sterilized scent of apprehension all around me. I hated hospitals. Three hours, fifty-three minutes. No word. We should have heard something by now. Anything besides, "We're still trying to stabilize her."

"You saved her life. Starting compressions that fast. If... when she's stabilized, it will only be because you were with her."

"She didn't tell me," I muttered, dropping my head. "Could you please explain before I lose it?"

"She has hypertrophic cardiomyopathy. Her heart has thickened to the point that she has an obstruction and struggles to pump her blood. We were lucky with Paisley, and we've been able to monitor it, but we only caught it because we lost Peyton. Her heart failed without warning one morning after PT. Sudden cardiac death."

The SCD triggered a memory. "Sergei Zholtok."

"I'm sorry?" Carter asked, taking the seat across from me and stretching out his legs.

"A hockey player who died from HCM during a game. It caused sudden cardiac death in the locker room." Shit. Everything we'd been doing the last few months raced through my mind—the bungee jumping, the ATVs, the sex. Every spike of adrenaline, every time her heart rate must have skyrocketed, caused more damage than she could afford. My stomach turned another degree sour. I could have killed her. Maybe I had. "God. I did this. She wanted to go bungee jumping today, so I took her. I never would have done half of the things..." My throat closed.

"I know." General Donovan placed his hand on my shoulder, but it didn't feel as awkward as it could have. "This isn't your fault. Bungee jumping was probably the stupidest thing you could have done—"

"Try the actual stupidest thing." Carter growled, finally loosening his tie. Mine hadn't made it out of the car.

"—but you had no reason to suspect what was going on with her." He glared at Carter and stood slowly, his eyes tracking his wife as she paced, but she waved him off.

"Why wouldn't she tell me?" The knot that had permanently wedged itself in my throat tightened again.

"She didn't want you to know," Carter answered. "She wants to feel normal, and you give that to her...gave that to her."

I ignored his assumption. "But you knew?"

"Of course."

"And you didn't think I should?" I leaned forward on my knees, embracing the rush of heat that inched its way through me, replacing the numbness.

"I told her to tell you; you needed to know. There was no way you could take care of her without knowing. I'm still not sure you're capable."

General Donovan cleared his throat, his weight shifting side to side. "Boys, Paisley made a choice, and it's not like arguing that point is going to get us anywhere at the moment. Bateman, the only answers you're going to get will have to come from her. We've all been trying to get in her head for months, and she won't let us in."

"It's not like she really let me in, did she?"

"You're one to talk, because she looked pretty damn shocked to meet your father." My jaw flexed. "This is just one thing," Carter added. "You know everything else but this one tiny part of her."

Everyone else had known. Her parents. Carter. Morgan. *Morgan*. Shit. Someone needed to call her. I reached over to the chair next to me and picked up Paisley's purse. A quick look, and I had her cell phone in hand.

"I've already called Morgan, if that's what you're thinking. She had to wait for her mother, but she's on her way," Carter said.

"Of course you already did," I replied. I slipped her phone into her purse, and it fell off the seat, scattering the contents on the foot-worn linoleum floor. She didn't carry much, just her phone, a tube of lip gloss, a small wallet, and a folded piece of paper that landed between my feet. I put everything back in and picked up the paper last, carefully unfolding its worn edges.

Short, tight handwriting lined the page, accompanying small boxes on the left-hand side. Some were checked off in green, and others in orange. Some were still open and blank. This was Paisley's list. I ran my fingers over some of the entries, remembering how we'd done some of it together, and wondered when she'd found time to do the others.

"What is that?" Carter asked.

"It's her little bucket list," I answered. "Everything she wanted to get done before graduating college." Carter raised his eyebrows in a look I'd seen many times since we started flight school, the figure-it-out look. "Oh, shit. It's because of her heart."

He nodded as a doctor was paged overhead.

My chest tightened, the paper wrinkling under my grip. "What the hell? Everything on this list can get her killed."

"Hence why I told her no every time she asked me to do something." My eyes narrowed at him. "Hence why she chose you. She wouldn't even let me see the damn list."

I thumbed over some of the orange boxes—they were the ones I'd done with her—and let those words sink in. Paisley chose me for a reason, and she'd chosen not to tell me for the same reasons I'd chosen not to tell her about my father. We'd been happy in our bubble, as she called it.

The doors swung open, and my breath caught, but it was only Morgan and her mom, followed closely by Masters. I shoved the list into my pocket before reading the rest of the boxes. General Donovan met the women and directed them to his wife. Grayson crossed the room, dropped a black backpack at my feet, and consumed the seat on my left, taking my coffee and handing me a bottle of ginger ale without so much as looking at Will. "It'll help with the nausea."

"How did you—"

"Just drink it."

I unscrewed the lid and took a swig, the bubbles washing the dryness from my mouth. "How did you know I was here?"

"Yeah, funny story. This Robert Redford look-alike knocks on our door with a giant bodyguard a couple of hours ago. Turns out he's the ranking member of the Senate Armed Services Committee, and he's looking for his son...Prescott. Don't give me that look—I watch CSPAN. Anyway, I'm thinking he's off his rocker until he says Donovan's name. Then I'm thinking maybe he's not so crazy, and maybe I'm not the only one in the house who doesn't like to flay open his past. Since you didn't answer any texts, I found Morgan's number, and here I am."

I slipped my phone from my pocket and cursed at the dead battery. "Fuck. I'm sorry...for all of it."

He motioned to the backpack. "Don't worry about the phone, I brought you an extra charger. As for the rest, you don't owe me an explanation." Carter scoffed, and Grayson glared. "And you certainly don't owe second-choice Carter one."

Carter mumbled something that sounded like, "Go fuck yourself," and walked over to where everyone else huddled near the doorway.

"How is she?"

I twisted the cap on and off. "I don't know. They're trying to stabilize her. They haven't given us an update for about an hour or so."

"Shit day."

I dropped my head into my hands. The condensation dripped off the bottom of the cold soda bottle, leaving wet splotches on my pants. "What am I going to do if she doesn't... if they can't..."

"Don't." Grayson clasped my shoulder and gave it an awkward pat. "You open that door and it's all you'll think about. Focus on something else, anything but that."

"I can't." I tried to suck deep breaths in, fighting the urge to hurl as my vision hazed over. Existing without Paisley was a physical impossibility, like imagining a world without oxygen.

He reached in front of me, unzipped the small pocket of the

backpack, and thrust a yellow 5&9 booklet at my face. "Then quiz me."

"What?" I sat up.

"We have a test tomorrow, remember? Quiz me." He shook the study guide, and I momentarily debated hitting him with it, but I took it instead.

Where was that focus that always pulled me through the worst shit? I would fly that fucking helicopter because that's what had gotten me this far. *Block everything else out. You're good at that.* But her name was all that came to mind as I quizzed Grayson for the next two hours. Photographic memory or not, my brain just didn't tune in.

At some point Morgan and Will took over the seats across from us. Morgan quickly fell asleep on Will's shoulder, and Morgan's mom kept the Donovans stocked in coffee. Six hours and seven minutes after we brought her in, the door swung open, and I stuttered over the last question I asked Grayson as the doctor addressed the Donovans across the room.

Mrs. Donovan's knuckles turned white against the dark fabric at the waist of her husband's blazer. They both nodded, but there were no tears. That had to be a good sign. I found my legs and stood, only to be given the universal wait symbol by General Donovan. They disappeared down the hallway, and every one of my nerve endings fired, desperate to crawl out of my own skin to get to her.

Morgan's mom woke her up. "Let's go, honey. She's stabilized for now in the ICU, but they're not going to let anyone but family in tonight. Let's get you home."

Stabilized. The knot in my throat loosened slightly.

Morgan blinked the sleep out of her eyes and nodded. "You okay?" she asked Carter.

"Yeah. If she's stable, I'll head home." He looked over at me. "Bateman?"

"I'm staying."

"They're not going to let you in tonight."

"I'm not leaving this hospital until they let me see her." I sank a little deeper into the hard plastic chair.

"We have to be on the flight line at seven thirty a.m., and there's a huge test in the afternoon. How are you planning on swinging that with no rest?"

"I'll be there, and I'll still be able to outfly you."

"Yeah, because this is adequate crew rest. Masters, talk some sense into him." He followed Morgan and her mom out.

Grayson motioned to the backpack. "I figured you wouldn't leave, so there's a clean change of clothes, a flight suit, shaving kit, and a shit ton of caffeine. You're going to need it." He was halfway out the door before he turned around. "Oh, and I left your boots under your truck since the door was locked. Just pray no one steals them."

It was another half hour before the Donovans came out. Mrs. Donovan's eyes were bloodshot, but she had a faint smile on her face. "She's asking for you," she said softly but crystal clear across the empty waiting room.

"Room 728," General Donovan called after me as I sprinted through the swinging doors. I slowed to a walk when I got a death glare from a nurse whose last name was probably Ratched.

I nearly stumbled when I caught sight of her. Her skin gave the sheets competition in the pale department, and her hair was piled limply on top of her head. An oxygen tube lay under her nose, and wires trailed out of her neckline. A monitor beeped in rhythm with her heart, and an IV dripped steadily. Her eyes were closed, her breathing deep.

The chair made no noise as I pulled it toward her bed, sitting close enough to her to ghost my fingers across her upturned palm. Her eyes flickered open, the normally crystal green a hazy moss color, and I took my first full breath since she'd stopped her own.

Everything I wanted to tell her, to ask her, sprinted across my brain. Every demand for information about her condition. Every condemnation for not telling me. Every whisper of thanks for what she brought to my life. Every hope and fear that consumed me, because I already knew she was my only possible future. Instead, I lowered the side railing of her bed and laid my head next to her hip so I could still see her as she struggled to open her eyes. "I love you. You're my entire world."

A weak smile floated across her face as she feathered her hand into my hair. "Thank goodness, because you're my universe." Her words slurred, and her eyelids drooped. "I love you, Jagger. Don't leave? Stay with me?" Her voice trailed off as she lost the battle with sleep, her breath evening out.

"Always." I glanced at the clock, knowing I needed to go—this week was going to be a bitch with tests and final check rides—and knowing I wouldn't. I couldn't take leave right now, not without failing primary, so I'd have to deal with the sleep deprivation.

It was six forty-five a.m. when I pulled myself away from her. I'd spent the night in and out of her room, leaving at intervals forced by Nurse Ratched. Grayson had nailed the hospital kit, so I got ready in her bathroom and headed out, kissing her forehead. Thankfully, no one had stolen my boots, so I made it to the flight line on time, but I was off my game, even with an energy shot. Not enough to crash us, but enough for my IP to shake his head. Carter tried to cover for me when I missed more than half the answers. But I made it through the morning, even with Paisley consuming nearly every thought.

By the afternoon, my mind was fuzzy, and I'd had enough caffeine to jump-start a racehorse. I tapped my pencil on the desk, mentally counting down the minutes until I could get back to the hospital.

Then I took out Paisley's bucket list and read over some of the boxes we hadn't checked off yet, trying to think of ways to make them happen for her. Some of them were so unlike her that I had to wonder how well I really thought I knew her. Go surfing—when she could barely swim?

"How are you doing?" Carter asked. I wanted to punch him a little less today. Either he was growing on me, or I was too exhausted for hate.

"Thanks. Surviving."

"It's a lot to take in." His eyes dropped to the paper. "Her list?"

"Yeah. Some of it just…I don't know. They're all amazing, wild things to do, but it's like she tried to pick the most out-there, dangerous things, and honestly, I don't think she'd enjoy doing half this shit. And get a belly-button ring is marked off, but I know she doesn't have one."

"Belly-button ring?" He reached for the list, but paused, looking at me for permission.

I nodded and handed it over. "Make a name for herself at West Point? What the hell is that even supposed to mean? I know she's hell-bent on getting all these done, but it doesn't even feel like her."

Carter's face drained of color as he scanned down the paper. "Why didn't I see it? Why didn't she tell me? God, Paisley. She never meant for this."

Chills erupted on my arms.

"All right, boys and girls, it's test time," our instructor said, closing the door behind him and passing stacks of tests down the aisles.

"What do you mean?" I asked Carter.

"It's not her list—not her handwriting, and those green marks? You're right, she didn't do those. The belly-button ring, the skinny-dipping, the mechanical bull…I was there for all of it that summer, but…not with her. I never even knew she'd made something like this." He dropped the paper on my desk like it had burned him. "Paisley's finishing Peyton's list—the one that got her killed."

The test hit my desk as my stomach hit the floor.

CHAPTER THIRTY

19. Think of someone else's needs first.

Mama flipped the page of her *Southern Living* magazine and sighed for the twentieth time in the last hour. When I didn't respond, she tried another tactic. "What are you reading?"

"Not much." *Everything.* When I'd first Googled "Jagger Bateman," nothing had come up but hockey scores and highlights. But when I entered "Prescott Mansfield"? A whole world opened up.

I needed to keep my mind off Will's phone call. The one that told me to be kind to Jagger because he'd bombed his flight today and scored a zero on the test this afternoon. He'd failed. Because of me. I'd become the one thing he'd tried to avoid— the worst kind of distraction. He'd be able to bounce back, I was sure of it. But not when I was dragging him down.

"Well, it must be interesting. You've had your head in that thing all day, and that's saying something seeing as it's going on supper time." She flipped another page.

"Why don't you head home? There's nothing you can do here, Mama." I finished another story, this one speculation on where Prescott and Anna Mansfield really were, directly questioning Senator Mansfield's request for privacy so his children could live free of the public eye.

She peered over at me with a look that withered lesser women. "Oh, no. I'm sitting right here. There's no chance I'm headed home to that sea of piranhas."

I gave up, powering off the tablet. My left thumb hovered over the little pain clicker, and I wished it made my mother disappear as easily as the pain in my ribs from the break. "I'm sure it's perfectly fine. No one is out to eat you up."

"Oh, no? You are well aware that Sue Ellen Watts has told *everyone*, and there will be dozens of messages to return. She never could resist a good piece of gossip." She flicked another page. "Besides, I'm not about to let you sit here all alone."

God, I wish she would. I shifted my legs in the sheets, stubble catching on the smooth fabric. I needed a good shower and a razor. I changed tactics as I adjusted my oxygen tube. "Mama, go home. Get some sleep. I won't be alone. Jagger should be here any minute." I'd been telling myself that every minute since the clock hit five p.m. It was going on six thirty now.

"Hmm. Yes, about that boy." She looked over the pages of her magazine.

"Jagger is where I draw the line. Not a single word."

"Don't you mean Prescott?" The magazine landed in her lap, right with my patience. "I mean, really, Paisley. What kind of young man hides the fact that he's a senator's son? Maybe if we'd known that from the beginning, we wouldn't have been so against you seeing him, seeing as he's a Mansfield."

"Mama, who he's chosen to be is so much more than what he came from. I'd actually prefer not to have your approval of Jagger based on his father, and I'm not kidding. He's not up for discussion." I never wanted to hear that name again. He was Jagger Bateman, and that was all there was to it.

"Well, if that's how you feel. I wouldn't want to do anything to upset your heart...like bungee jumping or anything, before you get this pacemaker put in." She kept her voice sweet and level.

"Those are matters you know nothing about." Heart attack or no, there would be no pacemaker.

She stood, smoothing the lines of her slacks. "Hospital bed or not, don't you dare sass me, Lee. How about I get you some ice?"

I swallowed the messy emotions I knew she wouldn't want me to voice. "That'd be nice, thank you."

"How about I escort you to the machine, Mrs. Donovan?" Daddy asked her from the doorway. He winked at me. "Hey, darling. I'm going to steal your mama away and give you a second with this gentleman I found wandering the halls."

Jagger stepped around my father, dressed in faded jeans and a ringer tee just tight enough to make me want to peel it off him, if I was ever going to be allowed to have sex again. "Hey." I smiled, my heart already breaking.

His smile didn't quite reach his eyes as he leaned over and kissed me lightly. "How are you feeling?" Tension radiated from every line of his body.

"Better now." I tugged the oxygen tube from under my nose.

"Hey, you need that." Jagger looped it over my ears and pulled Mama's chair closer so that he could hold my hand. "So what now?"

"Wow, right to it, huh?" I joked. "No 'how was your day, dear?'"

"Where are my manners?" A corner of his mouth quirked up, but his usual grin didn't appear. "How was your day, my dear?"

"Oh, you know, mostly spent it being lazy and getting waited on hand and foot."

"Sounds like a dream." There was the smile. "More of the same tomorrow?"

My smile fell. "I'm being transferred to Birmingham tomorrow, so it should include a glamorous three-hour ride." My attempt at humor fell flat. "My cardiologist is there. I have to...make a choice now."

"You're getting a pacemaker, right?"

I jerked back reflexively. "What?"

"I spent some time on Google today." His eyes shot to where my tablet lay next to my hand. "I'm guessing you did, too. Anyway, I did some research."

"I thought you had a test."

"Yep. I took the test, *and* I researched new pacemaker technology."

My stomach turned, but I couldn't be mad since I'd spent my day researching him, too. But how much had he learned? "I'm choosing septal myectomy. End of discussion."

He paled. "You want them to shave down your heart?"

Apparently a lot. "It's not as bad as it sounds."

He sucked his breath through clenched teeth. "I need you to explain your thought process."

Logic couldn't keep my hackles from rising, and besides, wasn't this what I wanted? "I know you deserve an explanation, but you're going to have to watch your tone. Nothing gets me madder than someone bossing me around when it comes to my heart."

The chair creaked as he shifted his weight. "Do you love me?"

"Yes," I snapped.

"Do you want a future with me?" His eyes lit with the same fire that had drawn me to him in the first place.

"Yes." *Which I can never have.*

"Then stop acting like you're alone in this, and explain your choice. I'm not saying I'll agree with you, and I don't have to, but we're at least discussing it."

He wasn't Will or my parents. He wouldn't bully me against what I knew to be right. "I just have this feeling...and I don't want to be here again. I want the septal myectomy, because then it's done. Other than monitoring, I'm not sentenced to a life of...this." I gestured to the monitors. "It isn't just a Band-Aid, it's a fix."

"It's got a five percent mortality rate over six years, it's only eighty-five percent effective, and it has a huge rate of bundle branch blocks afterward. The pacemaker is proven to regulate your heart and seems like the most logical first step before you ask them to crack your chest, especially since you have a family history of SCD. Septal myectomy isn't guaranteed to keep you alive, the pacemaker is."

Ugh, stupid photographic memory. "I don't want a pacemaker." I enunciated each word.

"Well, that's a shitty reason."

"Wait...you...you actually *want* me to have the pacemaker?" Heat flooded my cheeks and then my ears. "They fail!"

He pushed the chair as he stood. "Yeah, in 2 percent of cases, they do, in which case you get it replaced, no big deal. Those odds are a hell of a lot better than the other."

"And you think you know best?" I sputtered. "I've been dealing with this for years, and in twenty-four hours you're an expert?" Why couldn't I stop the wrong thing from flying out of my mouth?

He threw his hands up. "No. I think that I know how to fly helicopters—that's it. Yesterday around this time I was at dinner with my girlfriend, wondering how to keep my family from blowing up in my face, and today she's making choices about fucking heart surgery. I spent some time on the internet so I could maybe not look like a moron, and what I read scares me more than when you collapsed on me yesterday."

I deflated, my shoulders drooping. "I should have told you. I'm so sorry you found out like this."

"We should have told each other a lot of things." He sat down, resting his head in his hands. "I should have told you about my family, or that I spent that week getting Anna into another rehab. But the things I kept from you don't change who I am right now, and you..." He looked up, the defeat in his eyes nearly breaking me. "I didn't tell you what happened to me, or what effect it had on other people, but you hid something that's killing you from the inside."

"Most HCM patients are asymptomatic. They never have an issue." Dang it, my defenses were back up.

"But you do. Most HCM patients don't have a family history of SCD. You could have died yesterday." The quiet tone of voice didn't match the intensity of his eyes.

"Then I'm lucky that my lifeguard was there again." My smile trembled.

"This isn't funny, Paisley. None of it. You won't even consider the pacemaker?"

"I want to fix my heart and really live, not manage HCM."

"By taking the most reckless route possible? How long have you been showing symptoms?"

"Since that day you found me in the library."

His mouth dropped slightly, and his eyes narrowed. I'd never seen that look leveled on me before and would have been quite happy never seeing it again. "You've had *months* and didn't do anything?"

"It hasn't exactly been an easy decision!" My hands gripped my sheets, desperate to stay grounded as the argument spun out of control.

"Living is a hard decision?"

"What kind of life would that be, Jagger? One where my heartbeats aren't really my own? One where I steer clear of everything that makes me feel alive? The kind of life you would refuse to lead?"

"What are you talking about?"

"I can't be the kind of woman you want, the kind you deserve, with a pacemaker. It will escalate to an internal defibrillator, and then what, you get shocked when we're making love? Do I just stay home while you run off and...swim with sharks?"

"Swim with sharks? Do you seriously think I'm so shallow that any of that matters to me? I've got nothing to prove and no list to mark off—I only want you."

"You wouldn't want me like this! I would hold you back."
Don't let me.

"I wasn't the one jumping ATVs or begging to bungee jump. That was all you, with zero consideration for your own life while you marked off this ridiculous list." He lifted his hips, pulling the folded list out of his pocket, and tossed it on the bed. I would have felt less exposed if he'd read my diary.

I snatched the paper and ran my fingers over the worn folds. "It's a bucket list. People put ridiculous things on them. Isn't that the idea? To stretch your boundaries?"

"Sure, if they were things you really wanted."

Goose bumps raced along my arm. "What's that supposed to mean?"

"It means that you've been so busy trying to live for your sister that you nearly died for her instead." His eyebrows lifted in a challenge I couldn't meet, not when he knew what I'd worked so hard to keep to myself.

"How did you know? It doesn't matter. I don't expect you to understand why I have to finish it for her."

He jumped out of his chair again, pacing at the foot of my bed. "Oh, no. You don't get to pull that card on me, like I don't know what it is to sacrifice for a sister. I walked away from my entire life for Anna, and I don't regret it. When my father cut her off, left her to rot in a crack house in Boston? That's when I emancipated myself. It wasn't just to get away from him, it was so I could get control of my trust fund and pay for her rehab when he wouldn't—when she became worthless to him."

"Your sister is still alive. It's different. You can still talk to her, ask her questions, hug her. Finishing that list is all I can do for Peyton." He didn't understand. No one did.

"Maybe Anna is still here, but she's buried under so many layers of her addiction that I'm not sure I'll ever have *my* Anna again. She's been in rehab thirteen times, Paisley. Thirteen times I've tracked her down and admitted her. Thirteen times she's begged me to stay, and a couple of times I did and nearly lost myself in her world. I missed deadlines for term papers and hockey games because I was flying to Seattle, or Texas, or wherever she'd followed the latest boyfriend. I swore when I started flight school that I wouldn't be distracted by anything… or anyone, that I'd put my goals first for once." He braced his hands on the footboard of my bed, the muscles in his arms flexing as he gripped the plastic. "And what happened when she turned up in Chicago? I missed a week of flight training and went to get her again."

"Isn't that the same thing I'm doing, prioritizing my sister's life?"

"No, because when I realized what it was doing to me, that I'd jeopardized my ranking to select the helicopter I'd worked half my life for, that I'd run off to Anna and left you hanging—that's when I told her that I'll always be there for her, but I can't walk away from my responsibilities every time she does. My life is just as valuable as hers, and yours is, too!"

"Peyton didn't get a chance to finish…anything!"

"Stop making this about her. You're the one in the hospital bed. This is about your life now."

I lifted my chin, the words flowing from my mouth like an eruption of acidic lava. "My life. My heart. My choice. I choose to have the septal myectomy, and then I'll finish the list."

"So this discussion's over?" He moved away, his hands in the air like he was under arrest. "My opinion doesn't matter?"

"You don't get a say in what I do with my heart!" The monitors beeped, spiking in time with my breaths.

"That's right. Your heart in *your* body—"

"Yes! Mine! You don't own it or control it. I do!"

"God damn it, Paisley! You own *mine*! Don't you get it? I'm in love with you, so fucking wrapped up in everything you are— that we are together—that I'm not sure I can exist anymore if you don't. Every single risk you're taking with your heart, remember that I'm along for the ride, strapped in, because my heart is tangled with yours. Why can't you see what you already have? You're so hell-bent on ripping your chest open for a risky procedure because you think a pacemaker sentences you to a half life where you can't complete these insane little tasks? Am I getting it right?"

"Yes." I hated how he made me sound, how I must look through his eyes because he didn't understand.

"I *am* that half life. Me. A pacemaker guarantees you *me*, and if our future isn't a good enough reason for you, then I'm out of arguments." His eyes pleaded with me to choose him, and I was. He just didn't understand *how*.

"You want a glimpse of our future if I do what you're asking? Look around you, Jagger. *This* is our future. Hospital rooms, stringy hair, bloody noses from dried-out nasal passages and oxygen tubes. A pacemaker isn't guaranteed to solve the problem. We could be right back here in a year or two, making the decision for the surgery because the pacemaker isn't going to do a damn thing about the obstruction. I will eventually go to an internal defibrillator. I'll wind up in end stage, where I'll need a transplant. That is our future if I don't do this!"

"You're jumping two steps ahead instead of buying yourself time."

"I'm giving myself an 85 percent chance at a normal life with you!" Tears stung my eyes, hot and volatile.

"You're giving me a 15 percent chance of losing you instead of a 98 percent chance of a happily ever after."

The space that separated us was far more than the few feet it measured. "I'm done with people in my life telling me they know what's best for me. I can't control my heart, but I can control this choice, and I will. Peyton didn't get a choice, and I'm not going to let mine be taken away because you think you know what's best for me. I'm not a child." *I could be fierce.*

He laced his fingers behind his neck and looked at the ceiling. "I'm not going to pretend that I knew Peyton, but I can't imagine anyone who loves you wanting this for you."

"Well, I knew her," Will said, stepping fully into the door frame, "and I can tell you she didn't want this for you, Lee."

Oh, God. Please let this bed swallow me whole. "How much did you hear?"

He leaned against the wall next to Jagger, standing with him more than physically, but also blocking him from leaving. "Oh, you've entertained a few of us out there. Your dad blocked every nurse who wanted to stop this overly loud discussion because we were hoping that out of all of us, you'd finally listen to him."

I sat up straighter, but ruined my attempt at independence by having to untangle my oxygen tube to do it. I'd never felt so alone, or so attacked in my life. They were supposed to love me, right? Then why couldn't they understand that there was something in my soul screaming against a pacemaker? Against an unnatural piece of machinery under my skin, controlling my heart—controlling me? "I can't make you understand. None of you are in this bed with me; you all get to leave this hospital. I don't. I'm the one taking the risks while you two go and fly your helicopters all day. I just...I want Peyton. I want to ask her what she would do, because I know she'd have the answer. She always did."

"She didn't have the answer," Will interjected. "I was there, Paisley."

"Well, she would tell me not to get bullied into something that I didn't want. She would have known what to do if she'd been in my shoes—if she'd known her heart was a ticking time bomb. Peyton never would have given in to what other people wanted."

"And that's probably what killed her, Paisley!" Jagger dragged his hands over his face, then dropped them, his shoulders sagging.

My head snapped like I'd been struck. "Why would you say that?"

"Because she knew! You don't want to see it, but she knew about her heart."

"She did not! She would have told me—told my parents!" My spine straightened until it almost hurt.

"Lee—" Will tried to interrupt.

"William Carter, get out! This isn't a conversation you're welcome to!"

"Seriously—"

"Now!" I yelled, but he didn't budge.

"Use that beautiful brain of yours, Little Bird." Jagger's voice softened, but he seemed farther away than ever. "Why else would she make a bucket list? Why else would she have done all those things the summer before, or handed you that note the last time you saw her? She knew, so stop hiding behind her and that damn list, or what you mistakenly think I need, and make your own choice, because she sure did."

My brain overloaded, caught between trying to process what he implied and knowing that if I wanted to give him what he really needed, this was my chance. I took it. "You want me to make my own choice? Fine. This"—I motioned between him and me—"we're over." The words ripped through me, and I half expected the heart monitor to show it, but it stayed as steady as my voice. "My sister never would have kept this from me, not if she knew it was genetic." Maybe if she *had* known, she would have kept it from me, needing to spare me the same way I'd tried to spare Jagger. But it was too late for either of us now. I refused to be the distraction that sank him. I felt adrift in a giant sea of uncertainty, and I was pulling him down with me... so I cut him free. "Go find another girl. As I recall your past, that shouldn't be hard to do. We're done."

"We're not done, we're fighting. I might not be proud of my past, but you're the only woman I want. You are irreplaceable, which is why you're scaring the shit out of me with the choices you're making. You're my family, and we are not done."

He was perfect, and I loved him so much that I saw the line and walked right past it, my chest aching with every step it would take to push him over. "The son of a drug addict? I should have known better than to be with someone who didn't know the first thing about commitment and real family. You would seriously try to use my sister, my deepest pain to manipulate me? You really are your father's son. Get out."

He stumbled backward, every feature on his face slack with surprise. Hurt streaked through his eyes, and I watched his heart break as surely as I felt mine rip into shreds. *What did I just do?*

"Maybe you're right. Someone with no real family can't understand one. But you're right, I am the son of a drug addict, so I do know a little something about trying to change a woman who's too stubborn to walk away from her own self-destruction. I love you, Paisley, more than I ever thought possible. You own everything I am, down to the very breath in my lungs, and I'm sorry that's not enough. Not enough for you to treat me like a partner instead of the enemy, and not enough for me to stand here and watch another woman I love kill herself over something she has complete control over."

He was more than enough. He was everything, but I couldn't force the words past the tangle in my throat. "Jagger," I choked out as he made his way toward the door.

"Stop it, Paisley!" Will shouted. "Damn it, he's right! Peyton knew!"

Jagger paused at the door frame.

Gravity shifted, taking with it everything that had been holding me together. It was one thing for Jagger to speculate, but for it to be truth? She couldn't have known. Not really. "No."

"Yes." He didn't break eye contact with me, and I saw the truth and his embarrassment at hiding it. "She knew for months, since our scuba classes early that summer. She knew she couldn't stay at West Point if anyone found out."

Pain ricocheted through me, scraping every nerve ending raw. I closed my eyes on everything I thought I knew and opened them with tears streaking my face, washing away my anger, my pride, and my certainty. My soul started soundlessly screaming, but I was so hollow inside that I was sure everyone could hear the echo.

He'd been right, and I hadn't listened. "Jagger?"

He shook his head, his eyes hard as he turned around. "Funny thing about families, Paisley. They're not always biological, none of them are perfect, and even if they have all the answers, sometimes they fail the first test they face."

"Bateman," Will said quietly.

"Don't," Jagger snapped.

I'll be your family now. My own words cut through what remained of my heart, mocking the way I'd failed him.

He crossed the room toward me, pulled something out of his front pocket, and placed it in the palm of my hand. I couldn't look down, not when his eyes held me captive in my own stupidity and stubbornness.

"I won't be needing this anymore." He brushed a lingering kiss across my forehead, and my eyes slammed shut, fresh tears leaking down my face. He took a deep breath in my hair and pulled away. I looked up at him, but the hurt was gone from his face, replaced by the carefree grin I'd seen on the beach before we met. Only this time it didn't seem beautiful, or sexy, but lonely.

"Jagger," I begged.

"I like to think it kept me safe, and I hope it does the same for you on your flight, Little Bird. I'll see you around." He smiled again, firmly entrenched in the impenetrable shell everyone else knew him so well for. "Carter, I'll see you tomorrow."

My eyes followed his figure out the door, but I was incapable of speech or thought. There was nothing I could say that would erase what I'd said, or how stupid I'd been. But he was free. He'd bounce back. He'd get his dream, but I wondered if he'd ever realize that he'd been mine.

"Lee?" Will sat on the edge of my bed. "I should have told you, but I promised her that I'd let you make your own choice."

"I don't want to hear about Peyton. Not now." Losing Jagger hurt too much. I released my fingers from the fist I'd made, and the light instantly reflected on Jagger's nickel. "At least he'll get what he's worked so hard for, right? Without me distracting him?"

"That's why you did it—said that crap to him. You pushed him away."

"He deserves better than this. I know how hard he's worked, how much flying that helicopter means to him. He was exhausted this morning and had no business flying, and it will only get worse if he stays with me. At least now he has a shot. He can get his dream." Will's mouth tightened. "What? Don't you dare hide anything else from me, William Carter."

"He's got no shot at top of the OML. He'll be lucky to get into the top ten even if they let him retake the test."

I blanched. I clung to one last hope, knowing the aircraft numbers varied from class to class. "How many pilots?"

"Twenty-three made it through."

"How many Apaches are there for selection?"

"Six."

You just shattered him for no reason. He's not getting one anyway.

I'd done this to him, taken away the one thing his family hadn't been able to. I picked up my cell phone and dialed the number by heart. It rang four times and then went to voice mail.

I waited, and then spoke, my voice stronger than my determination. "Hi there, Dr. Larondy. It's Paisley Donovan, and I just wanted to let you know that I've made my decision, so you can go ahead and schedule that surgery. I'll be ready."

CHAPTER THIRTY-ONE

JAGGER

But when you have that thing worth fighting for, you claw, you kick, you beg. Mom taught me that. But I couldn't save her. And you didn't bother trying. I'm not going to make the same mistake twice.

I raised the beer to my lips and swallowed. A few girls danced in the corner of Oscar's bar, Marjorie one of them, but I didn't care enough to even notice what she was wearing. She was pretty damn loud when she drunkenly toppled over the speaker, though.

Six fucking days had passed since Paisley had kicked me to the curb, and I wasn't sure how I was still breathing, seeing as most of my blood supply was made up of alcohol. Oh, I'd shown up sober to fly and even aced that retake on the test, but it only served to get me through school. The original score was tallied into the OML. Selection was the day after tomorrow, and with only six Apache slots...well, I'd lost the two things I loved the most in one week.

It wasn't the helicopter that hurt the most. No, that was a gaping, festering gash in my soul, but at least it was something. But Paisley...I couldn't feel anything—not pain, or grief. Nada. I kept myself busy or drunk, because if I slowed down, even for a millisecond, and realized what had happened? I wasn't sure I'd ever breathe again, or have a reason to.

I took another sip and looked up at the flat screen. Go figure, there was my father on CNN at his first official reelection campaign rally. I ignored it until they flashed our last family picture, Mom included—never a good sign. "Can you turn it up?"

The bartender rolled her eyes but did it.

With the music playing, it took all my concentration to hear my father.

"...and I'll say it again: I respect the wishes of my children to live private lives outside the microscope of the press." *I just appear randomly and destroy them.*

"So we won't be seeing them during the campaign?"

"No, I won't be trotting them out to smile for the cameras. I chose this life. They did not. I can say that I'm sincerely proud of the strong, independent adults they're growing into. Of course, all that credit goes to my late wife. Now, how about we talk about this spending bill?"

Par for the course. Exemplary politician and a shit father. I tuned him out for the rest of the segment and put away two more beers in the next thirty minutes.

My keys disappeared off the bar, and I didn't need to look to know that it was Josh. "Grayson's got dinner waiting at home. Why don't we get some food in you?"

"How fucking domestic." I laughed and finished off the longneck. "I think I'll stay a little longer."

"We have our final check rides tomorrow. A bar is the last place we need to be."

"Then leave." I motioned for another beer, and the bartender complied.

Josh took the bar stool next to me and started peeling the label off my discarded bottle. "Jagger, I wouldn't be here if it wasn't for you. There's no chance I'm leaving."

"Yeah, well, all I did was suggest aviation. My dad pulled the strings to get us in, right? I don't even fucking belong here. I wasn't good enough to get in on merit, and sure as hell wasn't good enough for…" Shit, it felt like I'd sliced open my heart to bleed out internally. I couldn't even say her damn name out loud. Yeah, numb was better.

He watched me for a few moments before breaking the six-day-old ice. "You know she loves you."

"I know."

"You love her."

"Yep." Even after the vicious shit she'd pulled, I couldn't stop myself. Because something about the way she'd snapped just wasn't right, wasn't her. Then again, seventeen unanswered text messages, six voice mails, and a flat-out refusal to come to the phone when I called her hospital room wasn't exactly sending any another message.

"Then it's going to be okay. It sucks right now, but you'll find a way to work it out."

I slammed the bottle onto the counter, which was better than punching something like I wanted. "What kind of world do you live in now, Josh? Fairy tales and fucking unicorns? I couldn't be happier that you and Ember are perfect, that you make it work, but guess what? It doesn't work out for everyone. She might love me, but she doesn't want me."

"Then go beg."

"I've tried!"

"Try harder."

"This isn't the same as you and Ember. You had months to work your shit out. I have days. It's not the same, and I'm not you!"

"No, you're better, and a hell of a lot stronger than I am.

What? You don't think I know about my mom's medical bills?"

Shit. "How long have you—"

"A year. Now shut the fuck up and let me talk. It's not the money, it's the time it took you to track everything down and then cover the tracks so I wouldn't know. You're the only reason I could afford to stay in college, and therefore the only reason I have Ember. I've never known anyone as fucking stubborn as you are, and I get it now, seeing how you grew up. So use it to your advantage."

"I can't sit by and watch her kill herself." I cleared my throat after my voice broke, and ran my thumb absently over the inked letters on my arm.

Josh saw the motion. "C to G. Cradle to grave. I know all about the promise you made to Anna, and I know you think this is just like her, or your mom, but it's not. Paisley can't control this condition or make it stop. This isn't something she can quit, and there's no right decision. You're not right. She's not right. But you have to ask yourself, if you don't stand by her now, can you live with yourself later?"

The beer turned sour in my mouth as his implications hit me. What if something happened to Paisley and I wasn't there? "How did everything get so fucked up? A week ago I had everything I wanted."

"Man, she's still Paisley. You're still you. This shit isn't too far gone. Go Tuesday after selection. We'll be done by one, and you could be in Birmingham by four."

"I think that's a great idea," General Donovan interrupted, sliding onto the empty stool next to me. He flagged the bartender. "Can I get a seven and seven?"

"Sir." I tensed as the bartender jumped to fill his order.

"Relax," he ordered. "What? You've never seen a general in a bar before?" A ghost of a smile tripped over his lips as he sipped at the drink.

"Not this one, sir," I answered.

"Well, I wasn't always a general. I used to be a butter-bar lieutenant chasing after a sweet little southern thing who preferred the seat at the very end." He took another swallow, and I almost fell off my stool when Josh elbowed me in the ribs. Asshole. "Are you going to ask me about her or not?"

Hell, yes. "How is she?"

He angled on his stool to face me. "Heartbroken, both literally and figuratively, but she's stable. Morgan's staying with her tonight."

Heartbroken. I'd had my hand in both. "I'm so sorry."

"Jagger, I was outside that room and heard every word. She threw everything but the kitchen sink at you, and she got what she wanted."

"What exactly was that, sir?"

"To push you away. She knows she's not exactly free of complications."

My beer hit the bar a little too hard. "Her complications don't matter to me. I will take her, heart whole or chest cracked wide open. Didn't she trust me to stay?"

"Hell, yes, son. She knew you would. You're her biggest blessing and her worst nightmare. She doesn't want to be the reason you don't get your aircraft or graduate."

"She destroyed me," I whispered, looking down into my bottle like it had the answers.

"She thinks she saved you, and then to get blindsided by Peyton's secret… Well, you two have some damnable timing. I wouldn't normally meddle—I'm not her mother—but I don't think she can do this without you, or the fight you bring out in her." A wry smile lifted the corner of his lips. "You bring her to life."

I kept my face straight, as professional as I could. This wasn't the guy to lose my temper on.

"You don't agree?" he asked.

"Sir, I'm sitting in a bar, discussing my love life with the commanding general of the post. Let's not pretend this isn't awkward." Josh nearly spit out his ice water next to me, but I ignored him.

"I only see a dad talking to the guy his daughter is in love with," he answered. "Look, you two are like super magnets—it doesn't matter what's between you, you're still drawn to each other. I saw it from the first time she said your name. I hated it then, but I'm thankful for it now." He swirled the ice in his nearly full glass. "Now, are you ready for that final check ride in the morning?"

"Keeping tabs on all the flight school students, sir?" Josh asked with a grin.

He placed his hand on my shoulder. "Just the ones in my family. You need to know that you got through to her. She's going ahead with the pacemaker; we're just waiting for a date."

"What? She did? Thank God." Relief nearly took me to my knees, but a pit grew in my stomach. Paisley had been more than adamant. "What changed? How does she feel about the decision?"

"She's quiet," General Donovan answered. "Quiet is better than dead, right?"

I nodded but couldn't say the same. What was wrong with me? I'd pushed her for this, so why did it feel like I'd lost something?

"Walker, take him home. Oh, and I didn't tie your class rank to his. That threat was just to scare the crap out of you."

"Well, it worked." *Thank you, Go— Yeah.* I might have screwed my own rank, but I hadn't tanked my friends'.

He laughed, which scared me more than the original threat. "Right. Well, two things. The first is that she's in room 824 at Birmingham."

I looked away. First he told me to stay the hell away from his daughter, and now I was basically being ordered to her bedside when she clearly didn't want me there. "Second?"

He leaned forward, clearly changing into general mode. "I've known your father for years. I actually happen to think he's an asshole. An influential asshole, but the same."

"Sir—"

"All that goes to show you, Lieutenant Bateman, is that you're not a measure of the people you come from or how you grew up, but who you've chosen to be." His voice dropped. "Knowing Senator Mansfield, I can say you are your own man." I flinched. "Fathers want the best for their children. I can tell you that it only took a phone call to get both Peyton and Will an appointment for West Point, but I also know that your father made no such phone call to get you into flight school. I checked, Jagger. You got here on your own, as a Bateman, not a Mansfield, and for what it's worth, I would have kicked a Mansfield out over the polar bear, no matter how mildly amusing I found it."

"Eat it." Grayson shoved the plate of eggs at me.

"Yeah, that's not going to happen." I pushed them across the table and finished fixing my coffee, not that I was sure that would stay down, either. Fuck, my ribs hurt. The new tattoo was the size of my outstretched fingers and was about as comfortable as being rubbed continuously with sandpaper, but it was worth it. The pain wasn't helping the nausea, though.

"You nailed the check ride yesterday, and everything else is out of your hands. There's no reason to be nervous. It is what it is."

"You're not even a little nervous?"

He'd already consumed half his plate, which might have contained a full chicken coop's worth of eggs. "Nope. My name is already somewhere on that list, and I can't control what the people ahead of me are going to choose. If there's no Apaches by the time my name is called, then I'll deal."

My stomach flipped again. "I'm not sure I can."

He nailed me with a look that called me out as an idiot. "You need to make peace with your demons and decide what's most important to you. Flying Apaches? Or being a pilot in general?"

My phone buzzed. *Maybe it's...nope.* "Josh just got there. Inhale the rest of that like the good little vacuum you are and let's go." I stroked my thumb over Paisley's picture on my contacts list, opened a new text message, and closed it out before typing anything. I'd be there in seven hours, in her face where she couldn't ignore me.

He flipped me off but hoovered it while I stole the check and paid. He'd be pissed, but he'd get over it. He stayed silent as we drove toward the airfield. It felt like I was walking to my execution.

I couldn't wrap my head around it or separate the two. I'd fallen in love with the Apache when I was a kid. It was the whole reason I wanted to fly. I wanted the power, the precision, the firepower. When I thought about flying, that was all I saw. Not that Blackhawks and Chinooks weren't useful, but they just weren't...mine. Where did this leave me?

I parked Lucy, and Josh met us at the door. "I thought you'd be here before dawn."

"Ha-ha. Very funny." We were actually close to the last ones there. There were two giant blackboards in the front of the room. One gave the makeup of the available aircraft for selection—six Apaches, three Chinooks, and fifteen Blackhawks. The other, completely blank for the OML. "Why the fuck can't they just tell us?"

Josh laughed. "Just the first lesson that the army can fuck with you just for the fun of it."

Grayson slid into his chair and stretched out like nothing was bothering him. "Relax."

What did it say? Where was I? Twenty-three pilots and six

Apaches, not that everyone wanted one. But I did.

But what if I didn't get one?

Nausea rolled through me. Thank God I hadn't eaten.

Was I here to be a pilot or to be an Apache pilot? The answer was easy to me—an Apache pilot, and I was about 99.9 percent certain I wasn't getting one. So what did that mean? If they got to my name and all the Apaches were gone, would I say Blackhawk?

No. This dream had started with an Apache, the way the rotors looked against the sky from the cockpit. Anything less was failure, a half of a dream—a half life.

Fuck.

You're so hell-bent on ripping your chest open for a risky procedure because you think a pacemaker sentences you to a half life...

I was the asshole here. I'd been so focused on what I wanted, on my own fears, I hadn't stopped to listen to what she was really saying. It didn't matter how illogical it was to me, because it made perfect sense to her.

I hadn't stood by her. No, I'd made her choose her half life. I. Was. The. Asshole.

Seven hours. I'd be there in seven hours, and then I'd listen to every single thought she had on it. I'd go in without preconceived notions, or my own mind made up. If I trusted her judgment on everything else, including me, I had to push my fears aside and trust her with her own future.

The door swung open, and Carter walked in, looking as green as I felt. At least I wasn't the only one who was nervous. He startled when he saw me. "What are you doing here?" he asked, sliding into his seat in front of me.

"Wait, this isn't morning yoga? Shit. I guess I'll have to select a helicopter after all."

"That's not what I mean—"

"Everybody grab a seat," Major Davidson said, coming from

the side door. "We're actually going to postpone selection for a few hours." A collective groan sounded in the class. "We didn't get the scores tallied from yesterday's check rides, so we need to move it. We'll be ready by fifteen hundred."

I glanced at my watch: eight a.m. They wanted us to wait another seven hours? Shit. I wouldn't get to Paisley until the evening.

"Seriously, what the hell are you doing here?" Carter asked, glaring at me.

"Where else would I be?" What was up his ass?

"Paisley is going into surgery in a few hours, so I figured you'd be there with her."

"What? No. She would have told me." *Would she?*

"She knew we had selection, but she told me she was going to tell you."

Major Davidson was still talking, but I didn't give a fuck. "She didn't."

Carter looked at me like he'd never seen me before. "She really loves you. You love her. It's not just a fling. You two are the real deal."

"A fling? She's my whole fucking world. She's my oxygen, my water, and my solid ground. Nothing matters without her. I cease to exist." I looked at the board where the helicopters were listed and stared as my heart picked up speed. "None of this matters to me without her." I jumped out of my chair, sending it flying to the ground behind me, and the entire room turned to stare. "I have to leave," I announced to all the raised eyebrows.

"Right, we'll all be leaving in a minute, Lieutenant Bateman. Let me finish these announcements and I'll dismiss you," Major Davidson said, anything but amused.

"No, I have to leave *now*." I swung my backpack over my shoulder and moved toward the exit. He met me in the doorway.

"What are you doing?"

"She's going into surgery." I tried to sidestep him, but he

blocked me. Twice. "Do you want to dance?"

"It's selection."

"It's Paisley."

The lines on his forehead appeared as he pinched the bridge of his nose. "You're going to be the damn death of me, Bateman. If you leave, your class leader will have to select for you, or you will draw whatever is left over. Can you live with that?"

I didn't need to think.

"I can live with anything. What I can't live without is her." I turned around and locked eyes with him. "Hey, Carter. You want to show me some of that West Point honor you're always gabbing about?"

He lifted one eyebrow as a response.

"Select for me."

CHAPTER THIRTY-TWO

PAISLEY

Screw you and your list, Peyton.

"Everything looks good to go. Dr. Larondy will be in soon." The nurse smiled at me, clipped my chart to the end of the bed, and left me alone with my mother.

"You're making the right decision, Lee." She looked perfectly composed except for the thumbnail she chewed on.

Then why does it feel like the wrong one? "I'll be fine, Mama. There's nothing to worry about."

"Hey! I brought your phone charger from home," Morgan called out as she skipped in. She looked the opposite of how I felt.

"I don't need to charge it."

"Come on, Paisley. Don't you miss the outside world?"

No, I only miss Jagger. "Everyone I need is right here." I forced a smile, but she saw straight through it.

"Call him." She sat on the edge of my bed.

I adjusted my oxygen tube and shook my head. "No. It's

selection day. I don't want to be a distraction."

"You know, usually you're the most levelheaded person I know. But this time you've gone lost your godforsaken mind."

"Morgan!" Mama chastised. "She's about to have surgery!"

"She's about to lose what I would absolutely kill for. What any woman would kill for."

White-hot jealousy ran my mouth dry. "Jagger?"

She scoffed. "No, you can keep Mr. California to yourself. Love, Paisley. Love. I would give my left eye for Will—I mean, well, anyone to look at me the way Jagger looks at you."

I studied her, putting pieces together in my head that I hadn't realized fit before. "Oh, Morgan, was I that bad of a friend?"

Color bloomed in her cheeks, and she picked fuzz off my hospital blanket. "Why on earth would you say that? You're my very best friend."

"Ask him out. Promise me right now that you'll ask Will out."

Her eyes shot to mine, but she quickly masked her surprise with a careful smile. "Oh, let's be serious. I think that ship sailed."

"Because of me?"

She shook her head and fluffed my pillow. "Oh, no. I'd say right around freshman year when I asked him to Sadie Hawkins and he took Peyton instead. As friends, of course."

"Of course." I didn't take my eyes off her as she straightened my covers. "Morgan, I love you, and I want you to be happy more than just about anything. Ask Will out. Go away to college and get drunk at a frat party. Get out of our little town because that's always been your dream. Stop staying for me."

"Don't talk nonsense. It's just a pacemaker. In and out, right?"

Now I was the one forcing a smile. "Right." A healthy dose of fear lodged in my throat, and all I needed was the one person I'd shoved so hard and so far away from me that he was probably in Siberia by now. "Listen, just in case…well, I need you to tell Jagger that I—"

"Tell me yourself," he answered from the doorway, dressed in ACUs.

My fingers dug into my blanket to keep me from flying off the bed and into his arms. I didn't have that right anymore. "What are you doing here? It's selection day."

"You know, you're the second person to ask me that today. It seems everyone has a different idea of where I'm supposed to be." He crossed to my bed and took the space Morgan had quickly vacated. "I'm exactly where I need to be, if you'll let me." His hand stroked my face, and I leaned into it, breathing in the scent of his skin, peppermint and home.

"I said awful things," I cried, tears pricking my eyes. "I'm so sorry. I just wanted you to get your dream, but now you're here missing selection, so even that is messed up!" I pulled the sheet to my face, swiping at the stupid tears.

"Why don't we give you two a minute?" Mama handed me a tissue box, gave Jagger a small smile, and pulled Morgan out of the room.

My heart pounded as we stared at each other in silence, each taking the other in. His eyes were bloodshot, making them seem more blue, and the skin underneath hung in purplish bags. "You look awful," I cried. Oh, great, now I was dripping snot into my oxygen tube. I pulled it free and blew my nose.

He laughed. "Hey, at least I'm not in a hospital bed. And besides, this is the best I've felt in a while."

"I'm so sorry about what I said."

He leaned forward and kissed my forehead, lingering long enough to take a deep breath. "There's nothing to be sorry for. I wasn't listening to you."

"What?" I draped the tube under my nose again.

He picked up my non-IV hand and squeezed my cold fingers. "Explain why you want the myectomy."

My shoulders fell. "We're not going through this again. I agreed to the pacemaker."

"Please, explain it to me."

"Jagger, no." I couldn't do this again. My hand slid from his.

"I'm…" His eyes almost glowed in their intensity. "I'm begging you. Stop pushing me away, because I'm not going anywhere. I love you, and it's not the kind of love that wavers. It's the scary kind that doesn't fade. I look at you, and I see not just everything I want for my life, but everything I am, because you took the emptiest, darkest pits of my soul and filled them with you. You are as much a part of me as my own heart, and it doesn't beat without you. You pump through my veins and you fill my lungs. I may have saved you, but you're the one who breathes for me every day. Do you get that? Stop pushing me away, because you make me imagine things, want things I never thought I could. Words like 'forever,' and 'vows,' and…'family.' I know I'm not good at that last one—"

"Stop," I whispered on the last of my breath. I hadn't been able to take one from the first word he'd spoken. "What you do for your sister, the loyalty you show to Josh, to Grayson. Jagger, that's family. What I said was unforgivable, and untrue. Once, I said I would be your family, but even that was wrong, because you already have one that I could only dream about belonging to. I love you. I love everything about you. There's no one else for me, and there never will be."

"Don't say that." Fear jumped into his eyes.

I brought his fingers to my lips and pressed a kiss to them. "Not because of the surgery, silly. There won't ever be anyone else because you own my heart. It might not be in the best shape, but it's yours. Nothing is ever going to change that. You say 'forever,' and I can't breathe for wanting it so badly, to wake up next to you for the rest of my life, but Jagger, I can't promise you forever. I can't promise you tomorrow. You are quite possibly the most reckless man I've ever met, but I'm not sure even you should take this risk."

He braced one hand on the outside of my hip and wound his fingers through the messy bun of my hair with the other, then pulled me into him so our mouths were only a breath apart. "Don't you remember? I told you the best things are worth the burn, the risk, and there is nothing better than you, Paisley Donovan." Then he kissed me like it was the first or the last time. My mouth opened under his, and I whimpered as his tongue stroked along mine. I'd missed the taste of him, and he more than made up for it. I felt his kiss in the depths of my soul. My pulse jumped, and he pulled away with a grin as the monitors beeped. "I don't want to bust your heart just before you have it fixed."

"Temporarily."

"Tell me why you want the septal myectomy."

"Jagger, we've already established that my reasons aren't logical."

"So what." He shrugged. "Tell me."

I ran my fingers through his hair, unable to stop touching him now that he was here. "Why are you such a good pilot?"

His brows lowered in confusion for a moment. "The photographic memory helps for academics."

"But the actual flying?"

"Instinct," he answered. "I have really good hand-eye coordination and great instincts."

I ran my fingers down the back of his head and laced them behind his neck. "I have this feeling...that I need the septal myectomy. Call it an instinct, call it stupid, but it's there. Getting the pacemaker feels wrong with every cell in my body. I know that's a lame reason, but it's mine."

His breath shook as he exhaled, and the muscle in his jaw flexed. "Then do it."

"Are you out of your mind?" I skimmed my hands across his shoulders. "You hate that idea."

"Yeah, well, I trust you and your instincts." His thumbs stroked along my waist as he held me. "Maybe we should—" He hissed when I ran my hand over his heart.

"What?"

"It's nothing. I got a new tattoo, and it's still raw."

To Jagger, tattoos marked monumental events, and I had to know right now. His zipper on his ACUs was easy, and he laughed as I pulled his T-shirt free. "If I'd known you were going to strip me on sight, I would have gotten here sooner."

"Hush," I reprimanded, doing my best to ignore the lickable lines on his stomach. By ignore, I meant ran my fingers over them briefly as I pulled his shirt up and out of the way. He lifted his arms and looked down at me as I studied it.

Then I lost my breath. "Jagger, it's beautiful." It was a bird, its wings raised in flight. The colors were bright, unlike anything I'd seen on him, the wings and feathers immaculately detailed in little... *Oh, mercy*. Little paisleys. The outline of the bird wasn't just a line—it was made up of words.

"'For once you have tasted flight, you will forever walk the earth with your eyes turned skyward, for there you have been and there you will long to return,'" he recited as I gently traced the quote.

"For finishing primary?"

"For loving you. Because the first time I lifted you into my arms, I knew you belonged there. The first time I kissed you, tasted what it could be like with you, I was addicted. I realized that I loved you, that I was capable of really loving, and the first time I made love to you, I knew I was finally home. You're it for me, and it didn't matter if we were together or not. You'd always be it. You push me away, and I'll still show up here looking for you because you're all I want."

Before I could kiss him, heck, tear his clothes off his body, a knock sounded at the door. "Knock, knock," Dr. Larondy sang as he slowly opened the door. "Ready for me, Paisley?"

"Yes." *No.* Jagger zipped his top before he was fully in the room.

Dr. Larondy smiled down at us as he examined my chart. Jagger untangled himself from my arms and stood, but he held my hand. "How are you feeling about today?"

"Oh, good, we're in time." Mama sailed through the door, not so subtly checking the position of our hands. "Hmm," she noted with a slight smirk.

Dad came in right after her, winked at me, and stood next to Mama on the opposite side of my bed.

"Well, now that everyone is here," Dr. Larondy joked. "Paisley? You ready for today?"

I opened my mouth, but no sound came out. He looked at me with expectation, but still, nothing. Jagger squeezed my hand when I looked up at him for help. He shook his head with a soft smile. "This is all you, Little Bird."

I sought my mother, her anxious eyes and trembling smile. "I'm sorry, Mama, but I need you to trust me."

Daddy moved closer to me and rested his hand on my shoulder in support with a satisfied smile. "Let's hear it, Paisley Lynn."

I gripped Jagger's hand and met Dr. Larondy's eyes. "I'm sorry for all the trouble, Dr. Larondy, but I've changed my mind. I'd like you to perform the septal myectomy."

I ignored Mama's gasp and relished the supportive hands of the men in my life. Dr. Larondy smiled. "Let me see what I can juggle on the schedule." He walked out and shut the door behind him.

"There is no way!"

"Magnolia!" Daddy shouted, startling me. "The girl, as you say, has spoken her piece, and that is that. Be supportive, or be absent."

"I just don't want to lose you, too." Her voice broke, and she became fascinated with the ceiling lights.

"Mama, Peyton died because she ignored this. I'm facing it head-on, but I get to choose how."

Her lip trembled as her gaze darted between us. "Okay, Lee. Paisley. We'll trust your judgment."

An hour later, Mama and Daddy hugged me, then Morgan pretended not to cry as they wheeled me down to the OR doors, Jagger my only company for the walk. "This is as far as you go," the nurse said.

He leaned over me, grinning at the ugly cap that had my hair bound, and laced his fingers with mine. "You think this is as bad as it gets, right? In our life? This moment?"

"Well, I'm breathing, which tops some of our other moments by that fact alone, but I've never been this scared," I admitted.

"Me, either." Every line of his body was tense, and I knew it would remain like that until he saw me in recovery. "Well, if this is as bad as it gets, how do you think we're handling it?"

"Like pros." He was so close that his face consumed all of my vision, blocking out the hospital around me, and with it a portion of my fear.

"Right. I love you. You are the best thing that has ever happened to me. My life started the moment I breathed into you, and I can't think of a better use for my breath now than to use it to say, 'I love you,' for the rest of our lives. I'm going to marry you, and we're going to have gorgeous, green-eyed babies who will turn us gray with their recklessness."

My heartbeats paused, then hammered. "Is that a proposal?" I whispered, terrified of both answers.

He shook his head, his dimple making an appearance. "No, a warning. Trust me, when I propose, you'll know it."

I leaned up and kissed him, thinking of when he'd told me the same thing about his kisses. "Trust me, when I say yes, you'll know it," I whispered against his mouth. "I love you."

"I'm sorry, but we have to get going," the nurse said behind a small sniffle.

We didn't say good-bye. Jagger held my hand until he couldn't reach beyond the painted red line in the hallway, and then I was alone. When they told me to count backward from one hundred, I mentally counted the reasons I loved him, but I didn't get past ninety-four.

CHAPTER THIRTY-THREE

JAGGER

I'll be around, but you won't see me, because you never really did. But I'll find someone who will, and I'll start my own family, not as a Mansfield. Prescott can stay with you and drown with your expectations. Jagger will fly way above them. Way above you.

"**D**o you want to know?" General Donovan asked as he came into the waiting room. "I just spoke with Will."

I shook my head. "It doesn't matter." Nothing mattered except the blonde who currently had my heart out on the operating table.

She'd been in surgery three and a half hours for a procedure that should have taken a flat three. Each movement of the second hand took a minute. I counted twenty-three chairs in the waiting room, and one hundred fifty ceiling tiles. "You're driving me crazy," Morgan whispered.

"She should be out."

"No news is good news," she countered, flipping the page on

Paisley's Kindle.

"We're in a hospital. No news is usually dead." I cursed my slip.

"And they call me dramatic."

The door opened and a scrubbed doctor headed for the Donovans, but it wasn't Larondy. I was halfway across the room before I thought about standing up.

"We found something," he explained. A weird sense of calm swept over me, numbing the panic. "She needs to have her mitral valve replaced. We couldn't tell the extent of the obstruction until we were in there, and the valve isn't salvageable."

Mrs. Donovan sagged into her husband. "Right now?" she asked.

"It's best to do it while we're in there, yes."

"I didn't want this in the first place. Oh, Lee."

"Ma'am, this isn't a complication of her surgery, but of her heart. It's a good thing we did the septal myectomy. We've already removed nine grams, and the pacemaker wouldn't have helped the obstruction. She would have been back in here before too long." He lifted the clipboard. "Who wants to sign?"

Her instincts had been right. She'd saved herself. "Do it. She doesn't want another surgery. Get it done now," I ordered.

Her father studied me carefully, then nodded. "He's right. She would want you to do it now." He took the clipboard and signed, then handed it over.

We waited another hour before I couldn't take it anymore. I paced the hospital like a caged tiger, with no goal or destination in mind. They had her heart open. Right now. Doctors were touching the most precious thing in my world, and I had zero control.

People moved around me, oblivious to the fact that my world hung in a precious balance. Probably because theirs did, too, but the noise...the noise was too fucking much. I paused at the chapel and pressed in on the doors.

Blissful quiet came over me, and my ears slightly rang from the abuse they'd been taking all day. Even though I was alone, I picked a pew at the end and sat in a church for the first time since my mother's funeral. I bowed my head and began to pray. I made every deal I could think of with God, in the hopes that he existed and listened. I would do anything, give anything, as long as she lived. Anything.

I don't know how much time had passed, but my hands had gone numb where they supported my head, and I was no longer alone.

"She's out and in recovery," General Donovan said, his voice full of reverence that had nothing to do with where we were.

My head fell back, and my eyes turned skyward, where the small stained-glass skylight rained down color. "Thank you." He dropped a folded piece of paper into my hand.

"Paisley wanted you to have that. But I sure as hell wasn't going to deliver a death letter before she lived."

I turned the note over and shoved it into my pocket.

The halls of the hospital looked completely different when my eyes weren't fogged by fear. "Didn't take you for a churchgoer," he said as we took the elevator to recovery.

"I'm not, usually." *Ever.*

"Well, there are no atheists in a foxhole, right?" The elevator came to a stop.

"Something like that, sir."

"'Any reason is a good reason,' that's what Mom used to say."

"Mine, too, though for completely different circumstances," I finished awkwardly.

He shifted his weight uncomfortably. "Jagger, I know she seems pretty...put together, but if you ever need to talk to someone about your family, your mother or your sister, well, Magnolia might know a thing or two about growing up like that."

What? "Um. Thank you, sir."

"Well, you're family now."

"Sir, you're not going to hug me, are you?"

"Hell, no."

"Good. That could get awkward really quickly." He shot a sideways look at me and walked away.

It was another two hours before Paisley was awake enough for us to see her. They'd removed all her tubes except the IV and oxygen. She was pale and tiny, and had never looked more beautiful to me. I kissed her forehead and walked behind her bed as they wheeled her to her room.

"Hey," I whispered as I sat next to her and reached for her hand as they locked the wheels. "I love you," I said, just because I could.

A faint smile ghosted across her lips. "I love you," she whispered, her green eyes barely visible as her eyelids drooped drunkenly.

"Glad we agree. You can sleep, Little Bird. I'll be here." Forever.

She slipped into sleep, and I watched her breathe, feeling utterly content for the first time in my life.

"Hey." Josh shook me gently. "Everyone's awake but you, hot stuff," he joked, and I blinked myself awake.

"Whoa," I mumbled, sitting up straight in the chair. My eyes darted to Paisley, who smiled sleepily at me.

Morgan sat on the very edge of Paisley's bed. Will leaned against the wall behind her, with Grayson on the opposite wall. Josh stole the other chair and pulled it next to mine. "Are we having a party?" I asked.

"A celebration of sorts." He smiled.

I wrapped my fingers around Paisley's, the need to touch her more overpowering than anything I'd ever felt. "We have a lot to be thankful for," she said.

"Okay, enough, will you please tell him?" Morgan asked Will.

Selection. Right. "Let's hear it." I slid closer to Paisley.

"Grayson was top of the OML," Will announced.

"No shit!"

All eyes moved to him, but he just shrugged. "You two were too busy screwing each other up. I just studied."

"What did you get?" I asked.

"Apache."

"Congrats!" I knew he wanted it and couldn't have been happier for him. *Then there were five.*

"I pulled second," Will admitted, no malice in his features. *And then there were four.* "Two warrants selected Apaches next." *Two.* "Then one of the Chinooks, then another Apache."

One. It didn't matter, I had Paisley. But damn if my heart didn't seize up anyway.

"Fuck, how far down did I finish?" That stupid test. I hadn't even marked an answer, just turned the thing in blank, like my mind at the time.

"Ninth," Will answered, and my stomach dropped.

"Well, Blackhawks aren't all that bad."

"Are you going to let me finish?" Will asked.

"Please, continue. The sound of your voice is so soothing." Paisley shot me a look but rubbed her thumb over my hand to take the sting out of it.

"Josh was next." *And then there were none.*

I smiled over at my best friend, who had a shit-eating grin on his face. "Congratulations, man."

"Thanks, I think I'll like flying Blackhawks."

My mouth dropped open. "What?"

"Well, I can't fly medevac with an Apache, can I? I owe a little something, so I gotta pay it back. Besides, it's not like I can't transition easily over to Special Operations or anything."

I shook my head. "I had no idea you were thinking…"

"It snuck up on me, but it's where I want to be."

"And number eight?" The room went silent, and I knew. "Apache, huh?" They all nodded. *And then there were none.*

"Lee-Lee? I'll…uh…let you do the honors." Will guided Morgan out of the room, and the rest followed suit, finally leaving me alone with Paisley.

"How are you feeling?" I asked, perching lightly on her bed.

"Like I just had my chest cracked open," she joked. "But the pain meds are lovely. Do you want to hear the rest of the story?"

"About selection?"

She nodded. "I know how it ends."

"I won't mind flying a Blackhawk. I'll get to be with Josh, and hey, I'm still flying." I tucked a strand of pale blond behind her ear, rubbing the silk between my fingers. "And I get to come home to you, so what does it matter what I fly?"

"You selected the Apache."

My hand froze at her cheek. "What?"

Her smile could have lit the world. "You heard me."

I shook my head. "How? I counted. That's impossible."

"You didn't count, you assumed."

I went over the figures in my head again. "All six Apaches were selected before they got to me."

She shook her head. "Will deferred his choice for every turn until he was next to you. He took a Blackhawk. He selected the Apache for you."

"Why would he do that?"

"Because he said he would. You trusted him to select for you."

"He gave me his aircraft?"

She nodded, and I fumbled for words before I sprinted out the door and into the hallway. Josh and Grayson sat on the floor, braced against the wall. "He left already," Josh answered my unspoken question. A nurse slipped into Paisley's room behind me.

"Why would he do that? He wanted it just as badly." I couldn't understand.

"He mumbled something about honor and bit the bullet," Grayson answered. "Josh, you ready to head to Nashville? My flight is in five hours."

They both stood. "Yeah, let's get you there." Josh turned to me. "You going to be okay here?"

I nodded slowly. "Yeah, I think I am."

"Good," Grayson answered, pressing the button for the elevator. "I packed you a bag. It's in Paisley's closet, complete with a new set of Apache 5&9s. Start studying, and you might have a chance to beat me for top of the OML in the Apache course." He walked into the elevator without another word.

"Arrogant prick." I laughed.

"Who knew, right?" Josh joined in and then followed Grayson into the elevator. "How are you feeling?"

I grinned. "Living in a land of fairy tales and unicorns, man."

"Hell, yeah."

"You two are disturbed," Grayson muttered as the doors closed, leaving me alone with Paisley.

"There's a reclining chair if you'd like to rest near her," the nurse offered with a smile as she left Paisley's room.

The only light came from the bathroom as I walked in. Paisley mumbled something, and I sat in the chair next to her, noting that her IV bag had been changed. "Need anything, Little Bird?"

"Just you," she said, lacing her fingers with mine.

"You will always have me. That's never going to change."

"Still want to marry me? Or were those the drugs talking?" Her voice was sleepy.

"You're on the drugs, not me, and I meant every word." I leaned over and brushed my lips over hers in a soft kiss. "I'm going to spend the rest of my life loving you."

"Good." She smiled against my mouth. "Because I love you. And I want lots of kids. And a really big library." Her voice wavered as she slipped off to sleep.

"I guess it's a good thing that I have experience building those," I whispered as I tucked the blankets around her. Then I slipped her letter out of my pocket and opened it, reading in the dim light.

Make love on the beach. See the Statue of Liberty. Visit the Parthenon.

It wasn't a letter.

Oh, no. It said, "Jagger and Paisley's Bucket List."

And I was going to make sure she completed every last one… at least once…or more. That beach one sure looked promising.

EPILOGUE

PAISLEY

66 I'm older than you now. Do you know how wrong that feels? I keep thinking back to when I was five, and you were seven, and I was so mad that you could ride that roller coaster, and Mama kept telling me that I'd always be younger, and I told her that wasn't true. One day you'd be dead. I reckon I was not an easy five-year-old.

"I hated you for a minute there," I admitted as I pulled the grass between my fingers. "But only because I loved you so very much. If I had known, I would have spent more time with you that summer. I would have made you see reason and do something about your heart...our hearts." Another crimson leaf drifted down as the September breeze kicked up. It landed between my knees and the white stone that marked where my sister rested. As I brushed it away, sunlight caught on my watch. As much as I'd always detested it, I was more scared to let myself believe the truth—I didn't need it anymore.

"I don't get to hate you, because you're not here. I don't get to hate you because the choice you made cost you the most, but it cost the rest of us, too, Peyton. But mostly, I don't hate you because at the very end, it was your choice, no matter how wrong it may have been, that gave me the strength to make mine. You saved me. You were reckless." I laughed through the tear that escaped and brushed it away. "Incredibly reckless, but you died chasing what you loved, what you wanted. You died by really living, and I can't hate you for that." Movement caught my attention from the left as Jagger walked slowly up the path through the West Point cemetery. That sweet burn filled my chest, like it did whenever I saw him, and I smiled. "Because I finally understand having something not just worth dying for, but living for."

I took out the folded, worn piece of paper from my pocket and opened it. I brushed my thumb over number sixteen, and the check mark I'd added in her green. *Make a name for myself at West Point.* "I wish you'd found another way to check this one off, you stubborn thing. I didn't finish the rest of them, and I'm sorry, but I made my own list, Peyton, and loving him is at the top of it. I'm fierce, now, just like you wanted for me, so you don't need to worry. It's not your brand of fierce, or wild, but I'm exactly who I want to be. Well, I'm getting there."

Tingles swept my feet as I stood, the blood rushing back into them. "I miss you every day, and will always love you, Peyton."

I unclasped my watch and used it to weigh her bucket list down on the top of her stone. Then I pressed a kiss to my fingers and traced the outline of her name with my fingers, aching for the sight of her smile, the sound of her laugh, anything but the cool stone that was left in her place. "I'm going to live for me now."

The gravel on the path crunched as I walked toward Jagger. He opened his arms wordlessly, and I slipped into them, my head finding its place on his chest. His heart beat under my ear, strong and steady. Mine was finally a match for his, just like our lives.

We spent what was left of his leave down in Destin, Florida, finishing out the only break Jagger was going to get during the Apache course. It looked the same as it had a year ago, but I had irrevocably changed. *Just not in the modesty department.* I clutched my cover-up to my chest and breathed in the salty air.

"Let's go, Little Bird!" Jagger stood in the water, the waves rocking to his knees as the sun started its descent. He bounced, expelling the nervous energy that had been slowly leaking out through the tapping of his fingers on the steering wheel for the whole drive. I'd never seen him so nervous to start a new session of classes.

Another wave crashed, soaking him above his waist before receding. Water dripped down his stomach to his swim trunks, and my mouth ran dry. I knew what every inch of that skin tasted like, and I could never get enough, but it was the heart underneath those incredible looks that had me hooked. I walked forward, to where my toes hit the cool water, and watched a wave bury my feet.

"Still not close enough." He cocked his head to the side and grinned, but I held firm until that dimple made its appearance. It was my kryptonite.

I forgot about the depth of the water and what had happened the last time we were here and concentrated on the man standing in front of me. Then I unclenched my hands and let go, the ocean breeze sweeping my cover-up away. He held out his arms, and I walked straight to him, gasping as the water hit the tiny strip of skin exposed by my tankini. "Impatient today?" I couldn't fake being stern when his smile still took up half his face.

"Always impatient to get my hands on you." He grabbed my rear and lifted me against him. I wrapped my arms around his neck and my legs around his waist, reveling in the warmth of his skin over the cool water.

"People are going to stare," I murmured, leaning my forehead to his.

"Ask me if I care." He punctuated the last word with a kiss that consumed every protest I had. By the time he pulled away, I was beyond caring that we were making out on the beach. His biceps flexed as he lifted me even higher and ran a trail of kisses along the scar between my breasts, lowering me as he made his way to my mouth. "You taste like sunshine."

I slid my tongue across his lips, and his grip tightened on me. "You'd better not move, or we'll really give everyone a show," he whispered.

"You'd better cool off, there are kids on that beach."

He peeked over my shoulder. "There's one other group here, and I'd hardly call those teenagers kids. Now, are you ready?"

"Ready for what?"

He flashed me a wicked smile while he turned my back to the ocean. Then he threw me into the waves. I sailed through the air with a squawk and plunged into the crystal water. My toes hit the sand, and I pushed off, clearing the distance to the surface. I took in a huge breath and located Jagger a few feet away.

Then I splashed him. "Seriously?"

He laughed, the sound stealing all of my ire away. "Better to just jump in, don't you think?"

"That was a daring move, Mr. California." I treaded water, rising and falling with the waves as they gently swelled the surface around us.

"You want to see daring?" he challenged. "Follow me."

I swam after him as he crossed the small distance toward the pier. My heart beat in a steady rhythm as he cut us toward shore where he could stand, but I couldn't. My body hummed with energy, elation at what I'd just done. "I love this!"

He lifted me against him, the water swirling around his shoulders. "I'm incredibly proud of you." Fear flashed across his eyes, flattening his mouth, but he replaced it with a smile before I could ask what had crossed his mind. "I love you, Paisley."

"I love you, too," I said softly.

"I want to spend every day of my life telling you that." He swallowed and took a breath.

"Me, too. Jagger. Are you okay?" I rested my hand over his bird tattoo. "Your heart is pounding."

He walked us slowly toward the beach, until the water lapped at my waist, then turned so he was backdropped against the colors of the sunset. "Yeah, well, I'm nervous. Look, I know we're young, but if there's anything that the last year has taught me, it's that life is short, and I'm not going to stand around waiting for what I want." His eyes dropped to my scar, then up to my eyes. "I want you, in every way possible. I want to sleep next to you and wake up next to you. I want to fight with you, and make up, and give you everything you could possibly want, because I'm addicted to your smile, your laugh. I can't think of anything better than building you a library so you can read to our kids, or having the same last name. I'm not exactly known for rational choices, but you are, so I'm going to trust you."

My heart thundered, and my lips parted as I tried to breathe, to think. "Jagger? What are you—"

"Look up."

I turned my eyes skyward over his shoulder and gasped, my fingers flexing into his skin. Where the pier had been empty a moment before, a giant banner hung from the same place I'd been thrown from last year. I read it three times before I could suck air into my lungs, or even notice that our friends and family, even Anna, stood smiling behind it. Tears built in my eyes as I looked into his.

"Paisley Lynn Donovan, I can't imagine my life without you. You are my sunshine, my oxygen, and the captain of my soul. Will you marry me?"

My pounding heart leaped into my throat, and I took in everything about the moment, wanting to file it away so I would never forget.

"I could get down on one knee, but I don't think you could hear me underwater," he added, uncertainty springing to his eyes.

"Oh, no," I replied.

"No?" he whispered, every muscle in his body tensing.

"What? No, don't go underwater." I smiled. "Yes, I'll marry you, Jagger."

"Oh, thank God." He leaned his head back and shouted, "She said yes!"

The pier erupted in cheers, and the sky turned momentarily white over our heads as he kissed me breathless. The flap of wings caught my attention. "Are those—?"

"Doves." He watched my reaction like a kid on Christmas hoping he'd bought the right presents.

"Little birds." I laughed, needing to let some of my joy out before it burst me apart. "You're ridiculous!" I'd never felt stronger, happier, more loved in my entire life. He lowered me gently until I felt the sand beneath my feet.

"Well, I figured I'm only doing this once." Then he lifted my left hand and kissed my finger before slipping a classic, perfect engagement ring onto it.

I blinked the tears from my eyes and kissed him, tasting salt on his lips. "It's perfect. Wait. Where were you hiding a ring?"

He grinned. "You don't want to know. It was complicated."

I shook my head but couldn't stop smiling. "I will love you my entire life."

"I'm counting on it." He carried me onto the beach to the cheers of our little crowd—our family, both biological and chosen.

I looked up at him, my chest on fire with how much I loved him, and how little that word seemed to encompass this burning. "This is where you saved me."

"No. This is where you saved *me*."

He kissed me, and my heart took flight all over again.

ACKNOWLEDGMENTS

My first thanks goes to my Heavenly Father, whose plans always far outshine my dreams.

To my husband—for kicking me out of the house on weekends to write this little book. For every time you kiss me, every time you remind me that we're the lucky ones to have a love this strong. For being the guardian of my heart, the protector of our children, and my buffer to the outside world. Thank you to my children—words do no justice to the love I feel for you, or the way you inspire me to work harder, do more, be everything you deserve. Especially to our Little Miss, you're teaching us far more than we could ever teach you.

To my agent, Jamie, I love you enough to give you the last brownie. Thank you for being my friend and the gateway to my dreams. To my amazing editor, Karen Grove, I couldn't imagine anyone handling this series like you do. I couldn't do this without you. My phenomenal team at Entangled—Britt Marczak, Debbie Suzuki, Heather Riccio—thank you for always having my back with a smile. My publicists, Melissa and Sharon, thank you for taking me on and thrusting me out of my comfort zone with kindness and crazy levels of patience for my endless questions. To my cover artist, Britt Marczak, thank you for being generally awesome and giving me a beautiful cover.

Linda, squirrel chaser extraordinaire, I'm grateful for the insanity of my street team, but so much more thankful for your friendship. Thank you for holding my hair back when my nerves get the best of me. My awesome Epics, you rock my socks off.

Sarah, thank you for taking the time to read this at draft stage, and for making sure I got the complex world of heart conditions right.

To my writer friends who keep me sane—Mindy, Nola, Fiona, Katrina, Jessica, and Brenda—thank you for not judging my epic freak-outs. Lizzy and Molly, who read this chapter by chapter as it was written, and held my sanity together with kind words and clamors for more, you guys are utterly priceless to me. Amy, thank you for patting my head and telling me to breathe while you put a freshman at the prom queen table. I'm forever grateful. My Backspace Survivors—Sean, Alicia, Monika, Michael, Lauren, Malia, Ulana—still no Korean food. Just no. To the bloggers who helped make Full Measures a success by your reviews and your mentions, Jillian, Marianne, Jordan, Natasha, Aesta, Maryse, Alexis, Ashley, Lisa, Angie, Amy, and countless others, thank you for taking your time to promote authors. You all humble me.

To my friends and family who keep my feet grounded while I reach for whatever's next, thank you. Mom and Dad, for always coming when I call, no matter how far away we live. My brothers, Doug, Matt, and Chris, and my sister, Kate, thank you for not killing me when I was younger. I really appreciate that now. Lynette, Dori, and Matt, thank you knowing how quirky our family is and still choosing to marry into it. Emily, Christina, Donna, Thea, Sara, Kierstan, Jessica, and Mandy—I couldn't ask to have a better group of friends. Thank you for putting up with me when I'm in the writing cave, swearing to call you back. I really meant to, I swear.

And lastly, to my husband, Jason, again, because you're my first thought in the morning and my last prayer in the evening, no matter what continent you're on. Jagger's only amazing because there's so much of you in him.

Can't get enough of Rebecca Yarros?

Dive into the next book in the Flight & Glory series today.

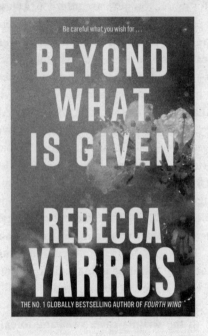

Falling in love is something neither Grayson nor Sam can afford, but love often finds you when you least expect it ...

Available now

Welcome to the Renegades.

*Six unlikely friends on a Study at Sea program will learn
that chemistry is more than a subject and the best lessons
aren't taught in the classroom ... but in the heart.*

Available now

JOIN OUR SQUAD

CADETS, SIGN UP TO OUR
NEWSLETTER AND KEEP AN EYE
ON OUR SOCIAL CHANNELS FOR
OFFICIAL CORRESPONDENCE
FROM THE EMPYREAN